One Day in May

CATHERINE ALLIOTT

PENGUIN BOOKS

For Al

PENGUIN BOOKS

Published by the Penguin Group
Penguin Books Ltd, 80 Strand, London WC2R ORL, England
Penguin Group (USA) Inc., 375 Hudson Street, New York, New York 10014, USA
Penguin Group (Canada), 90 Eglinton Avenue East, Suite 700, Toronto, Ontario, Canada M4P 2Y3
(a division of Pearson Penguin Canada Inc.)
Penguin Ireland, 25 St Stephen's Green, Dublin 2, Ireland (a division of Penguin Books Ltd)
Penguin Group (Australia), 250 Camberwell Road, Camberwell, Victoria 3124, Australia
(a division of Pearson Australia Group Pty Ltd)
Penguin Books India Pvt Ltd, 11 Community Centre, Panchsheel Park, New Delhi – 110 017, India
Penguin Group (NZ), 67 Apollo Drive, Rosedale, Auckland 0632, New Zealand
(a division of Pearson New Zealand Ltd)
Penguin Books (South Africa) (Pty) Ltd, Block D, Rosebank Office Park,
181 Jan Smuts Avenue, Parktown North, Gauteng 2193, South Africa

Penguin Books Ltd, Registered Offices: 80 Strand, London WC2R ORL, England

www.penguin.com

First published by Michael Joseph 2010
Published in Penguin Books 2012

004

Set in 12.24/14.5 pt Garamond MT Std
Typeset by Jouve (UK), Milton Keynes
Printed in England by Clays Ltd, St Ives plc

ISBN: 978-0-718-19260-0

Export edition ISBN: 978-0-718-19261-7

www.greenpenguin.co.uk

MIX
Paper from
responsible sources
FSC
www.fsc.org   FSC™ C018179

Penguin Books is committed to a sustainable
future for our business, our readers and our planet.
This book is made from Forest Stewardship
Council™ certified paper.

I

Maggie's look of fixed concentration as we hurtled up the M40 was to be encouraged, and for a moment I pretended I hadn't heard her last remark. Instead I simulated sleep. An in-depth analysis of my family would surely require her to take her eyes off the road, and since her lack of white van handling skills was legendary, I wanted them firmly on the Friday afternoon traffic.

'Hattie?' she barked above the lawnmower roar of the engine, not one to be ignored. 'I said, isn't your sister spoiled beyond belief these days? I haven't seen her for ages, but I seem to remember she had everything she wanted even then. Didn't you say she'd eaten one interior designer for breakfast already?'

I sighed, realizing my pathetic eye-closing ruse was going nowhere. I also remembered that whilst it was quite all right for me to have a go at my family now and then, I resented it when my friends did.

'I didn't say she was spoiled,' I said evenly. 'I simply said she's got some quite grandiose ideas. But then her taste has never been anything like mine, particularly when it comes to doing up houses. She likes everything draped and patterned and swagged, which is fine in the country, but it's hardly you and me, is it?'

'Hardly,' Maggie snorted with derision, then looked pleased. She returned her attention to the road and leaned sharply on the horn. A vast Hungarian juggernaut had dared to cut in front of us whilst we hogged the middle lane, rattling along at sixty miles an hour, which was all we could do when loaded to the gunwales, our cabin full of fabric, sample books and furniture, the tools of our trade.

'Pick a lane and stick to it!' she roared, betraying her own rudimentary grasp of motorway driving. She flashed her lights furiously as she got right up behind him.

I gripped the upholstery. Another white-knuckle ride. Maggie had recently admitted to an adrenalin rush when sparring with fellow truckers, and I felt it was only a matter of time before she boasted a tattoo and a wife-beater vest. At least we weren't in France, I reasoned, where we'd clocked up most of our miles together, and where Maggie's aggressive handling of Chalky, our white Transit van, had caused more than one *monsieur* to slam on his brakes, leap from his vehicle and demand an explanation. At least in leafy Buckinghamshire all we encountered were V signs and the odd McDonald's carton flung from windows in our faces.

'So why does she want us then?' Maggie yelled disingenuously as we lurched into the slow lane and beetled illegally past the lorry. 'Your sister.'

'You know why. Hugh wants us,' I said wearily. 'And even Laura knows better than to flagrantly go against him. And actually, I think it's jolly loyal of them to ask us to quote at all. Even if we don't get the whole house, even if it's just a few rooms, they'll still pay squillions.'

Maggie sat up a bit at this, silenced. When my brother-in-law had rung the shop and asked if we'd 'cast an eye over the place' for them, I too had been astonished. Saxby Abbey was hardly the French Partnership's usual commission, Maggie and my habitual territory being basement kitchens in Fulham, or, at the most, a small house in Parson's Green. But Hugh had been insistent.

PENGUIN BOOKS

One Day in May

'Her books are supremely readable, witty and moving in
equal measure and she has a brilliantly sharp ear for dialogue'
Daily Mail

'Possibly my favourite writer' Marian Keyes

'An addictive cocktail of wit, frivolity and madcap romance'
Time Out

'Sensitive, funny and wonderfully well written'
Wendy Holden, *Daily Express*

'Another charming tale of heartbreak from this wonderfully
warm and witty author' *Woman*

'A poignant but charming journey of self-discovery.
A bittersweet and captivating novel' *Closer*

'We defy you not to get caught up in Alliott's life-changing
tale' *Heat*

'A fun, fast-paced page-turner' *OK!*

Catherine Alliott is the author of twelve bestselling novels including *One Day in May*, *The Secret Life of Evie Hamilton* and *A Crowded Marriage*. She lives with her family in Hertfordshire.

'Laura's got ... well, she's got some rather extravagant ideas, Hattie,' he'd said nervously, and very quietly, even though he'd already told me Laura had gone to the village. 'She's got some London decorator coming down who wants to put silk everywhere. Even on the walls, for God's sake. I need you.'

Small and shiny – cheeks and bald pate – he might be, but the words 'I need you' delivered passionately by a peer of the realm are inclined to sway one. Besides, I was very fond of Hugh. He was a dear, kind man and, when let off the marital leash, could scamper like a frisky terrier and be terribly amusing in his cups.

'But, Hugh, Maggie and I do understated French charm, you know that. Shabby chic. A couple of huge garden urns and one or two baroque chairs in an otherwise bare room streaked with a bit of verdigris paint. It's not going to be Laura's *tasse de thé* at all.'

'Paint?' he'd yelped, like a Labrador after a scrap. 'Did you say paint? That can't cost much, surely?'

'Well, ours isn't cheap; we have it specially mixed. About thirty quid a litre?'

'And a litre covers about fifty metres of wall, doesn't it? Do you have any idea how much her silk Obsession wall-paper is?'

Ah. Obsession.

'About a hundred pounds for one metre. And the Abbey must have ... ooh ... 20,000 square metres of wall space at least!'

There was a silence as we both did the maths.

'Please come,' he'd implored at length. Which, hot on the heels of 'I need you' found me not just swaying but melting. 'Come, and bring your partner too. I swear to God I'll make it worth your while.'

'You don't have to do that, Hugh,' I'd muttered feebly. 'I mean, overpay us or anything. We'll charge our usual rates. But Laura—'

'Laura will be fine,' he'd interjected, quite firmly for him. 'Leave her to me. Oh, and by the way, your mother's here too,' he added, in something more like his habitual nervous tone. 'The pair of them are flying from room to room clutching swatches and bits of wallpaper shrieking, "Yes! Yes!" as they hold them up to windows, like a couple of born-agains. Their Bible seems to be an enormous book by the prophet Bennison, which they clutch to their breasts, open reverently and dribble over.'

I smiled; could just picture it. Mum and Laura, both tall, blonde and gorgeous. Laura in jeans and T-shirt, Mum in Bond Street's finest and, now that it was back in fashion, fur-trimmed too, around her collar, cuffs, tops of boots … As Dad said, it was only a matter of time before it made it to her eyebrows. And boy, they'd be busy. Hastening around the Abbey shiny-eyed, discussing, conferring, holding up rolls of silk, Mum running to the lavatory when the excitement got too much for her middle-aged bladder, both thrilled to bits to be *finally* getting their hands on the pile, which Hugh's parents had *finally* vacated, allowing Hugh, Laura and their three children to move from the tiny cottage in the grounds where they'd spent their first fifteen years of married life.

'And it was only supposed to be five,' Laura had complained to me once when she'd come to see me at my shop in London. 'When we got married, Hugh's parents said five, or maybe six years max, then we'll swap, it'll be too big for us. And, Hattie, I could have handled eight years, even ten. But now I've got two hulking great teenage girls hitting their heads on the beams and throwing Ugg boots up on sofas, and Charlie's bouncing off the walls, and we're *still* in the cottage!'

Maggie had been crouched in the shop window at the time, pretending to polish a ball-and-claw sofa foot. She'd made a 'lucky-you-to-have-a-free-cottage' face at the floor as she'd rubbed. But I'd felt for Laura, actually. To be fair, apart from this little outburst, she'd sat firmly on her resentment as her eighty-year-old parents-in-law rattled round an enormous twenty-room house, and whilst a family of five, plus dogs, squeezed into a tiny three-bedroom lodge at the entrance to the estate.

'Well, why don't they move then?' had been Maggie's exasperated reaction when Laura had gone. She sat back on her heels in the window as she watched my sister go off down the street, blonde hair swinging. 'Why don't they buy their own house, like everyone else does?'

'Because every time they decide to do that, Hugh's parents get all batey. His mother starts muttering about family loyalty and Hugh's father flies into a towering rage, so Hugh says they must stay a bit longer. Not upset them.'

Maggie had harrumphed at that and resumed her dusting with a vengeance, muttering darkly about people not having enough backbone to lead their own lives. But I'd ignored it.

I'd also looked at Laura that day, as she'd sat in the back room of my shop in Munster Road, on a shabby Louis Quinze chaise longue Maggie and I had recently hustled back from a *brocante* in Paris and lovingly re-covered in a few yards of thin but exquisite tapestry found in a flea market, and wondered how we'd ever reached this juxtaposition. My big sister: blonde and beautiful beyond belief, who, in June 1992 had graced a cover of *Vogue* that bore the legend: 'Britain's latest beauty' – oh, yes, seriously good-looking. Who'd given it all up to marry Hugh; who'd said goodbye to the photo shoots and the catwalk to live in the country and have children. Who'd made a resounding success of her life; and here she was, pouring her heart out to the one who'd made pretty much a bish of everything. The one who'd failed to marry at all, let alone successfully. The one who'd scuppered her chances early on in her twenties by adopting an orphaned boy from Bosnia, thereby accruing baggage 'no sane man would want', as my mother had put it crisply at the time. Who'd poured any paltry money she had into a risky and competitive business – the French Partnership wasn't the only French décor shop in Munster Road, let alone in London: French Dressing, French Affair and Vive La France all prevailed. Who lived in a tiny terraced house with a crippling mortgage at the wrong end of Lillie Road, and yet here was my sister, blue eyes filling as she sat in her Marc Jacobs coat, fiddling nervously with the socking great diamonds on her fingers, insisting she'd been the one to bog it.

As a tear rolled down her cheek – Laura even cried beautifully, no slitty eyes and swollen nose for her – I'd passed her a tissue and moved to sit next to her: joined her on the faded pastoral scene. I put my arm round her shoulders and gave her a squeeze.

'Nonsense, you haven't bogged it. Just give it a bit longer and the old dears will see sense. God, they'll be incapable of getting up the stairs soon. And Hugh's even put a Stannah stair-lift in for them at the cottage, hasn't he?'

'Which will be broken soon,' she said with a mighty sniff. 'The children haven't walked upstairs since it arrived. But, yes, we have. And if that isn't a hint I don't know what is.'

'They'll wake up one morning and realize they can't manage any more. Can't carry on. You'll see.'

Laura had turned huge damp blue eyes on me. 'Or maybe they won't wake up at all.'

'You don't mean that!' I'd gasped, knowing she didn't. Laura was the gentlest of creatures.

'No,' she sighed. 'Of course not. You know I'm fond of them. Even if Cecily is foul to me and Lionel still scares the pants off me.' Hugh's parents were a formidable duo, even in their eighties. 'But the mind works in mysterious ways, Hattie,' she went on wistfully. 'I don't want to hate them. I don't want to be this person. But I do resent them, and that's not nice. I know I'm selfish, and many women would kill to live in a cottage like mine.' Maggie scrubbed even harder in the window, her mouth set in a grim line. 'It's just … at my age, at my time of life, I expected more,' she finished sadly, giving a little shrug.

Ah, yes. Expectation. The route to all disappointment. Which was why I expected so little.

'And Hugh won't push it?'

'No, he's far too nice. I was the one who bought the stair-lift,' she added guiltily. 'So there I am, lying in bed beside him, wondering if Cecily's motorized buggy, which she wobbles round the village on, roaring at the locals, ordering them to pick up litter, might one day hit a rut in the lane and send her soaring over the handlebars, feeling nothing as she somersaults to the ground. Or if Lionel, at six foot four, bellowing that he can't find his whisky decanter again, might one day fail to detect the doors he ducks so assiduously, and just walk straight into one – boof. How horrible is that, Hatts?' She turned despairing eyes.

'Well, as long as you're not actually fiddling with the brakes on the motorized buggy, or removing those tassels Lionel hangs from the door frame to remind him to duck—'

'No. Never!' She clutched her handbag on her lap.

'Then thinking is very different from doing. And your guilty secrets are safe with me.'

That had been a few months ago. And then spookily, days later she'd rung, breathless, to say that Cecily and Lionel were moving out. Not to the cottage, which Cecily had apparently always disliked and dismissed as poky and damp – join the club, Laura had yelped – but to Shropshire, to be near Lionel's sister. They'd be gone by Easter.

'At last, Hattie, we'll be in. We'll have the Abbey!'

I'd almost expected her to add, 'It'll be mine – all mine!' together with a cackling Hammer House of Horror laugh, but she'd refrained. Then she'd reined in enough to remember her manners and added, 'And you must come and stay.'

Like I say, that had been months ago. And what with all the moving and hectic reorganization and settling in of her parents-in-law – plus, to be fair, I'd been to Paris on business – I hadn't been summoned.

But six months had passed now. Not since I'd seen her, because she came to London regularly and we always had lunch, and she'd excitedly tell me her plans for the house. But six months before I got the call from Hugh. The summons. And a tiny bit of me had thought – oh, thanks very much. Not an invitation to stay, but to work. But the thing was, I'd secretly been dying to go. When they were in the cottage we'd spent a lot of time there, my son, Seffy, and I. We'd all cram in having a jolly time, boozy kitchen suppers, the cousins littered on the floor watching television, or roaming the grounds together, and I suppose I was disappointed that an arrangement I'd expected to become more fluid when space wasn't an issue had become static. And I also missed Laura; was hurt she didn't miss me. I wrestled with all sorts of feelings on the end of the line to my brother-in-law.

'I need you, Hattie, I really do. I can't seem to get through to her at the moment. And she listens to you. Come for the weekend.'

I'd licked my lips, standing as I was at the time when my mobile had rung, on a seventeenth-century console table, fiddling with a delicate crystal chandelier. The weekend. I was supposed to be quoting on a house in Battersea on Saturday.

'And don't worry, I know you decorators all charge consultancy fees these days,' he said quickly. 'I've factored that in.' He went on to mention a sum of money so huge I had to climb off the table before I fell off.

'Well, that's extremely generous of you, Hugh,' I said, trying not to wonder, if that was a consultancy fee, what the entire job would yield. Trying not to mentally pay off the mortgage and Seffy's school fees.

'Oh, believe me, it's a fraction of the price I've been told someone called Ralph de Granville charges, who will otherwise be unleashed in my house. D'you know him?'

'Only ... by repute,' I'd said, holding on to the console table now. I mouthed at Maggie – who was transfixed by this conversation, standing stock-still in the middle of the shop, a pair of gilt rococo cherubs in her hands – first the amount of money, then the name of the competing decorator. The first she gaped at; at the second, looked horrified. She shook her head and made an eloquent throat-slitting gesture. I turned back to Hugh, vertebrae stiffening.

'We accept, Hugh. We'll come this weekend and price the job up for you. Expect us on Friday.'

'Perfect,' he'd purred in relief.

'Are you mad?' Maggie squealed as I snapped my phone shut. Ralph de Granville? If we go head to head with that man we'll be the laughing stock of London! If that's who Laura wants there's no way she'll have us. We're chalk and cheese! *Fromage et froufrou*, in fact. Remember Albion Close? That woman proudly showing us her "de Gran-ville" bathroom with the tart's knickers hanging from the window? That blind had more colour and pattern in it than one would care to see in an entire house! Hugh clearly has no idea how different we are. He just thinks one decorator is much the same as another.'

'I'm not so sure,' I said slowly. 'Hugh knows what we do, and he likes it. And at the end of the day, Maggie,' I flicked her a look, 'it's his house, not Laura's.'

She pursed her lips. 'Right. Blimey. Not much has changed then, has it? I mean, since the days of Mr Darcy and Miss Bennet.'

'Not a lot,' I said shortly. 'As Carla discovered to her cost.' I climbed back onto the table and resumed my inspection of the chandelier. Carla was Hugh's first wife: a fiery Italian who'd left him after a few years of unsat-isfactory marriage for a Formula One racing driver.

She'd received a handsome settlement but if she'd expected half the Abbey, she'd been disappointed.

'Tricky for you, though,' Maggie mused behind me, still weighing up her cherubs and the implications. 'I mean, Hugh wants you, but Laura clearly doesn't.' Her voice couldn't resist a triumphant little rise at the end. I ignored her and carried on fiddling with the crystal droplets. Rather like Christmas tree lights, a dud one could jeopardize the entire show. 'And if we did get the job,' she persisted, 'we'd be there a lot, don't you think? I mean, weekends too, possibly?'

'Possibly.'

'Seffy would like that, wouldn't he? Now he's a weekly boarder.'

'I'm sure.'

There was a pause. I could tell she was building up to something. 'And Ivan?' Her voice betrayed a *frisson* of excitement.

Ah, Ivan. My other weekly boarder. The one that tended to stay during the week, and scarper at weekends, who knows where. I carefully screwed in the last glass drop, then reached out and flicked a switch. The chandelier sprang into fabulous light, dazzling our tiny shop. We gasped as it glittered.

'You see?' I said triumphantly. 'Just needed a bit of TLC. That'll transform someone's hall, turn it into Blenheim Palace. We'll sell it for a fortune!'

That had been the Monday, and the sudden illumination had silenced my friend spectacularly. On the Friday, however, as we rattled off the M40 and onto the main road into Thame, she returned doggedly to her theme.

'Will he come and stay, d'you think? Ivan?' Her face was pure innocence, but her mouth twitched provocatively. She made a show of studying the road.

I pretended to give this due consideration, determined not to rise. 'Why not?' I said airily. 'He might.'

She sniggered into the dashboard. 'God, I can just see Laura's face. And your mother's.'

Even my sang-froid wobbled a bit at this, but I held my nerve.

'Oh, I don't know,' I said lightly. 'They want me hitched. They'll be delighted I've got a boyfriend at all. Probably be all over me.'

'Until they meet him,' she grinned, shooting me a look. Her eyes widened at my stony face. 'Don't give me that look, Hattie. You know very well I'm deeply jealous and would give my eyeteeth to have an Ivan, but I can't help feeling a little bit of *schadenfreude* at your family's reaction. Oh my God – your brother!' She turned a hundred and eighty degrees and took a hand off the wheel. Clutched her mouth. 'Isn't he a vicar?'

'MAGGIE!' I screamed, grabbing the dashboard as, in a blare of horns, the whole cab was illuminated by flashing lights behind.

'Bastard,' she muttered, as yet another outraged lorry driver hurtled past, fist shaking, mouth a dark hole. I could tell she was shaken, though.

'Surely we're nearly there?' she snapped, distracted from her train of thought, gripping the shuddering wheel. 'I thought you said they were just off this main road, but no one ever mentioned it?' She scanned the surrounding scenery. 'Said everyone sat sipping Pimm's on the lawn, seemingly oblivious to the thunderous roar of traffic?'

'They do. In fact Hugh's planning a waterfall in the river to drown it out. Oh – here, quick, hang a left.'

'A water feature!' said Maggie gleefully, hitting the brakes and spinning the wheel at the last minute. 'They'll be putting decking on the terrace next. Down here? My, but this is grand. Is this really their drive?'

It was. We'd shot through a pair of white gateposts flashing in the hedgerow and down a slip of tarmac, which plunged like an arrow, straight through an avenue of pollarded limes. The trees appeared to be holding hands facing us, their topiary branches pruned to cling. Wide grassy verges were mown neatly at their feet. Beyond, behind the post-and-rail fence, green fields spread flatly into the distance, and creamy cattle grazed.

'Almost French,' said Maggie, surprised. 'I mean the avenue. The whole setting, in fact. They've even got the Charolais cows.'

'Exactly,' I said, pleased she'd noticed. I kept quiet, letting her take it all in.

'Keep going?' She'd slowed down for a little humpback bridge at the bottom.

'Yes, over the river. You see it runs in front of the house, which is unusual, isn't it? Normally in England the lawn runs down to the river at the back.'

'Does it now. Funnily enough I'm not terribly *au fait* with the layout of the grand country houses of England. Most of my friends live in Croydon. Where's the house then?'

'You don't see it until – oh, take the left fork.' She obediently swung the wheel as I pointed. As the drive divided sharply, the house loomed up before us.

'Oh!' She stared.

'What?' I demanded, keen to know, but not to prompt.

'It could be a château.'

Out of a clearing in a bank of trees along the flat valley floor, the Abbey rose up, its stone façade the colour of Dijon mustard. It was long and flat centrally, but had towers at either end, their conical slate roofs tapering sharply. Laura, when she'd first seen it, had wondered if, like Rapunzel, she'd be expected to let loose her blonde hair from one of those high windows as she sat spinning in an attic room. Dozens of windows flashed at us now in the evening sunlight, perhaps in welcome, perhaps not.

'Exactly. Albeit a rather titchy château. But look at the pointy steeple roofs, just like that place in Chevenon. And the shutters, and the double front door.'

'Tall windows too. Quite a lot of symmetry going on ...'

'It's by a Scottish architect,' I rushed on. 'And if you think about it, some of those Highland piles are very French. Look at that wide bank of steps at the side, tumbling down to the gravel terrace. Just cries out for one of our distressed café tables, don't you think? A few wrought-iron chairs, a well-placed urn ...'

'And look at your sister's face,' breathed Maggie, as we came to a halt in the gravel sweep at the front.

The very French double front doors had swung back and Laura appeared at the top of the steps, dressed in a gun-metal grey silk shirt and jeans. Her blonde hair was shining, and her face plastered with an anxious, reproduction smile. She was flanked by another blonde, my mother, whose smile was more practised, less nervous. Behind them a pair of baying lurchers bounded out, nearly toppling my mother, and then Kit, my brother, appeared, a dog collar under his jumper. He beamed broadly from on high, a wine glass clasped to his chest. No sign of Dad, sadly.

'Right,' I muttered, all courage deserting me. 'I think we just pretend we're delivering a house-warming present – that mirror in the back will do. We'll stay for drinks, then turn round and go home, don't you think?'

'Nonsense,' said Maggie, whose professional eyes were glittering as only a true Francophile's could. 'This place has got the French Partnership written all over it. I thought we were coming to some mouldy English pile, not a veritable Loire Valley pastiche. If you think I'm passing up a trillion-pound contract and the chance of having my name go down in the annals of interior design history with the likes of Mr John Fowler and Mrs Nina Campbell you're mistaken. We're here for the duration. This is working for me, Hattie. I've already picked my bedroom.'

She threw open the cab door and jumped out. 'Laura – and Mrs Carrington – how lovely! Kit, what a surprise, loving the surplice, incidentally; you carry that off terribly well. How wonderful to see you all!'

2

Laura's hug at least was genuine, and I realized the synthetic smile was masking apprehension, not antipathy. I was aware of my own face not knowing quite how to play this either.

'I should have rung you,' were my first instinctive words, muttered guiltily in her ear, because of course I should.

'You texted me.'

'I know, but that was cowardly. I should have rung and asked, not texted and told.' I remembered her curt little text back: 'Well, if Hugh has asked you 2 come of course I'd love you 2.'

I should have punched out her number there and then, except I knew she'd be cool and polite down the line, but warmer in the flesh, as she was now. She looked gorgeous as ever but, close up, there were circles under her eyes.

'Actually, I'm really glad you're here,' she murmured. 'Mum's driving me mad, and Kit could do with a little diluting.'

'What's he doing here?' I glanced at my brother, beaming a canonized smile from the top step.

'He's on some Bible-thumping course in Oxford, so he's staying.'

'Ah, I wondered. He's got that ecstatic look on his face he always gets when he's topped up his fervour. What about Dad?'

'Due tomorrow. There's a strike in Geneva, would you believe, so he couldn't get a flight.'

My father had pretty much retired as a journalist now, but sometimes took freelance assignments. Currently he was doing a travel piece for the *Independent*.

'Darling!' My mother, realizing too much chat was occurring on the gravel without her, and that if she wanted to know what was going on she'd have to drop the Norman Hartnell ex-model pose – chin up, right foot slightly at an angle and to the fore – expertly descended the steps in heels. 'How lovely, what a surprise!'

It wasn't, of course, but Mum was lining up with Laura, placing herself firmly in her camp. Not for the first time I felt a guilty twinge of relief that Laura now had a house big enough to accommodate my family and its foibles, all of whom I loved unreservedly, but didn't want to be proximate to all the time. In my darker moments, in my tiny house, with Seffy away at school, I sometimes fantasized about being attached, settled, having a proper family, but I was never quite sure about everything else that went with it. Part of me relished being the daughter who bombed in and then slid back to London: the one they no doubt discussed when I'd gone, worried about. If Mum had her way I'd be married to a nice GP in the village and work part time in a little antique shop selling Edwardian knick-knacks. I shuddered at the thought.

'Mum.' I kissed her fragrant cheek, marvelling at how she seemed to get younger: her shoulder-length ash-blonde hair was streaked with silver now, but the bones were still good, blue eyes bright, and she was slim and straight-backed as ever. 'You look terrific.'

'Thank you, darling. I've got a new girl doing my facials in Motcomb Street. It's all to do with the rotation of energy and fluids, apparently. You might try her; I'll give you her number. You're looking a little peaky, if I might say so.'

'Thanks.' I grinned. 'Oh, Mum, you remember Maggie, don't you?'

Mum, who at five foot ten, never stooped to accommodate lesser beings, peered. Maggie flushed, and almost curtsied. There was certainly a bit of a bob going on there.

'D'you know, I believe I do. Now, Maggie, you look awfully well. You clearly look after yourself, and you single girls should, you know.' She cast me a reproving look as she air-kissed Maggie's cheek. There, the first reference to my spinsterhood, and we'd been here, what, two minutes?

'Did you go and see Mr Auchbach, darling?' She was back to me, eyes penetrating.

'Oh, no, I haven't yet.'

'I knew you hadn't. I could tell by your worry lines. For pity's sake, go.'

This, a reference to her counsellor, a complete stranger, to whom she poured her heart out once a week. Lord knows what about; she couldn't be more happily married or solvent. Me, the problem daughter, no doubt.

'And Laura tells me you failed to catch the Garnier.'

Not a bus, but an exhibition, by a little-known Cuban painter, thus completing, in under three minutes, the Hattie-will-not-be-beautified-analysed-or-cultured trilogy. Not bad, I thought, in awe.

'A record, surely?' murmured Kit, who, in his languid manner, had finally managed to stroll down the steps to kiss me, hands in pockets.

'Must be,' I muttered back. 'She's only got to mention Seffy's long hair and alcohol consumption and things will really get provocative.'

'Oh, we've already done that. I thought I'd get it out of the way early. I told her a bottle of wine a day was quite normal for a fifteen-year-old, especially one who's spent so much time in France.'

I giggled. 'Thanks.'

He moved on to shake hands with Maggie; all six foot two and eyes of blue, with cheekbones and swept-back blond hair to boot; surely the most decorative and affable vicar the Church of England was ever likely to get. My family are red hot in the looks department, or at least most of them are. I'll come to me and Dad later. I saw Maggie swoon visibly.

Hugh was amongst us now, muttering, '…how marvellous, thanks for coming, splendid, splendid …' as he kissed and shook hands, palpably relieved, I think, that we'd actually made it, and that his wife wasn't sulking at being outmanoeuvred. However, as we all climbed the steps behind him – his hair had finally retreated, I noticed, apart from two plucky outposts above his ears – and he pointed out architectural features and turrets to Maggie, who was exclaiming politely, Mum helpfully sticking her tour-guide oar in when she felt her son-in-law wasn't being effusive enough, Laura linked my arm – held it, rather – and we fell back. She discreetly got down to brass tacks.

'Presumably you know I've got Ralph de Granville coming to look at the place?' she said softly.

'I do, and listen, Laura, he's streets ahead of us in design terms. Whoppingly famous and totally different, too. You stick with him, if that's what you want. Maggie and I can just give you a bit of advice on – I don't know – the odd spare bedroom or something?' I waved my arm vaguely, upstairs somewhere.

'Or I thought the kitchen,' she said eagerly, 'because that's the sort of thing you do so well, isn't it?'

Basic, functional, utilitarian rooms: yes, we did, I thought, heroically holding my tongue and trying not to think about the elegant drawing room we'd just done in Chester Square, or the morning room in Wiltshire, or indeed the entire house in Streatham.

'In fact, tell you what. Why don't we leave the others to get a drink and I'll show you what I mean?'

I knew, though, because I knew her kitchen. It was the only room I rated. In the old days, when Cecily and Lionel were away, we'd creep around the house together, feeling slightly treacherous – reorganizing, giggling, making plans – and I'd praised the kitchen's simplicity, its integrity, said I wouldn't touch it. It was with a sinking heart, therefore, that I obediently followed her through the great domed hall, which managed to be both huge yet claustrophobic – busy Victorian floor tiles and oppressive oak panelling – mentally painting it a pale mouse colour and picking out the beading in something slightly stronger – down towards the back corridor.

'Hughie, darling,' she called over her shoulder, 'will you get everyone a drink? I'm just going to show Hattie the kitchen.'

The look of panic that crossed Hugh's face, as he stopped *en route* to the drawing room with the rest of the crew, told me this was not going to plan.

'Oh, I think Hattie would like a glass of wine too, after her long drive, wouldn't you, Hatts? Why don't we all have a drink, and then do the house together?'

There was a silence. Laura swallowed. 'All right, darling.'

She about-turned and we all trooped into the shabby drawing room – one or two good pieces but far too much furniture, every available surface crammed with doodahs and whatnots. All eyes were firmly on the threadbare Persian carpet. Laura and Hugh went into a furious whispered huddle over by the fireplace, Kit suavely engaged Maggie in conversation and escorted her to the window to show her the view, whilst Mum held my arm.

'Don't get involved,' she said in a low, portentous voice.

'I'm not getting involved.'

'Yes, but you're here to quote.'

'Because Hugh asked me!'

Mum made her famous face: the one that suggested I'd overstepped the mark. I counted to ten.

'This is something they have to sort out for themselves,' she went on in the same, *gravitas*-laden manner. 'And poor Laura is terribly upset and emotional at the moment.'

'Yes, but why?'

Another well-known expression: the one with pursed lips. 'Personally I think it's hormonal.' Mum's answer to most things. She drew herself up importantly. 'Speaking of which,' she peered at me critically, 'when did you last have a Well Woman?'

'I've never had a woman, well or otherwise,' I quipped feebly.

'Don't be fresh, young lady, you know I mean – a gynae.'

He-lp. I looked around desperately, but everyone else was occupied.

'You have got a good man, haven't you, darling? You're not still trotting down to that heaving surgery on the North End Road with the rest of south London?'

'Er, well, you know. Now and then.' I sank into the glass of wine Hugh had handed me. I wasn't going to tell her I let years go by, ignored countless reminders for check-ups; let them gather dust.

'It's about time you saw my man Stirrup. I'll give you his number. Oh, do stop smirking, Hattie. It really is time you grew up and stopped giggling at names. He's quite the best.'

'Right.' Hugh was upon us now, beaming nervously, rubbing his hands. 'That's decided then. Laura's going to take Hattie and Maggie to the kitchen. Apparently she wants you to see it in natural light, Hatts, before it gets dark.That's why she headed off there in the first place. The rest of us can stay here and chew the fat.'

Natural light my foot. He'd capitulated. Maggie and I obediently took our glasses and fell in behind Laura, who led us, pink-cheeked, head held high, out across the hall, then down the long passage to the kitchen.

Through a heavy panelled door we encountered a cool, high-ceiling room smelling slightly of ancient stone and polish. A giant baroque chimneypiece rose up before us from the old black range, and a vast oak dresser thick with copper pans flanked one entire wall. An old refectory table stretched centrally, a bench either side, and a white butler's sink sat on a cupboard under the tall window. Original grey slate tiles spread at our feet. The room hadn't been touched for fifty years, and although the peeling cream walls badly needed a lick of paint, other than that, it was perfect. Maggie stood still in the doorway, awestruck.

'Oh, but this is terrific. It's like a museum piece!'

'It is a bit of a relic,' Laura agreed, chewing her thumbnail and looking round.

'Yes, but that's the point. Apart from the walls – and I love that floor, by the way – I wouldn't touch it. I certainly wouldn't dress those windows, and that cracked old paint on the shutters is fab. Lucky you!'

'This is the room Laura would like us to do,' I explained helpfully.

'Oh.' Maggie's eyes widened. 'Right.'

'You see, the walls are such a state,' Laura rushed on, 'and in here too, the pantry.' She led us into another totally perfect room, albeit with peeling walls, but lovely slate shelving all the way round, more tiles on the floor. 'Needs totally revamping.'

'Yes,' said Maggie, faintly.

Hugh stuck his head around the door. 'Just come for the ice.' He smiled and reached into the freezer for the bucket. 'Don't forget to show them the breakfast room.'

'They're not doing the breakfast room, Hughie,' said Laura. 'Ralph is doing that, remember?'

'We'll go,' I said quietly to Maggie later, as we climbed the stairs to get changed for supper. 'If they haven't agreed this beforehand between themselves, I can't get involved. This has all the makings of a family feud and I won't be caught in the crossfire. I'm annoyed with Hugh, actually, for putting me in this position.'

'Nonsense, it won't turn into a feud. It's only decorating, for heaven's sake.'

'Remember Lambrook Gardens?' I intoned darkly.

Maggie paused on the stairs, shaken. Forty-one Lambrook Gardens had housed a recently married, loving young couple, with diametrically different tastes. Things had finally come to a head when he slashed her suede headboard and punctured the water bed with a knitting needle, but not before she'd tap-danced in studded rugby boots all over his highly glossed and varnished floorboards, which ran throughout the entire house. The decree absolute was through in six months.

'But he's adamant, Hattie,' Maggie insisted in a low whisper as we went on upstairs to the gallery. 'He's got it all planned out. He told me when he showed me round. He wants all this horrible oak painted in the hall to lighten it—'

'And she wants it all French-polished,' I hissed. 'She told me!'

'And he wants to get rid of all the chintz and heraldic stuff—'

'And she wants more chintz and more heralds. Wants to recreate a Victorian country house, as far as I can tell. Doesn't want to modernize at all.'

She frowned. 'I thought Laura had style?'

'She does,' I said loyally, 'but it's a conventional sort of style. She certainly doesn't do minimalist.'

'Maybe there's a compromise?'

'No, there isn't. This is a disaster, Maggie. I'm so sorry to have dragged you in and it's all my fault for not sorting it out properly, but we'll leave in the morning.'

'Don't be silly. We're here now; we can at least stay the weekend. It would be rude not to. Ooh, is this me? I can't remember.' Maggie pushed a door into what was palpably not the spare room she'd been allocated. We stood surveying Hugh and Laura's master bedroom, complete with four-poster bed, hideous parrot wallpaper, and matching curtains and bedcover. Parrots do require the lightest of touches and there were more here than one would care to see in a rainforest.

'God.' Maggie boggled. 'How do they stand it?'

I shrugged. 'Well, it was Hugh's parents' room up until recently. That's the point: they want a revamp.'

'Whoever does it, it'll cost a fortune,' she murmured, going to the window, feeling the ancient cloth. 'This place is huge. Each room to be stripped, repapered, recurtained ... has he got the moolah?'

'Easily. That's why Laura and Mum are so twitchy with excitement. City bonuses still go a long way these days.'

'She's quite shrewd, your sister, isn't she?' Maggie dropped the cloth and turned to me, narrowing her eyes. 'I mean, she's nabbed an aristo, but he's not a chinless wonder: he's got brains too. Most of them are penniless and stupid, aren't they?'

'No, she's not shrewd,' I said shortly. Maggie was an only child, and sometimes I sensed she resented the closeness Laura and I shared. Single girlfriends can be awfully possessive. I ushered her out before we were caught loitering in the master bedroom. 'She loves him,' I said simply. 'Always has. She certainly didn't marry him for his money. After all, money doesn't buy happiness, does it?'

She gave me an arch look before going into her bedroom, the one she'd been shown to. 'Maybe not,' she drawled, 'but it certainly helps.'

*

Supper that evening was a sparky affair. Toxic, even. No children as yet, to lighten it. Laura's brood, like Seffy, didn't come home from school until tomorrow lunchtime after matches, so we were missing the high spirits of the young, and more than usually prey to the quixotic undercurrents of bubbling bad temper of the adults. We ate in the kitchen, Laura coaxing a roast chicken out of the oven, pink-faced and muttering darkly as she nearly dropped it, whilst Hugh popped corks, keeping up a resolutely chirpy banter. Maggie, at the table with Mum, Kit and me, looked on in an alarmingly anthropological manner. She was quiet too: always a bad sign.

'D'you ever use the dining room?' she piped up eventually, innocently, but I could tell this was going somewhere.

'Never,' said Hugh cheerfully. 'At least not for ten years or so. The aged Ps never liked it. Fiendishly cold and dark, ridiculously large too. I remember the odd Christmas in there, as a boy, but other than that, no.'

'But you'll use it, won't you?' she persisted. 'I mean, eventually?'

'Oh, well, I suppose the odd dinner party. But kitchen suppers are more the thing, aren't they? Much cosier.' He put the bottle on the table and sat down.

'And you don't use the morning room or the billiard room, the ones you want us ... the ones that need decorating?'

'Christmas,' said Hugh again. 'The morning room, that is. When the village children come to sing carols, we pop them all in there. Quite jolly.'

'But the billiard room?'

'Well, I don't play billiards!' he chuckled, pouring everyone a glass of wine.

'What about that blue room, then? The one off the drawing room through the double doors.'

'That's the Blue Room.'

'But you don't use it for anything?'

Hugh looked bewildered. 'It's not really for anything.'

'So … why d'you live here?'

I cringed.

'I mean, if you only use one or two rooms downstairs, and hardly any upstairs, and you've got so much work to do, which will frankly take ages and cost a small fortune, why not sell it and buy somewhere smaller?'

Laura's eyes boggled into the chicken as she brought it to the table on a board. We were short of men so she was next to me. 'Don't be silly, we'd never do that. Hugh's family have been here for two hundred years.'

'Yes, but two hundred years ago people had servants, masses of them, so there would have been about twenty people living in a house like this, which would have made sense. All those attic rooms would have been full of maids and now they're empty. The coach house would have had grooms sleeping above it, and even though you're a big family, you'll rattle around in it. Surely you're perpetuating a patriarchal way of life that simply doesn't exist any more?'

Maggie had read Sociology at Newcastle. She'd also had two large gins.

'What you mean is, isn't it rather selfish to have all these empty rooms when so many people have nowhere to sleep at all?' enquired Kit slowly. Disingenuously too, as if the thought had only just occurred to him.

Laura put down her carving fork and rolled her eyes. 'Oh, yes, marvellous, Kit. All those people sleeping in bin bags in London – they could all come down and get a bed here, couldn't they? Why not?'

'Well, why not?' asked Kit mildly.

Maggie blanched, unused to my brother's simplistic method of taking away the sins of the world.

'But then where would you stay, Kit, hm?' enquired Laura. '*En passant* from Oxford, if all the rooms were full of poor homeless souls shooting up. Under the billiard table, perhaps? You might be glad of it then. Gravy, anyone?'

'Well, no, I didn't mean that, actually,' said Maggie nervously, more used to flexing her argumentative muscles in Notting Hill of a Friday night, where discussions took less of a knee-jerk turn. 'I was thinking more from Hugh and Laura's point of view. It's quite a thing to be saddled with. Quite a responsibility.'

'Ah, but it's only entrusted to me for a length of time, that's the point,' said Hugh. 'It's not mine to do what I like with, just to keep going for the next generation. In point of fact it's Luca's, really.'

'Luca,' muttered Laura, viciously stabbing the carving knife into the chicken breast. 'Hughie, come and do this, would you? Before I massacre it.'

Hugh obediently stood and moved round to take over. 'Of course, my darling. You only had to ask.'

'Luca?' asked Maggie, with a frown. 'I thought your son was called Charlie?'

'Luca is Hugh's son by his first marriage,' explained Mum smoothly, pussycat smile firmly in place. 'Now, Maggie, can I pass you the mangetout?'

'Who'll probably sell the place anyway,' said Laura, 'the moment it passes to him, which, if Hugh gets his way, won't be when we're under the sod, but when he deems we've had a Jolly Good Crack At It and it's time for the young to have a go while they've still got the energy. While I've had to wait fifteen flipping years and am definitely out of energy!'

Maggie, grasping the finer nuances of the situation, opened her mouth. Shut it again. 'Oh. So how old is—'

'Twenty-two,' interjected Mum.

'And where—'

'In Florence, with his mother.'

'So how often does he—'

'Not often, just once or twice a year, generally in the shooting season. More broccoli, Maggie?' Mum was purring away like an old Bentley, flashing her vivid smile.

'Won't you?' Laura demanded of Hugh, not deflected.

'Won't I what?'

'Pass the house to him?'

'Well, I certainly won't wait till he's too old to enjoy it.'

'Like we are.'

'And I don't see the point,' he went on quietly, and in what was clearly a practised fashion, 'of decorating it up to the nines, at vast expense, if Luca decides in a few years' time he wants to redo it.'

'Few years! *Few years?* Is that all you're saying we've got?'

'I'm speaking figuratively. Of course we've got more than that. But you must see, darling—'

Whatever it was she must see, though, she didn't. With a strangled sob Laura pushed back her chair, and ran from the room, throwing down her napkin on the way.

There was a silence. Somewhere upstairs, footsteps thumped along a corridor. Then a door was heard to slam.

Maggie cleared her throat. 'I'm awfully sorry. That was entirely my fault.'

'No, no, it's been brewing for some time. I'll go.'

Looking grey and daunted, Hugh got to his feet to go after his wife. I put a hand on his arm.

'Actually, Hugh, can I?'

He sat down again, heavily. 'With the greatest pleasure.'

I got up and followed my sister from the room.

3

I found Laura in her bedroom, prostrate on the bed, face down amongst the birdlife. Her body was shuddering with sobs. I sat quietly beside her for a while, my hand on her back. Eventually she calmed down. After another moment, she stopped completely: flipped over and sat up, drying her eyes on a pillow.

'Stupid. So stupid,' she muttered. 'And I am so spoiled.'

'No you're not.'

'Yes I am. I'm horrid. Ghastly. Beastly to Hugh, snappy with the children. I've been revolting for months.'

'But why?'

She clutched the pillow fiercely to her chest, threw her head back and blinked at the ceiling, blue eyes huge and wet.

'Because ... oh, Hattie, I can't explain. At least not to you. It's why I haven't seen you.'

I felt a lump rise in my throat.

'My little sister, who works hard all day, weekends too, who's permanently juggling bills and trying to make ends meet. And I'm bellyaching about not having a manor house – for ever. About not being able to pass it on to Charlie.'

'But you knew that. You always knew that.'

'Yes, but I'd pushed it to the back of my mind because I had other fish to fry. I had to get my hands on the place first, so all my energy went into that. I was so intent on getting our feet under the table, and now that we're here, I've moved on. I'm obsessed with something else, with staying. And I do want to do it all beautifully, not skimp – not that using you would be skimping.' She reached out and touched my arm. 'But Hugh says, if it's only for a few years, what's the point in spending so much money? And I think — well, what's the point of being here at all? — and I get so depressed.'

'Have you said all that to Hugh?'

'Well, you heard me tonight, and it's not the first time. And the moment I voice it, it sounds so terrible, like snakes and venom coming out of my mouth. These six months have been the unhappiest of our married life,' she said sadly. 'And they were supposed to be the happiest. I thought, once we were here I'd never want anything even again. But I do, I do want more. And I am so disappointed in myself. That's what it is. I simply don't like me,' she said vehemently.

I swallowed. 'Everyone thinks like that. Everyone always want more. It's human nature.'

'Not always. Not you.'

True, I didn't really. Not materially. I loved my little house, my shop, my work, my son. If I could have had more, if I had that longing she spoke of, it would have been years ago, and would have taken human shape. In the form of Dominic. Laura could have any man she wanted: she only had to walk in a room and smile, so I supposed it was natural her lusts were more worldly. Dominic I could never have because he was married, and then he'd died, so that had been that. Even now, though, if anyone mentioned his name, I caught my breath. Felt trembly. Or if I thought about him, I had to sit down: stop whatever I was doing. Years ago, I got a white light in my head, which dazzled me, prevented me from seeing anything else, and I suppose Laura had lived the last fifteen years seeing only this place, a blinding white light. She hadn't seen the complications, only her dream. But dreams have a way of becoming nightmares if too many years lapse before they're fulfilled. Where once Laura had been the ex-model with three small children waiting to occupy the ancestral pile and grace the pages of *Hello!*, now she was a middle-aged woman with teenagers poised to flee the nest, living in a ticking time bomb of a mausoleum as a wicked stepson debated when to turf her out.

Wicked? No, but difficult. And Laura had tried hard. Always. Right from the very beginning when she'd inherited Luca as a mixed-up six-year-old, shattered by his parents' divorce, born with a withered arm, brought up by nannies as Carla pursued her own ends, her film career, her social life. So Luca was shipped over to England in the holidays, to his father, and Laura and Hugh did their best. Lots of attention and time, holidays in Cornwall, fishing for crabs in rock pools, Laura newly married, then heavily pregnant, then with toddlers, but really feeling she was getting somewhere by the end of each summer, forming a relationship with him. She'd ring me elated: 'He let me put him to bed, read to him, we had long chats. I'm really getting through, Hatts.' And then next time he came, she'd ring me aghast: 'He's so different, so cold, so distant! What the hell do I do?'

'Keep at it,' had been my advice, and she had. But each time he was ruder, more confrontational, and I'd been shocked to witness his teenage years: druggy, surly, calling Laura 'woman'. But then he'd had countless operations on his arm, which had never improved. He slunk around the lodge frightening Biba and Daisy, Laura's girls, letting loose a stream of Italian at them: a sinister figure who scared even Laura, now.

33

'Has he improved? Luca?' I asked tentatively. 'Hugh says he comes to shoot. Has he gentrified miraculously? Head to toe in tweeds?'

'Of course not. He shoots in an old airman's jacket and ripped jeans, while Hugh looks pained and embarrassed but doesn't dare say anything. He's coming in a couple of weeks' time. I might rope you in for moral support.'

I smiled. 'Thanks.'

She sat hugging her pillow. Lay her face sideways on it. A beautiful, sculpted, sorrowful face. We were silent a moment.

She raised her head and went on in a low voice, 'You might not believe me, Hatts, but I'm honestly not upset for me. I'm upset for the children. To move them in here, then suddenly move them out when Luca marries—'

'Is that when it changes hands?'

'Not necessarily. It's at Hugh's discretion. But that's what he said the other day, apropos of nothing. "When Luca marries I'll hand it over, won't let him wait like I did." Well, he's twenty-two, Hattie. It could be a couple of years!'

'Unlikely. Most people don't get married till later, these days,' I mumbled. Luca wasn't most people.

'OK, but still, say five years. It's not so bad for the girls. They're teenagers, they'll be off in flats in London after university; home won't be so important. But for Charlie, who's only eight, to move out ...'

'Children move house all the time! He'll understand. Look at us – sixteen houses in twenty years!'

'Which is precisely what I didn't want!' She turned fierce eyes on me.

I sighed. I'd never thought it was so bad, our slightly nomadic lifestyle as Dad's job took us from place to place, country to country sometimes. But siblings raised identically often have totally different takes on their childhood. What Kit and I had thought exciting, Laura had thought muddled, unsettling.

'And the thing is, Hatts, years ago, we could have bought a perfectly nice house with Hugh's salary, made it a home. A lovely country house with paddocks, pool, a court, but manageable – oh, listen to me! Paddocks, pools, a court, as if they were staples!'

'It's only natural. It's what your friends have all got, so it becomes the norm.'

'Yes, but you do … slightly lose touch with reality. Lose perspective. Money does that. And you also become … a bit isolated.'

Ah. I'd wondered. I'd never envied Laura's life because I liked living in a road with lots of people. Loved London, loved waking up to its buzz, walking to my shop every morning, grabbing a cappuccino from Paulo's, exchanging a cheery word with my neighbours, couldn't imagine driving half an hour to see a friend, as Laura did. I knew Maggie was up the road, Sally round the corner, Ben and Steve in their art gallery, Mum and Dad a tube ride away. Dad.

'What would Dad say?' she said in a small voice, reading my mind.

'He'd be hugely sympathetic.'

'That I was upset, yes, but secretly appalled too. Troubled by a daughter who was seemingly so obsessed by wealth and status. He'd draw parallels with the American Dream, ask me gently if I'd ever read *Gatsby*. Quietly disapprove. Like he does with Mum. I am Mum,' she said sadly. 'I've turned into her.'

'You are not Mum.'

She blinked rapidly down at the bedcover.

'You're panicking,' I said firmly. 'And that's only natural. It's a huge undertaking, this place, and I can quite see you're nervous about pouring everything into it, only to have it taken from you—'

'Exactly!' She looked up quickly. 'Like – like bringing up a child, knowing you'd got to give it back. Imagine if Seffy's real parents hadn't died, and they'd shown up one day saying, we want him back!'

'Well, no, that would break my heart, Laura,' I said slowly. 'We're talking about a house, here. A pile of bricks.'

'Yes,' she said quickly, breathily. She looked appalled. 'You see?' she whispered. 'See what sort of a person I've become? How I've lost touch with reality? See?'

We were silent a moment. Both preoccupied with our thoughts. After a bit, Laura shifted on the bed. She brought her knees up to her chest and clasped them: a regrouping gesture.

'And I haven't asked you anything at all about yourself. I'm so obsessed with my own life, I've completely tuned out of yours. I'm sorry.'

I smiled, recognizing genuine contrition when I saw it. 'Don't be. Not much to tell.'

'Oh, yeah? Mum thinks you've got a man.'

I coloured. 'She does? Why?'

'Don't hedge. She says she rang you the other day and you were short of breath and said you'd been for a run. She thought, Hattie doesn't run for a bus, and then she heard a man laughing in the background.'

'Ah.' I remembered it well. It had been the turn of the airing cupboard to host that afternoon's erotic activity, which had been hot. That, amongst other things, had left me breathless when Mum had rung.

'Well, come on, who is it?'

'Um … you don't know him.'

'Of course I don't, but give us a clue.'

I scratched my neck. 'He's … just a bloke.'

'That's it?'

'No, obviously not, but …'

'But what?' She stiffened. 'He's married?'

'No.'

'Well, thank the Lord. I gather Maggie's got one of those. OK, so what's the problem? Oh – does he make you dress up? Wear rubber, or something?'

'Don't be silly. No, he's quite … you know.'

'What?'

'Young.'

Laura's eyes widened. 'Oh. Young. How young?'

'I'm … not sure.'

'What d'you mean, you're not sure. Haven't you asked?'

'Er, no. Not yet. Not very, I don't think. But he did take GCSEs rather than O levels. And he'd never seen a vinyl record before.'

'You've been spinning discs?'

'Well, the more modern equivalent.'

A light went on behind her eyes. 'Sex!' she breathed. 'For the sake of it.' She gazed at me entranced. 'Can't remember when I last did that and didn't tick it off my list of Things To Do. You know what Mum will say?'

'Where's it going!' I yelped, panic-stricken. 'I know, so please don't tell her, Laura, promise?' I gripped her wrist. 'Pinky promise?'

'No, I won't. But … be careful, Hatts. Is he good to you? Treats you well?'

'Of course!' I was aware of my cheeks flaming.

'And who picks up the restaurant bill?'

'Well, him, for sure, obviously.' I wasn't going to tell her we hadn't got to the restaurant stage. We're working backwards towards it, so to speak. From bed.

She raised her eyebrows, quizzically.

'I'm not a sugar mummy, Laura. He pays his way.'

'What – from his pocket money?'

'Don't be silly, he's not that young. And anyway, it's not that unusual, is it? Look at Emma Thompson and Greg thingy, and, um, Joan Collins—'

'Joan Collins! Her husband's known as the antique dealer!'

'Is he?' I was appalled. Licked my lips. 'Well, heavens, I'm not marrying the guy. It's just a bit of fun. Just a fling.'

How naïve it sounded, sailing boldly out of my mouth into the stratosphere.

'Oh, really?' She held on to those ironic eyebrows. 'That doesn't sound like you, Hattie. You don't do anything you don't pour your heart and soul into. You don't do flings. Don't do anything for kicks.'

I got up quickly from the bed in one fluid movement, wishing she didn't know me so well. Know how I ticked. I was falling in love with Ivan, I knew that, and couldn't seem to stop myself. Falling. Such an apposite word. Free-falling, face down, arms and legs out like a starfish, probably a heavenly sensation with a parachute to steady you, to add a note of caution, but not so funny without one and with a bumpy landing. And I'd been careful all these years not to do that. Since Dominic. Not to get involved.

I went to the window and narrowed my eyes to the gentle, undulating hills beyond. My phone vibrated against my thigh in my pocket, and in true Pavlovian response, I felt a thrill go up my spine. All those texts. Ten a day sometimes, designed to make the heart beat faster. 'Morning, my love, you're beautiful' or 'Can't stop thinking about you.' Not as many as Maggie, of course. She was on thirty a day. Like fags, I thought in surprise. I wasn't a chain texter, like her. Could I wean myself down to one a day, perhaps? Just a quick fix after breakfast? Maybe one could get a patch. On the NHS.

I sighed and leaned the heels of my hands on the sill, gazing out. It was beautiful, that view, but you couldn't live on a view. I wondered how Laura did. Oh, what, so texts and a toy boy were better? I pressed my forehead against the glass, trying not to think what might have been – years ago. Before there was any need for younger men. He'd grown up round here, of course. Dominic, not Ivan. Not in the grand, ancestral way that Hugh had, but on the edge of the village, which was how Laura met Hugh in the first place – through me knowing Dom. Through Hal, Dom's younger brother, who'd been a mate of mine at university. Yes, Dominic and Hal Forbes, who'd lived … well, over there, surely. I stared; turned to Laura, who still had her head resting pensively on her knees.

'Is that Little Crandon?'

'Yes. Why?'

'You couldn't see it from the lodge.'

'No, I know, but we're further up the hill now.' She got up and joined me at the window. 'I rather like it, actually. Don't feel quite so alone. I like to draw my curtains at night and see someone else in the village draw theirs.'

'And Letty still lives there, does she?' My heart began to pound.

'In The Pink House? Yes, look, you can see it from here. Left of the village, go two fields across from the church … then down in the valley where the sheep are, see?' She pointed. 'Their land marches with ours, as Hugh puts it, which always makes me think of thousands of blades of grass going left-right, left-right, in strict formation.'

'Letty and her daughter?'

'Yes, Cassie. Although for how much longer I don't know. Irony of ironies, Hal wants to kick her out too. We had a coffee the other day, Letty and me – well, turned into a bottle of wine – the main thrust of the conversation being how to keep one's relatives' thieving hands off one's property.'

'But that's outrageous. The house was Dominic's, and Letty is his widow. What right has Hal got to it? And Cassie … surely if it's anyone's, it's hers?'

'Well, I may have got that wrong. You know Letty: she's a pretty unreliable source. But Hal certainly wants her out. It's a lovely place, but again, quite isolated. A bit of a schlep from the village. You went there once, didn't you? With Dominic? Dispatch boxes and things?'

I nodded. Couldn't trust myself to speak. She meant when I worked for him. At the House of Commons for about a year. And yes, I did go there. And it was, indeed, lovely. As was Letty, his young wife, pregnant at the time. The whole thing was idyllic: a pretty, smiling, welcoming wife, stepping out of a sweet pink house with roses round the door – heaven. Which was why nobody, not even Laura, who knew how I ticked, had known, or indeed could ever know, how deeply, passionately in love with him I'd been. How loving, but not being able to love Dominic Forbes had altered the entire course of my life.

4

I met Dominic through his brother, Hal, who I'd been friendly with at Edinburgh. Hal and I were in our fourth year together, reading Law and English respectively; we also shared the same student house along with one or two other friends. Well, OK, I suppose Hal and I were slightly more than friends. He'd taken a shine to me, is how my mother would have put it: not a phrase to trip off a student's tongue in the nineties, but it did rather aptly describe Hal's devotion to me and my refusal to get involved with him. I don't think I even kissed him in a drunken moment, pining quietly as I was for the full back in the firsts: six foot two, spectacular thighs and fatal, devilish smile. I was flattered, and I liked Hal, but that was it: romantically he didn't press any of my buttons. It didn't seem to deter him, though. He didn't exactly carry my bags, but I'd often come out of a lecture theatre to find him lurking by the coffee machine, huge army greatcoat drowning him, dark hair long and scruffy, pushing his glasses up his nose, poised to get us both a milk and two sugars.

After one particular seminar, which had turned into more of a careers discussion and from which I'd emerged steaming, I'd been particularly grateful for the polystyrene cup he handed me. Everyone seemed to have a vague idea of what they wanted to do next, and some were positively shot through with conviction. My other flatmate, Kirsten, a narrow-faced, focused Scots girl with precious little *joie de vivre*, had even done something sinister called a 'milk round', whereby prospective employers kerb-crawled around universities picking up potential worker bees: Kirsten was now on course to work for Unilever for the rest of her life. I'd been stunned as she'd dropped this bombshell mid-seminar.

'But how d'you know you'll like it?' I'd demanded. 'Selling toothpaste, shampoo – how d'you know you'll be passionate about that?'

'Why do I have to be passionate?'

'Well, what's the point, otherwise?'

Our tutor had sat back with a watchful smile.

Kirsten's eyes, which already, it seemed to me, had been traded in for lightless, corporate ones, met mine coolly.

'The point is it's good money and it's one of the best marketing training schemes around,' she'd said in her thick Glaswegian accent. 'And the fast track to management level is infinitely better than in most PLCs.'

The voids of my ignorance opened before me. Trainee, management … I didn't even know what a PLC was. It seemed a long way from discussing the pastoral motifs in *The Mill on the Floss*. It also seemed to me that for four years we'd been encouraged to be idealistic in our work and hedonistic in our play, and overnight were expected to transform into thrusting, power-hungry executives. And it was typical of Kirsten, who was supremely organized – one of the reasons Hal and I lived with her was she had a fine line in acquiring decent student accommodation – to be ahead of the game. The public school contingent at Edinburgh, particularly the boys, called girls like Kirsten Wee Marys, whilst the Wee Marys in turn called them the Fucking Yahs. I didn't belong in the Scots lass camp, but didn't really fit into the other either, being a bit dubious socially: or as Kirsten sweetly and succinctly put it, 'Yer not really posh enough, are ye?' I lined up with the Yahs none the less. We were laid-back, nonchalant and cool. So cool we missed the employment boat.

'I don't have a clue,' I'd wailed to Hal in the coffee bar as we'd slopped our drinks across to a table. 'Everyone else seems to have a clear idea of where they're going and what they're going to do and I haven't given it a thought.'

I'd been far too busy: having fun, partying, dyeing my hair unusual shades, wearing lurex tights, drinking, smoking, meeting boys – so many boys but never the right one. As I'd looked at Hal then in the coffee bar I'd thought what a shame it was he was quite so skinny and sallow-looking, and why did he stoop? If you're tall, for heaven's sake, stand up. And that annoying way he had of clearing his throat before he spoke. Laura was right – she'd breezed through Edinburgh on a shoot for *Harper's* when Bailey had her draped around the castle walls in Givenchy – Hal was sweet enough, but drippy. Not in the ranks of the rugby-playing heroes I aspired to.

'Well, what d'you think you want to do?' Hal asked.

'I don't know, that's just it! Something arty, I suppose, but I'm not creative. And I like old things,' I said vaguely, staring bleakly into space. 'You know, china, glass, that type of thing. French stuff, mostly.'

'Like all that rubbish in your room.' This, a reference to my precious and nearly complete Limoges tea set.

'Antiques of tomorrow,' I'd told him tartly, lest it be thought I was starting some sort of bottom drawer; lest it betray my only real – and shameful – ambition: to get married.

'Well, how about working in a museum, then? Or a gallery?'

43

'Ugh, too stuffy.' I slumped forward miserably on the table, nose to the rim of my coffee cup. I tried to drink it without picking it up. 'It's all right for you, you know what you want to do.' I wiped my chin as coffee dribbled down it. 'Save the world.'

Hal was going to be a human rights lawyer.

'I don't know about that, but I wouldn't mind trying to make it a better place, at any rate.'

'You see?' I sat up. 'Caring, altruistic ... and you'll be at the centre of things too, where it's topical, where the action is. That's where I want to be,' I said suddenly. 'Where the action is.'

Hal pushed his lank and frankly greasy hair out of his eyes. Adjusting his spectacles he said hestitantly, 'I could always ask my brother, if you like? If you just want to tread water and get some work experience, you could maybe get a job with him for a bit.'

'Where does he work?' I'd asked, thinking it was a pity Sam McKinnon hadn't come in. He often had a coffee here after his History lecture. Before rugby training. Sometimes in his kit. I craned my neck round.

'The House of Commons.'

'The House of Commons?' My head snapped back: my neck came out of my shoulders like a tortoise.

'Yes, he's an MP. Well, a Government whip, actually.'

'A whip.' My, that sounded exciting. A leather-clad lothario wielding a hunting crop and bearing, oddly, a startling resemblance to Sam McKinnon sprang to mind.

'And what does he do?'

'Oh, bustle around making people vote, I think. Lobbies for support. He's sort of a party organizer.'

Like a party planner. Which had at one stage been an idea, but I'd dismissed it as too frivolous. Counting vol-au-vents and folding napkins into swans and so forth. But a political party planner … I rehearsed it in my head. I'm a political party planner.

'Which side is he on?'

'I told you. The Government.'

'Oh. Right …' My knowledge of politics was negligible in those days, but I was pretty sure that was the more, you know, right-wing lot. Stricter. Too many immigrants, too many hand-outs, too much welfare state, that kind of thing. Bit mean, but probably quite right.

I shifted uncomfortably. Well, I wasn't really fussy. Better-looking, I'd hazard. Nice spotty ties, good suits, braces. I wasn't sure what Dad would think of it, though. We'd been brought up on the smell of an oily rag, mostly in chattering North London – more Neasden than Hampstead – and my father was a bit of an armchair socialist. (For years I'd thought this meant sitting in an armchair being sociable, passing the peanuts.) He'd been a big Michael Foot man and was on walking-stick-raising terms with him on the Heath, and although when Neil Kinnock took the helm he'd lost heart and voted Monster Raving Loony in protest, I wasn't convinced he'd approve of me Crossing The Floor, as it were. Even Mum, in her youth, had apparently done some prison visiting – the mind boggled, jangling down to the cells in her Mikimoto pearls and her Chanel chains – and despite having morphed into a flog-em-hard-hang-em-high Tory who only bought her sausages at Fortnum's, she still had a photo of herself at a rally in Trafalgar Square holding a placard, admittedly without a hair out of place, which Laura and I had gaped at. I had an idea Toryism was something you were eventually allowed to slide into, at least in my family. I wasn't sure one should succumb so quickly: it was a bit like drinking Horlicks in your teens.

But it was only a stepping stone to other things, I reasoned. Research, maybe. Research. That sounded serious. I could tell Kirsten that. And what a chance! Seat of government. Corridors of power. I saw myself running down them in a very tight pencil skirt and heels, arms full of documents, behind a very good-looking important man: 'Tristan – Tristan, your speech!'

'Would you ask him?' I said eagerly, eyes probably shining into Hal's, which wasn't kind.

'Of course. Or you can ask him yourself. He's coming up in a few weeks for the graduation.'

And indeed he did. And I'd been expecting a corrugated quiff of Brylcreemed hair, a ruddy face, a bluff manner, wall-to-wall pinstripes, but someone tall and golden had appeared, with a fabulous smile and wise, amused eyes that crinkled at the corners; he also had a very muddy Spaniel, and a shabby Barbour and boots, which he apologized for when he came to our flat to change.

'We've been stalking in Fife,' he explained, slapping his little brother on the back and beaming at Kirsten and me, dressed as we were in our smartest, darkest Oxfam or Topshop graduation clothes. Our little basement kitchen had never looked so attractive as he bounded about, introducing his equally blonde wife, Letty. 'It was bloody freezing up there! We've only just thawed.'

Stalking. My first encounter with the clothes, the whiff of the great outdoors, the purple heather, the glamour,

46

the exclusivity, the money, the danger, the guns: it all seemed to breathe at me in that dingy Edinburgh basement kitchen.

'Brought you these, Hal; shot them in an idle moment. Or perhaps I should give them to the girls.'

Two dead rabbits, eyes glassy, heads hanging, were offered from a bag, and I just managed not to scream. Kirsten did, though, and took a leap backwards too.

'Skin them for you if you like?' Dominic said in surprise, as I reached and took them from him, trying not to heave. I'd never touched a dead animal. 'No, no, I'll do it. How kind!'

He smiled into my eyes, and it seemed to me we had a moment.

'I'll do them later,' said Hal, quickly taking them from me. 'You'd better change.' This to his brother. 'The ceremony starts in an hour.'

Dominic and Letty were *in loco parentis*, Hal's mother being abroad, his father dead. When they emerged from Hal's room and then later, as we all trooped across campus with our families to McEwan Hall, I thought how glamorous they looked: Dominic in a dark grey suit, Letty in a floaty cream linen dress, beads, quirky straw hat, witty little shoes: she had an alternative bohemian style and even my mother, stunning as ever in grey shot silk and never liking to be outdone, noticed them.

'Who is that very attractive man, darling? With your flatmate?'

'Oh, Dominic Forbes, his brother. He's an MP.' I couldn't take my eyes off him. Or keep the excitement from my voice.

47

'Of course. Darling,' she nudged my father. We were filing into the hall, now, finding our seats, 'it's Dominic Forbes.'

My father, who'd taken an order of ceremony sheet and put his reading glasses on to survey it, raised his head to peer over them. 'So it is,' he said in his soft Bostonian accent. 'The acceptable face of capitalism. Or so they tell us.'

'You've heard of him?'

'Of course,' said Mum. 'He's always in the papers. He's the youngest member of the cabinet for fifty years, and his father was Peter Forbes, the film director.'

'He's not in the cabinet yet,' murmured Dad, resuming his perusal of the programme. 'Still on the back benches.' But Mum was on a roll.

'Oh, yes, it's quite a dynasty. Go back another generation and the grandfather was the great explorer, Ernest Forbes. This one, Dominic, is supposed to be equally brilliant, and is hellbent on reforming his party and making it more – what's the word, David?'

'Slimy?'

'No, more modernist, that's it. Sweep out the old Tory blue-rinse image and introduce a more caring society – I read about it in the *Mail* last week. And there was a whole double-page spread on Her, all about what she did with the turkey on Boxing Day.' Mum was fairly palpitating with excitement now, and I wasn't far behind. The more she talked the more a shimmering glow seemed to surround Mr Forbes.

'Apparently he's got his sights on being Prime Minister one day, and why not? It's about time we had some young blood running the country.'

Dad was clearly going to let her run with this, but not without raising his eyes to heaven.

'But this article said he'd like to have a go at being Chancellor first. Sort out the economy, which badly needs doing,' she added sagely, as if it were a teenager's bedroom. 'Don't you love his pink tie?'

Dad finally cracked. 'Your mother's razor-sharp political insight into the man she's tipped to head up Her Majesty's Government seems to be based entirely on the colour of his tie and what his wife does with leftovers. Let's hope she's not indicative of the nation.'

'And *she* is the daughter of Lord Bellington, that eccentric impoverished peer who sleeps with greyhounds on his bed and whose sisters all write gardening books. They're always in the papers too. And her mother was a model like me in the sixties.'

Dad's eyes had now completely rotated because we all knew Mum's modelling career needed huge pinches of salt. She had once done some knitwear patterns – half-turn to camera, enquiring eyes, finger to chin – but it was hardly Christian Dior.

'I might go and work for him,' I said, unable to resist.

'No!' she breathed ecstatically.

'Well, not sure yet,' I said hastily, seeing her lurch forward and almost sprint across to wring his hand, check out his tie. 'Hal's going to try and fix it up for me.'

'Hal?'

'His younger brother, the one you met. We share a flat.'

'Ah, yes, the peaky-looking one. I must say, seeing them together, you'd never guess they were—'

'Shh.' Dad silenced her as the organ started.

'See you later,' I whispered, as I shot away to join the rest of the robed, mortarboarded crew waiting to go up on stage to face the proud parents. I muscled through to where Hal had secured me a seat beside him.

'Well?' I breathed, as we sat down.

'Well, what?'

'Oh.' My face fell. He grinned.

'He said he'd be delighted to have you on unpaid work experience for a couple of weeks. Can you type?'

'Yes!'

'Well then, he said you never know, after that you might get some typist going sick, and then you can fill in. And then if another goes on holiday or something one thing could lead to another. He can't promise anything, but as in all these clubby places, it's getting a toe in the door that counts. He can at least do that for you. Then it's up to you.'

'Oh, Hal. Thank you!' I gazed at him, covered in delight.

He gave an odd little smile and shrugged. 'My pleasure.'

I couldn't resist looking over to where Dominic was sitting with his wife, in the audience. At that moment he looked, and I caught his eye. He smiled. Half a gallon of adrenalin shot up the back of my legs. I grinned broadly back: winked too, which, in retrospect, perhaps I shouldn't have.

5

Everything about it was seductive; everything. As I stepped off the tube at Westminster and climbed the steps to emerge into hazy summer sunshine, crossed the road under the dappled shade of dusty plane trees, the Thames flashing before me, Big Ben looming, I felt excitement mounting. The air may have been full of blaring horns and toxic fumes, but as I skirted the cool oasis of green that was Parliament Square, hemmed in on all sides by Thursday morning commuter traffic, it seemed to me it was heady with possibility. A stationary white van, window open, blared out reggae music and I fancied I fell into step with London's heartbeat as I strode past it, bass note thumping, blood pumping. Parliament, in all its ornate gothic splendour rose to greet me, windows flashing in a honey-coloured limestone façade, and even the policeman, stationed at the towering iron gates, had just the right amount of amiable old-fashioned-English-bobby about him. I flashed him one of my very best smiles and we exchanged a cheery good morning as he checked my pass: through the archway I fancied I could see right into the lobby beyond; people were already gathering, hustling, barking into mobile phones and oh … my … god … wasn't that the journalist with the big ears? The one on *News at Ten*?

'You'll be wanting Portcullis House, luv.' He handed my pass back to me.

'That's it.'

'Back around the corner,' he turned, 'and across the square. See that tower block over the road there?' He

pointed in the distance to somewhere slightly less picturesque; slightly more chrome and concrete. 'First left
through the big glazed doors and take the lift to the fourth
floor.'

'Oh.'

Not quite the oak-panelled corridors of power I'd
envisaged then. Nevertheless I obeyed orders and crossed
back over the road, around the square, through the doors,
and took the elevator. I squeaked along the linoleum passageway, floor-to-ceiling plate glass on one side, a row of
closed doors that looked faintly clinical and forbidding
on the other. No matter: the atmosphere may be subdued
and humdrum, but at least – I turned my head wistfully
before knocking at the door to which I was bidden – at
least there was a view of Big Ben.

Katya, Dominic's private secretary, attractive in a
plump, middle-aged, powdered way, was sympathetic.
When she'd shown me where I'd sit, in a corner without
the view, and then where the photocopier was, in another
dark corner, she laughed when I casually mentioned the
location.

'Oh, no, only the cabinet have offices over there. In fact
it's quite nice to be at a distance; to go there and then
come back. You appreciate the contrast more. It's like
anything: when you get too close, it loses its appeal.'

'So you still get a buzz from it?'

'Oh, yes, it would be hard not to. Having said that, it's a
job, like any other. Routine and hard work. The excitement
and glamour – what there is of it – is in the chamber. I'll
take you over there later. It's Prime Minister's questions at
twelve o'clock. Dominic asked me to get you a ticket.
We'll go and watch.'

'Did he? Oh, how kind! So we'll all go together?'

'Well, Dominic obviously sits on the benches. We'll be up in the visitors' gallery.'

'Of course.' I sat where she'd shown me. 'Is he … terribly busy at the moment?'

'Extremely.' She bustled across to her own desk and picked up a great pile of papers. 'And I'm afraid you won't see a great deal of him. He's lobbying for support on a transport bill at the moment. We've got a few waverers, and there's a rogue member in Wales who's threatening to go Lib-Dem, probably about to lose his constituency, so he's sticking the knife in as usual – all hell's breaking loose. Why don't you sit and have a look through these bills and reforms and familiarize yourself with what he does?' She dumped them on my desk. 'His big thing is education, he's passionate about the primaries. Have a look at his latest proposals.'

Whilst Katya pounded her computer in the other corner, I spent a very turgid hour flicking through a mind-numbingly dull heap of documents, trying hard not to yawn, or even pass out. In my bag was a *Cosmo*, which I surreptitiously smuggled onto my lap.

After a while, I went to make myself a cup of coffee in the little kitchen. Katya was already in there, and before I went in, I heard her talking to another secretary behind the door.

'And of course Dominic takes all these students, and then flaming well disappears. What am I supposed to do with her?'

My hand came away from the handle. I stepped back. I was one of many: a student who wanted to see the chamber, the Strangers' Gallery, have a drink on the terrace overlooking the river, be introduced to MPs. Maybe even catch a glimpse of the Prime Minister. I went back to the office.

Moments later Katya fluttered back to her desk.

'There you are, dear.' She handed me a mug. 'And there's a couple of biscuits and a sugar. I'm sorry I haven't been very communicative, but when I've finished these letters and made a few calls, I'll take you across the road.' She hastened back to her seat.

'I can type,' I said. 'Accurately. My father taught me. He's a journalist. I used to type up copy for him sometimes. Why don't you make your calls and I'll finish that pile for you?'

She looked at me, surprised, over her glasses.

'I'm fast, sixty words a minute.'

'Well...'

I saw her hesitate. 'Where have you got to?' I got up and crossed to her desk.

She rose hesitantly. 'Well, you can have a go at his correspondence, if you like. These are responses to all his constituents, but his handwriting's appalling. I don't know if you'll be able—'

'I will.' I sat down eagerly. 'My dad's got terrible writing too. If I can decipher that I can read anything.'

I took the pile of letters from her, flicked up the screen, and shot a piece of Portcullis-headed paper into the printer. She hovered over me uncertainly as I rattled off the first one. Dominic's handwriting *was* appalling, but once I'd got my eye in I could see his As and Es were the only confusing elements and I could guess the rest. I handed Katya the letter to check.

'Very good,' she said approvingly. 'Well, if you could bear to wade your way through that little lot I can sit at the other desk and ring the party chairman with a whole list of worries and woes. Reply to some of Dominic's emails, too.'

'Absolutely. You crack on.'

I set off at breakneck speed, something all us Carrington children could do, almost as a party trick. Dad had taught us one summer, when there was no money for a holiday and we were kicking around the garden, bored. He'd lined up three old typewriters, which were being chucked out of the *New Statesman*'s offices, in the back yard – we'd hit Kilburn by then, not an address my mother favoured – and put boards over our hands to teach us not to look at the keys. Laura, Kit and I had races, the winner rewarded with an ice cream from the shop on the corner. I typed now as I'd typed in that Kilburn garden: competitively, lips pursed, imagining Laura rattling away beside me, whilst Katya made her calls. At ten to eleven she stopped me.

'You've been terrific,' she said, beaming gratefully over my shoulder. 'Truly, truly helpful. Come on, I'll take you across the road and we'll see what's cooking.'

I could tell she was pleased and we chatted companionably on the way across. She lived with her sister in Vauxhall, she told me; had worked for Dominic for five years, and before that for his uncle, who was also a politician.

'Really? I didn't know that.'

'Roger Forbes?'

'Oh, yes. I've heard of him. Didn't know he was his uncle.' Black mark to Mum.

'They're a very distinguished family. Rather like the Attenboroughs, everyone is talented. But quietly, and in different ways. Charming with it.'

'So you like working for him?' We dodged a motorcyclist on our way across.

'I love it. It's my life,' she said simply, and somehow that didn't sound so sad. Yes, OK, she was unmarried and lived with her sister, but for eight – no, probably eleven – hours a day she was a vital cog in the ever-spinning wheel of one of the world's most modern, constitutional governments. In this great edifice of parliamentary democracy, she was in the engine room. She wasn't your archetypal role model, I thought as I followed her thick calves and swinging hips into Parliament, waiting as she paused to reapply her over-pink lipstick covertly in a compact before we went in, but in that moment, at that particular time, I wanted to be her. Wanted to purr 'Dominic Forbes's office' down the phone to whom it may concern, but wanted, especially, for the man himself to turn as we approached in the busy lobby, thronged with people hurrying too and fro, sweep back his blond hair and come towards us eagerly.

His eyes lit up as he saw Katya.

'All well?' he asked anxiously.

'Yes, fine. Ted Mallory wanted to know if we could reconvene on Tuesday and I said not unless the Whips' Office could have a say in the final proposal – he said he'd let us know. Colin Mercer called to say yes in theory, but no to the extended budget. Oh, and we need an amendment here –' she handed him a paper – 'Section B apparently should read "centralized", not "ministerial", and then a signature here ...' she handed him a pen and he scribbled, '... and here.'

He signed again. 'And I've cancelled your trip to Delhi on Friday and rearranged it for the following Tuesday so you can still vote on the health bill.'

Whilst she'd been speaking, periodically punctuating her flow with a proffered piece of paper, he'd nodded, muttered 'Right' or 'OK' occasionally, but by the time she'd got to the end, his face had cleared.

'Good. Well done. I'm pleased you managed to put the India trip off. Did you check it with his lordship?'

'I did, and then had to ring the world and his wife and rearrange their diaries. But it helped enormously having Hattie. She waded through your correspondence, bless her, whilst I haggled.'

He turned; seemed to see me almost for the first time. 'Did she, by Jove? Hattie, I'm so sorry, I didn't recognize you without your mortarboard. How marvellous that you've been such a help.' He smiled and I glowed. 'I've certainly never heard Katya say my attempts at integrating students were anything more than a hindrance. You've clearly earned your keep!'

Another dazzling smile, in which I basked like a salamander, determined to do even more that afternoon.

'I've got to dash to the chamber,' he was saying to Katya, 'and I thought I'd ask the nursery school question if the Speaker's on form. What d'you think?'

'I would,' she urged. 'Tom Paine was saying the other day that someone's got to ask it, and it might not be popular, but eventually the Opposition will wonder why we haven't.'

'Exactly.' He strode off.

I gazed at her in awe. Oh ... my ... God. She wasn't just a secretary, or even a researcher. She advised. She was trusted, wise. And he not only asked for her advice, he acted on it. My estimation of her went up tenfold as I fell in step behind her and we went up to the gallery. I even wondered, should I invest in American Tan tights?

Tiny, compact and green, arranged like a chapel but much more raucous, the chamber was brimming with braying MPs waving bits of paper: full, actually, of testosterone, albeit with a few token pink suits and silk scarves scattered around the front benches. I loved it; was spellbound. It was particularly atmospheric today, Katya explained, because a controversial bill was being voted on later tonight, so all elected representatives were present and correct. Questions were being hurled at the Prime Minister, who, leaning confidently on the ballot box, swiped some away like dirty flies but gave others a longer, more considered response. Finally Dominic, looking slightly nervous, smoothed down his tie and got to his feet, but before he could get to the end of his question, he was shouted down by a rude fat man opposite. I bristled indignantly. Dominic forged on none the less, was encouraged to do so by the Speaker, and the Prime Minister had no choice but to reply, albeit in a rather offhand manner, clearly not welcoming criticism from his own benches, and was then jeered by the opposition for the feebleness of his response. I was completely riveted.

As we saw Dominic on the way out, horribly aware that my eyes were shining, I couldn't help but put my hand on his arm as he hurried away.

'Can I just say I thought you were fantastic. Absolutely fantastic. He may have pretended to dismiss you, but you really rattled him.'

He'd been striding off down the corridor with a couple of cronies and they all turned to look at me in wonder. The other two threw back their heads and roared.

'Well, someone's got your vote, Dominic. Even if the rest of us are agin you!'

Much baying and waistcoat slapping at what I realized must have sounded corny and gushing, but Dominic's eyes, although amused, were kind.

'Thank you. At least some of my office recognize a killer question when they hear it.'

More snorts of derision greeted this, and then they strode off in a wall of grey flannel, but not before Dominic had turned to flash a smile over his shoulder.

The week went by: flew, from my point of view, but, happily, I was there for another. The second would go even faster, I knew, and I tried not to think about it. Tried not to think about going home, when on day twelve – and I swear to God I didn't touch her – a minor miracle occurred. The sort of thing that never happens to me. Katya put her back out. The previous evening, in her flat in Vauxhall, she'd tried to clean her French windows, fallen off her stool, and was now doubled up in agony. She didn't come in the following day, and was then off work for another two, which was unheard of, Dominic told me. She'd never had a day sick in five years. That afternoon at five, she rang to say she couldn't walk: wouldn't be in for at least a fortnight.

Of course I didn't take over. I wouldn't have had a clue. But a competent temp who worked regularly at the Commons stepped in, and Dominic asked me to stay two more weeks to help with the typing. Just before Katya was due to return, he thanked the temp: asked if I'd been a help.

'Of course she has. You know, this is the only whip's office that doesn't have backup. I can't understand how Katya does it all. I certainly couldn't be doing without a typist.'

Well, it could have been worded better. 'Without Hattie's incisive judgement and invaluable political acumen' perhaps, but the point had been made.

When Katya returned she went into his office for a word – quite a long word – and came out pink and flustered.

'Right. Well.' She patted her hair. 'You've obviously done rather well. Dominic wants you to stay on to help out, although I'm sure you've got other career plans. Don't want to be a typist for ever. After all, you're a graduate.'

'Oh, no, I'd be delighted.'

'Would you now. Right, well, pop in,' she said crisply. 'He wants to see you.'

Dumbly I walked to the door. I'd barely been in this hallowed, book-lined sanctuary, Katya had seen to that, and certainly not when he'd been in it. Dominic was behind a huge leather-topped desk, signing papers, and I thought how young he looked to be in such an important position, with such weighty responsibility. He looked up and smiled as I approached.

'White smoke?'

'Oh, thanks.' I whipped out my Marlboro Lights and lit up, perching on a chair.

'No,' he laughed. 'You know, when they choose a pope? Except I hope I've chosen a typist.'

Shit. I looked around for somewhere to stub it out. Heavens, I'd thought we were settling down for a clubby moment with cigars.

'Oh, don't worry, puff away,' he said. 'I'm not averse.'

I held the wretched cigarette low; so low the smoke billowed around me as if my ankles were on fire.

'Of course you may not want it, but I've been aware for some time Katya has too much to do, so if you could see your way clear to becoming full-time dogsbody – I'm afraid that's what it'll amount to to begin with: tea lady, photocopying—'

'Oh, no, I'd love to,' I burst in. 'Honestly, it's my dream.'

'Really?' He looked at me with new interest. 'I didn't know. Did you read Politics? Here.'

He handed me a saucer for my cigarette and I stubbed the wretched thing out.

'No, English. And I don't know the first thing about politics, but I love working here and I'm sure I'll develop an interest.' I licked my lips. Took it more slowly. 'I mean – I'm already very interested. My dad's a journalist,' I threw in widly, 'so it's always been a kind of ... family thing.'

'Oh? Called?'

'David Carrington.'

'Ah, right.' He frowned; leaned back in his chair and tapped a pencil thoughtfully on his blotter. 'Good of you to mention it. Many people might not.'

'Really?'

'Well, your father's very left wing, Hattie. The *Guardian* is not necessarily my paper of choice.'

'No. Of course not.' Damn. Why was I so clueless? 'But ... he's a very fair man. And it doesn't really matter who's on what side, does it? I mean if we all want a better country? Eventually?'

'Noo,' he said slowly. 'Although I suppose I'd want to know you're fundamentally on our side. But I agree, essentially we should all be after the same thing, the common good. Which personally I see as a better education for all.'

'Oh, I couldn't agree more.'

'Our schools are chaotic.'

'Ghastly.'

'Some are downright disgraceful.'

'Crap.'

I was nervous, OK?

'I mean, I was lucky enough to have a very privileged education. But the majority don't, and it breaks my heart.'

'Mine too,' I said firmly.

'Really? Where did you go?'

I thought quickly. I had any number to choose from. Laura always said St Mary's on the grounds that it sounded private though it was in fact state, Kit plumped for one in upstate New York (two terms), but I tended to gauge it to whoever I was talking to.

'Stockwell Comprehensive.'

'Really?' I could see he was impressed. 'Well, your father clearly put his money where his mouth was.'

'We didn't have any money.'

'No. Quite. So you know the situation then. Know the problems.'

'Oh, I do,' I said gravely. 'Terrible place.' I'd had a ball at Stockwell. An absolute ball. Had made masses of friends of all creeds and cultures and found it far more lively and vibrant than any of the stuffy convents I'd been to.

'Well, that's my particular hobbyhorse, gripping the inner-city comprehensives. And how fascinating that you've got first-hand knowledge. Presumably quite recently?'

'Yes, I only left a few years ago.'

He stared at me, almost in awe, as a botanist might a rare orchid. I felt myself glow. Felt many cosy hours of glue-sniffing-drugs-and-knives chat coming on, with me as his inside girl. Perhaps on that sofa over there, legs tucked kittenishly beneath me as I filled him in on yoof culture. Showed him how to roll a … no, perhaps not. I listened as he went on to outline the job, which, as I already knew, was pretty much bang that computer, and then he got up and turned to the window, which meant I got to look at the back of him. I swallowed.

'One more thing. Katya is … very protective of her position here, and frankly marvellous. I suppose the reason it's taken me a while to hire anyone to help is I've been sensitive to her feelings: of her wanting to do it all herself.' He turned. Gave me a searching smile.

'That's only natural. This is her patch. You're very much her baby.'

'Figuratively speaking.'

'Of course. Like the Pope.'

I was quite pleased with that little sally. He looked bemused, then smiled. 'She's already admitted you've been a huge help. But I just wanted you to be aware of …' He looked awkward.

'Her toes?'

'Exactly.'

'I won't step on them.'

'Thank you.'

He grinned at me and I grinned back, an understanding arrived at. In fact I'd go so far as to call it a meeting of minds. After a few minor incidentals, like money and hours and time sheets, I left, on air. Positively hovering.

When I resumed my position, Katya, I could see, was wrestling with herself.

'I'm so pleased,' she said as I sat down. She was trying hard. 'Really, I mean it. I know I'm overprotective and I know it had to be someone, eventually, and I'm glad it's you.'

I saw her eyes glisten and knew, in that moment, she was in love with him. I also knew 'I'm glad it's you' meant, not someone more his age. I was still very young and gauche and scruffy. What she didn't want was some sophisticated thirtysomething desk-perching and crossing her legs, flicking back a mane of expensively high-lighted hair, and reeking of Chanel.

I think she might have seen my flash of recognition, because she went on hurriedly: 'Of course, you must meet Letty now. She's delightful, and terribly friendly.'

Well, I'd already met her at the graduation, but meet her again I did, that very Friday.

Dominic thought it was important I had an all-round view of the job, and that meant going to his constituency, where he disappeared to most Fridays. Who was I to demur? Apparently it was where his surgery was.

'Makes you sound like a doctor,' I said as we purred down the M40 to Thame in his rather sporty low-slung car. He was looking fairly sporty and low-slung himself in jeans, a checked shirt open over a white T-shirt, sleeves rolled up, tanned arms at the wheel. So unlike an MP I could hardly breathe. I lifted my legs off the seat beside him to make them look less fat.

'Well, in a way it's not dissimilar. Local people come to me with their worries and I try to sort them out. The problem is, by the time they get to me, they've exhausted every other avenue. I'm their last hope. They've already harangued the council, or their school, or local authority, but I do what I can. And to be honest that's the bit I love most, the bit that makes it seem slightly ...' he hesitated.

'Vocational?' I offered.

'Yes.' He glanced at me, pleased. 'When I get a result, I feel like punching the air. Feel I've really made a difference.'

Aware I was staring, I closed my mouth.

'Although, of course, you do get the occasional oddball who comes regularly, and you know there's no hope of ever helping them. Barking Brenda is my particular cross to bear. She runs the village shop and thinks it's possessed. She wants me to exorcise it. The Church have washed their hands of her, but she's convinced things are moving of their own accord – baked beans into the freezer, shampoo mysteriously appearing in the fridge – although in fact it's just her losing her marbles and forgetting she's put them there.'

'Oh! Sad.'

'Very, and what she really needs is a doctor, but then she might be sectioned, and is she really ready to be? She might lose her shop too, where she's worked all her life.' He shook his head. 'The whole thing is fraught. But if everyone pulls together – MP, GP, vicar – we just might be able to help her, and that's how it should be. Everyone working together to create a better community, a better way of life.'

It seemed to me his hair had grown to his shoulders and he wore white flowing robes; a halo round his head.

He was saviour, no doubt about it. I was working for a saviour, who'd come down to earth in the body of Johnny Depp.

He was swinging the wheel about expertly now, negotiating some winding country lanes, the sun on his face. It occurred to me I had my own vocational family member to draw on.

'My brother, Kit, feels like that. Giving something back and all that. He's in Bosnia.'

'Really?' He turned, surprised.

'Working for the International Red Cross. He's eighteen.'

'Good grief, that's brave. Even though they're diplomatically protected that's bloody dangerous.'

'I know.' I felt myself clench inside instantly. I didn't want to be told Kit was brave. To have his danger confirmed by one who knew. In fact, I wished I'd kept quiet. But Kit had rung last night, and was therefore on my mind. I turned to stare out of the window to ward off further conversation; tried not to think about my little brother, whose gap year adventure had turned into a nightmare.

A month in Florence had been the plan, plus a couple of weeks travelling round Italy, with a boy from school. But this boy's cousin worked for the UN, and he'd announced, when the six weeks was up, that he was going to cross the border, to help his cousin in Croatia. The ICRC needed volunteers, he said, and he couldn't look at any more Botticellis or knock back any more Bellinis while fifty miles away – fewer, even – a war was going on. I remembered the boy: very bright, focused, heading for Oxford; knew he'd be shot through with conviction. Kit, conversely, was a blithe, handsome, possibly even frivolous soul, certainly unencumbered by any social conscience, but he'd gone along for the ride; for the craic as they say in Ireland.

'Can you imagine how this will look on my CV? How many other fledgeling ad execs with have "Aid worker in Sarajevo" he'd said down the line to Dad from Florence. 'Looks a bit grittier than work experience in Harrods, don't you think?' He'd got an awful lot more on his CV than he'd bargained for.

Most of the time we heard nothing, but when he did ring, he sounded strained, far away. Last night he'd got me on my mobile and we'd made a show of chatting about incidentals, Laura's new flat, his sunburn.

But then he'd said, apropos of nothing, 'Did you know that there are concentration camps out here?' his voice attempting to be airily matter-of-fact. 'That's what they say, anyway. The stories you hear, the ones that come out …' he'd faltered and I'd sat up very straight. 'And us lot, the Red Cross. God, it sounds great, doesn't it? Red Cross – like the Seventh Cavalry or something, roaring in with ambulances. But it's tiny, minuscule. And … and anyway, what can you do?' My little brother. Sounding terribly lost and far away.

I gave myself a little inward shake as I sped down the lanes in Dominic's Alpha Romeo, brambles brushing the sides of the car. Tried to dispel all gloomy thoughts of camps and ambulances. I didn't want to go there. Where Kit was: a dusty, war-torn country, awash with despair. I wanted to be here, now, beside my attractive new boss in his sexy convertible, on the way to his sumptuous country pad: I wanted life to be optimistic and glowing with possibility.

After a bit the lanes got narrower. One, I noticed, even had grass growing down the middle. We were well off the beaten track.

'Here we are,' he announced, as we turned off through an open five-barred gate.

A pink house, long and low, thatched and creeper-strewn, with roses crawling round the two bay windows either side of the front door sat centrally in a gravel sweep. It was beautiful but modest. Not a sod-off house, but a comfortable family one, the sort of thing Laura and I would have given our eyeteeth to grow up in. I got out, trying not to look too enchanted.

Letty had heard the car and come to open the door. She was wearing cropped jeans and an oversized man's blue shirt and her feet were bare. Without the heels she'd worn at the graduation I realized she was tiny. Her long blonde hair was slightly tangled, and her huge, luminous grey eyes beautiful. I seemed to be catching my breath a lot today. She welcomed us warmly, ushering me in, kissing Dominic, who held her tight and kissed her hard on the lips, which surprised me.

'We don't usually snog when we see each other,' she assured me, seeing my face, 'but I've been down here all week.'

'Oh, of course.'

'Normally I come up to town, but I've been as sick as a dog. Thought I'd rather lie in a shady garden and puke than puke in London.'

I was about to enquire, sympathize, when I realized her tummy was slightly swollen. I was too young to know what to say to pregnant women. Finally I managed, 'Congratulations.'

She grimaced. 'Thanks. Come on, come through. Even I'm allowed one glass of wine. We'll crack open a bottle.'

We did; a very cold white one, which she grabbed from the fridge as she padded around the kitchen in bare feet, Dire Straits blaring, chatting away, hair swinging: an easy grace. And then out of the French doors we went to a terrace at the back, where a table sat under a wooden pergola dripping with ancient pink clematis. The sun was still low and unseasonably warm in the sky, and there was a view of the hills, sheep in the meadow, a brook at the bottom, the lot.

'So you slipped through Katya's radar? I can't *imagine* how she let that happen; you're far too pretty!' she grinned at me, as Dominic brought out the glasses. 'Crisps, darling?' She glanced at him.

'Have we got any?'

'In the larder.'

He turned back, and I thought, all week I've seen this godlike figure telling everyone else what to do, and now here he was, obediently trotting back to the larder.

'In a bowl!' Letty called after him, just as he reappeared with a huge packet. He stopped and went back to get one from under the island.

'Hattie rather cunningly became indispensable,' he explained as he rejoined us. 'So Katya was effectively kiboshed. Didn't have a leg to stand on.'

'I think she's happy enough now, though,' I said loyally. Katya had actually been very kind to me.

'I doubt it. But I should think she's relieved you're not Estelle Butcher!' Letty giggled and sipped her wine. 'Ooh, that's good. First of the day.'

'Estelle Butcher?'

'Mike Katz's private PA,' she explained as Dominic rolled his eyes to heaven. 'Big tits, short skirts, French too – hot. She's deeply in love with Dom, pantingly so, and has been itching to join the department, which would have sent Katya reeling. The other day she asked if he played squash, and when he said no, she said, "Shame."' Letty affected a husky French accent. '"I want to do something sportif wiz you."' She snorted. 'Katya nearly had to be given brandy.'

As she giggled into her wine, I regarded this merry, lively girl: clearly aware that half of Westminster fancied her husband, certainly aware that at least two women were in love with him, and not just the repressed Katya, but Estelle too, whose description I now recognized, and who was indeed one very saucy, *clever* babe. Yet there she was, laughing and confident, in the country all week, not batting an eyelid. And I could see why. Why would he want more? Why, when he came home to this beautiful creature who looked no older than me, but must have been a good eight years, who was having his baby, in this deeply settled domestic scene, in this perfect house, with its creepers round the door, basking in a secret fold of the Buckinghamshire hills? Why would she be even faintly worried?

As the sun sank, rosy and glowing in the sky, settling almost in benediction on the pair of them, on their shiny blond heads, a deep sigh unfolded from the soles of my trainers. I tucked them under my chair, aware how vast they looked beside her tiny bare toes, and reached for the crisps. I'd been starving myself for three weeks, but it seemed to me it didn't really matter how fat I got now.

6

The following day, as promised, Dominic took me to his surgery to get the bigger picture. It was located in the local market town, and the action took place in a back room of the town hall, which flanked the main, cobbled square. Cold, sparse and smelling of floor polish and dust, it was less than salubrious, with just a table and chair at the far end for him, and another at the door for his constituency secretary, Amanda. Amanda was a hefty woman in a navy-blue jersey two-piece, who puffed and blew like a small chugging engine as she moved, but who mostly sat squarely at her post like a sentry, muttering darkly about the nutters in the waiting room.

'Nutters?' I stuck my head round the door, expecting to see a room full of jabbering delinquents, like something out of Hogarth's illustrations of Bedlam. Instead, several grey, quite ordinary-looking people gazed opaquely back. Amanda chugged back to her desk from shutting the front door.

'Have you ever been to see your MP, Hattie?'

'No.'

'Have your parents?'

'Don't think so.'

'Brothers, sisters, friends?'

'Er ... no. Not to my knowledge.'

'Precisely. I rest my case.' She shuffled her papers, still blowing hard. 'If you ask me, they're all a bit peculiar.'

Dominic frowned at her, but it wasn't without a twinkle, and as the first one came in, I hurried to sit beside him to listen. Drains were the problem, apparently, which stank. No help from the council. Dominic said he'd see what he could do. Then a woman who'd tripped on a paving stone and wanted to sue the local authority. Dominic pointed her in the direction of Legal Aid. Next, a Sikh family with immigration problems: a father and daughter, the father fragile and bewildered, barely speaking English. Dominic was endlessly patient and kind. Then, just as I was wondering what on earth Amanda was talking about, a smartly dressed woman in a tweed suit burst in before Amanda, who'd got to her feet and bustled round her desk, could stop her.

'There you are!' the woman declared, hastening towards Dominic and me at the far end. The carpet slippers seemed at odds with the rest of her outfit.

'Why didn't you come home? I did liver, your favourite.'

'Barking Brenda?' I muttered.

'No, Mad Martha. She thinks I'm her husband.'

'Oh!'

Martha gripped the table 'Is this her?' She glared at me.

Crumbs. I pushed my chair back.

'Little chit,' she spat. 'Little squinty-eyed whore.' Her eyes blazed.'

'Perfectly harmless,' Dominic murmured in my ear as Amanda bustled up to strong-arm her out.

'Come on, Martha,' she soothed.

Martha shook her off, eyes still sparking. 'Not till I've had my statutory two minutes. I know my rights!'

'Yes, quite right,' agreed Dominic. 'That's fine, Amanda. Do sit down, Mrs Carter.'

'Martha!' But she sat.

72

'Martha. Now, how can I help?'

'You can start by fixing the handle in the downstairs loo and then you can see about that damp patch on the landing wall.'

'Righto, I'd be absolutely delighted,' Dominic said with exaggerated courtesy. He picked up his pen and scribbled away studiously. 'Anything else?'

'Yes, you can put your shirts in the bucket outside the back door to soak like I showed you so I don't have to scrub the collars, and then set to in the garden. It's getting ever so late for bedding plants.' She seemed to have calmed down somewhat.

'Of course. My pleasure.' Dominic's face was a picture of contrition as he wrote. Then he put his pen down with a flourish, stood up, and smiled broadly as he came around the desk. She got to her feet too.

'And it's the whist drive on Tuesday,' I heard her mutter, less forcefully now, shoulders sagging.

'So it is!' said Dominic as he took her arm and escorted her out. 'What a treat. I shall look forward to it. Couldn't be more thrilled. Goodbye, Martha!'

He waved her off at the door, beaming excessively, then turned and came back, looking weary.

'You go along with it?' I gaped.

'Only way forward. Contradict her and she gets punchy and we end up calling the police. Any more, Amanda?'

'No, that's it.'

'Thank the Lord. Come on, let's pack up and go home.'

The rest of the weekend flew by in a relaxing, country house manner, the like of which I wasn't accustomed to.

It was punctuated by huge fry-ups, long walks, pub lunches, and culminated with a drinks party on Sunday evening hosted by the Forbeses.

'A grisly little ritual we Tory wives are supposed to throw on a regular basis,' Letty confided to me in the kitchen as we sliced lemons and cucumber. 'I do about one a year. All the great and the good come. Most are over seventy, and even the men are lavender-tinted. You'll love it,' she promised with dark foreboding.

'But who wants to turn out on a Sunday evening?'

'Oh, never underestimate the snoop factor.'

True enough, on the dot of six, the house filled up with what looked like a Saga holiday coach tour. Bright eyes darted around the sitting room like magpies, not missing a trick. Amongst the wrinklies, an old boyhood friend of Dominic's called Hugh, whose parents lived in the big house on the hill, and who was down from London for the weekend with his wife, Carla, a sulky-looking beauty who folded up her long limbs on the sofa to chain-smoke, occasionally hissing in Italian at her little boy, a skinny, plain child with a withered arm, who slunk about miserably. Hugh was sweet, though, and funny. He pointed out all the local gentry to me, chatting genially as they came up to wring his hand enthusiastically. Then, as they tottered away, he'd mutter in my ear, 'Chartered Accountant. Two months for white-collar fraud in an open prison in Hastings.'

'No.'

'See the wife? Dear old soul in beige? Shot her sister in the knee in '67 to stop her running away with her lover, who turned into the accountant.'

'What about the one with the eye patch?'

'Disgraced standard bearer from the British Legion. Turns out he was never in the army at all, and there's nothing whatsoever wrong with the eye. They took away his flag last Remembrance Day. He didn't give it up without a struggle, though. Nasty scene at the war memorial on the village green.'

I giggled, and thus a merry evening was filled, fuelled by buckets of Pimm's, as I listened to Hugh's no doubt apocryphal, but colourful take on the community.

'So you don't see yourself coming back to live here then, amongst the good burghers of Thame? I mean, presumably the house will be yours one day.'

'You must be joking,' hissed Carla, who'd left her perch momentarily to join us. 'If I had to leeve here, I'd slit my wrists. No, we leeve in London and Firenze, don't we, Hughie?'

'We do,' admitted Hugh, sadly.

'Come.' Carla stubbed out her last cigarette in a pot plant. 'Time to go. I can bear it no more. Poor, poor Letty.' This to her hostess, in commiseration. 'She will go to seed,' she lowered her voice in an aside to me. 'They all do, in this place. Her hair one day will be blue. You'll see.' She swept out.

'Lovely to meet you,' I told Hugh as I said goodbye. I meant it. He'd made me laugh.

'You too.'

'Back to London?'

'Yes, back to London.' And I thought he'd looked wistful.

'Nice couple,' I said diplomatically to Dominic and Letty later as we were collecting up glasses and ashtrays.

75

'He is. She's a cow,' Letty informed me cheerfully as she drained her glass. Her voice was slightly slurred. 'She got her claws into Hugh a few years ago, then suddenly she was pregnant, and that was it. Bye-bye, Hughie.' She threw her hands up for emphasis.

'Letty, should you be drinking?' asked Dominic mildly, not quite out of my earshot as I went back for more glasses.

She looked surprised. 'I'm not drinking, darling. I've had two glasses, which my GP says is absolutely fine. Do lighten up.'

On the way back to London in the convertible, bundled up beside him in a huge old overcoat he'd lent me, Dominic confided: 'Letty finds all the constituency stuff a bit of a strain, I'm afraid.'

'I'm not surprised,' I said staunchly. 'It's hardly her age group.'

'No, true,' he conceded. 'In fact, there's hardly any young blood in the party at all, apart from the Young Conservatives. But I always think that sounds so … well, preachy, doesn't it?'

''Fraid so. Like a church youth club. Cravats and blazers.'

'Exactly.' He narrowed his eyes at the road. 'The problem is, most young people aren't actually that interested in politics unless there's a whiff of the revolutionary about it. You're quite unusual, in that respect, Hattie.'

Me? I was startled. Oh … yes. Luckily it was dark.

But as we rattled along the M40 I wondered if this was my moment to fess up. To admit to not being that drawn to the bump and grind of the legislative process in Westminster, but more to the buzz and glamour. On the other hand, the roar of the engine was awfully loud. Quite tricky to be heard.

'D'you mind the roof down?' he yelled above the wind. 'I can stop and put it up?'

'No, no,' I snuggled down into the coat, which smelled of him. 'I love it.'

The weeks rolled by – months too – and Katya's back didn't improve. To her intense chagrin she found herself having to take more time off, and I, in turn, had to shoulder more of her workload. The pressure was on and I was literally learning on the job, but I'd studied at the feet of a master: I'd seen Katya deal with stroppy MPs or recalcitrant civil servants, who were the bane of Dominic's life, on the one hand forever wanting lengthy meetings, which he considered a complete waste of time when so much could be achieved by email, and on the other, barring his way to the people who really mattered. My job was to ensure those he wanted to speak to could reach him, and those he didn't couldn't.

'But I was told he'd be available for a meeting with the honourable member for Guildford at eleven o'clock?'

'Ah, yes, but something came up. At the moment he's with the party chairman discussing plans for the reshuffle.'

He wasn't. He was in his office writing a paper on the reintroduction of competitive sport in schools, a subject much closer to his heart, but it sounded scary and shut backbenchers up. I was learning to tell white lies, to box and cox as Katya and, to a greater extent, Dominic did. I was learning politics.

And the reshuffle, coming as it did, hot on the heels of an unpopular budget, was on everyone's mind.

'Tony Palmer's worried,' Dominic confided to me in the Ebury Street wine bar, which we often repaired to for a quick drink after work. 'The PM's rattled by all these sleaze allegations. He's threatening a comprehensive shake-up. And if Tony's worried, I should be too. I may lose my job as whip.'

'Don't be silly, of course you won't,' I soothed, as I did regularly these days; sometimes over supper too.

Well, it was lonely for him in that tiny flat in Westminster, and Letty wasn't having a very straightforward pregnancy. Driving made her feel sick and she loathed the train: she hardly came up at all. They barely saw one another, a problem – amongst others – we touched on occasionally. Sometimes I cooked him supper in the flat I shared with Laura, a rather swanky Pimlico apartment courtesy of Laura's modelling career. Dominic did a double take when he met Laura – everyone did, she was that gorgeous. Even nursing a broken heart as she was then, having just been dumped by a well-known brat-pack actor. She was bruised and tearful and didn't want to go out, but craved company, so it suited us all. Particularly me. I was very scared of how I felt about Dominic, and knew it was important not to be alone with him. No more Ebury Street drinks, no more suppers at Roussillon, I decided. Just here, at the flat, and only if Laura was around.

More numbers were added to my safety one evening as Dominic brought along Hugh. Except it was a different Hugh from the jokey, light-hearted one I'd met in Buckinghamshire. Carla had left him and gone with Luca to live in Rome, for good.

'She can't bear England any more,' he told us, white-faced, sipping a whisky. 'Can't bear me either, apparently.'

We embarked on a fairly drink-fuelled supper until, at ten o'clock, Dominic's phone went and he was called in to vote. I walked him down the three flights of stairs to the front door. As he turned to say goodbye, he regarded me a moment.

'Walk with me,' he said impulsively.

I caught my breath. Back to the Commons, on a beautiful early summer's evening.

'I'll only be ten minutes, then we can wander back here again.'

By which time a velvet night would have descended, maybe with a scattering of stars.

'No,' I shook my head. 'I'm tired. I think I'll have one more drink then go to bed.'

He nodded, but his eyes held mine for a moment longer than was strictly necessary. And then he turned and went.

As I went slowly back upstairs, my heart was pounding against my ribs. Oh God, oh God. Not good. Not good at all. I made to go back into the kitchen to join Laura and Hugh, but from the hall, saw two heads bent low over the kitchen table, both unloading tales of recent heartbreaks. The bottle of wine was going down rapidly. They didn't even notice me in the doorway. Instead I walked on down the corridor, and went to bed.

7

I'm not proud of this next bit, so I won't be lingering. In fact you may even get edited highlights. The reshuffle was scheduled for two weeks hence, and in the days leading up to it the atmosphere in the Commons was electric. Insecurity about jobs was rampant, everyone was tense, and Dominic, as whip, was presumed to have the PM's ear. As I swept down the corridors of Portcullis House beside him – Katya managing only three days a week now – arms full of papers, heels clicking in a spookily *déjà vu* way – dark-suited figures would emerge from the shadows: 'Can I have a word, Dom?'

Dominic would either stop and take two minutes to chat and reassure, or excuse himself politely on the grounds that he was in a tearing hurry, which he always was, but the eyes that followed seemed to say – does he know? Is he letting me down gently?

He was both respected and feared, and, as the right-hand girl I was rapidly becoming, I felt some of that powerful dust settle on me. I'd be sounded out by other secretaries, sometimes even MPs, who invited me for coffee, lunch in the Commons dining room. I wish I could say I was impervious to it, that it rolled off my back, but I loved it. I was twenty-three, barely out of university, and some of the most important and influential men and women in the country were courting me, canvassing my opinion. My head was not so much turned as spinning.

On the morning the reshuffle was due to be announced, the *News at Ten* journalist whom I'd recognized on day one, stopped me in the lobby.

'Any news, Hattie?'

'None whatsoever,' I muttered, hurrying on.

'Come on, poppet, be a sport. Any inkling?'

But I was on my way; my overriding concern to make sure Dominic was all right. We'd worked late the previous night, and he'd confided to me that, contrary to popular opinion, he barely knew about any cabinet positions: had had a meeting with the PM that morning and attempted to delve, but the shutters had come down and he'd been told nothing. I'd never seen him so rattled.

'Surely if my job was secure I'd be tipped the wink by now?'

'Not necessarily,' I'd consoled. 'He knows everyone badgers you for information. He might be protecting you.'

He'd regarded me suspiciously. 'No one protects anyone in this place, Hattie. You have to watch your back at every turn. It's every man for himself.'

Later that morning, one by one, the cabinet were called in. Dominic later said that the walk he took from Portcullis House, across the road, past Big Ben, and through the main gates opposite Westminster Abbey was one of the longest of his life.

Katya was in that day – oh, you bet, bent double, face racked with pain, but she was there. The two of us waited, each at our post, our computers, chatting nervously at first, and then, as the morning wore on with no word, turning to our screens for solace, typing silently, mechanically. This, surely, was bad news. A lengthy interview meant there was a lot of explaining to do on the part of the PM. A lot of thanks for all the hard work, effort, etc., followed by a pained, grave expression as he let the bad news sink in. Katya and I tapped and tapped, grim-faced. The phones were quiet. That was unusual too. Normally they never stopped and we were run off our feet answering them. Had other MPs heard something we hadn't? Was Dominic no longer the man to call, the man in the know?

The night before he'd confided to me that the post he hankered for, the one he lay in bed at night and fantasized about, Education Secretary, had gone, he thought. Not for sure, but the whisper was Tim Atkinson, from Environment.

At ten past twelve the door flew open. Katya and I spun round in our seats. Dominic stood in the doorway, eyes shining.

'Foreign Secretary,' he breathed.

'Oh!' We sprang to our feet, dumbfounded.

In a moment he'd crossed the room, taken me in his arms and twirled me around. Then he put me down and hugged Katya. We were all ecstatic now, and as we shrieked and jumped up and down and congratulated him, suddenly the room hummed again. Ken, the permanent undersecretary, appeared, beaming, phones rang as members called in their congratulations, doors opened and shut like a French farce as people flew in from all corners. Champagne was found – someone had belted to the off-licence – and Dominic, in the midst, like a tall blond lion, handsome face shining, genuinely baffled as well as delighted, was looking like a little boy, although now of course, a hugely important, influential man. I couldn't take my eyes off him. And now and again, as he turned to accept congratulations, wring hands, I knew those eyes came back to me.

The day passed in a blur. Journalists rang constantly, wanting quotes: at thirty-four Dominic was the youngest Foreign Secretary, it transpired, that century. Even Anthony Eden in Chamberlain's government in 1935 had been a ripe old thirty-seven when he achieved the same high office. Again and again Dominic went out to Parliament Square to speak to banks of cameras, news crews from all over the country, as we, his department, watched from the windows above.

Other results came in: some good, some bad. His great friend Peter Ward, a kind, intellectual man, had lost his job at Transport. He'd been shuttled to the back benches. Whilst Sally Turner, her of the sexy black suits, bright red lipstick and patterned tights, had a meteoric rise to Health. Health! We all giggled, high on champagne.

'Hope she doesn't give them anything,' remarked Katya tartly. 'Who knows where she's been.'

Katya was thrilled, but brisk with me, snapping out orders and I knew why. She'd watched as her boss of six years had crossed the room to hug me first, to sweep me up in his arms before her: her smile was broad but her eyes were like flints as she made sure I was edged out of any limelight that might be shining round our office. I typed away guiltily.

At close of play, yet another journalist rang, wanting a few words with Dominic for an evening chat show. But Dominic, by Katya's desk, was on another line and shook his head, frowning. He put his hand over the mouthpiece.

'Katya, pop down, would you, and say a few platitudes on my behalf? Or send Hattie, if your back's not great?'

'I'll go,' said Katya quickly, getting up not so smoothly and hobbling to the door. 'I'll say you're extremely honoured and looking forward to the tremendous challenge the job offers, shall I?'

'Splendid. If you would. You are marvellous, Katya.'

But she went out wordlessly, the damage having been done. Dominic was oblivious, though, and then, as Katya left, her phone rang and I found myself talking to our new counterpart office in America.

'It's Warren Christopher,' I breathed, 'wanting to congratulate you. D'you want me to …?' I pointed to his office, indicating I'd put it through in there, but instead, he just took the phone from my hand and perched on the desk.

I listened as he thanked and smiled, got up and walked around, swept back his hair, his colour high, walked around my room, and then into his room. At the door, still talking, he looked back and jerked his head at me. I frowned. He jerked it again, meaning for me to follow him.

Smiling and shaking my head, bemused, I did as I was told, shutting the door behind me. I hovered in the book-lined room as he thanked the American some more, still beaming, still pacing circles, still sweeping back his hair.

I walked to the window and gazed out, leaning the heels of my hands on the sill. A thunderstorm was gathering, and the light was fading fast, turning the sky violet over the ancient crenulated stone of Westminster. Down on the lawn I could see the camera crews, news teams from around the world, some beginning to pack up now, collapsing huge lenses: the remains of the day.

'Thank you so much … Oh, I agree … I agree entirely, and rest assured I will do my utmost to preserve it, nothing will jeopardize it … be assured of that … Many thanks, how kind … and many thanks again for calling.'

He put the phone down, an almost dazed look in his eye. An exhilarated one too. Then he walked to the door, locked it, came back and took both my hands in his.

'He wanted to touch base with his opposite number.' He reached up and pulled down the window blind behind me. I knew what was happening but felt powerless to stop it. 'Wanted to assure me of his support, and be sure he could count on me.' He took my face in his hands, steering me away from the window, leaning back on the light switch. As the room plunged into darkness, his lips found mine. He kissed me gently: once, twice.

'Wanted to be sure of our special relationship. To preserve it at all costs.' He was still kissing me gently, drawing me in closer. I felt my body melt into his.

'Do you feel that special relationship, Hattie?' His eyes were trawling mine, as dark as the violet sky outside. 'Do you feel it too?' he whispered, almost pleading.

'Yes,' I breathed. 'I do.'

Our eyes locked then in silent communion and he took me in his arms and kissed me properly. I shut my eyes, felt my bones turn to liquid, my senses swim: saw only a blinding white light and heard a roaring rush in my ears. I'd never lost consciousness before, but it seemed to me this might be how it would feel: reeling first, then spiralling in slow motion down somewhere deep and precipitous to oblivion. It was certainly an impediment to thought.

Down below, the traffic rumbled by; a distant soundtrack and a reminder of a world beyond this one, but muffled and indistinct.

Another noise, this time much closer: footsteps – voices too – and then the light snapped on. As the room exploded into terrible clarity, Dominic and I sprang apart in its glare. Standing at the only other door to the office, the one rarely used and only accessed via the coffee room, so therefore only by a Commons secretary, was Katya. Her eyes were bright and darting, her face grim but triumphant. Just behind her, luminously pregnant in a black and white floral dress, matching patent heels and handbag, her hair done professionally in a coil, all ready for the cameras, was Letty.

8

I left my job immediately, of course; Katya saw to that. Had seen to it, in fact, that very evening as, hands shaking, I went through my desk drawers, gathered any possessions – books, magazines – eyes lowered. Dominic went after Letty, who'd stumbled away with a strangled sob, one hand to her mouth: but not before her eyes had found mine, wide, grey and shocked. After that, she'd turned and fled.

Katya, of course, had stayed. Standing over me like an SS guard, seeing me off the premises.

Meanwhile I'd gulped things like, 'Can't stay.'

'No, quite. I can see that.'

'So sorry ... Can't think why ... so sorry. Explain why I'm going, would you? I can't ...'

'Of course.' Chilly.

'But don't say. Don't tell them about ...'

'Of course not.'

I knew she wouldn't. Knew, if Dominic were to keep his job, which she wanted at all costs, she'd keep her mouth shut. It was her life, this place, and the blood shed in it flowed through her veins. I found my handbag and she escorted me to the door.

'I can't think what ...' I was muttering. 'Don't know what came over me.'

'Don't worry.' She could afford to be kind now. She'd never see me again. 'Just go. I'll talk to Personnel. Tell them it was to do with your family or something. And I'll give you a reference.'

'Will you?'

'Of course.' She made her face smile. 'These things happen.'

'You mean—'

'Oh, no, never before. Never a hint of scandal. He's a good man.'

And I was a bad girl. Who'd instigated scandal. Trembling, I gathered my coat from the back of the door and departed. Would Hattie Carrington kindly leave the stage. Why? Why did I go, just like that? Years later, in retrospect, I'm not sure, but down the linoleum corridor I went, the one that had held so much promise, down the whispering elevator, and out into the night.

After the air conditioning, the humid night air ambushed me, wrapped itself around me like so many menacing scarves. I weaved shakily across the road, feeling it on my cheeks, like hot accusatorial breath, through the heavy traffic without waiting for the lights to change, amid blaring horns and furious-faced drivers around the square. Churchill loomed, then Palmerston; more horns as I crossed the road again towards the backstreets of Pimlico.

Laura was out when I got to the flat. There was a note on the kitchen table: 'Hughie and I are in Pitcher and Piano if you and Dominic want to join us.'

You and Dominic. You see, that was the problem. I'd let it become so. But he wasn't mine. We weren't a couple. And I knew Laura had worried, had tried to broach the subject more than once that we were perhaps too close, but I'd brushed her off, dismissed it. I wouldn't admit to myself, let alone to others, that I … I caught my breath. Loved him.

Despite my shame, despite his hugely pregnant wife in the doorway, the one who'd offered me hospitality, I knew this to be so. With the most burning certainty I'd ever felt about anything. And it was the first time. I'd got to the ripe old age of twenty-three without it. Had gone out with boys, but felt nothing like this. Nothing like the completely overwhelming sense of helplessness as he'd taken me in his arms in his office. In his office. How ghastly is that? How cheap? Yet to me, it seemed utterly romantic. And now, I'd never see him again. I'd lost my job, and I'd lost him too. The ramifications were hammered home, one by one, like nails in my head, delivered, it seemed to me, oddly not by Letty, but a contorted-faced Katya. I went to my bedroom and threw myself dramatically on my bed, still in my coat, pulled the pillow over my head, and burst into tears.

At length, the phone went beside me. I turned over. Lay there a second listening, then picked it up. Could it be …? No, of course not. It was Kit, ringing to wish Laura a happy birthday. Of course, Laura's birthday. Which was why they'd gone out.

'No, she's not here, but I'll tell her.' I sat up with a struggle, wiping my face, trying to steady my voice. 'How are you?' I lowered the mouthpiece and exhaled heavily, turning damp eyes to the ceiling. 'Having fun?' I managed.

'Fun?'

I came to, remembering where he was. The steel in his voice went right through me.

'Oh, Kit. Sorry, I—'

'Fun?' he repeated. 'You have no idea.' His voice was trembling. I could hear him trying to compose himself. I sat up and grabbed a tissue.

'Kit?'

'Oh, yes, great fun.' Harsh words tumbled out. 'The father of the family I'm staying with was killed yesterday, caught in crossfire on his way to hospital. A doctor. Snipers got him.'

I caught my breath, shocked. 'I'm so sorry.'

'Three children.'

'Oh, Kit. I'm so sorry,' I whispered again, lamely.

'That's nothing. At least it was quick.' His voice didn't sound familiar. It seemed to be coming from somewhere thin and dark. I felt completely disorientated, bounced as I was, in a heartbeat, out of my own drama and into his. I couldn't marshal my thoughts.

'At least he didn't know anything about it,' Kit was saying. 'Not like the ones who are rounded up every day. Boys, some of them, shitting themselves as they're herded into lorries and taken away, and all in the name of ethnic cleansing.'

My mind swam in a befuddled manner. I tried to grasp what he was saying.

'Ethnic cleansing my arse – it's genocide. I'm in Croatia, Hattie, not the fucking King's Road.'

'Yes, no, I – I forgot. No – didn't forget, of course I didn't, but—' I swung my legs over the bed, massaged my temple hard, willing myself to think. To be there for him. But it was all such a world away. Such a very long way away. I forced myself to stay with him, to keep up, but my mind was a blur.

'Kit, I – don't know what to say,' I said eventually, hopelessly. I didn't. And then a considerable silence elapsed. 'Are you going to stay?' I ventured at length. Like he was at a sleepover.

'Of course I'm going to stay!' he almost screamed, making me leap. 'Haven't you seen the pictures?'

I panicked. Pictures. Oh – yes, I had. Dimly. A while back. Shocking pictures of a camp. A couple of journalists had sent back photographs that looked as if they'd been taken in Auschwitz fifty years earlier.

'Over four thousand people died in that place,' Kit went on in a low, unsteady voice. 'Tortured, beaten, whole villages wiped out. They just don't exist any more, like – like Chipping Sodbury or somewhere, just disappearing.'

'I'm so sorry, Kit. Forgive me. I am so very sorry.'

I heard him breathing heavily on the other end. Trying to collect himself. I apologized again. Inadequately. After a bit he calmed down. Muttered something. But I only caught, 'OK, OK.'

I tried to talk to him then, help him. But he was distant, quiet. I made myself jabber away about the family, Mum's new car – bright yellow, would you believe. Laura's modelling, humdrums, anything. And after a bit, I heard him sobbing quietly on the other end. I was terrified, but I let him cry, realizing perhaps I was the outlet he needed. The only place he could go. In my mind I was frantically wondering how to get him back. Dad should go out, of that I was convinced. Mum and I had talked about it, Laura too. But my father was strangely reticent on the subject.

'Shouldn't we go and get him?' Laura and I had pleaded. 'Shouldn't we get him back?'

'Not if he doesn't want to come back,' had been Dad's measured response.

Kit and I talked some more. I didn't want him to go until I felt he was truly calm, but he couldn't be calm, he said. Not really. Not any more. Never would be. Nothing would ever be the same again. And I couldn't ease his pain.

*

If you'd told me an hour before that I'd go to bed that night thinking of anything other than myself, my own particular drama, I wouldn't have believed you, but eventually I dozed off in some strange dusty country, a darkening land. Kit in khakis, in a tented encampment, similar to something I'd seen on *M.A.S.H.*, was running with his hands on his head, past trucks emblazoned with red crosses, flinging himself to the ground as mortar shells dropped and exploded around him.

Amazing how the ego thieves back in, though. Stealthily. Quietly. The following morning, although Kit was still on my mind, my own problems loomed large. The morning papers had moved on too. The Balkans war was still just on the front page, bottom right, two columns, but a young man of thirty-four had been appointed Foreign Secretary. The *Mail* led with that. My heart thudded as I picked it up off the doormat. A huge colour picture of him and his wife, she, heavily pregnant in a black and white dress, a golden couple. You'd have to look very closely to spot the strain around her eyes.

I switched the answer machine on. Dominic rang about an hour later, and my whole body leaped at his voice, but stoically, I didn't answer. Knew I mustn't. Loved the fact that he'd rung, though. Played the tape over and over: 'Hattie, it's me, I'm worried about you. Will you ring?'

Laura had flown off early that morning for a shoot in Paris. The flat was full of flowers from Hughie for her birthday, white roses everywhere. I sat amongst them, hands pressed together. Dominic rang again at lunchtime. Again I didn't answer. And anyway, I was out, I'd gone out to buy the *Standard*. Princess Diana had replaced Dominic on the front page, but inside was a profile of the young man who was to be Our Man Abroad, heading up the Foreign Office. More photos of him: one as a schoolboy at Harrow, another as an undergraduate at Cambridge, and one of him leaning over a five-barred gate, smiling, taken outside The Pink House. No Letty, this time. I couldn't take my eyes off him. The following day, in *The Times* – I bought all the papers – a serious article by Michael Jenkins, entitled 'The Man Who Would Be King', all about Dominic being the young pretender, potentially the next Prime Minister. I read it three times; cut it out and stashed it away with the others.

Funny how the mind works: left alone, to my own devices, sitting in the flat, going to the window periodically to press my forehead against the glass, I wondered idly if I could have my job back. If that was why he was ringing. If Letty could … if Letty could what, Hattie? Below, on the pavement a skateboarder skidded into the gutter. Understand? Forgive? How was that little scenario going to play out then, hm? Or – or maybe I could work somewhere else in the Commons? So I could be near him. The skateboarder got up and brushed himself down. Because, what was so terrifying, what was making me hyperventilate, was the thought of never seeing Dominic again. Which unless I was there, in the Commons, I wouldn't. Panic rose within me. The idea grew, from a little seed. Yes, I could work in another department. Defence, perhaps. A friend, Rebecca, worked there, for that nice woman Fiona Snell. Perhaps in a few months' time, when the dust had settled, I could go back? Reapply, when it had all blown over? After all, I'd been on a career ladder. I couldn't just abandon that, could I?

I left the flat at lunchtime, as was now my routine, when I knew the first edition of the *Standard* came out, leaving Tanja, our help, in the flat. When I came back, she was putting her coat on, getting ready to go.

'A man called, for to deliver a letter,' she told me in her broken English.

'Oh?' The world stopped on its axis. Swayed. 'Who?'

'Yes, tall man. Nice face. He no say who.'

My heart kicked in. 'And the letter?'

'On your bed. I put it.'

I rushed down the hall, throwing the *Standard* on a chair. I heard Tanja open the front door, and close it behind her. An envelope was indeed on my pillow. I opened it with trembling hands. Darling, please come back? It's you I love? Somehow we'll work something out?

I spread open the thick creamy sheet. It was from Hal. Two words.

'You whore.'

9

Split airport was as sterile and formulaic as any other European terminus, but there the similarity ended. As we emerged from Customs, the concourse was heaving: noisy, hot and impossibly airless. Fear and panic were tangible: on the faces of the women in headscarves clutching children by their wrists, in the voices of the men, shooting up an arm and shouting for them to follow, in the old and bewildered, darting frightened eyes, struggling under the weight of precious bundles. Nearly everyone was leaving, or trying to leave. Unlike us. We were going against the tide, skirting the main clot of traffic, keeping to the walls, bumping against armed guards with cold rifles and stony faces as we kept the UN passes around our necks firmly to the fore.

My father had rung some contacts, reluctantly, when Kit had said yes, I could come out as an aid volunteer. But only packing food parcels. And only on the coast, where it was safe. But yes, he could cut through the red tape, such as it was. It was chaos; they just needed help. Nevertheless, papers of some kind were required and Dad, sensing something had happened to me, that I really needed this, had used his press connections. He'd also quietened his distraught wife, who was beside herself at the thought of two of her children in a war zone, and, together with a photographer from the *Independent*, I'd flown out.

'Will you be all right?' Paul, my photographer friend, shouted to me as, alarmingly, we began to get separated in the crush. He headed towards a man in sunglasses waving his name on a card. I panicked. No, was my overwhelming reaction, no I won't, and I attempted to follow him through the teaming mêlée. But then I saw Kit.

'Yes – there's my brother!'

Except I barely recognized him. Two stone lighter – and he'd been thin anyway. His cheeks were sunken, his hair long, face very brown. His eyes scanned the crowd.

'Kit!'

He saw me and muscled across. We embraced. He quickly introduced me to a fellow ICRS man, Brett, a Dutchman, equally brown and lean, and they hurried me outside. Through another swarm of people we dodged our way to a Bedford lorry down the street, engine running, a girl revving it impatiently. She had a tank full of petrol, Kit explained as we ran towards it, which was like gold dust. Didn't want anyone stealing it at gunpoint. Brett ran to leap in the back and Kit bundled me in the front. Behind us, in steerage, three young Irishmen, all aid workers, were huddled with their backpacks. They'd also just arrived, apparently, and Kit assured me he wouldn't have been able to collect me, to leave his post, but for these three: I'd have had to make my own way through Italy and across the border. As Brett banged the roof in the back, Fabianne, French and tight-lipped, let out the clutch, and we rumbled down Split's main highway, dotted with bombed-out buildings and teaming with military. We weaved through the armoured vehicles, leaving clouds of dust in our wake. The sun was a huge shimmering orb on the horizon, and despite the obvious tension in the air, on the faces of my brother and his comrades, I couldn't help feeling exhilarated as we swept through town. I was here. I'd made it.

Kit and Fabianne were silent until we'd left the city, their eyes constantly roving, watchful. Only when we were speeding towards surprisingly green, panoramic countryside, did they relax slightly; nod to each other in relief. I was awestruck by Kit's new mantle of seriousness; even more so as the new aid workers in the back, aware we were now out of immediate danger, leaned forward to ask questions. Fabianne cut in occasionally in broken English, but it was Kit who did the talking. I listened to his answers in silence. About four thousand, he reckoned, killed at Omarska, including most of Prijedor's intellectuals: teachers, lawyers, politicians – those were the sort of people they were after, but anyone would do. Anyone with an education, or who was in the way. Universities had been raided by the military in Srebrenica and Sarajevo, and professors and students were rounded up daily. Their families too. Some were shot on the spot, some sent to camps. No one knew who to trust. I learned that people knew their torturers, had grown up with them, gone to school with them.

'Like the Jews in Nazi Germany?' My only contribution, in a small voice.

'Exactly. And no one thought it could happen again.'

The boys in the back were far more informed than I was. I listened as they had confirmed that which they'd already feared: atrocities they'd gleaned through Reuters, information agencies back home. All true.

At length, on a long stretch of dusty road, we fell silent. We were approaching the mountains now, beautiful majestic scenery rising before us. Fabianne shifted clunking gears as we lurched about, then began to climb. In the foothills, a little village would materialize, or the

remains of one. A shattered mosque here, a few roof-
less houses there, endless piles of rubble. Hens pecked
in the dirt, and a skinny brown dog slunk by. A clutch of
people stood at the roadside: one or two old men and a
tall woman, a few children peeking around her skirt like
mice. The woman followed our lorry warily, her
eyes dull.

'Are they frightened of us?' I asked.

'They're frightened of everyone. But they see *"Aide
Humanitaire"* on the side and they know it's OK.'

Kit pointed out the shelled school, then a tent used as
a makeshift hospital. His hands were brown and sinewy,
his voice strong, not broken as it had been on the phone:
informative now, not emotional. I felt very proud. Humble, too.

Serb checkpoints had to be crossed, papers checked.
Very young soldiers with guns at right angles to their
chests came to the window. My heart began to pound as
they checked my papers, then Kit's, then Fabianne's. They
went round the back, checked Brett and the boys', came
back and asked Kit some questions, aggressive now. He
shrugged. They cursed, then went round the lorry and
offloaded some boxes from the back.

'What were they doing?' I whispered as they finally
waved us on.

'Taking food parcels. And they're pissed off because we
usually carry a lot more, but not today.'

'Why not?'

'Because we knew they'd take it. We usually travel at
night when there's only a couple of them on the checkpoint and only a few boxes get dragged off. But during
the day they swarm like locusts. They say it's going to

Serb civilians, but that's bollocks. They keep it for themselves, for the military. It's their rations for the next few weeks.'

'But that's outrageous. You're neutral, aren't you? Protected by the UN?'

Kit shrugged. 'What can you do? Nothing. Not unless you want to be accused of smuggling arms into the city.'

'So how much do you usually carry?'

'About twenty tons is our limit, and we've got five trucks. Other agencies have more, but we're quite small.'

'And you deliver? The food? I mean, you personally? I thought you just packed it.'

'I do now,' he said, shortly. 'Only recently. And usually only to villages, which is reasonably safe.'

'So where's not safe?'

'Sarajevo.'

'Have you ever been there?'

'Yes.'

'How often?'

'Once or twice.'

'Do Mum and Dad know?'

'No. Well, Dad might.'

Taking aid into Sarajevo. I didn't even ask how dangerous that was. Knew that, even with the humanitarian message on the side, rules were broken here and he was risking his life.

'But where we're going now,' he swept on, reading my thoughts, 'which is essentially the Dalmatian coast, is safe. You'll see.'

Except for the father of three, I thought. Kit's doctor friend, the one shot by snipers. Only relatively safe. Rather like the road we were on now, I decided, although 'road'

99

was pitching it high. A thin, elevated snake of potholed shingle wound through the mountains, either side of which crumbling rock fell away at an alarming angle. It seemed to me to have all the qualities necessary to facilitate a fatal accident, and I wondered how this unwieldy Bedford managed at night when they usually travelled. I voiced as much tentatively to Kit, who shrugged and said you got used to it, although of course it didn't help not having headlights.

'No headlights?'

'These hills are full of snipers. You don't want to announce yourself.'

Of course you don't, I thought, gazing down the steep embankment to the gully and certain death below.

'And although we're only going a bit further up the coast from Split, this route through the mountains is much safer than the coastal one.'

'Right,' I said weakly, shutting my eyes as two tons of articulated lorry shuddered and wheezed around a hairpin bend.

At Heronisque, where we were based, however, I relaxed slightly. A pretty coastal village with a Mediterranean feel to it, albeit shabby and clearly shelled in places, here life was going on in a relatively normal fashion. As the evening drew in, old men sat in a dusty square running beads through their fingers, a few women bustled into red-tiled houses with baskets: one or two children played in the street, and businesslike dogs trotted by. Every so often you could hear the odd pop of gunfire from the hills, which sounded like an old motorbike backfiring in the distance. Other than that, one could almost be in Italy, or Greece, I decided.

An old boathouse on the quay had been requisitioned as the packing station, and Kit took me there first.

Outside were the other Bedfords, and inside, checking and loading scores of boxes of food and other essentials, medicines too, were a dozen or so people. All nationalities were here: Swedish, German, French, Spanish. They broke off at the sight of us, looking tired and drawn, but were all very welcoming as Kit introduced me. That night, over a hastily prepared supper of tinned food heated over a Primus stove in the entrance to the warehouse, we sat around cross-legged. As I looked about me, listening to the chatter, I knew this was right. Knew I'd been right to come, even though, as the evening wore on, it became increasingly apparent that my brother wouldn't be staying.

'Where are you going?' I asked him as he began saying goodbyes all round, shaking hands. He glanced at me warily, leaving me till last.

'With the Irish boys to Telospique. We've got another packing station there and they need more people. More aid is coming in there from Sweden.'

'Where's Telospique?'

'About fifty kilometres away.'

I wanted to say – but surely, because we're brother and sister, surely we could be together – but I knew it didn't work like that.

'Closer to the fighting?'

'A bit, yes. Nearer the front lines, anyway.'

I nodded, silenced.

'But you'll be safe here.'

'I know.'

We hugged tearfully, then. Held each other close. It was dark: a sultry night had descended with a huge rusty moon, and only the lapping of the waves on the quay disturbed the silence. From behind us, one of the Bedfords started its choleric rumbling. I glanced round and saw the silent Fabianne behind the wheel, revving the engine. Kit got in beside her and this time, I didn't make it hard for him. Didn't ask if Dad knew. But as I watched them go I thought how, in the last few hours, I'd got closer to my brother than I'd ever been. And I wondered when I'd see him again.

I threw myself into my work in the warehouse. It was hard, physical labour, mind-numbing in its monotony – checking, packing, heaving boxes around, slamming a lorry on the back when it was loaded, then watching, hands on hips, a brief moment of respite as it trundled off into the hills in convoy. But I was glad of it. This was what I'd come for: to forget myself, to help, and whilst it was never enjoyable, it was therapeutic. I learned a smattering of French, Swedish and German from the people around me – even though everyone spoke English – and an awful lot about life. Particularly from the family I was billeted with.

In a half-baked, befuddled sort of way, I'd had an idea we aid workers would all be housed together, but of course that was impractical and we were spread about the town. Unlike the others who were mostly in the centre, I was on the outskirts, in a tiny house built into a hillside. Savage barking dogs lived in the yard outside, and three generations of family within. An ancient grandmother, who rarely moved from her high-backed settle by the fire, and dressed entirely in black, including some sort of bonnet on her head, headed up the family – or so it seemed to me. No English was spoken. An old man, her husband, equally wizened and bent double, spent a lot of time shouting at the dogs. The daughter-in-law, Ibresqua, known as Ibby, did all the shopping, cleaning, cooking and coaxing of meagre vegetables from the patch at the back, helped by her six-year-old daughter, Mona, olive-skinned, with pigtails. Ibby's husband, the old couple's son, was in the mountains, fighting the 'Chetchkins', I learned, and although the other men in the village came back weekly, he hadn't been back for a while. Ibby, pregnant with her second child, was kindly but preoccupied. Mona giggled shyly at me from behind her hand. The elderly couple didn't address me at all. Meals were taken in the boathouse with the other aid workers, and all this family provided was a silent bed. I took it gratefully. A slip of a room with an iron bedstead and skinny mattress, a tiny wooden table with crucifix above. On the opposite wall, a photograph of a burly young man with a luxuriant black moustache, who I took to be Ibby's husband. As I lay down every evening, exhausted after a day's work and the strain of being amongst strangers who spoke little English, I looked at Ibby's husband, before I went to sleep. Only then did I allow myself to think of Dominic.

The weeks trudged by. Once or twice I saw Kit, but only because he'd made an effort to come back to Heronisque *en route* from a convoy, I felt. The last thing I wanted to be was a burden, so on his next visit, I assured him in the strongest terms I was fine. I didn't see him again.

Day after day I packed and loaded and slapped that lorry, and night after night, after supper, I slipped quietly back into my house in the hillside, the dogs no longer trying to tear my ankles off.

Then, three months into my stay, dysentery descended on our little community. Gretel, the German girl, got it first, then Brett, and then one or two of the other boys. They'd be fine, I was assured by the others, it was an occupational hazard out here, but for the moment, we lacked drivers. I'd been out on convoy once or twice before, but only as lookout. Now, for the first time, with a new young Italian boy beside me, I was behind the wheel. Initially I only went to villages close by, then, presumably when they saw I could bring the Bedford back in one piece, I went further up into the mountains. Always at night, almost always in convoy, always with no headlights. Sometimes, though, the length of the journeys and the state of the roads meant dawn was breaking as we returned. I'd grip the wheel with Pablo beside me, both of us scanning the road, not just for boulders to take the front wheel off now, but for bandit gangs too: modern-day highwaymen with AK47s, ready to commandeer the truck, and then who knows what fate befell the occupants. Each time I bumped back down those perilous dusty roads and felt the empty Bedford lurching into the familiar potholes that led to the village, I sent up a silent prayer. Thank you, God.

Gradually I got to know my way around, and one or two of the villages became familiar. I'd smile or attempt to greet the women who slipped silently out of the houses in the dark to take our food, but got nothing in response. Most places were denuded of young men: just women, children and old people. All fighting? I asked Brett one day, who'd recovered enough to pack for us again in the warehouse. 'Not all,' he said shortly, and I knew then they'd been rounded up. Thereafter I unloaded the food parcels in silence, the children falling on the tins of milk and sometimes bars of chocolate, the mothers retrieving it all with blank expressions.

I wasn't fooling myself. I knew what this was about. All this heat and dust and fear and lack of sleep, the bump and grind of someone else's war: it was about Dominic, whom I loved heart and soul, and needed to expunge from both. And yes, it helped. But it was about being good, too. A good girl. So all for me, this effort? Perhaps. But it seems to me charity work of any denomination can't withstand too much scrutiny.

And I wouldn't want you to think it was all hard slog either. There were days when I could sit on the Dalmatian coast and sun myself with my new friends, as, clasping our hands around our knees, sleeves rolled up, we rested our weary backs and gazed out to sea. There were days too, in the house in the hillside, when life got immeasurably lighter. Ibby's husband, Alam, returned from the mountains, and the joy, the relief – the love – that exploded in that little house is something I'll never forget. The old lady, her face wreathed in smiles I didn't know she possessed, took her son's head in her hand and kissed it hard. Mona jumped up and down shrieking and clapping. Ibby, by now hugely pregnant, laughed with joy, but perhaps the most affecting was Alam's father, who sat down and wept: his only son, back from the war, safe.

He'd been captured by Chetchkins, we gathered over a reunion supper in which I was included, but mercifully had escaped with a few others. His sunken eyes and gaunt frame bore testament to his ordeal, and he looked nothing like the man in the picture in my bedroom. That night we ate ambrosial cured ham running with yellow fat clearly saved for this occasion, drank very dark wine, soaked creamy cheese up with rough bread and rejoiced. Out of the horror of war, like scattered moondust, special moments.

Alam spoke a little broken English and I gathered my adopted family were refugees. They were not from around here, not from this town, and one or two things fell into place. Like the fact that they kept to themselves and seemed to know no one. They'd been driven from their home in Kosovo two years ago, all of their immediate family, uncles, cousins, killed. This, they seemed to accept with equanimity, considering themselves the lucky ones. I was later to learn that when they arrived here, they changed their name, from I know not what, to Mastlova, a local one. To do their bit for the war effort they'd taken me in, as if it wasn't enough that Alam had been fighting in the mountains for weeks on end. But fear was a powerful motivator, and behind most decisions in those days.

The party went on late into the evening, and the following morning, Mona was late for school. I watched her running off down the road, breaking into a skip, which I'd never seen her do.

'*Tata se vratio s planine!*' she cried to a friend, waiting for her on the corner, slightly cross at being kept waiting. 'Daddy's back from the mountains!' A shout of joy went up from her friend; a hug, a dance in the dusty street: the human face of war.

My own family were reassured by my domestic situation. In letters I was able to gloss over the fact that I fumbled my way through the mountains at night in a blind lorry, and give them snippets of domestic life instead. Mum even sent a doll for Mona and linen for the baby when it came, which the old lady pored over with delight. Kit, I told them, was working closely with an army chaplain in another depot, which I knew to be true. I didn't mention he was in Sarajevo, which the Serbs now had in a stranglehold, so that he was effectively incarcerated.

I'd suspected my silent family were kindly but frightened, but only after Alam returned did my relationship with them change completely. They asked me to stay for meals, which made a pleasant change from tins of beans on the warehouse floor, and I'd help Ibby prepare them. Ibby was only a few years older than me and most evenings, before I went out on convoy, we'd sit in the yard together shelling peas, the dogs at our feet, and I taught her a bit of English. She in turn taught me Croatian, laughing at my accent, and in a garbled fashion and with lots of sign language, she told me of the life she'd had before the war, as a teacher in Kosovo. When they'd fled they'd been accepted here in Heronisque only because they were Catholic – Croatia being a fiercely Roman Catholic country – and because Ibby's grandfather, now dead, had been a priest. One or two notaries in the town had heard of him, remembered his name, and it had proved to be their salvation. Pictures of him in his robes, long grey hair, were all over the house, I realized, under crucifixes, strung with rosary beads, and it was his name the family had taken.

We'd sit in the evening sun and watch Mona play with the chickens, whilst the men played a board game of some kind behind us, chequers I think, not backgammon, a tiny glass of something strong apiece, and as the old lady slept bolt upright inside on her wooden settle. At length Ibby would get to her feet, one hand on her swollen belly, another in the small of her back, and together we'd go and get supper.

And then one night, I came back from a convoy that had taken us to the ancient town of Mostar, closer to the front lines, horribly shelled, almost parallel with Serb trenches. The crack of gunfire had been even closer. I was very tired and my nerves were shot because daylight had been breaking towards the end. When I finally left the warehouse and got back to the house it was empty.

The door to the room where the old couple slept downstairs was wide open, and when I ran up to Alam and Ibby's room, which Mona shared, it too was deserted.

I fled into town, to raise someone, anyone, who, although the Mastlovas kept to themselves as refugees, they might know. But it was four in the morning and my banging and hollering fell on deaf ears. Finally, a woman appeared at a doorway in a shawl. She recognized me. Exclaimed. Came out and gripped my wrist. She tried to explain through the language barrier, her words coming fast like gunfire, arching her hand high over her stomach.

'Ibby? The baby?'

She nodded, fearful: then began to wail, turning her face to the sky, shaking her hands in the air. Yes, the baby.

'What? What?' I cried.

At my voice her teenage son appeared behind her in the doorway, bleary-eyed. The woman turned to him and spoke rapidly. His face darkened; he knew this story. He turned to me. She was taken to hospital, he explained in broken English, the baby was coming, they borrowed a car. They all went, all the family, to Dubrovnik hospital. But on the road, on the way, the car was shelled.

'Oh God.' I sat down in the dust. 'All dead?'

'Yes, except the young mother. She survived and they got her to hospital, I think. I don't know.' He shrugged; looked wretched. The woman began to wail again, pray and cross herself as I sat there, stunned in the dust.

Moments later I was up and running to the warehouse, stumbling as I went. Alam, his parents, Mona – all gone. Oh, Ibby! I had to stop and clutch my stomach. Take a few moments. Finally I reached the quay, and between sobs, told Pablo, the Italian boy, who was still there, what had happened. I needed a Bedford, and I needed him to come too, right now. He hesitated. The lorries were empty from the night's convoy, but still, we shouldn't. In a few hours' time they'd need to be loaded again. Tears streamed down my face as I begged him, and in another moment he was sitting beside me in the nearest one as I started the engine.

I drove as I'd never driven before down that baked, potholed road towards Dubrovnik, a long plume of dust spreading out behind us over the fields like a smoke-screen. 'Aide Humanitaire' on the side got us through the checkpoint outside town, the red crosses doing their work within the city too. At the hospital, in the busy main street, Pablo sat outside in case the lorry was stolen, whilst I ran in.

Other atrocities were never far away: a residential area had been hit in the same shelling that had taken out the Mastlovas' car, and inside, a mass of terrified relatives swarmed, demanding news of loved ones, hospital staff struggling to put up lists of the injured. I pushed through the mêlée and, on a hunch, made for the stairs. People were sitting on the floor the entire length of the corridor, some bandaged and sick, some waiting for treatment, some for news. I caught hold of a harassed-looking nurse. Maternity? Third floor, I was told.

As I staggered up the staircase I wondered if Ibby knew, had been told, that her husband and child ... Oh, Mona! In my mind I saw her running to meet her young friend on the corner, satchel swinging. Had to stop on the stairs to steady myself. Then I stifled a sob and stumbled on.

The news I was given outside the delivery room was bad. Ibby had died from her wounds as she'd gone into labour. And the child? The child had been delivered by Caesarean section. The baby was weak, but alive.

I don't remember a great deal about what happened next, but I do remember the confusion. The floor seemed to tilt from under me, and as I slid backwards, I felt the eyes of the rows of people sitting on the floor rise above me, gaze down. I imagine I was taken somewhere. I don't know where. I don't know how long I was out for either, but when I came round, someone was leaning over me, the same doctor who'd given me the news about Ibby: very young, in a bloodstained white coat.

'Was the baby a boy or a girl?' I asked.

A boy.

'And was he OK? Was he going to live?'

Yes, he was.

The doctor went to sit down beside me a moment, but a shout went up outside in the corridor. The door flew open. A nurse spoke rapidly, clearly in distress. The doctor hurried from the room. I turned to the woman beside me in the next bed: a school had been shelled, I gathered, close by; they were bringing the injured in now.

Kindergarten age. More horror, more chaos and confusion. I just wanted it all to go away. To go away. I shut my eyes.

Sometime later I left the hospital: stumbled numbly down the corridor, down the stairs and away. I didn't expect Pablo still to be there and he wasn't but miraculously he'd alerted another young driver, who was revving nervously in the street. One look at my face told him I'd had terrible news, but he didn't ask more than was strictly necessary. No one did in those days. He drove me back to Heronisque in silence, although at one point, I had to tell him to stop the lorry so I could throw up by the roadside.

The shock rendered me speechless for two days. During those days I stayed inside the Mastlovas' house and saw no one, telling Pablo to tell the others I'd be back at the warehouse when I was able. We all needed to do that from time to time, so I knew I could. I sat in that cold empty house, in the grandmother's upright wooden settle, by the fire, which I didn't have the energy to light, the dogs around my feet, feeling numb and empty. On the opposite wall, the priest, Ibby's grandfather, gazed back. It seemed to me his eyes never left me.

Two days later, Brett, who'd been on a week-long convoy all the way over the other side of the Balkans to Masticstan, came to the house. More savvy than Pablo, he persuaded me to talk. Once I'd started, I couldn't stop. Couldn't stop crying, either. The family Brett was living with had a car, a beaten-up old Peugeot, and when I'd recovered sufficiently, Brett and I went back to the hospital.

The baby had been taken to an orphanage, we were told by a nurse. It was housed in a convent, and operated out of a bombed castle on the outskirts of the city. Brett knew it. It was run by nuns he told me, strictly Catholic, and by all accounts the best amongst many in the city. The least grim, at any rate. I asked him to take me there.

In some godforsaken wasteland on the edge of town, towering grey crenulated walls rose up from a sea of bricks and rubble. We banged on the huge studded door until finally it was opened. A young nun in a blue habit and starched headdress stood there, stony-faced. I explained. A baby had been brought here, another victim of the atrocities; his mother, father, sister, grandparents, all dead. Could we see him? Such stories were common-place in this city. She crossed herself and said a silent prayer. Then she turned and led us down a corridor.

We followed her down the echoing stone passage, doors either side flung wide. Inside were rows and rows of cots with tiny babies, then a room full of older children, who, in a gentler age might just have been starting school or nursery, but who were also in cots. Their eyes followed us, dull and listless as we passed. In a smaller room, a few newborns lay asleep in makeshift cribs, drawers from chests, I realized. The baby I was looking for was amongst them, I was told. The one on the end: dark hair, swaddled.

A different sister appeared, elderly, no English, in a blue habit, a huge bunch of keys on a chain around her waist. We hadn't spelled it out to the first nun for fear of not getting in, but she was given to understand, through Brett's minimal Croatian, why exactly we were here. She was wary, doubtful. Many foreigners wanted these children: couples from Florida sending emissaries waving cash, particularly the tiny babies. They had to be very careful. No, it wasn't possible. She disappeared and we were shown out.

The following week, we were back: this time with the full weight of the UN and its aid agency behind us. The same sister appeared and in as many moments as she'd efficiently dispatched us last time, this time gave us her consent. The Foreign Office, it transpired, had already been in touch. Papers had been sent, permission had been given, red tape miraculously severed. At that time, in the chaos of civil war, in the former Yugoslavia, anything could be obtained with money, influence and papers, and I had all three. I was deemed the official adoptive parent and Seffen – as I knew Ibby intended to call a boy – left the orphanage in my arms. We returned to England three weeks later.

I'd been almost eight months in Bosnia, or Croatia, or Herzegovina, or whatever you wanted to call the Balkans, depending on your creed, your culture, your background, which, apparently, was what the fuss was all about. I'd experienced first-hand the terror of living in a war zone: I'd lived with people who'd feared for their lives and lost them, and I'd feared for my own at times. I'd seen what hatred can do to a beautiful country, brought to its knees by its own people, but I'd felt such love and kindness too, such as I don't think I ever felt again. Seen horror, but humanity too. Kit, I'm sure, saw more. We never discussed it. Kit lasted longer than me: he didn't return to England until the war ended the following year, in 1995. He'd been working out of an aid station in Sarajevo with a chaplain from the Italian forces, which regularly came under heavy artillery fire. He was lucky to escape with his life. Brett was not so lucky. Ten days after I left, he was killed on a convoy to Bechistanova, his Bedford lorry shelled and engulfed in flames. Pablo, Gretel and the others survived, although I never heard from them again.

When he returned home, Kit, who'd been working under the aegis of the Catholic Church in Sarajevo, ditched his place to read Business Studies at Durham, and enrolled instead at Wycliffe Hall Bible College in Oxford to read Theology. Thereafter, he became a priest. He came back from the Balkans with God, and I came back with a baby. The spoils of war, you might say.

10

As I leaned on the warm bonnet of my car outside Thame station fifteen years later, waiting for Seffen to emerge with Laura's daughters, Biba and Daisy, it struck me how, all things considered, the years had been kind to us. To Seffy and me. The first had been tricky admittedly. Mum had been beside herself with anxiety, convinced I'd 'wrecked my life', but Dad, after the initial shock, had understood. Kit obviously did, and so too did Laura, because coincidentally, she was about to have a baby. After the shock of discovering she was pregnant by her boyfriend, who was not yet divorced, she then declared herself the happiest girl alive when Hugh, the happiest man, promptly proposed, pending his decree absolute from Carla. So two babies landed unexpectedly in the Carrington family lap that year, and as even my mother admitted later with a sigh as she fussed over them in their cots, what, in a way, could be nicer?

I watched them now, coming through the station concourse together, arguing hotly, which wasn't unusual. Both tall and slender, Biba blonde and Seffy dark with beautiful, leaf-shaped eyes: two cousins brought up together from the year dot, whilst Daisy, fair and dreamy, lagged behind.

'Hi, Hattie.' Biba kissed me abstractedly, her cheeks pink. 'Seffy says the girls at my school are known as the Slutty Stevens – how gross is that? Why are boys so vile? Is it because they're basically immature and scared of us?'

'Undoubtedly,' I agreed, kissing my son. 'Hi, darling.'

'Mum, all I said, right, was that St Steven's girls are generally messy, using slutty in its true literal sense and not its more modern usage to imply a woman of loose morals, which obviously would be an outrageous slur on their character. What's wrong with that?' His eyes widened in mock outrage as Biba went to thump him. He caught her flailing wrists, laughing.

'Ooh, hey,' he soothed, 'relax. You're all stirred up.'

'You are soo horrible!'

'Just breathe,' he commanded, 'breathe.'

I ignored them and greeted Daisy.

'Hello, darling.'

'Hi, Hattie. Have you seen my girls?'

'Not recently, but the last time I looked they seemed in fine fettle. I'm afraid chickens aren't really my thing, though, so perhaps I'm not the best judge.'

'Bantams,' she corrected as I relieved her of her bag, which weighed a ton. Why these girls brought their entire wardrobes home for one weekend was beyond me, whilst Seffy, of course, in true, teenage-boy style, appeared to have brought nothing. Not even a toothbrush or a pair of pants, I observed, as he ducked into the back of the car laughing, still under attack from Biba's fists. She told him precisely what the girls at her school thought of the boys at his, which seemed to be arrogant gits without a brain cell between them, whilst Daisy chimed in to divulge that her friend's dad was a TV producer and was thinking of doing a documentary on the boys at Lightbrook, where Seffy was, in Berkshire, calling it Chinless Charlies. Seffy bellowed with mock indignation.

'What have you got in here?' I hauled Biba's case into the boot as she got in the back with Seffy. It was even heavier than her sister's.

'I wasn't sure how smart tonight was 'cos Mum said there was a dinner, so I brought a few things.'

'A dinner?' Seffy and Daisy looked horrified.

The whole point of an exeat weekend was to come home – which Seffy regarded as either our house in London or here with his cousins – adopt a horizontal position in front of the television for thirty-six hours, eat and drink solidly, preferably while still horizontal, argue about who took command of the remote control, but otherwise do nothing. The last thing anyone wanted was a smart dinner.

'No, no,' I reassured them hastily, 'it's only us, plus Kit and Granny and Grandpa. Oh, and Maggie.'

'I like Maggie.' Daisy brightened. 'She's the really cool one you work with, isn't she?'

'She is. She's also Seffy's godmother.'

'Who's going out with a married man,' put in my son helpfully.

'Really?' Biba was all attention. 'Does his wife know?'

'Thank you, darling.' I eyed Seffy sternly in the mirror as I turned the key in the ignition. 'Yes, well, Maggie is minus the married man tonight. And then tomorrow a chap called Ralph de Granville's coming. He's an interior designer.'

'Like you?' asked Daisy, putting her belt on in the front seat beside me.

'Yes, like me.'

'But why? I mean, I thought you and Maggie were doing the decorating?'

'Yes, but Mum's got some fixation about this Ralph person,' Biba informed her from the back. 'He's much more, like, fashionable? More flamboyant, apparently. No offence, Hattie.'

I grinned at her in the mirror. 'No offence taken.'

'But won't that be a bit awkward? I mean, if you're, you know, all there together? As competitors?' asked Daisy.

I was inclined to agree, and had been horrified when Laura had rather nervously told me that Mr de Granville, although originally coming the following week, now found himself otherwise engaged in Italy looking at some marble, and the only day he'd be able to get to the Abbey, was this Sunday morning. Obviously he realized weekends were precious, so alternatively, he could possibly squeeze something into his diary three months hence, pending other commitments …

'It'll be all right, won't it, Hattie?' Laura had asked me anxiously, fingers twisting at her waist. 'Having you all there this weekend? I mean, you're all professionals – you're not going to scratch each other's eyes out, are you?'

'Well, it's a little unusual, Laura, to have competing decorators in the same house. But I suppose Maggie and I could go to the pub. Make ourselves scarce.'

'I'll cancel him,' she said quickly.

'No, don't be silly, it'll be fine. You're right. We're all grown-ups. And I'm your sister, for God's sake. I might just be there for the weekend, not in any professional capacity.'

'Exactly. With your friend—'

'The interior designer?' I'd finished drily.

Maggie, though, was far from put out when I'd told her privately.

'Oh, goody. I've always wanted to meet this jerk. Let's see if he's as risible as his publicity suggests.'

'You don't mind?'

'Of course not. Hope he stays for lunch. And while he's getting stuck into the Bloody Marys I'll snitch his bag and snap his pencils and hide his tape measure.'

'No, no, we're all mature adults,' I told Daisy now as we sped off down the lanes. 'There won't be any silly jealousies.'

'I prefer your sort of design anyway,' she said thoughtfully. 'I don't like flamboyant and fashionable.'

I shot her a grateful look, beside me in jeans and a sweatshirt, unlike her sister in the back, swathed in Camden Market's finest: three or four layered tops, a tiny skirt over leggings, masses of messy blonde hair and bling. There were only eighteen months between them, but Biba had embraced her teens with gusto – boys, parties, action, bring it on – whereas Daisy seemed to be resolutely clinging to childhood and her pets. She had a flock of bantams – 'the girls' – which were her pride and joy.

And Seffy ... well, Seffy had always been more like Daisy: in less of a hurry. Quite studious and musical – he played the cello beautifully – he was a prolific reader, but then a year ago ... well, they were bound to grow up, weren't they? I swallowed. Narrowed my eyes to the road. Bound to want to push the boundaries. And the rules at his old London day school had been so petty and ridiculous, just asking to be broken. So he'd got into a bit of trouble, which was unlike him. As the headmaster had said at the time, totally out of character; but then he'd been led astray. Nothing terrible, a few smokes in the park, a bottle of wine ... but he'd seemed to be kicking against something. So I'd moved him to Lightbrook, a boarding school in the country – a huge financial stretch – but what Seffy had wanted. Had indeed asked to go to. Insisted. Well, I imagine it was rather quiet for him at home, with just me, no brothers and sisters, and certainly he seemed to be thriving there. He'd settled down a bit, was starting to work again, which he hadn't been doing at Westminster, where he'd totally lost interest. And he was a bright boy, he'd catch up. For a while he hadn't come home much either, even though he could at weekends, which had hurt a bit, and then when he did, he was much less affectionate. They all were, Laura assured me. Biba was just the same; they move on, which is away from us. But Seffy and I ... well, being just the two of us, were so close.

I gave myself a little inward shake. But that was last year. This year, these past few months, had been better. He'd rung me more, been more communicative, and his grades were steadily going up, hopefully in time for GCSEs.

'How's the play going?' I asked him in the rear-view mirror. Was it my imagination or was there always a slightly guarded look now, just fleeting, before he answered me?

'It's good, going well. We've still got a way to go, but rehearsals are OK.'

'What's the play?' Biba demanded.

'*King Lear*.'

'Oooh,' she said mockingly. 'Ambitious, Seffy-boy. And who are you, the crazy king?'

'No, I'm Edmund, a rather dashing young earl who I'm playing with one hell of a swagger, I can tell you.' He flicked up his coat collar and smouldered at her, waggling his eyebrows.

'Oh God,' she spluttered, 'please don't tell me you're the love interest.'

'Honey, I'm the sex interest.'

Both girls roared and I smiled at them all in the mirror. He liked playing to the gallery, making the girls laugh, they loved having him around and I knew they were proud to call him their cousin. Tall, good-looking, floppy-haired, he was considered cool, even though he didn't try, and his rather exotic background didn't detract either: son of Croatian revolutionaries whose father had fought and died for his country, and whose family we'd tried but failed to trace any further back than the priest grandfather.

When Seffy had been about ten he'd become very absorbed with his background and asked to go back to Croatia. We'd taken a package tour one week in the summer, and found a very different place from the one I'd left. The Dalmatian coast, quite rightly, had become a tourist resort. Full of holiday-makers, the picturesque little quayside villages were crammed with tavernas spilling onto pavements and heaving with families, in flip-flops and shorts, buying postcards. A very different atmosphere prevailed from the one I'd left. I'd shown him the house where his parents had lived and where I'd stayed, freshly painted now, bright blue, with bougainvillaea trailing from pots in the yard. But a suspicious dark-eyed family lived within, who, I think, fearing we were laying some sort of claim to the place, were reluctant to let us in. Neither could we find anyone who remembered Seffy's family, the Mastlovas being refugees anyway, and before it got too depressing, we moved on, to a resort down the coast for some sailing and snorkelling. Seffy, I think though, had been pleased to see it. On the beach, I'd often see him swim out, then turn round and tread water, narrowing his eyes to the hills behind, which I knew he was thinking his father had fought so bravely for.

The Bosnian war was still topical and it gave him a bit of glamour, I think. He used to talk about it a lot, although these days, less so. In fact, not at all. And he was impatient when it was mentioned. My father, who'd often got maps out and spoken to him about it, thinking it was important, had been surprised at the brusque way Seffy no longer wanted to discuss it. But Mum said it was only natural: he was English, for heaven's sake, at an English public school. All his friends were called Tom, Sam and Harry, he wanted to fit in, move on, not be different. He was growing up. He was. Up until he was about twelve, he'd still crawl into my bed for a cuddle. Not now, of course.

When I next went to speak to him, I saw he was already watching me in the rear-view mirror.

'Hungry?' I smiled.

'Starving. Breakfast had finished by the time I got up, so I missed it.'

'Oh, Seffy, don't they make you get up in time? What's that matron doing, filing her nails?'

'We're deemed Responsible Adults.' He made ironic quotation marks in the air. 'Old enough to get ourselves up.'

'Yes, but still,' I grumbled as we pulled into the front drive and crunched to a halt. 'They should make some provision for adolescent torpor. Left to your own devices, I'm surprised you get up for lessons.'

'I don't always,' he said softly as he climbed out of the car, then seeing my horrified face: 'Joke, Mother. Chill. I've haven't missed one at Lightbrook yet, OK?'

Although I missed quite a few at Westminster, was implicit in that, I thought as he slouched up the drive, hands in his overcoat pockets, to the house. Biba and Daisy, behind him, were yelling that he could at least help

122

with their bags, or didn't they teach those sort of manners at top public schools any more? He turned and
walked backwards towards the front door, cupping his
ear, quizzically, aping deafness. What? Can't hear. They
appealed to their mother who'd just that minute pulled
up beside us in her four-by-four, Charlie in the front seat,
fresh from his prep school, looking impossibly gorgeous
and freckly, his face lighting up when he saw Seffy, banging on the window to attract his attention. Laura, though,
when she'd got out and hugged her daughters, refused to
censure her nephew.

'Well, if you girls worked harder on your charm, perhaps he might help. I always found the delicate-flower
routine worked wonders.'

Seffy stopped walking backwards and widened his eyes in
mock delight. 'Oh, I love delicate flowers,' he assured his
cousins. 'Now if you were a bit more like your mother, a bit
more…' he wrinkled his brow, 'gentle, feminine…' He didn't
get any further, though, as, roaring like banshees, the girls
chased him into the house, Biba taking off a shoe and hurling
it at him, Charlie on their heels, shrieking with delight and
shedding his blazer as he raced after them. Laura and I sighed
and stooped to pick up the heavy bags, obviously.

Supper that evening was a noisy affair. Mum and Dad,
down from London, were there in their favourite role as
grandparents, Kit was relaxed amongst his family, and
Maggie made an easy guest. As a single girl she was accustomed to singing for her supper and could be very droll,
but also thrived on drawing people out, something no
one in my family needed, but were all delighted to do,
given the opportunity. She was leaning her chin in her
hand at the kitchen table now, making huge eyes at Kit.

'It must be wonderful having a calling, a vocation,' she was saying as Laura and I hustled vegetable dishes to the table, Laura telling her daughters they could at least lend a hand, instead of poring over her latest copy of *Hello!*. They shut it grudgingly, and slouched to the table.

'Oh, I feel very blessed,' Kit agreed.

'And you really stepped up to the plate, didn't you? Gave up so much. I mean, materially, if you were thinking of going into the City. I think it's wonderful.'

Kit's chest was expanding and Laura and I exchanged smiles. Of course it was wonderful how Kit had answered the call, given up so much, and we were all very proud of him. Particularly what he'd done in Sarajevo. But it was interesting how, over the years, he'd somehow reverted to type, albeit within the Church. The gritty parish in Tower Hamlets that he'd talked of reforming at Bible college had, after three years of cycling around Oxford, become less of a burning issue, and even though he'd been offered just such a parish in Tottenham, when he'd also been offered a curacy on a vast country estate – a duke's estate, a famous one belonging to a friend of Hugh's – with its own idyllic church in perfect Jane Austen parkland, and where most of the parishioners were over sixty and feared God anyway, and where he was to be in possession of a dear little brick and flint vicarage, the sort people pay squillions for in *Country Life*, he'd found himself accepting. Far from being at the cutting edge of the ministry, Kit was firmly at the upholstered end.

'Done much shooting lately?' enquired Laura innocently, as she shepherded Charlie to the table by his shoulders, flicking me a look.

'A bit last season,' Kit conceded.

'You shoot?' Maggie blinked.

'Kit has fishing and shooting rights on Richard's estate,' explained Hugh. 'I gather you caught a whopper on Saturday. A twenty-pounder, no less.'

'Yes, but that was a bit of a one-off,' said Kit uncomfortably. 'Normally at weekends I can't get away from parish duties,' he explained to Maggie. 'Visiting and so on.'

'Ah, yes, the needy of Henley-on-Thames,' grinned Dad, sitting down and spreading his napkin on his lap. 'Quite a challenge getting round all those manicured lawns, trudging up those crunchy drives. Keep it up, laddie.' Kit grinned good-naturedly as we guffawed. 'Actually, we mustn't tease,' Dad went on soberly. 'Kit does sterling work kissing for Oxfordshire.'

Kit took a mock bow to our cheers whilst Maggie looked bewildered. Years ago Kit had made the mistake of kissing an old lady on the cheek after the service at the church door – '*purely* because she proffered it and purely because it seemed rude not to!' he'd declared hotly later. But the very next Sunday, every old dear in the parish had lined up, cheek at the ready for this attractive young vicar to peck, standing their ground resolutely if he even looked like hesitating. Kit claimed he now kissed so many powdery cheeks on a Sunday his lips were white by the end of it.

'Manufacture a cold sore,' Biba suggested. 'Or a great big zit, just here.' She curled her lip.

'Like this.' Charlie helpfully demonstrated with a blob of mashed potato on his sister.

'You are so dumb.' Biba flicked it off with her finger, whereupon the Labrador caught it like a fly.

'I don't like this word dumb,' remarked my mother imperiously as she handed round the carrots. 'It's an Americanism.'

'You're married to an American,' yelped my father.

'Yes, but you wouldn't say it, darling. You're an educated American.'

'Why, thank you, my flower.' He inclined his head ironically. 'Nice to know I'm winning the Darwinian struggle.'

'It comes from watching too much television,' Mum observed. 'Too much *Friends*. I mean, you wouldn't say "sidewalk", would you?' she demanded of Biba. 'And you wouldn't take out the garbage?'

'No,' Biba agreed, 'I'd take out the trash.'

As the young dissolved, Laura retorted: 'Chance would be a fine thing.'

'You've been rinsed, Granny,' Seffy informed her.

'I'm always rinsed, darling.' She patted her hairdo. 'I make my girl do it twice, to get out all the conditioner.'

This struck them as unbearably funny, but Mum ploughed on undaunted, turning her gaze on someone else. 'And speaking of taking out the rubbish, I gather you've got some young man to do just that, Hattie?'

That stopped the laughter instantly: silence descended. I glanced, appalled, at Laura, who got up, pink-cheeked, on some spurious excuse to grab the tomato ketchup bottle. She hissed, 'She-made-me!' at Mum's back.

'Rather young, I believe. But at least Seffy likes him.'

'Yeah, but I think he does more than take out Mum's rubbish,' drawled my son. I gaped, red-faced, as everyone roared. Seffy shrugged at me, grinning. 'Sorry, Mum, but, like my aunt says, she made me. I was tortured. You try not answering Granny's questions.'

'You just tell her to mind her own business!' I sput-tered, but I was secretly pleased too. He liked Ivan. I thought he did, but I was pleased to hear it: publicly too.

'How young?' Biba was mouthing across the table to Seffy, clearly gripped, and clearly annoyed she hadn't been in the loop about this. She boggled as Seffy mouthed something back.

'Hattie. You've got a toy boy!' she squealed.

'I have not got a toy boy!' I roared, the colour of the tomato ketchup bottle now.

'Well, if he makes Hattie happy, I think that's wonder-ful,' said Laura, grovelling for all she was worth, having spilled the beans, and shooting her daughter a look.

'I agree,' said Dad staunchly. 'It's about time you had a boyfriend, darling. I couldn't be more pleased.' I sent him a grateful look. 'And if he's still in short pants with a cata-pult in his pocket, it's all the same to me.'

More hilarity. Oh, splendid.

Later that evening, after coffee and much more drinking, and when Maggie and I turned in for bed, she stopped outside my bedroom door, cheeks flushed.

'Your family are great,' she observed. 'I'd forgotten. You're so lucky.'

That had never really occurred to me, and I was sur-prised. My family were loud, opinionated, quarrelsome, easily offended, sparky and often intensely irritating, but great fun on the whole, and I supposed I was lucky. We got together very regularly to bicker and snap and roar, and couldn't really go a couple of weeks without seeking one another out. Mum, Laura and I certainly spoke most days. It struck me I knew very little about Maggie's family.

A widowed mother in Hendon, no brothers or sisters. She had lots of lovely girlfriends, though, many more than me: the phone was always going in the shop and it would be Hannah, or Sally, or Alex, but when I'd commented on this she'd say, 'That's because you don't need them. People from big families never do.' I knew she lapped up my family's affairs, regarding it as a never ending soap opera, particularly here at the Abbey.

As we said good night, though, I thought how it made a change to feel blessed. Most people, apart from Maggie, regarded me with a hint of pity: late thirties, no husband, a single mother, and when they pressed me on what I did now that Seffy was at boarding school and I said, 'Oh, work, mostly,' I could tell they were thinking: poor Hattie. It was competitive, life, wasn't it? I shut my bedroom door and crossed to the window. Like in that *Two Ronnies* sketch with John Cleese, I felt slightly sorry for Maggie with no happy extended family and no child, but looked up to Laura, with a husband, three children, and a huge house; yet Laura looked up to friends who could live in their houses for perpetuity. Where did it end? When did we ever stop wanting more?

I didn't ask myself that in all seriousness, though, because I knew, with gut-wrenching surety, that if I could have had what I wanted, what I'd always desired, years ago, the only man I'd ever loved, I'd never want for more. Never. I reached up to pull the curtain across and saw a curtain draw simultaneously in a house in the valley, in Little Crandon. It affected me like a few thousand volts. I stepped back from the window. It was The Pink House, where Dominic and Letty had lived, but I knew it would only be Letty doing the pulling now. On her own, like me.

11

Dominic was killed in a terrorist attack in London in the summer of '95, two years after I'd left the House of Commons, one year after I'd come back from Croatia. I say an attack, but they hadn't actually been targeting him *per se* as an MP, not like the Brighton bombings, nor the bomb in the Commons car park that killed Airey Neave. No, this was the usual, random, cowardly, bomb-on-a-bus routine, designed to kill and maim ordinary civilians and cause general unspecific terror. Imagine their delight, then, when one ordinary civilian on the number 14 bus turned out to be the Foreign Secretary, the honourable member for North Oxfordshire. One Dominic Forbes MP, who, not as a matter of course, and not on any regular daily basis, had caught the bus into Westminster one Tuesday morning, purely because his driver had failed to turn up, purely as a matter of expediency. Imagine the jubilation in the terraced house in Kilburn, which the police eventually raided and found deadly incendiary equipment within. Imagine the revelry in the house of the Brothers of Jihad.

I'd been in France at the time, a country I'd achieved via a circuitous route. When Seffy and I came back from Croatia my parents had insisted I live with them for a bit in order for them to help with the baby, which I gladly did, having not a clue which end of an infant was which. Mum and Dad by then were in their sixteenth house in their twenty-seven-year marriage, which remarkably they're still in today, and which, thanks to no school fees, they own outright. Thanks also to Dad finally being recognized as a voice of sanity rattling in the broadsheets of a morning, culminating in a regular and prestigious weekly column, which rendered them comfortable. Sod's law, as he said, having been uncomfortable all those years when he'd really needed the money, when he'd had a young family to support. Nevertheless a small terraced house at the wrong end of Elsworthy Road – which put it in Primrose Hill as far as my father was concerned, and in St John's Wood if you asked my mother – became home to us all. And it was perfect. Particularly for Seffy and me. The park was on our doorstep, that great, green, glorious slope to trudge up every day, arriving at the summit panting and glowing, my baby on my chest in a papoose, the whole of London spread before me.

Mum was brilliant, and made me hand Seffy over for an entire day once a week, so I could 'get out there', as she put it: get back to the real world, keep my hand in.

'In what?' I'd wail as she shooed me out of the front door.

'Whatever you want,' she'd say firmly, jiggling Seffy in her arms. 'Go and think, go and walk the streets. See what appeals.'

Yeah, right, I'd think as I trudged up Avenue Road to the underground. Whatever appeals: as if the world were my flaming oyster. But Mum, for all her glamour, was a hustler. It was she who'd rung up newspapers demanding they see her husband's work when Dad was too reticent to harangue them, it was she who'd marched Laura into Storm, the model agency. I couldn't help thinking she was dreaming here, though. I could hardly get a job as a secretary for one day a week – which I'd loathe anyway; the only reason I'd tapped a keyboard was its proximity to

Dominic — and I'd equally be laughed at if I enquired about working in a shop or a café for just a day. What did she expect me to do?

But my mother's not only a hustler, she's also brighter than she looks and the time alone did me good. I'd invariably come back fresher and more energized than I went out, probably with a few bits of faded old porcelain, or a French goblet from Portobello for Mum and Dad, who wouldn't take rent, but loved old pieces almost as much as I did.

Often I'd track further west, taking the District Line and alighting at Sloane Square. One stall I used to frequent at Antiquarius in Chelsea was run by a corpulent Frenchman, his face the colour of the glass of claret he kept under his counter and sipped surreptitiously from time to time. Breathing appeared to be a problem and he'd wheeze and splutter over his wares, hovering protectively as I fingered the Gustavian tureens, the old French bistro glasses, the beautifully turned Sèvres candlesticks.

'You can 'ave that for fifteen queed,' he wheezed, unplugging a cigarette from the corner of his mouth as I fondled an ancient milk jug lovingly.

'It's got a crack in it,' I told him, turning it over.

'Which ees why you can 'ave it for fifteen queed.'

Exchanges like this between the two of us were commonplace. He had the best — and cheapest — stock of continental china and glass of the type I liked in London, and the best and cheapest lace too. With the exception, perhaps, of an elegant po-faced French girl three stalls down. Her prices were monstrous, though, and she wouldn't haggle, or even speak to me as Christian would, but kept her nose firmly in her *Paris Match*, crossing her slim jeaned legs tapering to beaded pumps as she perched on her stool.

'I'll give you ten,' I told him.

He laughed. 'No way. I *buy* it for ten, in Boulogne! How much my petrol there and back, hm? Fark off.'

I shrugged. 'OK, I'll offer you ten next week. See if you take it then.'

It was a ruse that often worked with Christian. If he still had it a week later, he might give in.

'I won't be here next week, or any other week after that. My doctor say it's too much for me, working here every day weeth emphysema and every month back to France for stock. And so cold in this buggering marketplace in winter.' He rearranged his wares gloomily. 'So I pack eet in.' He shrugged.

'Oh. What will you do?' I'd grown accustomed to his wheeze. And his foul mouth.

Everything went up Gallically: shoulders, hands, eyebrows. 'Who knows? Go back to Nantes, *normalement*, but my wife, she like it here. So I don't knows. Work part time in a shop, maybe. You want the jug?'

'Um, yes. I'll give you twelve.'

'Done.'

The following day, having walked around Primrose Hill a good deal, Seffy having migrated to my back now he was older, and feeling ridiculously nervous despite having survived nearly a year in Croatia, and worked in the House of Commons – amazing what being at home with a baby does to your confidence – I rang him. I had his card from aeons ago, had picked it up from a little stack at the front of his stall. 'Reeng me if you change your mind, I save it for you,' he'd say as I walked away. 'Christian Belliose,' I read now, 'Dealer in Fine French Antiques'. He answered in his breathy, guttural way, and listened as I outlined my plan, bullet points before me at the kitchen table, Seffy on my lap biting a rattle, my parents out.

There was incredulity at first, and a great deal of spluttering of *'Merde!'* and other more scorching profanities, but he didn't put down the phone. He let me get to the end of my spiel. A pause. Then guarded questions: who the devil was I, anyway? What did I know? But I'd done my homework. We'd talked, over the months, and I knew he favoured the southern markets down in Provence: knew he considered the Paris flea markets expensive. Knew his preference was for Limoges over Sèvres in porcelain, and fluted glass over crystal, as was mine. I knew what made him tick. And he was tempted. I felt him dangle on the end of my line. Felt him hesitate.

'You do three days and I do two, but we split the profits sixty-forty my way?' he repeated.

'Yes, and I do all the trips to France so you don't have to travel any more.'

'Why? What make you do it? Work for nothing?'

I took a deep breath and raised my eyes to the ceiling. Oh, a myriad of things, I wanted to say. To be out in the real world again, to be working. Not to feel invisible at twenty-five, too young to fade into the background. I could have told him about fear too. Of course I loved Seffy, but I was lonely, isolated: no friend of mine was even married, let alone had a child. Did I even have secret doubts I'd done the wrong thing? No, never. Not even in my darkest moments. But still …

Instead I told him of my love of antiques, too strong to let this opportunity slip by. I told him of my passion for all things French, quite true, and I told him how he'd done the groundwork, built up the business, whilst I'd just be bombing in. How it was only fair.

'OK,' he said slowly. 'And what's the catch?'

'Well, the catch is you have to trust my judgement, obviously, in the markets. But I know what you like, what you'd buy—'

'And the real catch?'

I caught my breath. No flies on this *monsieur*, emphysema or not.

'The real catch is I have a baby.'

There was a pause. Then he laughed. I felt my heart drop like a brick. Out of the question, of course. A baby in an antique market – what, under the counter? Screaming at the customers? Although I had seen one or two older children running around. He was wheezing now, coughing.

'I'm wasting your time,' I said flatly.

'No, I laugh because I know. You smell.'

'What?' I flushed.

'Of babies. Sick. Eets fine. You juggle *le bébé*, and I'll talk to the management. We'll manage.'

We did. Christian, having been a stall holder for twenty-odd years and part of the fabric, let alone the antique furniture, had considerable sway in Antiquarius. In the day when the King's Road treasured its eccentrics, he was regarded as something of a character. The people there were kind too. They didn't want to see him go, forced out by illness; knew it was his life, his passion, and if his partner – his partner! – could enable him to stay, they were delighted.

'And the baby?' I breathed down the phone to Christian when he rang to report back. 'What did they say about Seffy?'

'They say he be fine, but bound and gagged.'

'What?'

'No, no, I tease.'

I was beginning to see why Christian's reputation went before him.

'No gag,' he wheezed, 'just doped. Drugged, and they say he be fine.'

They were an eclectic bunch at Antiquarius: shabby, but faintly glamorous, in a bohemian sort of way, and I soon realized everyone was juggling something. Pamela, next door (oriental china), had her incontinent mother, whom she couldn't bear to put in a home. Paddy, opposite (clocks and watches), had his wealthy gay partner who wanted him beside him at the bar of the Chelsea Arts Club, and came in to drag him out in a strop. Sally-Anne (ancient garden implements) had teenage children who constantly called to say, 'What's for lunch?' Everyone seemed to have a dependant of some kind. And they loved Seffy. He was a good baby and was passed around with much indulgent clucking. Even one or two sniffy old-school types who'd muttered about having 'a screamer' in their midst, softened when they crouched down to his pushchair and he instantly beamed. He smiled at everyone. Customers, tourists, and particularly the two little girls who belonged to Marie-Therese (maps and military prints), and who had a lovely time wheeling him around when they came home from school, flying up and down the aisles to make him chuckle. The market spawned a little community, and Seffy and I became part of it, although without Christian's sheltering wing, I dare say it would have taken a lot longer.

Françoise du Bose, or 'French Living', as she called herself – or 'feelthy copy cat', as Christian referred to her – was the only one who kept her distance. She hardly even deigned to look up from her stunning collection of wooden bowls full of dried herbs, fabulous old church lanterns, plaster busts, statues and huge garden urns as I walked past her stall every morning. I always gave her a cheery hello, but never got anything more than a tight little smile back. I gathered she was new too, which surprised me. Her *savoir-faire* suggested she'd been here for ever.

'She won't last, either,' Christian told me. 'Stuck-up beech. What her problem? She no speak to no one.'

'Needs a good seeing-to,' observed Toby (antique books), opposite. His answer to most things. He sniffed and blew some dust off one of his books.

'Her stuff's good, though,' I said. 'Lovely and rustic.'

'Ah yes, she 'as good taste,' Christian conceded. 'But she should learn to smile a beet more, she 'as a mouth like a cat's arse. Now, Provence ...' He turned to me anxiously as Toby wandered off in search of a Pot Noodle. 'I worry about this trip, Hattie. Ees not like Caen, just across the channel. Ees a fuck of long way down.'

'I know, Christian, I've looked at the map, and don't worry, we'll be fine.'

My last – and inaugural – trip to France, I felt had been an unqualified success. Just me and Seffy across on a night boat, then rumbling on in Christian's Transit van to Caen. We'd found the market easily and parked without difficulty, and although the sun had burned through an early mist and Seffy had got slightly uncomfortable – quite a bit of squawking, and I'd had to run off and find him a hat, fast – we'd managed. I'd given him a bottle and a feed under a shady café awning, my eyes trawling the emerging stalls, then flicked out the pushchair and rocked him to sleep.

Moments later I'd raced around those stalls with my buggy like someone who's won a free ten minutes with a supermarket trolley. I knew I didn't have much time, had to buy and haggle while he was asleep, and actually, the pressure worked. I bought instinctively, instead of dithering too much and losing something, and once I'd got my eye in, knew instantly what was worth having.

I'd seen the French girl, Françoise, at a distance, but knew she'd arrived later than me. Knew the night boat had given me the edge. Once I'd secured my booty I'd race back to the van to dump it, bags hanging from pushchair handles. And then it dawned. The pram. With crucial shopping basket underneath, which I'd brought in case Seffy needed a flat-out sleep – perfect. I assembled it quickly, lifted my sleeping child in, and hurtled back. Here and there I collected treasures stall holders had kindly held for me when I'd explained, in faltering French, I'd be back, their Mediterranean faces melting at *un bébé*. When the basket below was full I'd squirrel my finds carefully around Seffy's head, his feet, calling out my *mercies*, hurrying on.

When I'd returned to England, Christian had been surprised. He'd shuffled out of Antiquarius in his baggy fawn trousers, cardigan and cravat, cigarette dangling from his fingers, and helped me unload in the King's Road.

'You've done well,' he observed as he admired a beautiful Haviland Limoges bowl, translucent in its whiteness and with a magenta and gold rim. He turned it upside down to look at the mark. 'I thought you come back weeth crap, but is OK.'

I felt faint with relief. In my heart I was sure I'd done pretty well, but this was high praise from Christian.

'All the more reason then,' I told him now, a month later, 'to let me go to Provence.'

He made his outraged face: mouth down, everything else up – eyebrows, shoulders, hands – and I knew I'd won. I beamed and gave him a hug.

Crazy of me not to have allowed Mum and Dad to have Seffy as they insisted they should. Crazy of me to take him with me. But the pilgrim soul in me wanted to prove something: wanted to prove Seffy and I against the world could do this, that we could cope.

Unfortunately, Seffy was teething, and the dreaded *autoroute* went on and on in a horrific shimmering mirage of heat, all the way down to the South. However much I stopped in service stations and tried to pacify him, rub his gums, give him a bottle, a dummy, he didn't stop crying. Under a blazing sun, no airconditioning, poor Seffy wailing beside me, I coaxed the van on, which seemed to be ailing – oh, please God, don't break down – willing us to make it.

Finally, eyes gritty with tiredness and concentration, I found myself sitting outside a café in a square surrounded by high medieval walls. Even in my strung-out state I could see it was astonishingly beautiful. My sleeping babe was beside me in his pram, face still pink from crying, and a large glass of rosé was before me. I sipped it gratefully. A formidable *madame* dressed in black, whose chin ran into her not inconsiderable chest, put a plate of juicy figs and the thinnest ham in front of me, together with a basket of crusty bread, none of which I'd ordered. I explained. She flashed me a toothless smile. '*C'est normal.*' As the church clock chimed nine, fairy lights, strung amongst the plane tree branches, sprang into light to proclaim the town was *en fête*, and bunting fluttered in the breeze. In that moment, I felt something unclench and relax within me. Although my head felt like a thousand bees had hived in it and my tongue was like leather, under those twinkling lights, with Seffy beside me, the Provençal sun setting in a rosy hue, I knew why I wanted to do this. Why it made sense.

I didn't have enough money for a hotel, so after taking Seffy for a walk down by the river – he was toddling now, his chubby hand in mine – we went back to the van to sleep. I stretched out in a sleeping bag in the back whilst he lay in his pram top beside me. I slept fitfully, parked as we were just off the market square, thinking any minute a gendarme would knock on the window crying, *'Alors! Fiche-moi le camp!'* Happily we were left in peace.

We awoke to a hazy pink dawn, the sun streaming through the van windows. I sat up and pushed aside one of the shirts I'd hung as a makeshift curtain. Stall holders had begun to set up trestle tables under the plane trees. Some just spread a blanket on the ground, loading it with piles of bric-a-brac, whilst others used the backs of their ancient Citroën vans to display their wares. Above, swinging from the trees, a huge banner bore the legend *'23ème Fréjus Brocante'*.

An hour later the sky was sailor blue, and Seffy and I hustled to our café for breakfast. The same toothless *madame* beamed in delight – not at me, I realized, as she played with Seffy's bare toes – and the bar began to fill up. Old men drifted in for their pastis or café cognac, girding their livers before a hard day's work, sometimes in the fields, but more often playing cards outside, or a strenuous game of boules.

The stalls were now fully loaded: pagodas of books, lamps, pitted mirrors, coronas, candlesticks and commodes wobbled perilously. Entire domestic histories, it seemed, were reduced to one table, whilst the ubiquitous Louis Quinze chairs with shredded silk upholstery – looking faintly embarrassed to be outdoors and not in a salon – stood by. As the church clock chimed eight, I lifted Seffy carefully into the pram. Happily, after a huge bottle of milk warmed in the microwave by *madame*, his eyes closed like a doll's and I shot round the stalls. I bought quickly, but, I hoped, shrewdly, trusting my instinct.

Feeling rather pleased with myself I awarded myself a break at eleven o'clock, a cup of coffee, thinking I'd earned it. I'd wake Seffy for a feed, I determined, and then have another look: make sure there was nothing I'd missed. As I went towards our usual café, I paused at a shop to buy an English newspaper. That's when I saw it.

FOREIGN SECRETARY KILLED IN TERRORIST ATTACK

As I picked it off the stand I remember feeling a great throb, a rush of blood. I stared at the photograph: a wreck of a bus. Read the first few lines. But the realization that he was dead was not immediate. I felt only terror, and a desperation for the terror to end. I read his name again; 'Dominic Forbes, 36'. I began to shake violently. My knees gave way and the next thing I knew, I was sitting on the floor. A baby in a pram began to wail beside me. My baby. But I couldn't get up. Someone crouched beside me: a helping hand was on my arm, then another. A girl's face, the French girl's, Françoise, close to mine. Her voice, urgent: 'Are you all right?'

I couldn't speak. The newspaper was still clenched in my hand. Consternation was intense in the background now. Large Frenchwomen were flapping around offering advice, a small crowd was gathering, gesticulating, their voices shrill. Françoise was helping me to my feet and leading me away, one hand pushing the pram, another supporting me. We went towards a café, an umbrella in the shade. I sat dumbly. She ordered me a drink, a pastis, one for her too, but I couldn't drink. My eyes kept going back to the paper. I felt the blood drain from me, felt cold without it. I remember covering my mouth with my hand as I screamed. Françoise reached across the table to seize my arm in alarm, her eyes wide, but the scream had relieved the first terrifying pressure of the truth, the first shock of certainty. I felt both trembling hands cover my eyes as I wept noisily. I remember Françoise lifting a wailing, frightened Seffy from his pram to soothe him as I cradled my head to the table, catching my breath in great heaving sobs that seemed to come from the centre of the earth.

I don't remember much about the following sequence of events, except that she had a hotel room in the square, which she took me to. I lay on the bed and she let me cry on: on and on, face down into the pillows, up to the ceiling on my back, curled up in the foetal position. And then some time later, she slipped me a sleeping pill and I slept. After all, I'd been up most of the previous night.

Some hours later, I woke to find her on the balcony with Seffy. I could tell by the light it was early evening, and he was standing on her lap, his sturdy legs and bare feet bouncing on her thighs, as she pointed to the crowds below. The children's carousel, its lights flying round and round, flashed patterns on the bedroom wall: the smell of chestnuts roasting drifted up.

Later that evening when the low sun bathed the ochre roofs from our window in a warm glow, and when Seffy had been fed and changed and was asleep in his pram again, we went downstairs to a café. I felt weak, exhausted, but I finally drank that pastis. More than one, actually. And I told her about Dominic. About how I loved him, or had loved him, and how no one had ever come close to rousing such feelings in me. How my soul ached for him always, every day when he was alive, and now that he was dead … he can't be dead. I'd stare into my drink, tears streaming down my face in blank disbelief.

She'd reach out and squeeze my hand, rocking the pram with the other, being quiet, occasionally murmuring sympathies. Later, as I slumped back wretchedly in my chair, she told me a bit about herself. She was older than me, thirty, and she told me how she'd loved a boy for seven years. A Parisian, how they'd lived together, bought a flat in Montmartre. And then one day he'd left her, without too much explanation, and weeks later, became engaged to a friend of hers. This friend was expecting his baby in August. She told me how she, Françoise, had been unable to stay in Paris knowing the two of them were round the corner, how she'd come back to England just two months ago.

'Come back?'

'Yes, because I'm half-English, you see. My father was French, but my mother's English.'

'Ah.'

I'd wondered about the London accent, not a trace of Franglais. She told me that Françoise du Bose was just her professional name to reassure punters of the authenticity of her *brocante*: that her real name was Maggie. She'd come to England when she was ten, when her father died, been brought up in Hendon. Not far from me, we discovered, since to my mother's chagrin, I'd started life in Neasden. For a while, Maggie said, she almost couldn't speak with the pain of losing Étienne: didn't want to get involved at work, at Antiquarius, didn't want people to get to know her, ask questions. She said that although Étienne wasn't dead, he might as well be. And sometimes she wished he was.

She got me to eat a bit, even though I didn't want to, and later, made me have the bed back in the hotel, whilst she slept on the floor with a pillow, even though I insisted I was fine. I felt too weak to argue.

The following morning I woke up and the bedroom was empty. No Maggie, and Seffy was gone. I ran to the open French window. The muslin curtain billowed dramatically, and I cast about the square in horror, eyes wild. I didn't know this girl. Didn't know her at all. And then I saw her. Down below in the square, on the children's carousel: Maggie was slowly gliding round on a painted golden horse, Seffy on her lap. She waved. I waved back. Nausea rose in my throat as I remembered Dominic, but I knew, too, that moment of panic for Seffy had been worse. That he'd been the first thing on my mind as I woke and that nothing, absolutely nothing, was as strong as my love for him. It helped, a little.

Maggie and I stayed another two nights in Fréjus. I rang Christian and told him what had happened. It was Sunday anyway, so the market was closed, and I just said, a friend's died, I'd like to stay longer in the sun. He understood. Perhaps he knew it was more than a friend.

Those few days I spent with Maggie were the closest I'd ever got to anyone, bar Dominic or my family. We talked and talked. The newspapers, even the French ones, were full of Dominic: pictures of him, of Letty and him, sometimes with Cassie, their infant daughter. Double-page spreads in the *Sunday Times*, the *Telegraph*, lengthy full-page obituaries. I pored over them, reading bits out to Maggie, who'd smile, rocking the pram. I marvelled at things I didn't know – the starred First at Cambridge, Head Boy at Harrow – I was greedy for details and devoured everything. Maggie didn't try to take the papers away. I think she knew it was part of my grieving process.

On our final evening I managed not to talk about him. Instead I listened as she outlined an idea she had, for a shop, an idea she'd had for some time. She had a bit of money, and wanted to take out a lease, sell only French artefacts. She wanted to come to the *brocante* fairs not with a van, but a lorry – a ruddy great one – and take back not tea sets, but furniture: rococo consoles, armoires, mirrors, sets of chairs, *sièges courants*. Back in London she'd arrange them in vignettes – 'like in a room set, you know?' She'd accessorize them with candlesticks, piles of books on tables, huge lanterns above, a *trumeau* mirror on the wall. 'D'you see, Hattie?' I'd nodded. She said how she had to be quick, though, because other people were doing it. A shop called French Home had already opened in Clapham; another, Le Français, in Putney. Oh, it wasn't original, but she thought she could do it better. Thought

Fulham, Munster Road, would be ripe for it – all those terraced houses being gentrified – and she'd seen something suitable, tiny but central. We'd have to be quick, though. These shops went fast.

'We?'

Oh. Didn't she say? She wondered if I'd go in with her. She'd seen what I bought, what I liked, thought we'd work well together. Complement one another. My eye for detail, hers for the huge statement. And with her experience – she'd been dealing for six years and spoke the language – and my beginner's luck – like Christian she'd been secretly surprised at the Limoges bowl: '*C'est magnifique*,' she told me now – we couldn't fail.

'But I've no money.'

'No, but I've got a bit, and you can pay me back. And we can get a loan too.'

'From who?'

'From the bank, of course. How d'you think small businesses start?'

'Oh ...' I said slowly, no idea about anything. 'But ... what about Christian?'

'I know, I thought about that. But we can sell his stuff from the shop, it's not a problem. He'll sell more from us, in a proper shop, than he does in Antiquarius. And you can still source it for him. What d'you think?'

I remember looking at her over that gingham tablecloth under the awning outside that café in the starry night, her dark eyes keen and eager. She was trying to disguise the eagerness, though: it was the guarded look of one who'd been hurt before. I gazed beyond her then, so as not to be influenced by her vulnerability; by the wine, the warm night air. After all, I had my grief to nurse and nurture;

I'd be busy. And I'd only just met her. But I do remember thinking too, as the stars twinkled back at me, that although something had died out here, something could be born. The beginning of me as someone else: someone whose life wasn't going to revolve around being in love, around a man. It was perhaps the birth of the career girl in me, channelling passion into something I could control.

I took a deep breath. My eyes came back to hers. 'Why not?'

Ralph de Granville burst into the Abbey kitchen on a blast of fresh air as the Carringtons sat around the table in various stages of soporific Sunday morning stupor. At least, some of us did: the elder teenagers were still in bed, it being only nine thirty, but Daisy was amongst us, gazing dreamily into space in her dressing gown. Mr de Granville, all svelte good looks and resplendent in a lime-green silk coat with mandarin collar, voluminous white trousers and thonged sandals, seemed to have been beamed down from another planet as he suddenly appeared in our midst. He smiled delightedly, hands clasped, as Hugh, who'd gone to the back door thinking it was his gamekeeper, introduced him apologetically.

'Um, darling it's Mr de Granville. He's a bit early because—'

'Because a fiendishly difficult client in Henley wants me to pop in later and adjust her curtains before I go to Italy, would you believe?' He swept back his floppy dark hair and adopted an almost balletic pose, centre stage. 'So I popped in here first. Says she doesn't trust herself to touch them, I've arranged them so beautifully, but as I said to my assistant, it would take more than a curtain twitch to ruin that room. It's symbiosis is pinkie perfect, if I say so myself. "Twitch away, madam, twitch away!" I told her on the phone. But she's the sort of woman who doesn't trust herself to pick her own nose, if you know what I mean.' He made an arch face. Then beamed. 'How d'you do? Ralphie de Granville. How d'you do, hello, hello ...' and around the table he went, shaking every single astonished hand, including Charlie's, who had to transfer his boiled egg spoon to receive him.

Laura was on her feet now, pink-faced, following him and doing the introductions as he worked his way round.

'My daughter Daisy, my son, Charlie, my mother—'

'Mr de Granville, what an absolute pleasure,' beamed Mum, recovering first. She almost bowed: almost kissed his hand. 'I'm such a fan.'

The decorator squirmed delightedly.

'I'm always in your shop at Chelsea Harbour, aren't I, darling?'

'You certainly are,' agreed Dad, getting to his feet. 'See my credit card on this one.'

As he took Dad's hand, Ralph's heels snapped together and he lowered his head with a deferential, 'Sir.' My father's mouth twitched.

'And, um, my sister Hattie,' Laura finished, flustered. 'And her partner, Maggie du Bose.'

'Du Bose?' He reared back a bit, hands spread on his chest, fingers splayed. He glanced from Maggie to me, eyes wide. 'The French Partnership?' His smile didn't waver: only froze a little.

'That's it.' Maggie smiled thinly.

'But I saw your spread in the *Standard* only last week! Marvellous what you did with that poky little house in Tooting. All those dado rails and ghastly cornices. Quite a challenge.'

'Thank you.' Maggie inclined her head politely, not easily flattered.

'Were you given *carte blanche*?' He shot out immaculate green cuffs and folded his arms, head cocked interestedly.

'Not entirely, but we had a very sympathetic client. We worked well with her actually. She had some good ideas.'

'Really?' Ralph blanched: sucked in astonished cheeks. 'Personally I only take commissions these days if I'm given total control, but then I explained that in my email, didn't I?' He reached out and touched Laura's arm lightly with his fingertips. 'I can't be doing with putting up an expensive studded suede headboard only to find some hideous floral bedspread has been flopped beside it.' He shuddered. 'Not that you'd do that, of course.' He touched Laura's arm again, whilst Hugh, looking aghast at studded suede headboards, sat down heavily.

'Well, quite. Although I'm afraid you won't have total *carte blanche* here,' said Laura rather bravely, swallowing. 'Hattie and Maggie are here to, um, have a look at the more informal, family rooms. The playroom, the kitchen – that kind of thing.'

'Oh?' His eyes widened in surprise; darkened too, as he realized he had competition. I was grateful to Laura for spelling it out early.

'But obviously you'll have control within your own space,' she soldiered on.

'Obviously,' he purred.

'Given that we accept your quote,' said Hugh, firmly. He crossed his legs and folded his arms.

'*Naturellement!*'

My father, I could tell, was enjoying this hugely. He sat back with a small smile and a Mr Bennet air about him. Ralph de Granville strutted across the room to the Aga, executed a little pirouette, and turned to face us again, one hand on the rail.

'Well, you'll have a field day in here, won't you?' he drawled, eyes roving around the kitchen. 'Marvellous proportions … lovely tall windows, too.' He strolled across to them, the better to peer out. Then he turned and cocked an eyebrow at Maggie. 'It could take some really dramatic colour, don't you think? A Russian red. Or a vibrant jade, perhaps? Mouse on the doors and windows, of course … skirting boards too …' he mused, 'and then some fabulous steel cabinets along here …' His eyes narrowed professionally as he ran a hand horizontally across an imaginary work surface. 'American fridge here …' he went on, strolling to the corner, 'and maybe just one solid glass curtain rail, as a statement …' he gazed above the window, 'up there …' He put a reflective fingertip to his lips.

Maggie cleared her throat. 'Actually, we thought we'd leave it pretty much intact. The walls we'll take back a shade to catch the morning sun, but the freestanding furniture will stay, although we'll distress it so it's less uniform. We won't need a pole at the window because we won't be dressing it. And the fridge is in the pantry. Where it will stay.'

Ralph turned slowly to face his informant. Maggie's eyes were steady: her famous hundred-yard stare.

He blinked. 'Is that so?' he said softly. 'Well, I'm sure that will work equally well too. In a …' he smirked, searching for the word, 'traditional kind of way.'

'I'm a traditional kind of girl.'

'Aren't you just?'

A silence descended.

'Well!' Laura finally broke it. 'There we are then. All sorted. Splendid. Um. Perhaps you'll come along with me, Mr de Granville.'

'Ralphie,' he purred, eyes still on Maggie.

'Ralphie, and I'll, er, show you the formal rooms. The drawing room, the dining room and the … what have you … rooms,' she finished lamely.

'Delighted,' he murmured, shooting Maggie a final glittering look. 'Couldn't be more thrilled.'

He swept out of the door Laura had held open for him, green coat flying, closely followed by Mum, who, despite Laura's frown, clearly thought she was Of The Party.

'Oh my Lord,' Dad said with a sigh as he picked up his copy of the *Independent on Sunday* again. He folded it, the better to peruse the crossword. 'That man will have my wife eating out of his silk-lined pockets before he's through, no doubt about that. I like your style, Maggie.' He shot her an approving look before attending to One Across.

'Oh dear.' Maggie turned, distressed, to Hugh. 'I hope I wasn't too … you know …'

'Punchy? Not in the least. Frankly, I'd like to tell him what to do with his solid glass curtain pole, but I'm afraid Laura's smitten.'

'D'you mean up his bum?' asked Charlie, who, at eight, delighted in all things scatological.

'My advice, Hugh,' said Dad, reaching across to swat Charlie on the head with his newspaper, 'is to give in graciously. You'll have to eventually, so you may as well do it now. I speak from experience here. Spot a campaign early, that's what I say. Whether it's a new dishwasher or a new dog, these women lobby till they've ground you down.' He shuddered. 'Why more of them don't go into politics beats me.'

'You're probably right,' agreed Hugh gloomily. He picked a bit of dried egg off the tablecloth. 'I'll probably have absolutely no say in the matter, as usual.'

'And you, young man, can come with me.' Dad got to his feet. Charlie was mincing around the kitchen, flapping his hands camply and aping Ralph's effeminate voice: 'Pinkie-perfect fridge *here*, mousy-mousy thingy there …'

Dad caught his shoulders and steered him out of the door. 'We're gonna check out Daisy's bantams.'

'Oh!' Daisy, who'd remained pretty much inert and abstracted throughout the whole episode, jumped to her feet. Pausing only to shove her feet into wellies by the back door, she ran after them, dressing gown flapping.

'Wait for me!'

Under the circumstances, Maggie and I felt the great outdoors was probably the best place for us too. We went upstairs to grab jackets, and then, whilst Mr de— Ralphie, prowled the great indoors, the two unmarried ladies, as befitted their station – and for all the world like a couple of Jane Austen characters, we decided with a giggle – took a turn about the rose garden.

'Although I'm not convinced they'd chain-smoke their way round,' I remarked as Maggie paused to light her second cigarette of the morning. There was a stiff breeze and she had her work cut out, bent double, hands cupped.

'Oh, I don't know.' She straightened up, sucking hard to keep it going. 'I'm sure Emma would have been puffing away in the shrubbery given half a chance. And anyway, I've been provoked,' she remarked as she blew out a thin line of smoke. 'Did he get his personality out of a dictionary, d'you think? Under P for parody?'

I smiled. 'Ah, but you see, Mum and Laura would be upset if he wasn't like that,' I pointed out as we strolled between the formal beds, white roses nodding in the breeze. 'It's totally and utterly what they were expecting. All that flamboyant, artistic director stuff – right up their alley.'

'Makes my skin creep,' she shuddered. 'He'll be prancing around in there,' she jabbed her cigarette back to the house, 'waving his arms about and shooting his cuffs up, droning on about festoons and filigrees, and they won't have a bloody clue what he's talking about. I hate that kind of crap, blinding people with science. He'll be getting them to have coronets above the windows for pelmets and … oh my God …' She stopped. Stared back at the house. 'What did I tell you?'

'What?'

Ralph was at the dining room windows, chiselled profile to us, hands cupped in the air as if demonstrating a coronet shape. He saw us. Froze. Then glared and turned abruptly on his heel, sweeping on, whilst across the windows, like a couple of little mice, Mum and Laura scuttled after him.

'Prat,' Maggie spat with feeling.

'Ignore him,' I soothed. 'He'll be gone soon. Be prancing around Italy looking at marble.'

'Oh, I shall,' she seethed. 'I shall snub him entirely. But before he goes I might just accidentally spill my drink on his calf-skin attaché case.' The thought clearly cheered her and she smiled. Turning her back on the house, she gazed about her. 'Meanwhile I shall enjoy this ridiculously grand country house while I can. Blimey, look at this garden.' She blinked down at the statue at the end of the lime avenue. 'Or is garden de trop? Unspeakably vulgar.' Her lip curled. 'Parkland, no doubt.'

I shrugged. 'No idea. Dad calls it the backyard.'

She barked a laugh up to the sky. 'Good for him!' She looked admiringly at me. 'I like your dad.'

'Most people do.'

'Your mum's great too,' she said politely.

I grinned. 'She grows on you.'

'But your dad ... well, he's comfortable in his own skin, isn't he? Not impressed by any of this nonsense.' She swept her arm around dismissively.

'No,' I said slowly. 'But it doesn't get his back up, either.' She glanced back at me. Sniffed. 'Hm. Lovely air, anyway,' she said, changing the subject. She took a drag on her ciggie. 'Definitely smells different from London, doesn't it?'

'Definitely,' I agreed as she cupped a rose in her hand and lowered her face to smell it. A startled bumble bee shot out, just grazing her nose.

'Shit!' she squealed, dropping it hastily. Her gaze around the great outdoors was rather more nervous now. 'Come on, Hattie, this place is beginning to scare me. I think I need an espresso, fast. Let's walk to the village.'

'What do people do all day?' she marvelled as we strolled down the back drive towards the lane. The banks frothed with milky cow parsley and nodding ox-eye daisies, and beech trees cast an occasional pool of dappled shade. 'What does Laura do?'

'Oh, she says there's masses.' I said vaguely. 'She has to organize all the people who work here, don't forget, the housekeeper and the gardener, and then there's people at the Home Farm too. Tenants, that kind of thing.'

'How d'you mean, organize?' she pounced, sensing tyranny.

'Well, if their washing machine breaks down, or something, she's got to fix it. Or at least get it fixed.'

'Oh.'

'And she sits on committees and things too.'

'What, discussing the church roof?' she sneered.

'Amongst other things,' I said loyally, determined not to let Maggie take aim at my sister whilst she was under her roof. Even though, I recalled guiltily, I could be persuaded to on occasion as we sat behind the counter at the shop in London, cradling mugs of coffee.

Maggie twigged and made a face. 'Oh, well. Each to their own, I suppose. Although personally this place would drive me bonkers.'

'Oh, I don't know, I think you'd rather enjoy it. They're much more social in the country, you know.'

'Oh, come on,' she scoffed.

'No, it's true. I know we're out most nights in London, but only to a civilized drinks party or a film or something, and always tucked up in bed by midnight. Down here they might only go out Friday or Saturday nights but boy, do they party hard.'

'In what way?' said Maggie, chippily.

'Oh, you know. Roll back the carpets, dance—'

'Gee whiz,' she mocked.

'Smooch each other's husbands, drink heavily, shove illicit substances up their noses …' I was making it up as I went along.

'Do they?'

'God, yes. Then rattle home in swerving Land Rovers at three in the morning, singing at the tops of their voices.'

I was in a scene from *Four Weddings* now, but she didn't spot it. 'When was the last time you stayed up till gone three?' I demanded.

Maggie blinked. 'Can't remember. But then again I do have to get up to go to work in the morning,' she said pointedly.

'There is that,' I agreed.

'But meantime,' she straightened her back as we approached the village, 'bring it on, I say. The last thing I stuck up my nose was a Vicks nasal spray, and I'm very happy to have my arm twisted into some illicit sex while I'm here.'

'Oh, yeah? And what would Henry say to that?'

'He'd probably watch,' she said gloomily.

I laughed.

'And if I took the blinkers off my eyes,' she went on lightly, 'and listened to my friends, I'd hazard it's what he gets up to in New York anyway. So why the hell not? What's sauce for the goose, and so on ...'

This, an allusion to Maggie's beyond disastrous relationship with an unbelievably handsome married man, who not only cheated on his wife, but, as Maggie was increasingly being forced to believe, his mistress too. She didn't look at me, clearly not wanting it confirmed right now, but there was a telltale blush to her cheeks. Let me accept the poverty of my situation gradually, she seemed to be saying, at a drip, drip pace. We walked on.

'Where's your brother?' she asked suddenly.

I jolted at the juxtaposition.

'At work. Big day for him.'

'Oh,' She nodded in surprise. 'Of course. D'you ever go and watch? See him – you know, preach? Or whatever he does?'

'Of course.'

Maggie looked surprised. Her Sunday morning devotions generally revolved around a bistro in Chelsea.

'People do that in the country, I suppose,' she mused.

'In towns too,' I said, suppressing a smile.

'Any good?'

'Who, Kit? Yes, he is rather. In a subtle sort of way. He doesn't go in for fire and brimstone. Rather quiet and reflective. D'you want to go in here?' I asked, suddenly wanting to change the subject, and deflecting her rather neatly, I felt. We'd reached the edge of the village and were outside a dreary-looking coffee shop.

'Is this all there is?' She peered warily through the frosted window at the depressingly empty room. A solitary carnation in a specimen vase sat wanly on each table.

'Were you expecting to perch your Armani-clad backside on a zinc barstool perhaps? Admire your reflection in the mirror as *garçons* in white aprons swept by?'

'Actually, I was expecting to sit outside a thatched pub and watch the cattle go by. Off to market or somewhere.' She looked around wistfully. A car swept past, much too fast, down the main street. She jumped back from the kerb in alarm.

I laughed. 'This is north Buckinghamshire, Maggie, not deepest Devon. There is a nice pub, actually, but it's a hell of a hike. And if the cattle were going to market they'd find it's been turned into a gift shop now.' I nodded to it across the road, 'All manner of expensive knick-knacks in there. I'll show you in a minute.'

In the event we didn't stay for a coffee, the establishment having an even more depressing air within than without. The surly proprietress did little to alleviate it either, and even the air had a stale eighties feel. Instead, we got a couple of Fabs from the freezer and walked across the road to the gift shop, licking them.

'Charmless old witch,' grumbled Maggie. 'How does she expect to attract clients with social skills like that?'

'Well, quite.'

'And speaking of clients ...' She stopped at the gift shop window. 'This is clearly the sort of place Ralphie-boys go to for their tasselled tie-backs. Their nests of limed oak tables.' She gazed gleefully at the cramped, lively display of occasional tables, gilt table lamps and mirrors. Cherubs and hearts gambled cheerfully over pretty much everything, and every shade had beads hanging from it. 'Gilt-plated *objets d'art*,' she purred happily.

'Some people like it,' I said, feeling rather tired. Maggie seemed intent on rubbishing the country and I intent on defending it.

'Well, they shouldn't,' she spat. 'It's tasteless tat. I bet they charge like wounded rhinos for it too, bet they're raking it in. God, it's huge. Look, it stretches all the way down there.' She waved her hand down the street at the extensive shop front.

'I told you, it was the cattle market.'

'Well, it's a bloody emporium now. And it's open too. On a Sunday!'

'Sign of the times,' I said. Then quickly added, 'So perhaps they're not raking it in, after all?'

I was rather pleased with this little sally but Maggie had moved on, her keen eyes spotting a door opening further down.

'Oh, hello, here's one satisfied customer. Let's see what she's bought.' She took my elbow and hustled me along the pavement. 'Ooh, look at those deeply hideous candle-stick lamps!' Maggie breathed in my ear in awe. 'I'd pay not to have them!'

A fair-haired woman, tiny, swamped in a huge fur coat, was clutching a pair of tall skinny glass lamps wrapped in tissue as she emerged from the shop.

'Trophy wife, do we think?' murmured Maggie. 'Actually, perhaps not. More like a bag lady. Check out those trainers. With a mink! Hattie?'

But I was too busy wondering where to run, where to hide. Couldn't pay attention to the footwear. As the fur coat shuffled towards me I felt my heart kick in. Nowhere to run to actually, no escape, as her pale grey eyes widened in uncertain recognition. She stopped.

'Hattie?'

'Letty.'

'Oh – how lovely to see you!' she smiled.

I caught my breath, but strangely, didn't feel she was being sarcastic. Or lying. Her face, a bleached, shocking imitation of the one she'd had sixteen years ago, was eager, open.

'You too,' I managed, as a slim, strikingly pretty blonde girl materialized beside her. Just behind the pair of them, turning back to shut the door, which tinkled merrily, was a tall man in a blue jumper and jeans. He turned to face us. An older, darker version of … oh my God.

'Of course you know Hal Forbes, don't you? But have you ever met Cassie? My daughter?' Letty's face was twitching slightly as she shuffled from foot to foot. Her daughter took one of the lamps from her before she dropped it.

'This is Hattie Carrington, darling. Laura Pelham's sister.'

'Oh – hi!' Cassie smiled at me in surprise.

I cranked up a smile. Laura Pelham's sister. Not, the girl who worked for your father. Or, the girl your father … I had a sudden flashback to Letty standing in the doorway, in a black and white print dress, heavily pregnant, her hand on this child.

'Hello, Cassie,' I managed. 'Hal.' But I didn't look at him. Only heard him murmur, 'Hattie.'

I'd rehearsed this moment many times in my head. Sometimes I ignored him, even turned on my heel. Sometimes I'd smile and greet him coolly, perhaps planting a social kiss on each cheek, as if nothing had happened. As if I got letters of that nature on my pillow every day. It was a surprise therefore, when we finally traded a look, and his eyes asked if I remembered a time before Dominic, before the letter, when we were friends, and my eyes replied that I did.

'And I'm Maggie du Bose,' purred Maggie, absolutely lit up at Hal's name, perking smartly to attention. She knew. Oh God, she knew. But actually, I was grateful to her, for causing a diversion; for keeping a breezy conversation going. I couldn't speak.

'How long are you here for?' Letty was asking. Me, presumably, but Maggie was doing the answering.

'Oh, we're just here for the weekend. We're here to look at Laura's house ….' and off she rattled.

Stupid of me to let her talk me into coming to the village, I thought furiously as she explained. I never did, never, just in case. Had always just disappeared into the Lodge when Hugh and Laura had lived there. But now they were at the Abbey, it was as if I'd been lulled into a false sense of security. And I'd deliberately never got involved in Laura's socializing either – drinks parties, lunches – not that she socialized with Letty, who looked terrible, terrible, I thought in horror, as I allowed myself to glance at her face. I heard Maggie tell her about the decorating project at the Abbey, how we were back off to London today, but would definitely be here again, to sort the downstairs rooms out: had lots of ideas, plans. I couldn't bear to look at her any more; lowered my eyes as the two women talked. Hal's eyes, I knew, were on me and I felt my cheeks burn. I longed to get away, but the daughter was addressing me now, hazel eyes wide, fair hair scooped up in a messy bun, so like her father I almost couldn't breathe. She was definitely addressing me though, through her mother.

'Don't you remember I told you, Mum? I met Laura's nephew.'

'Oh, yes, darling. At a school dance.'

'So you're Seffy's mum.' She turned to me.

I was startled. 'Yes, that's right. You know him?'

'We met at a social at my school. One of those cringy boys v. girls things, which can be really grim, but this one was OK because it was a supper party, so at least no one was forced to dance. I sat next to him.'

'He didn't say,' I said, before realizing it sounded rude.

'Oh, it was ages ago,' she said hastily, blushing. 'He probably forgot.'

'And teenage children tell one so little, don't you find?' said Letty, her hand trembling as she pushed back her hair. 'I ask Cassie where she's been and she says, "Around," and I ask what she's been doing and she says, "stuff". If I ask who she's with, she just says, "people"!'

'Slight exaggeration,' put in Cassie with a grimace as her mother gave a shrill, unnatural-sounding laugh.

'But then, perhaps it's best to be left in the dark,' Letty mused. 'As my nanny used to say, what the eye doesn't see, the heart doesn't grieve about. And when there is so much to grieve about, one rather wishes one had shut one's eyes more. I know I do.'

I couldn't breathe. Was she talking about me?

'Don't you think these are terribly attractive?' Letty was appealing to me now, rustling the tissue paper down around the lamp, the better for me to see: almost as if I were an old friend from her past, not someone she might justifiably never want to see again in her life, or indeed cosh on the head with her new glass purchase.

'Very,' I agreed.

'I couldn't resist them. I bought them for Hal, for his wedding present. But actually, I think I might have to keep them. Put them on the mantel at home.' She held the lamp out at a distance eyeing it critically. Then her eyes widened back at me. 'Did you know Hal was getting married?'

'I didn't.' I licked my lips. 'Congratulations.' I couldn't avoid looking at him now. I found his gaze was already on me.

'Thank you.'

His face was older, obviously, but improved, actually. Much better-looking. He'd grown into his nose and those hooded eyes. Guarded eyes now. I couldn't read them as I had a second ago.

'How marvellous – where's it going to be?' The irrepressible Maggie again. 'The wedding?'

'In Provence.'

'Oh! Why France?'

'Because my fiancée's French.'

'Oh, really? So am I, actually. French. Well, half.'

Hal smiled politely.

'Whereabouts?' Maggie again. 'Only Hattie and I go to Provence a lot, don't we, Hatts? There's a fabulous antique fair we go to down at Aix. I'm Hattie's partner, by the way.'

'Ah.'

'So whereabouts?' she persisted.

He cleared his throat. 'Not far from Aix, actually. A little further north. It's a market town, called Fayence.'

'Fayence? Fay*ence*? Oh my God, that's a *hea*venly little town. Remember, Hatts, it's the one we stop at when we're nearly there, nearly at Aix, but simply can't go on any further. We lurch into it gasping for a glass of rosé. It's the one with the cobbled market square, and the dear little church you always like, with the blue clock.' She turned back to him. 'Don't tell me that's the one you're getting married in?'

'It is, actually.'

'Oh … my … God.' She clutched my arm. 'Remember, Hattie, we saw a bride going in with her father? That beautiful lace dress? And you made me sit and have another glass of wine in the square until she came out again with her groom? Went all misty-eyed and said if you were going to come out of any church, on any man's arm, it might just as well be that one, remember?'

'No,' I growled.

'And will you live out there? When you're married?'

I could hardly breathe.

'I'm not sure.'

My eyes were on Hal's shoes. As if I were thoroughly absorbed in the way he'd tied the laces.

'We haven't really decided.'

'They'll probably live in my house!' cut in Letty with another shrill, unnatural laugh. 'They're trying to chuck me out of it!'

This was beyond embarrassing.

'Come on, Mum,' said Cassie quickly, taking her arm.

'We'd better be going,' agreed Hal, taking the lamp from her. They said their goodbyes and, between them, helped Letty away.

'It was lovely to meet you,' called Cassie over her shoulder, as we watched them go up the lane.

'Well,' Maggie declared after a moment, still shading her eyes. 'So that's Hal. You didn't tell me he looked like *that*! Hattie? Hattie!'

But whatever else she said was lost in the wind. I'd turned on my heel and stalked away from her, in the equal and opposite direction.

13

'Don't be silly, you're exaggerating. I wasn't interrogating him, I was just being polite.' Maggie was trotting to keep up with me, but I was setting quite a pace as I stalked up the hill towards the woods, taking the short cut.

'Polite? I'm surprised you didn't ask to see a photo of her! Reach for his wallet and thumb through it!'

'Oh, you're being absurd. I was merely showing an interest. And it *was* a coincidence, him getting married at that church that you said yourself, in your wildest dreams, if you and Dominic—'

'Me and *Dominic*.' I stopped and spun round to face her, fists clenched. 'Wildest *dreams*, a confidence to a friend, certainly not one to be shared with his brother or his widow! Christ, any minute now I thought you'd give *that* an airing. Don't you see how awkward it was?'

'Well, I wasn't going to mention that, was I? The fantasy groom. I'm not a complete fool.'

We plunged into the woods in silence, following a dry rutted track through avenues of dark pines, our eyes taking a moment to accustom to the gloom. I was fuming with her but angry with everything. Seeing them all like that had completely thrown me. I'd carefully avoided meeting any of them individually for years: having them turn up together in one bumper package was certainly not in the script. Released from having to behave and make polite conversation, I gave in to the shock, let it rock me. My breathing was shallow now and I subjected Maggie to complete silence as she stumbled to catch up with me in her highly inappropriate wedged heels. I strode mercilessly on, snapping twigs and pine needles underfoot, feeling sharp stones through my thin ballet pumps, punishing my body as my mind reeled away down some dark and ancient abyss.

After a while we found ourselves walking up the back drive. My heart rate had come down a bit and I was breathing more steadily. Self-preservation dictated I rationalize the last half-hour as quickly as possible: square it away and recover. And I was surely a past master of such disciplines. I would be calm. In the distance, behind the parterre and the rose garden was the tennis court. Seffy and Biba were playing languidly in jeans and bare feet. They saw us and raised their rackets from afar. I waved; gave a tight smile back.

'Is Hal very like Dominic?' Maggie asked, pleasantly enough, and no doubt trying to embark on a cordial subject. But she was unaccustomed to making placatory opening gambits and could have chosen better.

I shrugged. 'Kind of.'

'I mean, I saw Dominic's pictures in the papers, obviously, and it strikes me Hal's a sort of darker version? Bit sallower, maybe?'

'Maybe.'

'Terribly attractive, don't you think?'

I ignored her and walked on across the lawn.

'Well, I thought he was gorgeous. Not surprised some French girl's snapped him up. I bet she's a looker. Although he's left it late, I must say. He must be nearly forty, but perhaps he's been busy playing the field. Getting it all out of his system. And he's obviously a bit of a cad if he's tipping his sister-in-law out. Poor thing, she didn't look quite with it. Very shaky paws.'

'She drinks.'

'Ah. I wondered. Lovely daughter, though. And she clearly remembers Seffy.'

'Who does?' The tennis duo had left the court and come up behind us. Daisy was trailing them, holding a hen in her arms.

'Oh – *sweet*!' cooed Maggie. 'Is it real?'

'Course she's real. You can stroke her, if you want.' She proffered the bundle of golden feathers. Maggie reached out a tentative fingernail and almost touched its head.

'Who remembers me?' repeated Seffy.

'Letty Forbes's daughter,' I said shortly. 'Who won the match?'

'Seffy, as usual,' complained Biba. 'It's so unfair, he should be made to serve underarm.'

'Apparently you met her at a social?' prompted Maggie.

'Oh, yeah. I remember. She was nice. Where d'you see her?'

'Just now, in the village.'

'She's at St Hilda's,' said Biba, throwing up an imaginary ball and serving it with her racket. 'I've played lax against her. She's really pretty.'

'Who is?' asked Daisy.

'Cassie Forbes? Her dad's dead and her mum's an alchy. It's really tragic. I feel really sorry for her.'

'I wouldn't mind being tragic,' remarked Daisy. 'Everyone's always really nice to you and feels sorry for you.'

'Don't be silly, Daisy,' I snapped, then regretted it instantly. Daisy's pale blue eyes widened in shock.

'Sorry,' I muttered quickly. 'Seffy, we should get going straight after lunch. You've got a play rehearsal this evening.'

'I'm going back with the girls.'

'What – on the train?'

'Yes.'

'But that's madness. You've got a hell of a walk from Newbury station. I can take you to the door!'

'I like walking.'

'But I wanted to pop in and see your housemaster.'

Seffy was already walking, though, off towards the back of the house, where the summerhouse was, and where the rackets were kept: ignoring me.

'Seff!'

He turned; continued walking backwards. Widened his eyes. 'I'm going back with the girls, OK?'

Biba and Daisy trailed after him. I watched for a moment, then, tight-lipped, turned and followed Maggie, who, unused to country ways was heading resolutely for the front door. Well, it was wide open and actually, I decided, trying to breathe, trying to calm down, it was probably best I didn't follow him; say something I regretted later.

The entrance hall at the Abbey was about the size of the tennis court the children had just vacated, complete with vaulted ceiling and domed skylight. A grand staircase to our right divided in two halfway up, then ran around the first floor as a gallery. Laura had rather sensibly put comfy armchairs down the far end of the hall under a window that caught the morning sun, and where Dad was installed even now, working his way through the rest of the newspapers, as was his wont. Meanwhile, in the main, echoing, and rather gloomy body of the hall, with its terracotta and blue Victorian tiled floor, were gathered other members of my family. We'd clearly interrupted a master class. Mum and Laura were listening, rapt, to their mentor.

'Now this is where I'd like to see some real drama!' Ralph was saying, twirling around, arms aloft. 'You've got space … use it! Emphasize it, don't clutter it! I'd clear all those chairs away.' He waved an imperious hand at the offending items, which included my father. 'Get rid of them all. And I'm thinking conch.'

'Conch?' Laura asked.

'Yes, a conch.'

Laura and Mum looked bewildered, as well they might. They willed themselves to understand.

'Like ... a couch?' Mum asked tentatively.

'No, no, dear lady, not at all!' Ralph was horrified. 'It's a shell, you know. But gigantic.' He demonstrated its vastness with huge sweeping arms.

'Oh, a shell!' said Mum, as if all was revealed and every home should have one. 'I see.' She nodded emphatically.

'A tropical marine gastropod.'

'Yes, yes.' Mum shut her eyes, palms up, as if no further explanation were necessary.

'I can get one sent straight from Peru, with a great gaping mouth, like this –' Ralph opened his jaws wide; Mum stepped back in alarm – 'suggestive of birth and renewal. A new family in situ, see? And we'll put it at the far end of the hall, so that once we've passed the stairs,' he tripped prettily past them, 'we encounter, it here ... voilà.' He stopped and unfolded his palms towards Dad.

'Oh!' My mother clasped her hands. 'Yes, I see. A sort of symbolism, Laura.' She turned to her daughter.

'But ... won't it be terribly uncomfortable?' Laura looked confused. 'I mean, is it to sit on? Or—'

'No, no, it's to walk around, to admire. To wonder at, to marvel. It's living art.'

'Expensive?' put in Hugh, who just happened to be listening behind a door.

'My dear Lord Pelham, it's coming from darkest Peru, like Paddington. It's rare, it's ancient, it won't be cheap. But you'll have it for ever, and no one, absolutely no one, wherever you go, will have one. You will never see it again.'

'With good reason,' murmured Dad into his *Tribune*.

'I see.' Laura liked this. 'And, around it …?' She made a helpless gesture with her hands, walking to where Dad and the chairs were.

'*Rien*,' Ralphie said firmly, following her. 'No clutter, no furniture, no pictures on the walls. Just one, very good, very important piece.' He held on to the 'c' in piece for longer than was absolutely necessary.

'Mollusc,' put in Dad.

Ralph inclined his head enquiringly, eyelids flickering.

'It's a mollusc,' Dad explained. 'A shellfish.'

Ralph smiled thinly, in grudging assent.

'Well, we'll think about it,' breathed Laura. 'And the floor?'

'Will have to go.'

'Go?' She looked down at the tiles.

Ralph shuddered. 'Hideous. Turn of the century. No age. Arts and Crafts revival at its very worst. I'm thinking French limestone throughout.'

Hugh yelped and disappeared. Laura, aware that she was in the grip of a formidable talent, but that she'd soon be in the grip of a divorce if she didn't watch out, looked flustered.

'Oh, um, look,' she faltered, scratching her leg. 'The thing is, the floor might have to stay. Only, you know, it's a family thing. Hugh's parents would be dreadfully upset.'

Ralph looked as if he'd sucked a lemon.

'But the um, shell – conch – I'm sure, is a very good idea,' she enthused.

'Along with the statue of Saint Somebody-or-other in the dining room, and the vessel in the drawing room,' remarked my father.

'Vessel?' asked Maggie, who'd heroically held her tongue up until now.

'Frightfully symbolic,' Mum whispered to her. 'And Mr de Granville firmly believes one should have one Good Piece,' she too held on to the 'c', 'in each room.'

'Oh, me too,' agreed Dad, folding up his paper. 'Give me a Cézanne or a Gauguin and I'm a happy man.'

'And it's just so wonderful that he can simply look at a room and tell right away,' Mum told Maggie, all sparkly eyed. 'He walked straight into the morning room and said, baroque. Early seventeenth century. Harpsichord in the corner. And then in the dining room we're going all North American Indian.'

My father made a choking sound.

'Naïve, indigenous art,' Ralph explained.

'Take a look upstairs, laddie,' said my father, 'on Charlie's bedroom walls. Plenty of naïve indigenous art up there. In point of fact, Laura's kept all the kids' paintings.'

'It's not quite as simple as that,' Ralph smiled politely.

Dad blinked. 'Is it not?' He nodded thoughtfully. 'Oh, OK.'

'But I think that's probably enough for one day,' Ralph said, looking rather tired suddenly. He half closed weary lids: plucked a fawn, kidskin attaché bag from a table and tucked it neatly under his arm. Maggie eyed it beadily. 'One wouldn't want to overdo it.'

'No, one *wouldn't*,' agreed Mum warmly. 'And it must be so exhausting, creating on the spot like that. I don't know how you do it. You've been wonderful, hasn't he, Laura?'

'Wonderful,' Laura agreed, trotting after him as he made for the door. 'And so kind of you to come, when you're just off to Italy.'

'Oh, yes, I *do* hope the trip goes well,' agreed Mum.

'Thank you. And will I order the slab of black Tuscan marble while I'm there, Lady Pelham?' he enquired, turning at the threshold.

'Um, d'you know, I might have to check with Hugh first. Can I ring you?'

'Of course, no pressure. But don't leave it too late. I'm only there a couple of days, and Tuscan marble goes,' he snapped his fingers, 'like that.'

And with that he sashayed down the steps and off to his car, shoulders back, bottom tucked in, one hand swinging behind his back, the other clutching his bag. Mum and Laura hastened to wave him off.

'That's … a three-metre slab of black marble to put on a plinth and make into a dining room table,' Dad informed Maggie and me over his glasses. 'To replace Hugh's folks' fine old mahogany one. Apparently it's not Georgian. And if it's not Georgian, it's gotta go. Nothing under two hundred and fifty years old can stay. Of course, in fifty years' time it'll be a full-up card-carrying antique, but this guy can't wait. By then it'll be firewood.'

'He was rather rude about some of the furniture,' agreed Laura, coming back in and biting her thumbnail nervously. 'Apparently there's a lot of repro.'

'Apparently!' hooted Dad. 'You see you didn't *know* that. You were blissfully unaware. It *looked* nice, you *thought* it was good – what difference does it make?'

'Well, except now I do know. And I'll know everyone else knows.' She turned to Mum, worried. 'I think he's right, don't you? If it's not antique – I mean antique enough – we'll go modern. Cutting-edge contemporary.'

'Definitely,' agreed my mother.

'I'll talk to Hugh.'

A slightly fraught lunch ensued a while later, with Hugh yelping things like: 'Harpsichord? But no one plays!' Or: 'A saint? What, like a shrine? We're not effing left-footers!' He was cheered by the vessel, though. 'A bowl? Some sort of potpourri thing?'

'Except it's six feet in diameter and carved from three-hundred-year-old wood,' Dad told him. 'You'd get an awful lot of dried lavender in it.'

'So … what do we do with it?' Hugh looked horrified.

'Oh, I guess you could always get in it of an evening. Rock about a bit. Sing row-row your boat.'

The children giggled.

'It's a talking piece,' announced my mother grandly.

'Maybe it could be like one of those hot-tub things? Where you take all your clothes off?' suggested Charlie.

'Now wouldn't that be grand?' agreed Dad with a smile at his grandson. 'Really get the party going. Give the neighbourhood something to talk about too.'

'Don't be silly. It's modern art. It was sculpted in an atelier in Bolivia,' Laura said testily.

'What's an atelier?' asked Daisy.

'A workshop,' Dad told her.

'Look, Dad, I'm just trying to bring this place up to date a bit, OK? Trying to bring it kicking and screaming into the twenty-first century, make it less like – like a mausoleum!'

'Of course you are,' said Mum, making her don't-say-another-word face at my father.

Dad held up his hands in defeat. 'OK, OK. I'm just trying to stop you being taken for a ride, that's all. Seems to me this house is pretty neat as it is. A bit tired, granted, but nothing a few coats of paint and some new couches wouldn't solve. But, hey, who am I to say? I'm just an old dinosaur who'd be happy living in a hut with a pile of newspapers and pizza delivered regularly.'

'Precisely,' said Mum.

'But if it was a case of paint and new sofas,' said Hugh bravely, 'then, Hattie, you and Maggie could, you know, see to that, couldn't you?'

'Oh, marvellous,' spat Laura, before Maggie and I could murmur some sort of awkward assent. 'Make me feel bad about not giving the whole commission to Hattie. Make me feel guilty in front of my entire family about spending too much on a fancy interior designer!' And with that she pushed back her chair and swept out.

Daisy looked distressed and made to go after her, but Hugh laid a hand on her arm. 'I'll go. She'll be OK in a minute.' He got up and followed Laura out.

'But why's she so upset?' said Daisy, blinking. 'It's only decorating.'

'I think,' said my mother, widening her eyes expressively at my father and employing her best *pas devant les enfants* voice, 'there are other affairs going on here. Pass the cheese, would you, Seffy, please?'

'You mean like Luca inheriting instead of Charlie?' asked Biba.

'Biba!' My mother couldn't get over how young people just spoke right up these days.

'I don't see why it would go to Charlie anyway,' objected Daisy. 'You're the eldest. It should be you.'

'Or why just one person?' said Biba. 'He's so old-fashioned.'

'Yeah, you should split it between all of you,' said Seffy. 'Like the French do.'

'That would be cool,' agreed Biba. 'Then we could sell it and each buy our own house in Chelsea.'

'Biba!' said Mum again. 'How can you even think of such a thing when your mother is working tirelessly to turn this into a beautiful home for you?'

'Sorry, Granny.' Biba blushed.

'Maybe she's got issues?' suggested Charlie helpfully with his mouth full. 'Maybe she's run out of eggs?'

'No, Charlie, there's a box of twelve in the fridge,' Mum told him.

'I meant in her ovaries.'

'Don't be silly. She's not old enough for that,' snapped Biba. 'And what d'you know about that, anyway?'

'They teach us at school in PSHE. Apparently, when the lady's young she gets really stressy just before she drops her egg – that's called PMT – and then later on, when she's really old, about forty, she runs out of eggs, and gets all wrinkly and depressed again, suicidal, sometimes. That's called the men-or-paws.'

'Thank you, Charlie,' I said quickly. Mum looked as if she were about to pass out.

'What kind of school does this kid go to?' asked Dad in horror. 'I hope you're taught a little football too?'

'Only when we're truly in touch with our feminine side,' Charlie told him, both hands clasped to his heart. He fluttered his eyelids expressively.

Dad snorted. 'Is that so? That could take a little while then. So what time do you guys have to get back to these visionary, emancipated educational establishments?' He looked at his watch.

'Soon.' Biba, beside him, turned his wrist so she could see the face.

'Twenty after two. And how are you getting there?'

'We'll get the train,' she told him.

'Anybody want a lift?'

'Oh, yes, please!' said the girls.

'Seffy?'

'Sure. If you don't mind?'

'Not at all. I'd like to see your new pad. Haven't clapped eyes on it yet.'

I blinked. Opened my mouth to protest. As a general clearing of the table ensued and everyone got to their feet, Seffy shrugged at me.

'Why not?' he murmured. 'He hasn't seen it yet.'

On the way home in the car, Maggie tried to placate me.

'Boys of that age don't always want their mums fussing around. He wants some independence. I can understand that.'

'But he was perfectly happy for Dad to take him back!'

'Because he was taking the girls anyway. Come on, Hatts, how much time does Seffy spend with his grandfather? Not a lot, I'm sure.'

'I suppose. And Dad did want to see the school ...'

My father always made a huge effort to be even-handed with his grandchildren. If he went to a concert at one school, he liked to go to one at the other. He'd always been like that with us as kids. Comparatively recently he'd given Kit, who earned diddly-squat, an old car he'd been about to trade in, and then tried to hand Laura and me the corresponding amount of money. We'd handed it back, touched, but as Laura had said, 'I'm hardly on the breadline, Dad. You don't have to give me money!'

Never penalize success, though, had always been his mantra. And Laura had certainly made a success of her life. Would he say the same about me? I was never sure. I knew it quietly saddened him that neither Kit nor I was married with children of our own – although he loved Seffy as if he were my own – and I was aware that he, almost more than Mum, worried I'd left it too late. Which of course I had.

'Exactly,' Maggie was saying.

It took me a moment to remember what we'd been talking about. Oh, Seffy. My chest tightened in its familiar fashion, but not as much as it would have done a year ago. Things were definitely better between us, but I still had the feeling he was deliberately distancing himself. Perhaps I'd been too overprotective, when he was younger? Too smothering? But then he was my only child, and I his only family too. He'd seemed to need that extra strong bond; we both did. But I knew some of his friends treated their mothers much more casually; kept them at arm's length. Perhaps Seffy was embarrassed by our closeness. Didn't want to be a mummy's boy. Perhaps he was just doing the same.

I'd wanted to ask his housemaster how he was getting on, but I suspected Seffy knew that and didn't want me to. Didn't want to be discussed; examined minutely from every angle – who would? And the awful thing was, whenever I talked about Seffy, I got horribly emotional. Often in the most inappropriate places. The last thing I wanted was to have a box of tissues passed silently to me by an embarrassed housemaster. There'd been enough of that at the last school. Perhaps it was as well he'd gone back with Dad.

I dropped Maggie off at her house just off Fulham Palace Road and drove the few blocks round to mine. The moment I was alone all vestige of pretence left me, and I felt the skies descend. My spirits dived in a way that couldn't just be attributed to general Sunday night gloom. Shoulders up, I hunched over the wheel. Not a great day. Not great at all. The encounter with Hal and Letty had shaken me more than I could say, and now Seffy – withdrawn, defensive. As I purred round the backstreets, I experienced a sense of foreboding that rushed at me in a nightmarish, ghostly fashion. It was one I knew of old and associated with inescapable loss.

As I turned into my road, though, remarkably, my spirits lifted, just perceptibly. They always did as I crawled down this tree-lined street to home. Home. My house. Small and terraced in a row of identical cottages, but how I loved it. Loved the pretty Victorian façade I'd painted clotted cream, the tiny front garden where I grew roses and sweet william, a lupin if there was room, the Peter Pan statue I'd found in Lyons and set amongst the fauna. I loved the fact that I could impose my taste on a small area and make it look so different from the neighbours'. And I'd done just the same inside. It was a real two-up two-down, but I'd knocked the two-down into one long sitting room: tacked a conservatory onto the kitchen too, which gave onto the garden. Now that really was a back-yard. I smiled when I thought of Laura's. I'd personally cleared it of rubble with the help of Kit and my father when I'd bought the place, chucking out broken bricks, an old bath, masses of green and brown bottles, turning it from a rubbish heap into a tiny walled enclosure, with a patch of grass. It was here that Seffy had splashed in his paddling pool, then later tricycled around in circles – just – and now lay on his back in the sun, feet up the wall. It was small, but enough for us. Or so I'd always thought. As I switched off the engine I glanced at it anxiously, willing it to do its magic. Willing it to relax my fraught nerves. It did, a bit.

In these enlightened days of residents' parking – no more dragging of smelly dustbins into the road to reserve a space – I was able to park right outside. I walked the few steps up the front path, deliberately taking time to savour the musky scent of the tobacco plants I'd placed strategically in pots by the front door. Always gloriously heady in warm evening air, they were really earning their keep tonight. I inhaled their fragrance deeply; smiled. Then I reached in my bag for the key, but as I put it in the latch, I realized the light was already on in the hallway, shining through the stained-glass door panel. I froze. Music was drifting out from within. Shit. Seffy? No, obviously not Seffy. He was *en route* to Lightbrook with Dad.

It could only mean one thing. He'd got back early. Had said he might, from Toulouse, but I knew that trip: hadn't really imagined he would. And yes, I had said come round, in the unlikely event. And he'd have found the spare key, the one I always kept for Seffy under the geranium pot, and which I moved periodically, leaving a note in Latin, hoping the burglars weren't versed in the classics. I didn't have a bit of food in the house, not even an egg. But more to the point – more pressingly – I didn't have any make-up on. Not a scrap. No eyeliner, no mascara, no hideously expensive Touche

Éclat, which I needed to erase the dark circles from under my eyes, the lines from my mouth, the tiny spider veins from my cheeks. No transfiguration unguents, which, when applied, went some way to ensuring I resembled not a dewy twenty-six – that would be downright impossible – but at least a sophisticated creature the right side of forty. Right now, all I had on was my Sunday night, greasy-haired, bare-faced cheek. The one I reserved for my family or old friends like Maggie, who'd seen me open-mouthed and snoring as we slumbered in the back of a lorry, waiting for the sun to rise over some distant *brocante*; who knew about the ravages of time and had seen the whole difficult, intricate process of living etched on my face.

But not this individual. He certainly hadn't. In that moment, all morbid thoughts of Hal, Letty – Seffy, even – were dispelled in a trice. With something approaching panic I leaped behind the dustbins, riffling furiously in my hand-bag like an old lady fumbling for her keys, except this one was after lippy. Lippy lippy lippy. Oh God, lippy! Hands trembling, I'd just managed to pull it out, twist it erect, and was poised to slather it on furiously – when my front door swung wide.

There, in the doorway, tousled and blond, in a crumpled white T-shirt and trailing jeans, feet bare and tanned, looking very much the dewy twenty-six I couldn't hope to achieve, was Ivan. He blinked in surprise as I hunched, paralysed over a dustbin in the moonlight, my compact mirror in one hand, a stick of Chanel's appropriately named Sunset Rose in the other.

'Oh, it *is* you. I heard the key in the door and couldn't work out why it didn't open.' He peered at me in the gloom. 'Have you been swimming?'

14

'Um, yes.' *Swimming*. God, I did look rough. I put my head down and made to slide past him. 'Desperate for the loo, though. Won't be a tick.'

'Hey, not so fast,' he laughed, stopping me with a huge arm and giving me a bear hug. 'Haven't you got a kiss for your old man?'

Old he certainly wasn't, but I liked the possessive article, and even though it was under the glare of my ghastly over-head light, I succumbed to his embrace. I made a mental note, eyes shut, mid-kiss, to remove the bulb. I'd removed all the other overhead bulbs in the house when I'd met Ivan, replaced them with extremely low-voltage table lamps, but hadn't got round to the hall. In the first place there wasn't room for a table – no matter, it could sit on the floor – but neither had I envisaged being ravaged here. I can't imagine why, I'd been ravaged most other places in the house, and this thought clearly occurred to Ivan as he began to peel off my jacket, eyeing the twelve square feet of carpet speculatively. But I wasn't having that.

'Won't be a mo!' I gasped, as I finally came up for air. I wrenched myself free from his arms and stumbled into the downstairs loo, locking it firmly behind me.

Happily, a full set of beauty paraphernalia was to hand – I kept make-up in most rooms, these days – and I franti-cally got to work. Not the full rig, I thought, scrubbing off too much blusher – that might be a bit obvious – but I outlined my eyes, glossed my lips, then threw my head down and tossed my hair back to add bounce. I sucked in my cheeks and eyed my reflection critically. Better.

Nothing would improve the nose Dad had given me, Roman and distinguished on a man, less so on a girl, nor the fullness of my face, but the fullness also extended to my lips, and together with my brown eyes and dark lashes, contrived to create a luscious, if slightly bovine look. If only I was taller, I thought, standing on tiptoe, but since most of the time I was horizontal with Ivan, it didn't really matter. I came out, licking my teeth in case Sunset Rose had strayed, and remembering to pull the chain behind me.

He was watching television in the sitting room, softly lit, but still too bright. I snapped off a lamp as I came in and groped towards him in the gloom.

'So how was it?' I asked, sinking down beside him on the sofa. David Attenborough was lying prone in the undergrowth before us, whispering excitedly about a female gorilla behind a tree. Poor girl. I have many problems, but wearing my sexual organs on the outside is not one of them.

'Oh, averagely ghastly,' Ivan groaned. He put his arm around me and I snuggled up, tucking my knees beneath me in a youthful manner. One of them clicked. 'The usual merry-go-round of rip-off merchants and tat, with the occasional lucky find. Our friend Monsieur Renard had the best, as usual, but he wasn't prepared to part with it for peanuts. I ended up paying well over the odds for a pair of château shutters, but they're excellent. You'd have fought me for them.'

I smiled. The first time I'd met Ivan we'd both been after the same piece in Boulogne. I'd seen it first: a plaster bust of the goddess Daphne, slightly wounded, it has to be said, but nevertheless, she'd sit beautifully in the landing window of a house Maggie and I were doing in Putney. But the fellow was asking a lot. I'd haggled and got him down a bit, but he wouldn't budge any more. Also he wanted cash.

'Save it for me,' I told him as I went grudgingly off to the bank to accommodate him. When I got back, Ivan had just bought it.

'That's my Daphne!' I said, as the Frenchman handed it over.

Monsieur Renard raised shoulders and dismissive eyebrows. 'He pay more. What can I do?'

I turned, furious, to my competitor: a tall blond chap in a leather jacket.

'I'd reserved that bust. You could at least have waited to see if I was prepared to outbid you!'

He'd widened cool grey eyes. 'Oh, is that how it works? A sort of gentlemanly *entente cordiale*. And there was I thinking antique dealing was every man for himself. Had no idea there were conduct rules.'

Monsieur Renard sniggered as he pocketed his euros.

'Well, you're obviously new to the game,' I snapped. Maggie and I knew most dealers' faces, particularly the English ones in the markets, and this was a new one on me. 'As a rule we don't tread on each other's toes and we do try to maintain some sort of decorum.' This was quite untrue. We'd snatch an object from each other's jaws if necessary.

'Is that so? So the little episode last week in Montauroux, when two girls were seen physically assaulting an elderly gentleman before whisking a campaign bed away in the back of a lorry, was totally uncharacteristic?'

This, a reference to an unseemly little tussle with Billy the Bastard, as he was known in trading circles, who'd tried to buy a bed Maggie had in fact already secured, and was just waiting for me to bring the van around to collect.

Naturally we'd dealt with him in a robust manner, since any other manner would be lost on Billy, but I wasn't prepared to go into that with my blond rival right now. I just wanted my Daphne back. But he was already making off with it.

'Where d'you think you're going?' I squealed.

'I was going to pop it in the back of your lorry for you – it's quite heavy. You can line up the *café au laits* in the bar.'

'Oh.' I stared after him.

Over coffee, I'd tried to pay him for the bust, but he wouldn't accept it.

'It's a present.'

'For me?'

'Why not?'

'Don't be silly, you can't buy it for me.' I was embarrassed now. 'I'll only sell it on at a profit.'

He'd shrugged. 'OK.' His eyes held mine over the rim of his coffee cup. Smouldered, might even be the word. 'Your choice.'

I hadn't, of course, sold Daphne. She was still with me today, on a console table in my bathroom, her beautiful face – lips pursed, eyes half shut – a comfort to me in times of stress, although Seffy said she looked like she was straining a turd. And that day in Boulogne, I hadn't hurried back to the *brocante* either. After all, there was another fair in Legele the following morning, and it was a long time since I'd been chatted up by a man at least ten years younger than me in the back room of a smoky bar, the low winter sun glancing off the tobacco-stained walls, our knees almost touching as coffee turned into a jug of wine, which turned into lunch, smiled on indulgently the while by knowing waiters, in a seduction scene that seemed to me, as I toyed winsomely with my tarte tatin and glanced at him under my lashes, to be straight out of a Jean-Claude Van Damme movie, but may have had more to do with yet another sozzled, middle-aged woman being easy prey for a young, slightly down-at-heel Lothario. Certainly as I weaved to the ladies for a monumental and long overdue wee – had my waters broken? Surely one didn't get pregnant toying with tarte tatin? – I clocked a few sly grins from the locals, as well as one or two dealers I knew.

Having picked my teeth clean in the loo – note to the older woman: ordering rocket salad might flag up fit, body-conscious babe, but it stays with you for three courses – I reapplied my lipstick and weaved unsteadily back through the restaurant. As I negotiated the tables, which seemed to have become a maze, and tried not to nudge too many elbows – 'Sorry … oops, sorry,' – I dimly registered that the sly smiles had turned into broad grins. No matter, this man was hot. Granted he wasn't strictly my type, but where had my type got me in the past? He was also uncomplicated. Most men I met were either married, or divorced with small children, and most wanted to give you the works up front so as not to be accused of being a shit later. But this one had no baby photos to show me, no horror stories of an unfeeling, frigid wife who'd gone off the boil since she'd had them. In short, he was perfect. What he saw in me I've no idea, and see me he did that day, in broad daylight, for the first and only time. Ever since then I've worn sunglasses whatever the weather – yes, even in the rain, like Anna Wintour. Hats I like too, and then obviously there's complete and utter darkness for the bedroom. In fact, these days, I'm not sure Ivan has any idea who I am at all.

He had a room above the restaurant, and my only excuse is that the attraction was immediate, and that two bottles of

Sancerre made it even more immediate. We repaired after coffee, and I awoke the following morning entangled only in a sheet, a new man and a warm glow. I couldn't wait to tell Maggie, who, happily, was minding the shop at the time.

That was five months ago and, astonishingly, here he still was, beside me on my sofa: huge, blond, gorgeous and raring to go. Oh, don't get me wrong, I hadn't fallen in love with him or anything inconvenient like that, nor he with me. No, this was a simple, straightforward relationship that suited us both, but I was surprised he was staying the course. Ivan had plenty of pretty female friends his own age, mostly from Camden Passage, where he worked, and whom I'd met, though through shaded glass, naturally. On one occasion I'd walked past a wine bar and seen him hand in hand with one of them, but pretended I hadn't. So I wasn't naïve. I think the truth was he was lazy, and I also suspect the young fillies wanted more from him than he was prepared to give, so this arrangement suited him. We had a laugh, we could witter on about antiques – he had a very good eye, I'd joke, that's why it had rested on me – and Seffy liked him, which was a relief.

I'd never really foisted a boyfriend on Seffy before, and although I'd had one or two, had never brought them back: always played away. But Ivan lived flipping miles away, in Crouch End, with a couple of other lads, in what can only be described as a dive. On the odd occasion I'd stayed there, I'd woken up on a hideously uncomfortable futon, stepped in a bowl of stale cereal *en route* to the loo, picked my way back through the detritus of empty beer cans and overflowing ashtrays to fill a kettle in a sink full of stale washing-up, and wondered groggily if my playing away days weren't over. I'd cleared up once, after they'd all left the flat. Got the place gleaming like a new pin. But that had only made me feel like their mother, so I'd taken a deep breath and changed the venue.

And, as I say, Seffy liked him. I think he was also relieved I had an interest other than him – there'd been a few hints – so he was probably prepared to like anyone, within reason. One night when I'd coyly and, brick red with embarrassment, asked if he'd mind if Ivan stayed, Seffy had barely taken his eyes off his computer as he replied: 'Well, I didn't think you'd been playing Monopoly, Mum.'

True, when Ivan wasn't there he called him my toy boy, and for my birthday had given me dumbbells for my bingo wings – marvellous, but you have to keep at it or the muscle reverts to flab – and had once also remarked that Ivan only seemed to come across after nine in the evening, but I'm being picky. On one occasion, when Ivan hadn't shot out of the door after breakfast, we'd even all walked to Bishop's Park together, where the two of them had kicked a ball around, and although there'd been an ironic look in Seffy's eye which had said, gee, Mum, here I am kicking a ball around with your young man, I'd been pleased.

So, yes, Ivan was still with us: padding back right now from the kitchen, where he'd gone to get us each a glass of wine. He bent over and kissed me on the lips as he handed me mine, then sank down beside me.

'So where did you go?'

'I told you, my sister's.'

'No, swimming.'

Luckily it was quite dark, as an unattractive blush swept up my neck like a high-speed elevator.

'Oh, um, Putney.'

'Really?' He turned from the gorillas, interested. 'They've reopened it?'

'Sorry?'

'It's been shut for ages for refurbishment. I tried to go the other day.'

'Oh, yes, right. You're quite right. I did go to Putney, but it was … still shut. So I – went somewhere else.'

'Oh, OK.' He waited, interested now, because of course Ivan swam. Lengths and lengths. Powering up and down the pool in what seemed to me a fairly mindless manner. Surely once you'd been to both ends you'd pretty much covered it? Was there one in Fulham? Fulham Pool, Fulham Baths, Fulham Lido … no, didn't ring a bell. He was still waiting. I licked my lips.

'Yes, a chap was passing, saw me trying to get in, and told me about one in Roehampton. D'you want some crisps with that? I've got loads.' I nipped off to the kitchen to rummage in a low cupboard, head down.

'Roehampton,' he was saying thoughtfully, following me out. 'Quite near then. Whereabouts?'

'Oh, miles away, nowhere near here really, right on the edge. More Brentford. Dodgy area too, and so crowded. Smoky bacon or plain?'

'Yes, but still. While Putney's shut … and Fulham's so expensive.' Damn. Fulham. Wouldn't you know? 'I'll Google it.' And he turned to sit at the computer in the corner of the kitchen.

'No, you won't find it,' I said, darting across, as indeed he was failing to, 'because actually, it's not public. I remember now, this chap owns it. He just let me use it because I was – you know – desperate.'

'Private?'

'Yes. In his garden.'

Ivan blinked, as well he might. For what we had now was a man who hung around public pools mid-refurbishment in order to lure women back to his house in a dubious area of west London, which none the less boasted a pool in its back garden, and was crowded with similarly desperate souls. It's worth mentioning I haven't been to a pool for about thirty years, and the only time I trouble the water is in the Mediterranean, with temperatures nudging ninety, and even then only in sunglasses and a hat.

Ivan's brow puckered. He looked confused. He also looked like a little boy who needed distracting. In a trice I'd slipped onto his lap at the computer and reverted to plan A. His plan A, admittedly, but needs must.

'Anyway, since when have you been so interested in my secret fitness regime?' I wrapped my arms round his neck and nuzzled his ear. 'What is this, twenty questions?'

Clearly not. There was no confirming and no hesitation, he just nuzzled right back. In fact he did more than that, and before long, I was shedding clothing again.

I wouldn't say the trouble with going out with a younger man is their insatiable carnal appetite, but there are times when a boiled egg in front of a Sunday night period drama, just me and my spectacularly greasy hair, appeals. When the sex kitten in me is not necessarily purring ferociously. Having said that, if anyone can persuade me to lay down my boiled egg spoon and take the hand that leads, not necessarily up the stairs, incidentally, to a king-sized fully sprung divan, but to who knows where, it's Ivan. Which brings me to another occupational hazard of not punching one's age weight: location. Or location location location in Ivan's case, because really, it could be anywhere. The kitchen floor has seen a fair amount of action in its time, as have the stairs, and even the cupboard beneath them, where a Hoover attachment in my back ensured spine-shattering sex in every sense. Ivan was the master of invention, and tonight, whilst one hand attended to a tricky belt buckle on my jeans, another was already clearing the computer table – Victorian pine, stripped to within an inch of its life, not unlike its owner was about to be – for action. The kitchen lights blazed down like the Gestapo – I made a long arm to snap them off – and over Ivan's shoulder, my son on my screen saver looked on in a quizzically amused fashion. It wasn't terribly conducive to the moment and I lunged for the mouse, pressing randomly, convulsively, only for Seffy to be replaced by a stern warning: 'Stand By'. Yes, indeed, I thought, turning my full attention to Ivan's appetite and shutting my eyes. You don't have to tell me.

Later, when I'd fled to the bathroom and the supreme comfort of a long hot bath, Ivan languishing happily on my bed in front of the telly in a dressing gown he kept here, I thought: this is more like it. I stroked the bubbles right up to my nose. More like marriage, perhaps. This – afterwards bit – at any rate. The cosy familiarity. I wondered if he'd stay. He did, occasionally. But then again, he often went home, claiming it was closer to work, and he was so appalling at getting up in the mornings. I'd rung once, when he'd gone, to tell him he'd forgotten his wallet, something making me ring his land line instead of his mobile, and a girl had answered, bright and breezy. His flatmate's sister, he'd said quickly when he came on the line. I didn't pry. He had to get back at weekends too, when Camden Passage was certainly at its busiest, but tomorrow was Monday: a quiet day. And it was well after nine now. Surely he was here for the duration?

Moments later a head came round the door, followed by a fully dressed Ivan.

'See ya.'

'See ya.' I grinned gamely back. Ah.

He came across to the bath and kneeled down. Naturally I'd carefully arranged the bubbles to cover me completely, and naturally the room was candlelit.

He carefully cleared a few bubbles from my lips and kissed me. 'I'll be back for more next week,' he warned, resting his arms on the bath edge. 'I thought we might go to that new Italian on Lillie Road.'

'Sure, why not?'

Out. We didn't generally do Out, Ivan much preferring In, regarding anything further afield as a retrograde step. Which was fine by me. I'd got over that stage of needing to be wined and dined long ago. And anyway, we did a lot of that in France, on our jaunts, which were frequent.

'Or on second thoughts,' he said, clearing a few more bubbles and gazing contemplatively, 'perhaps I should just hop in with you?'

'Perhaps not,' I smiled, rearranging the bubbles.

'You haven't finished your wine.' He plucked it from the tiled shelf at the side and put it to my lips.

I took a sip, but wrinkled my nose. 'I can't drink in the bath,' I confided. 'It gives me wind.'

'That's erotic.'

I grinned. 'It was supposed to be. Go home, Ivan.'

He ignored me and kissed me again; languorously this time, his tongue like a warm sea snake in my mouth. 'Oh, you'll have to do better than that, Miss Carrington,' he murmured. 'I'm rather enjoying this trapped and supine scenario. In fact, if I didn't have to see a man about some eighteenth-century firedogs …' He resumed the kiss, long and luxurious, and, despite myself, I began to join in, when a sudden burst of Vivaldi stopped us in our tracks.

Ivan sat back on his heels and pulled his phone from his pocket. 'Hello? Yes … yes I know. I'm on my way now.'

'Man about the dogs?' I enquired lightly.

'Hm?' He looked at me vaguely as he pocketed it. 'Oh, yup.' He sprang to his feet. Gave me a lopsided grin. 'Night, Miss Carrington.' He bent to kiss me, but this time it was a peck.

'Night.'

And he was gone.

I reached for a face cloth to wipe away my mascara, kept on until the last minute as an insurance policy. Yes, this suited me, I thought as I heard the front door slam behind him; listened to his footsteps going down the path. I balled the flannel and tossed it in the water. Maggie was right. I had all the fun of a man, with none of the aggro. No snoring lump beside me – but then Ivan didn't snore – no one drinking me out of fruit juice then, or demanding supper. No one hogging the computer. It was perfect.

Later, downstairs in the kitchen, in my dressing gown, not the slinky silk one I reserved for Ivan, but my comfortable old towelling one, I locked up and made myself a cup of cocoa. On the way back upstairs I tripped on a bit of rucked-up carpet I'd been meaning to fix for ages; spilled some of my drink. Annoyed, I went and found the hammer in the kitchen drawer and banged in a few tacks. Then I mopped up. When I eventually got into bed with the remains of my cocoa, I took a sip. A skin had formed; clung coldly to my lips. It wasn't ideal.

15

Laura rang me in the shop the following morning. Maggie was out getting the skinny lattes at the time, and I had a blonde woman browsing, picking things up and peering incredulously at the prices: not the most convenient time to be interrogated by my sister.

'You didn't tell me you'd seen Letty and Hal in the village?'

'Didn't I? I must have forgotten. There was all that Ralphie de Granville business when we got back. Must have slipped my mind.'

'So what did you think?'

'Of Letty?'

'No! We all know what we think of Letty: a poor lost soul who's never got over her husband dying and has embraced the bottle with brio. No, Hal.'

'Oh, Hal.'

'Yes, Hal! Don't you think he's completely gorgeous?'

'Laura, I've known Hal for years. I know what he looks like.'

'Nonsense,' she scoffed, 'he didn't look anything like that when you knew him. I came up to see you in Edinburgh, remember? He was a skinny, sunken-chested yoof with long greasy hair. He's filled out beautifully now, and those dark brooding eyes – heaven. Very like his brother, don't you think?'

'Not in the slightest,' I lied. It hadn't escaped my notice that the family resemblance was more marked now that Hal was older: a good few years older than Dom had been when he died, I realized with a start.

'He's getting married in the autumn, in Provence. It's going to be huge, apparently.'

'Yes, he said.'

'What, that it's going to be huge?'

'No, that he's getting married. Or Letty said, I think. Um, yes, that's right, seven hundred and fifty pounds …' This, to the heavily highlighted woman who was reaching up and fondling the chandelier, peering at the price tag. 'It's turn of the century and each drop is crystal.'

'Of course, he had the hots for you years ago.'

'Years ago,' I said brusquely. 'We were a couple of teenagers at university, for God's sake.'

'Well, early twenties, by the time you left. And you know what they say: the first cut is the deepest and all that.'

'Laura,' I said with studied calm, 'where exactly is this going? You've just told me he's getting married.'

'Oh, I know, it's just that when I saw Letty in the butcher's just now, she said Hal was so affected by seeing you again, yesterday. Went all quiet and thoughtful and snapped at her when she asked how many invitations they were sending out.'

'Letty?' I scoffed derisively. 'She barely knows what day it is, poor thing. I don't think I'd trust her to gauge anyone's inner turmoil.'

'Oh, I wouldn't say inner turmoil,' Laura said briskly. 'Just went a bit quiet.'

I ground my teeth silently at my sister's well-aimed parry. 'I'm afraid that's sold.' This, to the blonde, who'd turned her attention to a Napoleonic jardinière.

'Anyway, I was really ringing to see if Seffy wanted to shoot here. Hughie's got a few locals coming on the twenty-fourth of October and thought Seffy might enjoy it. It's a Saturday, I think.'

'Oh, he'd love it,' I said, instantly brightening. Seffy, under Hugh's guidance, and after some initial sneering about it being a toffs' sport, had recently enjoyed going off with his uncle to shoot a few rabbits for the pot, which had led to a few pheasants, and the odd day's shooting. I had a wholly unsustainable antipathy to the whole thing, which I kept under wraps, accepting Seffy's very valid argument that battery hens had a far worse time of it and the pheasant the best and most natural. I just knew I could never pull the trigger. Nevertheless, I loved seeing Seffy striding off with his uncle, jeans tucked into wellies, uncharacteristic flat cap on his unruly long hair: loved seeing him come back flushed from the exercise and the hunt, bubbling with enthusiasm, looking so bright-eyed and healthy and more like the Seffy of old. I grabbed at any opportunity for him.

'Good,' said Laura. 'And you'll come too?'

'Of course.'

'Because I've got Luca coming. Carla's just rung.'

Ah. That would explain the brittle, combative tone to her voice. The needless, initial needling. A common trait in our family: lash out under pressure.

'He'll be fine,' I soothed, 'don't panic. You said yourself the last time he was over he'd improved, and Seffy said he was easy.'

'Seffy's never intimidated by anyone. He's got the in-built confidence of generations of proud Serbs behind him. The girls are still scared of him though, especially Daisy. And I hate it that she has to spend her precious few days at home wondering where he is.'

'You're exaggerating,' I told her. 'Daisy's just at an age when she's nervous of any boy.'

I smiled an insincere goodbye at the blonde, who'd left without buying anything, and with a look that told me, before she banged the door shut, what she thought of saleswomen who sat on the phone whilst customers browsed, and wasted her time by having items already sold on display. Sold to me, some of them, if I couldn't bear to part with them, or didn't think they were going to a good enough home. Maggie despaired of me. Particularly when I told her I could have sold the lovely Chambéry table I'd found in Nantes, but the woman had wanted to cut the legs off and make it into a coffee table, so I'd hurriedly made up some story about ringing my partner to check its provenance, and been told, by a dialling tone, that actually it had already gone, been sold yesterday.

Making up stories. Yes, I was good at that, I reflected as I got off the phone to Laura and went to shut the door, which had bounced open with the force of the slam. Had told quite a few in my time, and indeed, had told one just now to my sister, about not having given Hal a second thought. Not quite true. I'd wondered about him over the years – of course I had – and sometimes wondered if he'd thought about me. I knew he hadn't married, and wondered how I'd feel when he did. Sometimes I even checked the paper for an announcement. So how did it feel, Hattie, hm? Now I knew? I tried to gauge my feelings honestly, straightening up and folding my arms as I faced the street. A twinge of regret for our youthful selves perhaps – laughing our way to lectures, going to parties together in his beaten-up Beetle –

a sentimental glance back in an *à la recherche du temps perdu* kind of way, but no more than that. Definitely no more than that.

I turned briskly and made my way back to the counter through the artfully arranged vignettes that made up the shop. A decoratively carved buffet table lined one wall, accessorized with a lamp, candlesticks, and a pile of antique books; a curvaceous console flanked another, between a pair of exotic blackamoors. Centre stage sat a beautiful, button-backed bergère, long, low and feather-stuffed, upon which, two hundred years ago, a grande dame would have settled, the seat wide enough to prevent her crinolines from creasing. That was what I loved about our pieces – I trailed my fingers along the bergère's intricately carved frame – the past. The wondering who'd touched, sat on, glanced in the mirror of, swept by in their hoops, and yes, you could pick up something shinier and brighter in Heal's, but did it have soul? Did it have a history? What secrets did that group of *fauteuils* hold, those small, upright gilt chairs, which would have lined the walls in some grand salon: what emotions had they been privy to, what glances seen traded, or tender moments heard whispered behind fans?

I realigned a row of silver apostle spoons on a table on my way back and sat down at the counter: an old apothecary's desk we'd found in Fayence, the town, incidentally with the blue church clock where Hal was getting married. I gazed through my treasures to the street. I had, in idler moments over the years, wondered if perhaps Hal hadn't married because he'd never forgotten me. Idle, silly, vain moments, as it turned out, because now I knew. As Letty had said, he'd been playing the field, until he landed the biggest catch of all: a beautiful French girl to sweep up that idyllic aisle. I smiled. Reached for my glasses and opened the client book. But of course.

A few minutes later, the door jangled open and Maggie burst in with the lattes.

'Look who I found lurking in Luigi's and trying to sneak away without coming to see us.'

Christian followed her in, lumbering over the threshold in a vast tweed coat, puffing and blowing. I crossed the shop to embrace him.

'How dare you!'

'Is not a question of not coming to see you,' he wheezed, 'is more to do weeth not wanting to be the bearer of bad news – again!'

Maggie and I exchanged guilty glances like a couple of fourth-formers. Christian, retired and arthritic now, did our books, Maggie and I both being numerically dyslexic, and he despaired of ever balancing us, let alone getting us to make a healthy profit.

'It's Hattie's fault,' said Maggie, striding to the counter and putting the coffees down. 'Most of the stuff in here isn't for sale because the prospective homes aren't deemed deserving enough.'

'And the things that are for sale,' I countered, 'Maggie puts exorbitant prices on, so they never sell anyway.'

'Well, I'm not selling for peanuts like that Magpie shop on the corner. They're practically giving it away.'

'Girls, girls,' wheezed Christian, coming to join us in a cosy circle behind the apothecary's desk where we had a faded brocade sofa (not for sale) and a brace of Louis Quinze chairs (so highly priced they'd never sell) to sink into. He settled in one of them. 'You got to be realistic. You running a shop here, not an orphanage, Hattie. Ees none of your business where your lovely Limoges plates end up. And, Maggie, you got to stop imagining you top end Mount Street or a museum curator!'

'Some of the stuff here could grace Mount Street,' muttered Maggie, but without much conviction because she knew he was right. We'd got too precious, lately. Weren't commercial enough. And new shops had sprung up in the vicinity, undercutting us, selling similar pieces – not as good, Maggie would insist – for a fraction of the price, whilst we sat reading our horoscopes and sipping our lattes, letting the world slip by.

'You've grown complacent,' Christian told us, opening the books on the table. 'Look. This two years ago, see?'

Maggie and I peered from the safety of our body language: crossed arms and legs.

'A whopping twenty per cent profit, yes?'

We nodded, uncrossing a bit: this, the result of a wonderful coup with an Edouard Honore bowl I'd found in Montmartre that had sold for £10,000 at Christie's, and a mirror of Maggie's – very nearly a museum piece – worth a staggering £20,000. Both had made huge inroads into Maggie's mortgage and Seffy's school fees. But that had been two years ago. And they'd been one-offs. Last year we'd done quite well with the furniture – the contents of a château in the Loire had yielded some fine old pieces – and we'd turned in a ten per cent profit: still pretty good. This year, however, not a lot.

'You rest on your laurels. Not good for reputation or business,' Christian said sternly, and then, just as I was about to take a bite from the enormous muffin Maggie had bought me, added, 'or figures.'

I put it down guiltily. Christian might be vast himself but he had an uncompromising Frenchman's view of spreading behinds.

'We need to go to France more,' Maggie said decisively. 'We've got lazy.'

'Or,' Christian threw up his hands, 'you just do commissions. Give up the shop.'

This was where we'd recently made money, doing up people's houses, so the shop had suffered a bit. To be honest, these days I thought of it as a nice place to go to chat to Maggie, to discuss said commissions, which of course was an extravagance. But the thought of closing it, of sitting at home like a couple of housewives playing at interior design, horrified us. This was our respectable working-girl front: we liked dressing up and marching into work in our clever, high-street-take-on-designer clothes. But rents had soared in Munster Road and we were paying through the nose to read *Interiors* wearing Boden.

'It's sheer laziness,' Maggie said firmly again. 'We used to go to France four times a year. We only went once last year.'

'But we did well,' I reminded her. 'Only one lorryload, but we made more than we would have done with four lorryloads years ago. We've got better.'

But I knew what she meant. The moment we were solvent, we lost our drive. Without the worry of wondering where the next cheque was coming from, or whether the shop would be a success, we relaxed, lost our edge; and a bit of me, at nearly forty, wanted to relax. Surely one didn't have to battle through life for ever? Surely we were allowed a spot of complacency, a bit of middle-aged spread? But Maggie was already consulting a diary.

'Montauroux is on the fifteenth,' she said, squinting and rooting in her bag for the reading glasses we both now needed: she perched them on her nose. 'And Fréjus is on the twenty-third. We'll go to both.'

'Ah. Slight problem. I've just told Laura I'll go and stay with her on the twenty-fourth. There's a shoot at the Abbey.'

Despite having just spent a very spoiling weekend there, the words 'Shoot' and 'Abbey', juxtaposed with my very privileged sister, were designed to send shock waves down Maggie's spine.

'That's OK,' she said evenly. 'The fair's on the Friday. If you drive through the night like we used to, you'll be back in time for the slaughter on the Saturday.' She sent me a flat stare over her spectacles: less best friend, more partner. I wriggled briefly, but the eyes had me pinned.

'Right,' I conceded weakly. 'France it is.'

Christian smiled, enjoying this little exchange. 'I think she right, you know. You need the stimulation,' he advised me.

Maggie gave me a triumphant look and swivelled to the computer screen – as much as one can swivel in a Louis Quinze – to make the ferry reservations.

'Oh, and by the way, Lucinda Carr rang,' her back informed me as she waited for P&O to flash up their wares. 'She wants one of us to look at her dining room. The Gustavian Grey has not turned out as planned, apparently.'

'Well, why can't you go?' I yelped. Lucinda Carr was a terrifying Chelsea housewife: pencil thin and waspish, the wife of a wealthy investment banker. She scared the pants off me. The client from Hades in Hermès.

'Because I'm doing this, and you know how hopeless you are on the computer.'

There was no disputing this, but I realized she'd deliberately lined herself up a task so I could be dispatched.

Grumbling I gathered my coat and bag. Christian was already pulling out a heaving drawer from the desk, spewing forth bills and paperwork, preparing to set to. I bent and pecked his cheek. He sent me a sympathetic smile.

'She eat you for breakfast, no?'

'Who, Lucinda Carr or Maggie?' I said, glaring at my friend. 'And anyway, what am I supposed to tell her?'

'Tell her it's fine,' Maggie replied without taking her eyes off the screen. 'She wants reassurance, that's all. You know what she's like. I told her you'd be there at eleven.'

'Did you,' I muttered as I slunk to the door. Childishly, I let it bang shut behind me.

Once out on the street, however, standing a moment to breathe in the heady mixture of carbon monoxide, coffee, and delicious restaurant smells wafting on the cool air, I relaxed. If truth be told I needed a walk. And I loved to walk in London: loved sauntering past the bars and cafés in our street, greeting my friends – the Italians and Poles clearing morning coffee, laying their tables for lunch – seeing what the competition was up to. Munster Road fairly bristled with antiquarian activity – lighting shops, carpets, fabrics – and one or two French establishments too. In the main they were less formal than us, more pine-based and farmhousey, and despite our supposed rivalry, we were friends with all of them.

'How's it going?' I called out to Penny, who ran Magpie on the corner. She was wheeling a distressed green wheelbarrow full of terracotta pots outside.

'Slow,' she groaned, setting it down with a bump. 'And you?'

'The same,' I agreed.

'Where are the tourists? she wailed.

'In the King's Road, paying silly prices,' I called back. She gave me a despairing shrug then, with a wave, went back into her shop.

I walked away from Fulham and its sprawling grids of redbrick terraced houses, and made my way towards the wider avenues of more gentrified Chelsea. It was quite a hike through Parson's Green, along New King's Road and on towards Stamford Bridge, but I enjoyed the exercise, and after a while, the houses grew taller and whiter, the pavements squeakier, the window boxes more luxurious, and the door knockers shinier.

When I'd lived with Laura in Pimlico, I'd walked past similar houses on my way to work in Westminster. In an immature sort of way, I used to imagine living in one, and indeed, a whole other life could flow, pretty much uninterrupted, under my everyday existence. I'd peer into basement kitchens and within a twinkling be breakfasting in one myself, with my pinstriped husband and my little blond children, waving them off to school in their straw boaters and blazers. Even back in those days, as I swung my Topshop handbag and smacked the pavements with the flip-flops I'd swap later for heels, I was disinclined to be trapped at home, so I'd invent a part-time job for myself, a spot of charity work perhaps. Not tin-rattling in the cold, you understand, more arranging balls in the warm, with other well-dressed women with tiny ankles. Later I'd change into something sexy and expensive – Ungaro, maybe? Or was that a country? – issue instructions to my nanny, and hurry to my taxi, purring outside my perfect house, pausing only to breathe to the cabbie, 'The House of Commons, please.'

I rocked to a standstill in the street. Where was I? Oh. Yes. Standing outside another perfect house. Mrs Carr's, in fact. I gave myself a moment, marvelling at the magnitude of my youthful gall. Then I took a deep breath and looked up. White, stuccoed and occupying four floors – a waste, I thought scathingly, since everyone knew these women lived in the basement – it was by anyone's standards, a supremely elegant house. But these days, I wasn't envious, only a little wistful. And not for the house, but for the way of life. Naturally I'd dreamed of having a more conventional family. Naturally I'd have liked a husband, a few children, a nice house, but life had decided otherwise. And occasionally, I had to quell the feeling it had treated me unfairly. I pulled myself together, but as I mounted the steps and pressed the bell, I was alarmed to find tears pricking my eyes. Would I be this person for ever? I wondered. This working girl, with her colour chart in her handbag, her boots that needed heeling, in her five-year-old coat, waiting for Mrs Carr, or someone similar, to open the door?

She did, moments later, still dressed in a pink jacket and sunglasses, having clearly just returned from dropping her children at school. An expensive carrier bag swung from her hand.

'Oh, it's you. I've literally just walked in.' She looked at me accusingly. 'I had to pick my dress up from Bruce Oldfield, for the Aids ball tonight. Didn't the other girl tell you eleven?'

'The other girl did,' I said smoothly. 'And I'm sorry. You're right, I am a few minutes early.'

'Well, you're here now. You'd better come in.'

What – as opposed to waiting outside on the step while she took off her coat and had a cup of coffee?

'Thanks,' I murmured.

'I'm just going to take my coat off and put the kettle on. Won't be a minute.'

I assumed I wasn't to follow, and waited in her black-and-white tiled hall, watching as her pert little backside went downstairs to the basement kitchen. Her heels echoed in the vast empty house. On the Pembroke table beside me – nice enough, but not a great deal of age – were framed photographs of her family. A studio shot of two blonde teenage girls caught my eye, the ones that years ago, I'd have been breakfasting with in the basement kitchen. They were probably reading History of Art at Newcastle now, or on a gap year in Thailand, prior to Mummy finding them work at Sotheby's. And what of Lucinda, I wondered, now they'd flown the nest? What was her life like now? Maggie insisted all her smart married friends had their work cut out keeping their successful husbands, and she didn't mean feeding them. Said that these days, nipping to Harvey Nicks wasn't a joy, but the deadly serious task of maintenance. Facials, hair, nails and clothes – it was all about keeping one's man, whilst at work the younger women circled like sharks and desk-perched. Just as I had circled and desk-perched too, I realized, as I looked up with a jolt from the smiling teenage faces, to this woman, who had my life. She was clip-clopping back down the passage towards me, still slightly irritated, but plastering on a smile. She had the grace to apologize.

'Sorry. You caught me on the hop, rather.'

And I had the grace to accept it for what it was: an attempt from a woman, whose life no doubt looked immaculate, but wasn't necessarily all it seemed, to remember her manners.

'Trust me,' Maggie would warn, 'you wouldn't want to be in their gilded cages, however cushy you think their lives are. They're all on antidepressants.'

'On the whole I'm very pleased,' she was saying, leading me down the passage and through some double doors. Thank the Lord. 'Your partner's got a very good eye, and she's caught just the theme I wanted. But the colour's a disaster.'

I followed her into the dining room which Maggie had indeed done well. I recognized the round, wrought-iron table we'd found in Grasse, originally a garden table from a château terrace, but working beautifully inside a London house. Around it were iron chairs, painstakingly sourced from a bistro in Paris and newly upholstered now in a modern grey check. On the wall opposite the open French windows, flung wide to dispel the smell of paint, hung a huge oil by Claude Vessan. The painting, along with the distressed corner cupboard for glasses and the walnut sideboard, were all pieces I'd personally found, but hadn't seen in situ. I felt a surge of pleasure at seeing them so well appointed.

'It's looking good,' I told her.

'It is, but the walls simply aren't working for me. This is not the Gustavian Grey I ordered.'

I nodded. 'Hi, Greg.' This to a painter she'd failed to acknowledge, who was crouched by the skirting board in the far corner, applying the finishing touches.

'Hattie.' He turned, nodded.

Lucinda's mobile rang and she answered it.

'No, I told you, two inches below the knee, not above. I can't go to the opera looking like a call girl, can I?'

She strode out through the French doors to continue her conversation on the terrace. Greg straightened up and showed me the tin.

'Gustavian bleeding Grey.'

'I know,' I muttered. We'd mixed it specially for her. Or had our mates at Perfect Paints do it for us.

'What on earth will my husband think?' we heard her say as she paced up and down, one arm clenched around her minuscule waist. 'It's for tomorrow night!'

'Her husband won't give a monkey's,' remarked Greg. 'He's in a maisonette in Battersea most afternoons after work, with his secretary.'

'How d'you know?' I said, appalled.

'I'm painting her kitchen, aren't I? Lilac Wine. Recognized him.'

Lucinda was back and Greg sank gnomically to the skirting again. She tucked her phone in her jeans, so tight over her skinny hips she could barely get it in, and turned to me. A fine fretwork of lines framed the azure eyes that gazed from a once very beautiful face.

'Well?' she demanded. 'Any ideas?'

Happily I had.

'The skirting boards and ceiling are brilliant white,' I explained, 'and they need to be softer. Off-white certainly, or even palest grey, or taupe.'

'Oh.' She blinked. 'But I always do them white.'

It was as if I'd suggested a radical rethink of her underwear drawer or something equally personal.

'Yes, but in a French themed room like this, they need to be more muted, otherwise the contrast is too stark. Too Dulux.' This had the desired effect. She froze. Dulux, to a woman like this, was a worse word than fuck. 'All the colours need to blend in,' I went on, 'so you don't notice them. One of these will be fine.' I fished in my bag and pulled out a National Trust colour chart – always useful *in extremis* – flopping it open on the table.

'Something like Pontoon,' I pointed. 'Or even Dead Salmon.' Greg smirked, but then decorators always did: at the bloody silly names, and the hated paint that went on like water, and needed three coats, not having any plastic in it.

'Oh, I see.' She peered. 'I rather like Muff.'

'Don't we all,' Greg muttered.

I shot him a look.

'Muff's a bit dark,' I told her.

'Beaver's nice, though,' Greg couldn't resist, mouth twitching. 'I reckon your husband would like Beaver too.'

'I can't see Beaver,' she frowned.

'It's been discontinued,' I said quickly, rolling up the chart. 'But if you're not sure about these, I can get one mixed specially for you, if you like? Something that fits in exactly?'

'Oh, *would* you?' Suddenly she was all charm and smiles, and I wasn't an annoying interior designer who'd got it wrong, but a magic wand waver, who really was awfully clever. 'Thank you so much. I'd be so grateful.'

'Not at all,' I murmured as Greg smirked into the skirting some more. He knew full well I'd pop a splodge of colour into a pot of cream paint, shake it up, put a homespun label on it, and charge her eighty pounds, which, with two hundred for the house call – house calls were pricey – plus VAT, netted a clear three hundred pounds. By anyone's yardstick it was a rip-off, but then, as Maggie said, women like Lucinda Carr deserved to be ripped off. She wanted to tell her friends her paint had been 'specially mixed' and she certainly didn't want me charging her twenty quid for it, either.

I sighed as I bid her goodbye and went down the steps to the street. I wouldn't tell Maggie about the husband, I decided. She'd love it too much. Maggie had recently become more gleeful about our friends' marital disharmony, and although a bit of me in the past had secretly exulted too, these days I felt uncomfortable with it. Surely women – all women – deserved our loyalty? Our support? Somewhere within me, I realized, I believed in something woolly and indeterminate called the sisterhood: I didn't want to be rubbing my hands at my married friends' misfortune. If I said as much to Maggie, though, she'd say sharply, 'Why not? They deserve it. They bring it on themselves.'

'In what way?'

'By not doing anything with their lives. By relying on a man.'

But what could they do? I thought as I walked on. Women like Lucinda Carr? What else did she have, besides the institution of marriage? Not a career. That, she'd never had, and never thought she'd need, either. And now it was too late to start one. So what could she do but marshal what forces she had: her fading beauty, her money, keep doggedly at the highlights, the manicures – never say die? Shouldn't we feel the pain and recognize the bravery of women like that? What could she do but plaster her walls with photos of her offspring – a constant remainder to her husband – restlessly tart up her house and her wardrobe, slap on a smile and hope for the best? Hope to still be here in ten years' time, and actually, if she could get through the next five, she probably would. Brave? I thought so.

As brave as being alone at forty? I turned down Sydney Street and felt the cool breeze on my cheeks as I headed towards St Luke's. That, of course, depended on the day. Depended on whether one woke up full of beans and optimism, or awoke, slowly opened one's eyes, and stared down the barrel of loneliness: at the years stretching ahead. I turned the collar of my coat up against the breeze, which, I recalled, always whistled very keenly down this particularly wide and gracious street. Then I put my head down and marched on.

16

Weeks passed and Provence beckoned. Historically, Maggie and I would spend the time leading up to a trip to France making plans. Heads bent over the apothecary's desk, excitement mounting, we'd draw up detailed lists: in one column we'd write what was selling and what was popular, and in another, what was passé, and what we should avoid at all costs. There was a bit of that this time. Lanterns, we decided were big this year, burnished and rewired. We sold masses. Armoires, too, for free-standing kitchens. Commodes were popular for putting TVs on, and overmantel mirrors flew out as soon as we'd shipped them in. But the larger mahogany pieces were anachronisms now. No one had houseroom for a vast old sideboard or a twelve-foot dining table, and likewise, wardrobes were a no no. We shuttled ideas this way and that, pacing the shop, sucking pencils, pausing to scribble or pontificate, both of us talking at once, and yes, a degree of excitement returned. Christian was right: Provence in autumn was just what we needed, and although we didn't fizz and buzz quite like we used to – years of experience ensured we could take a more relaxed attitude, leave more to chance when we got there – it undoubtedly put a spring back into the step of the French Partnership. Undoubtedly gave us a boost.

Which was why it was something of a blow when Maggie rang the night before we were due to leave, sounding dreadful.

'I'm really sorry, Hatts, I've come down with this ghastly flu,' she wheezed, coughing away from the mouthpiece.

'I'll join you out there for Fréjus, but I'm going to have to miss Montauroux, I'm afraid. I feel awful.'

'Oh.' I realized I was bitterly disappointed.

'But if I bring the van down when I come, we can fill that up as well. Get far more stock that way. It makes complete sense, actually, to have two vehicles,' she told me nasally. It did, commercially. But Maggie and I had never taken the sensible, commercial route, preferring the camaraderie of a giggle together in the lorry. It was the whole point actually.

'I suppose,' I said, wondering if her voice was brightening slightly. It seemed to veer from being extremely blocked up to perfectly normal. 'But what a shame.'

'I know.'

'You seemed all right in the shop. It's awfully sudden, isn't it?'

'Very, but that's how this bug is, apparently. My cousin had it. One minute you're as fit as a fiddle and the next, you're at death's door, feeling lousy.'

'Which cousin?' I asked suspiciously.

'Um, Cousin … Alfred.'

'Never heard of him.'

'No, well, he's kind of the black sheep of the family. No one really speaks to him.'

'And yet he rang to confide the details of his appalling malaise?'

'Yes …' Maggie was nowhere near as consummate a liar as I was.

A scuffle could be heard in the background, then a deep cough. I cleared my throat.

'Maggie, is Henry with you?'

There was a shocked silence. Then: 'How did you know?' she hissed. No sign of a blocked nose now.

'I can tell. Why didn't you just say, "Look, Henry's appeared out of the blue, he's back from New York, can I join you down there?"'

'Sorry,' she said, chastened. Her voice dropped to a whisper. 'His wife's gone to her sister's for a week. I was going to ring back later and tell you, I just didn't want …'

Henry to hear her say it. Because for all her scorn of the Lucinda Carrs of this world, Maggie's life was equally poised on the whims and caprices of a man. A phone call from Henry could have her life veering off in a completely different direction, away from her career, her friends, her commitments. Henry rendered her permanently pivotal.

'I wasn't going to lie to you, I promise,' she hissed, clearly having fled to the sanctuary of the bathroom now. I heard a door close. 'But I didn't want him to think I was dropping everything just because he's back.'

'Which you are.'

'Hattie …' she sighed, and implicit in that sigh was: you know.

I did know. Had heard all her arguments. About how she only got to see him about twice a month, about how every moment was precious, but that one day, all their moments would be precious, because they'd be together for ever. He'd leave his wife for her. And yes of course she felt guilty about deceiving another woman, but Henry had fallen out of love with Davina years ago, and who, after all, deserved her loyalty? This woman she didn't know, or Henry, the man she loved? We'd sit for hours in the shop, cradling coffees, analysing the relationship this way and that: Maggie trotting out clichés about not being able to choose who one fell in love with and only having one life, me trotting out ones about how Henry was never going to leave his wife and was having his cake and eating it with two women at his beck and call. But as her face collapsed, I'd be kinder. Agree that it was terribly painful all round. Difficult for everyone. And after all, who was I to moralize? Hadn't I once fallen in love with someone I had no right to fall in love with?

I wondered too if she really would have told me the truth, or if in fact she knew that what she was doing was so desperate, she wasn't sure even her best friend would understand? I did, though. I knew how nothing else mattered. How everything became irrelevant. How you'd let friends and family down, drop everything to be with the object of desire, and yes, feel ashamed, but still hurtle on towards that bright, blinding white light, trampling everything and everyone in its path.

'Be careful,' I warned her, as I'd warned her a million times before.

'Oh I will!' she exulted, knowing this was the green light to her white one. Knowing, by not being angry, I'd given her the nod of friendship and complicity. That I'd somehow condoned it.

'And I'll see you in a week or so, I promise. Meanwhile, I thought I'd work on your sister's place?'

'Meanwhile?'

'Well, obviously Henry has to go to work in the day.' Ah, right. Not wall-to-wall bonking then. 'So I thought I'd pop down on a daily basis and see how Rod and Kenny are getting on.'

These, our two wonderfully capable, experienced workmen, who'd been with us for years, and whom we'd installed at the Abbey, knowing once briefed, they'd need no guidance whatsoever. I frowned. Then it dawned. Christian was lined up to take care of the shop, a job he

214

loved occasionally, looked forward to, in fact. Now his wife had died, it got him out of his flat, made him feel useful, which he surely was. He'd be bitterly disappointed to hear the plans had changed. So yes, Maggie's love affair, without this frantic damage limitation, could have had a devastating domino effect. And of course she couldn't just sit at home and wait for Henry while Christian minded the shop. Even Maggie at fever pitch had pride. Where could she go?

'You say "pop down",' I said slowly, 'but Little Crandon's hardly down the road.'

'Oh, it's only an hour or so,' she said breezily. 'I don't mind.'

'OK. So ... d'you want me to check with Laura?'

'No, it's all right, I already have.' I nearly dropped the phone. 'She, um, says it's fine to come. I emailed her.'

I could almost feel her blush radiate down the phone.

'I didn't know you had her email?'

'I looked it up on yours.'

'Right ...' I said faintly. 'Well, it looks like you've got it all sorted, Maggie.' I couldn't resist a little edge to my voice. She'd gone to Laura before consulting me, so desperate was she that her plan should not fall through?

'I'm sorry,' she whispered, glimpsing for a moment the scale of her nerve. 'I just ... can't help it.'

No more she could, I thought as the lorry rumbled down the ramp off the ferry in Calais the following morning, yours truly perched alone and aloft at the wheel. No more than I ever could. But if we can't help ourselves, I thought, as I drove through the familiar, bustling town keeping firmly to the right, and more particularly, if my caustic, sharp, wise old friend couldn't help herself, what hope was there for us? Not for the first time I thought how neat and simple life would be if it weren't for love.

However, much as I'd have liked Maggie's company, happily I've never minded my own. Have been entertaining myself for years, in fact, and was content with the silence and my thoughts. Indeed, as the urban landscape gave way to a more rural one, as fields of golden brown stubble bristled to attention either side of the straight road ahead, I narrowed my eyes into the shimmering distance and felt myself relax, as I only truly did, I realized, away from home, particularly in France. I loved the anonymity of being abroad. Loved stepping out of myself, being someone else for a change. Dad would disagree. You can change your skies, but you can't change your soul, he'd say, and I'd hear it with an ache of dread. The truth, it seemed to me, doesn't so much have a ring about it, but a dull thud. And Dad had travelled a lot. I shifted in my seat. Well, if I couldn't change my soul, I could at least soothe it, and Burgundy's flat, anonymous, roomy landscape seemed to me the perfect balm.

There was also something faintly romantic, I always thought, about taking the lorry to France: something bold and heroic. To that end I always made sure I looked the part – hair freshly washed, a bit of make-up … I glanced at my reflection in the mirror. Yes, it was essential to look like the English chick abroad, cruising the markets and earning an approving nod from the louche Frenchmen – who, unlike their English counterparts, had no qualms about showing their appreciation – and, please God, never descending into the realms of a Woman of a Certain Age who still persisted in pitching up year after year. To that end, the mascara was on, the denim skirt long but wrap-around – ensuring fake-tanned legs flashed alluringly when I sat in a bar and sipped my cassis – the espadrille heels slightly raised.

And neither would I be totally alone when I got there, I thought with a sudden smile. I'd been frowning, I realized, hunched at the wheel. I straightened up. Ivan, who still doggedly trawled the smaller, cheaper fairs of France, which Maggie and I now eschewed, was on the coast in Montpellier, and although Aix wasn't a natural hunting ground for him he'd declared a drive of a hundred and thirty kilometers and an overpriced *brocante* not sufficient deterrent to keep him from my hotel room.

'Remember Castellane?' he'd demanded down the phone.

I giggled. 'I might not have a balcony this time.'

'Trust me, we'll improvize. We'll find a roof terrace. I definitely feel something a little al fresco coming on.'

I smiled to myself as I rumbled along the dusty roads behind an old Citroën van that looked in danger of collapsing at any minute, in the heat of a late Indian summer, the sun on my bare arm through the window. Yes, I too would have my share of love and laughter these next few days, so who was I to deny Maggie hers? And would I give Ivan up if he were married? Well, luckily he wasn't, I thought quickly, banishing the face of the girl I'd seen him with in the bar. Luckily, Ivan just had lots of good friends, at which point I reached, Pavlovian style, for my lippy in my bag beside me. I slapped it on.

Montauroux was heaving when I finally arrived, late in the evening. The main square was full of tourists who'd left it late and were looking for a spot for supper. Patrons at their awnings now turned away those who they'd recently sought to entice inside with promises of fresh *moules*, *escargots* swimming in garlic, or a fridge full of oysters on display. Seasoned antique dealers from London, however, did not leave so much to chance. They were already on their café cognacs and post-supper cigarettes, eyeing up the best sites for their trestle tables under the trees in the morning, preparing for an early night.

I greeted those I knew with a wave and a promise to yes, possibly join them for a drink later, and no, Maggie wasn't with me but would be along in due course. There was a camaraderie amongst us, as well as a fierce rivalry: we'd drink into the small hours together and laugh like drains, but the following morning, had no qualms about selling one another something we'd bought for half the price the previous week. In the early days Maggie and I had fallen for some classic ruses, but were unlikely to be duped now.

Amongst the French contingent of stall holders – most of whom looked like they were straight out of central casting – I spotted Antoine Renard propping up a long zinc bar. Jowly and bug-eyed, a Gauloise dropped from his lips as he ostensibly read *Le Monde*, but in reality scanned the crowd to see which of his rivals from the porcelain world were here. Jacques Dupont, he of the seedy dark looks, who'd smile and sell his own grandmother, was with him. At a table for one, under an awning, the once beautiful, now haggard, Madame Alain – never Pascale – with her dyed orange hair and tiny nervous dog on her lap, was impeccably dressed as ever, dripping with jet beads, and feeding Kiki the remains of her *plat du jour*.

'*Ça va?*' She smiled and tapped my arm with a heavily jewelled hand as I approached.

I kissed her three times, as was her wont.

'*Ça va*,' I agreed, '*mais fatiguée.*' I let my shoulders droop.

'*Ah, oui, c'est normal pour moi!*' Her own shoulders went up and her eyes popped as she let me know by her horrified expression that no one, however long they lived, or however far they travelled, would ever be as tired as she, Madame Alain.

I sat and chatted a while, wondering guiltily if she were the woman I dreaded becoming, then got up and moved on.

I booked into my usual hotel – no balcony, I noted with a smile – and once showered and changed, went back down to the square with my book. I deliberately made for a café down a backstreet, which I knew wasn't frequented by tourists, but did a very good plate of *saucisson*, which with a glass of wine, was all I fancied tonight.

Having settled myself at a table outside and ordered, I opened my book to read by the twinkling fairy lights in the trees above. As I did, a shadow fell over the printed page, blocking the light. I glanced up to see Hal Forbes standing over me.

I stared.

'Hello, Hattie.' He smiled, and then as if no water whatsoever had flowed under any bridges in the intervening years, indicated the seat opposite. 'May I?'

Still speechless I gazed as he sat down. Finally I found my voice. Took my glasses off. 'What on earth are you doing here?'

'Hm?' He looked around for a waiter, as if it were the most natural thing in the world to be sitting opposite me in a cobbled street in Montauroux, seven hundred miles from home.

'I live here. Or at least I have a house near here, in Seillans. Didn't I say the other week?'

I opened my mouth. 'Oh. Yes. Well – no. At least … well, I knew you were getting married here. I didn't know you actually lived here.'

'I've had a house here for five years. This is my local bar. They do the best *saucisson* for miles. Shall we make that a bottle?' he asked as the waiter approached with my glass of wine. 'You wouldn't want to stay here, though,' he warned as the waiter, recognizing Hal, broke into a wide smile. 'The rooms are dire. Pierre!'

He got to his feet to wring the patron's hand. I was staggered. This was his local? Of all the bars in all the world and I'd strolled into … He and Pierre were chewing the fat now, in quick-fire French: it gave me a moment.

'How far away is your house then?' I managed to keep my voice light and neutral as he sat down again, keen to get to the bottom of this.

'About five miles in that direction.' He jerked his head. 'It's an old farmhouse in the foothills of the Camiole valley, quite tucked away.'

'But I thought you lived in London?'

'I do, as a rule. My, you know a lot about me, Hattie. You're not stalking me, are you?' he grinned. 'Haven't seen you for years and first you turn up at my patch in Buckinghamshire and now here.'

I opened my mouth to protest, astounded. '*Your* patch! Little Crandon is very much my sister's patch, actually! And this, I'll have you know, is *my* patch. *My* antique fair, which I come to every year, have done for the last six!'

'Except last year.'

'Yes, except last year,' I said, surprised. 'We missed it. But how did you—'

'I saw you here the previous year. Didn't quite have the nerve to speak to you. Last year I looked for you, but you didn't pitch up. Thought I'd try my luck this time.'

I stared. His narrow dark eyes were steady, but I couldn't read them.

'So, in fact, you're stalking me.'

He gave a soft laugh. 'If you call stalking looking out for you once a year at a popular local fête, which I'd frequent anyway, then yes, I suppose. I wouldn't call it terribly committed tailing.'

'And yet, when I saw you the other week, you didn't seem particularly ...'

'Friendly? No, but then I was startled to see you out of context. Didn't have my speech ready, as I would have done here. Also, there were people around.'

The waiter came with our drinks and two plates of *saucisson*. I watched as Hal exchanged a few more fluent words with him, smiling the while. Yes, Laura was right. Very attractive. He'd filled out a bit. And his eyes seemed less intent and probing: there was more light to them, more confidence. Which came with age, of course.

'Your speech?' I said as the waiter departed.

'I ... want to apologize. For what I wrote all those years ago. And also for my silence afterwards. The ball was firmly in my court to make amends. We were friends, good friends, for years, and I ... had no right to judge you like that. I'm sorry.'

It was a simple, upfront, heartfelt little speech and, as such, affecting. Disarming, even.

'You had every right,' I said slowly. 'I behaved very badly. To you, to Letty ...' I felt myself blush under his gaze. 'You had every right, Hal.'

There was a silence. It seemed to me we travelled back in time together within it.

'You were young,' he said at length. 'You made a mistake.'

Funny. Even after all these years, I never regarded Dom as a mistake. Wouldn't have had it differently.

'I was young,' I agreed, 'but you were justifiably angry.'

'At the time maybe, but not six months, a year later. Not sixteen years later, certainly. Friends forgive, make up. I've always regretted not doing that.'

'But as time goes by it becomes more difficult. I can see that. It's nice to see you, Hal.'

It was. And as we smiled at one another, relieved to have got that out of the way, I realized I'd missed him. He had been my best friend, but I'd blocked his memory for years. It had hurt, at the time, losing his friendship, but not as much as everything else was hurting. I'd been so in love with his brother, it had seemed small beer in comparison. Losing Dominic, or rather not being able to have him, had been all-consuming. But as we chatted now, about old times, recent times, so much in between, the value of what we'd once shared, of what is, after all, a rare and precious thing, a friendship between the sexes without the sex, I felt something within me, some warmth I'd missed return. It was as if a battered old coin was being gently polished and burnished, recovering its gleam.

After a bit we were tumbling over our words, couldn't get them out quickly enough: about what we'd been doing all this time, me with the shop, him as a lawyer, but not human rights – too dull, too worthy – now a hotshot at a City law firm.

'You've sold your soul!' I told him gleefully.

'Didn't take much persuading,' he said with a wry grin. 'Although I still do legal aid.'

'For the sake of your conscience,' I retorted, 'which was always huge.'

He laughed. 'Which was always huge.'

As his laughter faded, his gaze across the table grew steady; fond.

'And what about you, Hattie? Fill me in from where we left off. What happened next?'

I told him about Croatia, about my own conscience, how I'd felt I had to go there. I told him about Kit, and about coming home with Seffy. He listened intently, his eyes never leaving my face.

'So now he's what – fourteen?'

'Fifteen. And gorgeous. You should see him.'

'Oh, I've heard. My niece is very communicative on the subject.'

'Your niece?'

'Cassie.'

'Oh, yes of course.' I blanched, startled. I knew Seffy and Cassie had met at a dance, but …

'I think they're quite good friends in a Facebook kind of way, which is nice, isn't it?'

'Yes,' I agreed after a moment, still taken aback. 'It is.' But I was hurt he knew more than me. Unsettled generally.

'How is Letty?' I asked, changing the subject.

He sighed, leaned back in his seat. 'Not good. Since Dominic died, she and the bottle have become inseparable.'

'Since before Dominic died,' I corrected quietly.

He frowned. 'I don't think so.'

I let it go. I knew so. Knew the marriage wasn't happy, hadn't been for some time; had witnessed her drinking when I went down to the country when she was pregnant. I knew Dom worried about it, had talked to me often about it, blamed himself for being away too much. But I wasn't going to go into that now. Wasn't going to rain on the Forbes marriage any more than I had already.

'And Cassie gets scared being alone with her.'

'I'm not surprised. That's not funny for a teenager.'

'So I'm trying to persuade Letty to sell up. Buy something smaller in London, where I can keep an eye on her, and where Cassie can be amongst friends and near me, not isolated in that house.'

'Oh. Well, you should know you've been cast as the baddie, locally. Trying to prise a poor widow from her house, her capital.'

'Bollocks. I want *Cassie* to have some money, before Letty drinks it all. And I want Letty to get proper help, go to AA, make friends, get a job perhaps. Not fester in that remote farmhouse drinking herself to death because she's lonely.'

I regarded him across the table. A good man. An honourable man. Always had been. A steady hand on the tiller. Yes, I'd missed his steer in my life. I felt an ache of regret.

'And now you're getting married,' I said lightly, apropos of nothing.

He held my gaze, which admittedly might have had something challenging in it. Inclined his head in acceptance of this fact, but said nothing.

'You've left it late?'

He threw back his head and laughed. A sudden, throaty, lusty roar I remembered of old.

'I like that! You haven't managed it at all!'

'Ah, but I've had baggage,' I grinned. 'I'm an unmarried mother, remember? Tarred and feathered.' I made a cross with my fingers as if to ward off vampires, and anything else.

'Ah, yes, Seffy. Your Good Excuse.'

He did know me well. But I wasn't deflected so easily.

'What's your excuse, Hal?'

He shifted in his chair and his eyes darted into his wine for a moment. Then came up to meet mine.

'Let's just say I never got round to it.'

'But you're getting round to it now.'

'Yes, I am now.'

'After how long?'

'Excuse me?'

'How long have you been going out together?'

'Oh. A few years.'

'Right. And engaged?'

'For three.'

'Three years! Why so long?'

He looked uncomfortable. 'We were going to get married last year, but her father died. So we put it off.'

'Oh, OK.'

'And then I had a big litigation case in Paris, which took me away for four months, so the wedding was put on the back burner again.' He shrugged. 'Just one of those things.'

I nodded, but it occurred to me to wonder why one couldn't pop back from Paris to get married? Hardly Dar es Salaam.

'Céline … wanted to have a long honeymoon in Mauritius,' he explained, reading my thoughts. 'I couldn't afford the time.'

'I see. And now?'

'Now?'

'Well – when's the wedding?'

'November.'

'And you'll get your honeymoon?'

'I guess.'

A pause.

'And it's going to be round the corner? I mean, the wedding? In Fayence?'

'That's it.'

'So where is she now? Céline?' Blood from stones. Teeth from heads.

'She's in London. We work for the same law firm – that's how we met. She's in the middle of a deal at the moment, so she's at our house in Holland Park.'

'Ah.'

What a nice life they led. Two glamorous, corporate lawyers, pots of money, two houses, one here, one in London, holidays in Mauritius … Not for the first time I wondered what I'd been doing with my life.

A waiter came to recharge the bread basket.

'*Une autre?*' He indicated the empty wine bottle.

I could have easily downed another, but Hal shook his head. 'I think we're done here, aren't we?' He looked at me.

'Absolutely,' I agreed.

'*L'addition, s'il vous plaît.*'

*

Later, as we strolled up the old cobbled street together, threading our way through the crowds towards the square, he nodded at my hotel.

'You're over there?'

'Yes,' I said, surprised. 'How did you—'

'I saw you come out,' he said quickly.

So he'd watched me all the way to the café. Had let me sit down before revealing himself. I had the feeling he could have kicked himself for saying that. He'd changed the subject now, this clever, corporate lawyer who'd tripped himself up. No. That was pitching it too high. I listened as he told me about the finer nuances of owning a house in France, the baffling bureaucracy, and as he talked I wondered about Céline: chic, intelligent, bilingual, no doubt – beautiful certainly, for this man was a catch. This man. And of course, I'd only known the boy: gauche, cadaverous, slightly awkward, but always wise, always clever. As he raked his fingers through his dark hair now, in the midst of some tale of corrupt planners, it was a gesture that took me right back to the student union bar, where, as he held forth in some intellectual way, raking his hair, running rings around everyone, I'd sit back, pleased with my friend. See? Look how clever he is? I seemed to say. Even then he'd had huge potential, but I'd had my eyes on the more obvious prize, the finished article: brother Dom. No vision, you might say, which was odd, considering I had plenty in other areas. Show me a wreck of a house and I'll mentally be knocking walls down, throwing up RSJs, yet Hal had passed me by. It was astonishing how like Dom he was now, aside from the hair colour, of course. But there was something else missing too. It came to me with a jolt. The smoothness.

Hal had charm, but no sugar coating. He wasn't fly. Shocked to find myself thinking of Dominic in anything like a critical manner, I attended to what Hal was saying, about his plans to get round the planners, build a pool.

'You could always get them over for a drink?' I suggested. 'Isn't that how everything's done in France, over a bottle? Pass around some foie gras nibbles?'

'Or maybe just a bowl of euros?'

I laughed. We'd reached my hotel now. A silence ensued as we came to a halt in front of it.

'Have dinner with me tomorrow night,' he said casually. We were standing under a balcony dripping with bougainvillaea and jasmine: the scent was heady. His slanting brown eyes gave nothing away. I hesitated. Then smiled.

'Why not? I'd like that.'

'Good. I'll come by at about eight.'

'Eight, it is.'

'Good night, Hattie.'

He took a step towards me, I thought to kiss my cheek, but instead, he reached out and gravely adjusted the collar of the thin linen shirt I was wearing, turning it the right way out.

Why should that small gesture rock me?

A moment later he was gone – into the crowds, the swirl of tourists, the still dark night.

I climbed the stairs to the second floor and let myself into my room. The first thing I did was to go to the window and throw it open, wanting more of that night air and bustle in the musty silent room. The second was to turn, cross to the bathroom, and look in the mirror. In the stark, overhead light, my cheeks were flushed, my eyes alight. Could have been the wine.

17

The weather held for the fair, and the following morning found me having breakfast on the hotel's terrace. It was slightly raised and fronted the bustling square, an excellent vantage point and one I knew of old. I was perfectly placed. Dipping my croissant into a bowl of *café au lait*, I watched as under a milky blue sky, trestle tables formed in a giant horseshoe on the cobbles, then steadily filled up as, bit by bit, treasures appeared from the back of old Citroën vans and trucks.

At the stall nearest me, an old man dressed in *bleu de travail* staggered under the weight of a huge and elaborately carved mirror, almost tipping him backwards. The glass was badly pitted, but it was clearly original, and worth a look, I decided, as he set it down shakily. Some terrible old carpets appeared next from his motorized Aladdin's cave, principally, it seemed, for his mongrel dog to curl up and sleep on; but then, not a bad wall clock with a decorative, chinoiserie face. I made a mental note to go there first. Already, though, I felt my mind wandering.

At five to nine we were under starter's orders. I drained my cup and got to my feet. The next few hours were spent in a mechanical and practised fashion, darting from stall to stall, arguing, haggling, expressing surprise and disgust at the prices, walking away as arms were raised behind me in disbelief, returning to haggle some more, and eventually, securing some beauties. A seventeenth-century lit bateau, a wrought-iron campaign chair, a marvellous pristine set of monogrammed linen sheets – these were amongst my finds. But for all my delight in securing them at decent prices, I knew my mind was chiefly on the evening ahead. Supper with an old friend: a much overdue catch-up. What could be nicer? Why, then, was I already wondering what to wear? How smart the restaurant would be – I had only jeans or my denim skirt – if I had time to nip to Aix for a skirt. Wondering what *he'd* wear, and generally feeling like a girl on a first date.

Get a grip, I told myself as I got out of the bath sometime later, rubbing my hair with a towel. Being short, that was all it needed, but nevertheless, I wished I'd brought a hair dryer. I'd already searched the room to no avail – it wasn't exactly a hotel, more a bar with rooms – and I wondered if I could nip downstairs and ask Madame? Don't be silly, no need, I told myself sternly. I none the less paid special attention to my fringe, which happily flopped dutifully into my eyes, poker straight.

How changed would he find me, I wondered as I gazed critically at my reflection in the mirror. Of course, men matured nicely, and he had, but surely my eyes, which I'd outlined with a touch of mascara, were still bright? My skin clear and mercifully unlined? Surely I'd pass muster? I pressed my lips together as I applied some gloss: left it at that. There. At least I didn't need the Ivan faceful. At least I knew Hal well enough to know he didn't like make-up, favoured serious, well-scrubbed girls, or at least, he had. I found myself wondering about Céline, though, as I dressed – no time to go into town, so jeans and a white smocky top. A lawyer. A Frenchwoman. She wouldn't be scrubbed, would she? I seized a jacket nervously before I went down, even though it was warm, and caught a glimpse of myself in the long landing mirror as I went. Well, what he was getting tonight was an old friend: jeaned, espadrilled, no frills.

He was waiting in the bar downstairs, as somehow, I knew he would be, talking easily to Monique, the *patronne*: fluent French, of course, which even after all these years I still hadn't mastered. But then he lived here. Well, had a house here. He turned as I approached.

'Hattie, hi.'

How easily he got up from the barstool, put an arm around my shoulders, drew me in to lightly kiss my cheek. Not the awkward Hal of old, hunched at a table in the library in that terrible old greatcoat, hair needing a wash, not even looking up as I plonked my books beside him and informed him I'd had a rubbish day and now a bitch of an essay to do, as he told me to lower my voice or we'd get thrown out. No, here, in a French bar, wearing a pink linen shirt, a blue cashmere sweater thrown casually around his shoulders, his tanned face was creasing into a lovely smile as he offered me a drink.

'Or shall we get on? We could have one there, if you like?'

'Sure, let's do that,' I agreed, not wanting to be under Monique's interested gaze, and feeling, surely, like the one in the greatcoat as I lumbered after him, wishing I'd packed some heels.

The car, naturally, was a convertible Italian jobby, and as we purred out of the square very close to the ground, I found myself lifting my thighs off the seat to make them look thinner, something I'd done with Dom in a very similar car, I realized.

'OK?' he called above the roar of the engine. 'Or d'you want the roof up?' His hand went to a button on the dashboard.

'You mean to protect my hairdo?' I yelled, patting my cropped locks ironically.

He laughed and shrugged as if to suggest some girls might and, once again, I glimpsed Céline.

Little did he know, I thought, settling back into the leather, that I had a cupboard full of decent clothes back home and could be as committed to good grooming as the next Parisian lawyer, if I felt like it. The fact that I didn't have to now was actually very relaxing. Was it always like that in a relationship, I wondered as the wind whipped through my hair. Someone making the effort, whilst the other party relaxed? I had the impression Hal had made an effort to seek me out, and it was not an unpleasant feeling to be in the courted shoes for once. In fact, as we left town and golden stubble fields swept by under a low sun, flickering on and off like a searchlight as it disappeared behind trees, I let my thighs spread defiantly on the seat.

Where are we going, was what I'd been about to say, when instead I caught my breath. We'd abruptly taken a left fork down a road so bumpy I had to hold the seat to steady myself. An old man wobbled on his bike beside us, knees at right angles to the wheels. Hal slowed down.

'*Bonsoir, Claude – ça va?*'

'*Ah, oui.*' The old man's livid face creased like a cheaper cut of beef as he smiled and we inched our way beside him down the potholed lane. '*Ça va!*'

'*Très mal, n'est-ce pas?*' Hal indicated the road.

'*Mais non, c'est charmant!*' Claude roared with laughter; had to pause his bike, in fact, to wheeze heartily. Hal smiled grimly as we bumped on, through fields of beefy white Charolais cattle.

'I swear to God this is the next thing I do,' Hal told me. 'The very next thing. I'll tarmac it from top to bottom, if needs be, Surrey style, with nouveau iron gates, which of course is what he wants.' He grimaced as the car hit another rut.

I glanced at him, surprised. 'This track is yours?'

'And Claude's. That's his farm down there.' He pointed. 'But the last thing Claude Labert is worried about is his tractor tyres or his bike so, naturally, it's down to me.'

'We're going to your house?'

'Is that OK? Everywhere else is still so touristy at the moment and I thought you might prefer it.'

'Oh, I'd love it!' I enthused. I really would, actually. Would love to slot the pieces of Hal's life together, but also knew, implicit in our coming here, was Hal's wanting to show me. He must be aware I knew that, but it didn't seem to bother him. I glanced at his profile, calm and impassive at the wheel. Well, after all, he was getting married in a few weeks, that surely gave him the impunity to bring any number of old friends back to his place while Céline was away. Would I mind, I wondered, if I were Céline? Obviously I'd be beside myself if it were Ivan inviting anyone: would stress and neurose about it for weeks, wonder exactly what sort of an old friend it was, as I had done when I saw his hand cover that girl's on the table in the bar. I shifted in my seat. But perhaps successful corporate lawyers were more mature. Perhaps they entertained numerous friends. They must take clients out constantly – Glyndebourne, Goodwood … Indeed, Hal was picking up his phone from the dashboard even now, glancing at a text, smiling. What did it say? 'With Jacques B. at La Coupole again. On his second plate of oysters – merde Cx' – or something equally urbane and sophisticated? I sighed. The only Other Man I ever had lunch with was Christian, and that was a Prêt à Manger sandwich, if I was lucky.

Hal's house nestled in the fold of a hill, in an idyllic spot in the valley. Vineyards rose up behind it in steep, geometric lines and before it, in long meadow grass, a gnarled olive grove made a more tumbled, haphazard picture. The house itself was stone and flat-fronted, with tall thin windows and streaky grey shutters. It had that slightly guarded, arrogant look French houses have. It was perfect and I told him so.

'Hal, what's happened to you?' I said as I got out and gazed around. 'You've gone all tasteful.'

'Oh, thanks!' He laughed, relieved I was making fun. But then I'd always known the way forward: knew instinctively how to lighten the indelible fact of his bringing me here. 'You mean I never was before?'

'Never. Not one ounce. Your clothes were dire. Remember that fur hat that looked like a dead cat?'

'I loved that hat! Bought it in St Petersburg. Still got it somewhere, actually. I'll dig it out if you're not careful.' We were passing through the front door into a cool flagstone hall.

'No, thanks. Remember when I tried to burn it?'

One bonfire night, pissed and giggling I'd run out of the pub, across the road, and into the recreation ground that was hosting our local firework party. Hal was running after me, roaring with indignation as I'd pretended to toss it in the flames. He'd caught up with me and seized me from behind, clamping my arms down, both of us gasping with laughter, an organizer bustling up to shoo us away – 'Bloody pissed students!' Hal, with his arms tightly round me, the closest we'd ever been physically, his face, as I turned, in the light of the flames, on fire too. Why was it that night, of so many, that I'd reached for and tossed between us, like that old hat, on this still warm night so many years later? Instinctively I saved us, reminding him of my own legendary good taste, even in those days; inviting him to scoff.

'Yours!' he spluttered. 'You used to go to parties in silver lurex tights and one of your father's old shirts.'

'That was actually a Bad Taste party, Hal, which, if you recall, you attended as an airline pilot with a white stick.'

'Inspired,' he grinned, as we sailed under an arch into a room full of squashy cream sofas and bright rugs. 'At least I'd given it some thought. And the white stick came in very handy later, if you remember.'

I'd gone into town with some hero dressed as Hitler, but Hitler had turned amorous outside the chippie, and when Hal came to find me at two in the morning the white stick had kept the dictator at bay as we'd legged it and flagged down a taxi.

Hal was crossing to open the French windows now, reaching up for the lock, his back to me. I ran a practised eye around the high-ceilinged room. The beams were all painted cream in the Provençal way – no zebra effect here – and the blue and white ticking-covered chairs I'd have chosen myself. The doors he flung wide issued onto an achingly pretty terrace, tumbling with Mediterranean plants, and a shimmering view of the hills beyond. No wonder he'd wanted me to see it.

I followed him out. Centre stage on the terrace was a table laid for two: napkins, flowers, the lot. For a moment I was lost for words. Hal was doing better. Pulling a cork from a bottle he'd plucked from an ice bucket, he was accusing me of sluttishness now, saying he couldn't really believe I was an interior designer.

'Your room in Edinburgh was a complete tip, as far as I remember.'

'No it wasn't, it was organized chaos, very arty.' He'd set the table and rigged up the ice bucket? My mind was busy as I sat down. 'And no worse than Kirsten's. Yours was just ridiculously tidy, Hal, verging on the anal. Don't you remember all your pens and pencils had to be lined up in strict formation on your desk? Does that still upset you?' I reached forward and messed up the knives and forks, as I used to mess his immaculate desk.

He smiled. 'Not as much as it used to.' He poured me a glass of wine and put a bowl of olives, little artichoke hearts, and tiny slices of cured ham between us. 'Your starter,' he warned, sitting down. 'So what type of houses do you do?'

I felt stupid with the haphazard cutlery before me and moved it back surreptitiously. If he wasn't embarrassed by the effort he'd made, why should I be?

'Whatever I can,' I answered truthfully, then wished I hadn't. Wished I'd stuck to skittishness. 'This looks delicious,' I said quickly, popping in an olive. 'Did you do it?'

'God, no.' He laughed. 'I'm pretty ham-fisted in the kitchen. I've got a housekeeper – she left it for me. There's some cold duck breast too.'

Questions crowded my mind. Is the housekeeper here when Céline is here? Do neither of you cook? Are you both so high-powered you don't need to, or do you banish the housekeeper when Céline is back and she rolls up her Dior sleeves and makes perfect profiteroles? It seemed indecent to ask just yet, and anyway, we were still on my life, which seemed to be shrinking by the moment: with every perfect glass I picked up, every which way I turned, glimpsing more beautiful rooms.

'Is it the sort of thing you see in magazines?'

'A bit,' I hedged. 'But magazine coverage is quite spasmodic. *Country Living* did an article about us a while ago, though.'

'I don't know that one. Céline gets something called *Interiors* sent from England.'

Yes she would, wouldn't she.

'Oh, yes, and of course, *Interiors*,' I couldn't resist.

'Really?' He looked interested. 'That's pretty ritzy, isn't it?'

'Pretty,' I agreed. 'And quite time-consuming too, so we don't always say yes.' Now I was turning down *Interiors*?

'But sometimes you do?'

'Well, publicity's always good for business. Not that we need much these days; our reputation pretty much goes before us.'

I was rather pleased with the way that had sailed out of my mouth. And after all, I hadn't said it was a great reputation, had I? He wasn't to know Maggie and I had not one, but two little disputes ongoing in the small claims court: one with a woman who hadn't realized the cherubs on her toile curtains were going to be naked and frolicking, and in her view pornographic, and another with a client who'd complained the distressed kitchen cupboards we'd done for her whilst she sunned herself in Marbella were too distressed. Positively weepy.

'Which edition?'

'Sorry?'

'Which *Interiors* did you do?'

'Oh, way back. Last winter,' I said quickly, sensing a recent copy might be lurking on one of those elegant coffee tables.

'Jan? Feb?' He was on his feet now, going inside to a veritable stack, under a table. It looked like a year's worth. My mouth dried as he crouched.

'Um, yes. But actually, I think it was the year before,' I mumbled. 'It was ages ago.'

'Oh, OK.'

He moved around to another pile, because of course the refined and organized Céline kept, as I did, all her precious copies from years back. I gazed, mute, as he ran his finger down the spines for the requisite month. I seemed to have swallowed my tongue. It tasted rank. As he pulled out a couple of copies, I found my voice.

'It was … American *Interiors*.'

He turned, magazines in hand.

'Yes, they love the French angle, you see,' I gabbled, 'being so … American. And as I say, it's all rather overdone in London. But in the States – God, they go crazy for us.' I rolled my eyes and shuddered, as if hordes of crazy Americans mobbed Maggie and me whenever we got off a plane at JFK. Black-and-white footage of the Beatles in a similar predicament sprang to mind.

'You go there a lot?'

My voice sounded unnatural. 'Whenever we can spare the time. But of course there are lots of Americans living in London,' I finished lamely. 'We have enough work at home.' And who wants to be jetting off to Madison Avenue or Beverly Hills, I seemed to be suggesting, when we can get the number 319 to Streatham Hill and rag-and-drag someone's spare room?

I felt weak. Lunged for my wine. Popped another olive in.

'So how many shops have you got?'

I nearly choked on the stone.

'One. Just the one shop.' Had he always been this nosy? 'Which I share with my partner, Maggie. The one you met in the village, remember? You'll love her.' Would he necessarily get to know her? I felt hot. Became garrulous to compensate for nerves. 'She's lovely, very outspoken and forthright, and she's always got a bee in her bonnet about something. At the moment it's people who let their dogs foul the pavements. She keeps a poop scoop in her bag, scoops it up, then runs after them saying, "I think you forgot something!"'

'Quite bold.'

'Oh, she's fearless. She's a bit older than me and she's convinced HRT is the secret to eternal youth, but her doctor won't give it to her 'cos she hasn't got any symptoms, so she's constantly banging his desk demanding it, claiming she's having hot flushes and things. The other day she sat in his waiting room bundled up in coats and scarves and when it was her turn, she threw them off and ran in saying, "See? Take my temperature. See how hot I am – phew!"'

Hal laughed. 'So did she get it?'

'No, he won't budge, so she's working on the mood swings now. Sunny smiles one minute and murderous rage the next – not hard at our age. Well, her age. She's a bit older than me, as I said. Ten years, ish.' Five, in fact, and would she ever forgive me? For telling a complete stranger her most personal details? Easily. Maggie told everyone her most personal details, and was vociferous on this topic: 'She's definitely on it,' she'd hiss as a Joanna Lumley type swept into the shop, or, 'See the alternative?' as a Nora Batty type shuffled out.

'And of course Margaret Thatcher swore by it,' I rambled on. I couldn't quite believe I was still running with this. 'Only needed four hours' sleep a night.' Hal was clearing the plates. I got up to help. Why weren't we tumbling over our words as we had been in Montauroux? Why was this more difficult? No teeming streets, of course, no background chatter. I followed him inside. 'But as I say, she's a bit older than me – Maggie, I mean. My Maggie, not Maggie Thatcher. Well, Maggie Thatcher is too, obviously. She must be— Oh.' Happily I was stopped in my tracks. 'Is that Céline?'

I'd been passing a walnut sofa table at the time, crowded with photographs. The largest of them was of Hal, sitting on some lichen-covered steps, his arm around the shoulders of a girl of such astonishing beauty, it fairly took my breath away. A relief all round, I should think.

Hal glanced over but carried on walking, plates in hand. 'Yes, a friend took it last summer.'

I stared. Couldn't help it. She was gorgeous. Long, silky dark hair swept back off a heart-shaped face, leaf-shaped eyes, full lips. She was laughing into the camera.

'How old is she. Hal?'

'Thirty-two.'

Right. Seven years younger than me. Him too, of course, which was fine for men, quite usual. But perhaps not so usual the other way round. I might keep quiet about that.

'And Ivan?' he asked as I joined him in the kitchen. I nearly dropped the plates.

'How d'you know about Ivan?'

'Letty mentioned that your sister had said something.'

'Oh! How news travels.'

He shot me a sympathetic look. 'Well, you know how it is. If you're single and over thirty, family and friends see it as their positive mission to help you settle down.'

'They do rather, don't they?' It was nice to hear it from another single, albeit affianced, one. 'They're so flaming smug,' I added, slightly more fiercely.

He grinned. 'Marriage is the Holy Grail, as far as they're concerned. So if Hattie's got a young man …' He wiggled his eyebrows knowingly at me. I laughed.

'Yes, all right, he is young. A bit younger than me.' I left it at that. To be honest I didn't actually know how old Ivan was. Hadn't asked. In case it was horrific. And he hadn't volunteered. Which meant it probably was. At the thought of him, though, my heart gave an exultant little kick. Ivan was like a guilty secret: I wasn't used to airing him in public.

'Is it serious?' Hal was reaching in the fridge for the duck breasts.

'Um, yes. Yes, it is.' It was, to me. And I wanted to have something as serious as Hal. To Ivan? Probably not.

'Good,' he said lightly. 'That's good.'

Yes it was, wasn't it? I thought as I followed him back to the terrace, head held high, clutching the salad bowl. It was absolutely bloody marvellous. My life was marvellous.

Hal ran me home later in his groovy convertible car. I was wrapped in an overcoat he'd lent me against the wind, a silk scarf around my neck, my right hand huge and bandaged. There'd been a bit of an incident. During pudding – plums in red wine left by the housekeeper, delicious, naturally – Hal had taken a phone call; clearly work as he mentioned a merger, or a takeover, and also mouthed 'Excuse me' as he left the table. He'd withdrawn down some steps to the lawn below. I'd watched as he'd paced up and down, talking. Tall, broad, one hand in his pocket, against a background of purple hills under a starry sky, head bent: he'd looked … important. That was the word. I'd toyed with my plums. Drank some more wine, thoughtful.

On he'd talked and, after a bit, I'd gone to the loo. On the way back, eyes swivelling as I drank in the perfect house, I couldn't help looking at the photo of Céline again as I passed. Only this time, I picked it up. The frame, old cherry wood, had collapsed, come to pieces in my hands, the glass slipping out like a guillotine blade. It smashed in pieces on the floor. Horrified, I swung round, but Hal was still pacing about in the gloom. I'd crouched hastily to pick up the bits, and one large shard had sliced my hand quite badly, right down to the quick. I'm not good at blood.

Moments later, Hal was back and I was trying not to faint. Unable even to stagger to the loo, I was kneeling on the floor, moaning and swaying. There was a fair bit of blood as I'd attempted to stanch the flow with my other hand, so it looked as if I'd attempted suicide. Slit my wrists.

Hal had hoisted me to a sitting position in a ticking-covered chair, put my head between my knees, held my hand in the air and talked to me in a voice one normally reserves for the educationally subnormal. When I'd recovered sufficiently so as not to pass out, he took me to the bathroom and washed and bandaged me, whilst I apologized profusely for breaking his frame. He insisted it couldn't matter less, that it was ancient, and I explained that I'd gone back for a second look because I'd recognized Céline's top. Had an identical one at home, which I'd bought in Primark – no, Paris! – which was quite a coincidence, I'd thought. Hal had accepted this explanation as if it were watertight, but as I'd glanced in the bathroom mirror, I'd seen his face as he wrapped my finger: handsome, composed. And also, the face of a middle-aged woman. Flushed, mascara smudged, eyes over-bright, looking as if she'd been at the sherry.

When he dropped me at my hotel in the square, the lights were twinkling in the trees above and people were still drinking on the terrace outside. I wondered if I should ask him in for a nightcap. Wondered if I could claw back some ground, some dignity. Have a serious discussion about Simone de Beauvoir over a pastis. But just as I was about to suggest it, he was hailed by a corpulent Frenchman drinking on the terrace.

'*Alors – Hal!*'

Plucking his brandy glass, he came swaying down the steps to shake Hal's hand over my head. I tried to look alert and interested, but after a while, felt silly sitting there as they talked across me, even though Hal had introduced me. So I got out. Hal immediately shunted into first gear and shot me an apologetic but grateful smile, clearly keen to escape the garrulous Frenchman.

'Night, Hal,' I called. 'Thanks so much!'

'Night, Hattie.' And off he drove.

I watched him go with a bright smile and a cheerfully raised hand for the benefit of his rear-view mirror. But as I turned, my smiled faded instantly and I felt indescribably heavy.

Odd, life, wasn't it, I thought as I went slowly up the steps to the terrace. He'd clearly sought *me* out, tracked *me* down. Yet now – unsurprisingly, since I'd turned into a woman who lectured on dog shit and hormone replacement therapy, smashed up his home and bled all over his floor – he couldn't wait to get away.

As I went inside, feeling a little bit worse for wear, I raised my bandaged hand wearily to Monique and the clutch of antique dealers propping up the bar. Despite Porcelain Pierre's entreaty for me to join them, I declined, although it was undoubtedly where I belonged. With Madame Alain and the other singles. I'd slot in seamlessly as they drank the night away.

Instead, I climbed the stairs to bed, glimpsing my face in the long landing mirror: tight-lipped, preoccupied now. It occurred to me I'd blown it. Blown what? What was there to blow? Something unformed, about having unwittingly laid some ghost of Hal's to rest, sprang confusingly to mind. Something about how he could now, unencumbered by any wistful niggling doubts, get on with the serious business of marrying his beautiful young fiancée. But as I say, it was a hazy and ultimately rather arrogant thought, I decided. Giving myself a little shake, I put the key in the door and let myself into my single room to go to bed.

18

Maggie rang the following morning, as I was getting dressed. At least, I'd got to the underwear stage, but since today was a holiday – no fairs until the one further south in Fréjus next week – I was taking a leisurely attitude to the business of starting the day.

'So how's it going?' she demanded, but then Maggie did rather demand.

'Fine. I did pretty well yesterday, actually.' I snuggled back under the duvet, smugly aware that I had a few coups under my belt. 'Two lovely balloon-backed chairs for 42 Westgate Terrace, an entire set of Regency dining chairs for Lisson Grove, which completely match their Georgian table so she's going to be thrilled, and some fab mirrors for Laura. Oh – plus, an enormous armoire for their playroom, which I thought could house all the old board games that are strewn around. I thought we could make that room much more of a cool teenage sitting room? Like a den? There's also a really nice coffee table made from old tea chests, which I couldn't resist. You're going to be thrilled.'

'Good, good.' She sounded far from thrilled. Distant and tense, in fact.

I frowned into the phone. 'Maggie? Are you all right?'

'Bloody awful, as it happens. Henry and I …' At which point she burst into tears.

'Maggie?' I sat bolt upright, clutching the duvet. Maggie didn't do tears. Not like me, who filled up if I was told it looked like rain: her upper lip was so stiff it was in danger of petrifying.

Eventually there was a fair amount of throat-clearing and snuffling and then: 'Split up,' she croaked. 'It's over.'

'Oh.'

I was shocked, but not too shocked. Maggie and Henry had a precarious, and obviously clandestine relationship, which was doomed to failure. On the other hand, it had lasted nine years.

'Oh, Maggie, I'm so sorry.'

There was a pause as she got herself together. Then: 'Probably for the best,' she managed gruffly. 'I mean, as you always say, where's it going, apart from his way?'

'Still incredibly painful,' I sympathized softly. And I didn't want to take the blame for anything. 'What happened? What did he say?'

She sighed. Took a deep breath. 'He didn't. I did.'

'You finished it?'

'Not quite. But I gave him an ultimatum.'

'Ah.' Something she'd been threatening to do for years, but had never quite got round to.

'After I came off the phone to you the other day, I felt so wretched. A trip we'd been planning for weeks … my best friend, my business, my livelihood … and I just drop it. Drop everything. I wasn't proud of myself, I can tell you.'

I didn't say anything.

'So when he came round that evening, arms full of flowers, champagne, huge beaming smile, I just couldn't raise my game. And always, always when he's appeared before I've been able to, because I'm so thrilled to see him, and nothing else matters. Everything else is usually irrelevant, except him.'

'But not this time?'

'No. I told him I couldn't go on letting people down, letting myself down, feeling small and used and convenient, that it wasn't very nice and would he please mind telling me whether he ever truly intended to leave his wife. He sat down heavily and put the flowers on the floor, almost as if he were laying them on a grave, and said no, he never would. That she'd given him too much to be left – three children, a home, the ability to follow his glittering career – that he couldn't abandon her now.'

'Did he ever intend to?' I wondered aloud, thinking Maggie too had given a lot.

'I asked him that. He said, truly, in the beginning, when he was so in love with me – yes; said he wrestled with it daily, didn't see how he could live without me. But as the years went by …'

He realized he could. Maggie had become a habit, a routine. No longer fresh and exciting: she, in a way, had become a wife. His second one. But because she didn't come with children and a home, she'd been much easier to shed. I wondered if it had even been a relief.

'I almost think it was a relief,' she said, disconcerting me. 'Henry's a kind man. He'd never have hurt me if I hadn't instigated it, but when I asked him to choose, I swear I saw a cloud lift from his eyes. And the awful thing is, Hattie, I think I've known that for a while.'

'That he wanted out?'

'Yes. But knew he'd never do it. So I suppose I knew, as I paced the flat, waiting for him to arrive with his flowers and champagne, what the answer would be. And I know I've just burst into tears to you, and Lord knows I've been crying on and off for two days now, but actually, honestly, deep down …'

'You know it's right.'

There was a heavy silence.

'I'll miss him.'

'Of course you'll miss him.'

'I feel so bereft.'

'But you're not bereft, Maggie.' I could feel her wobbling again. 'You've got so much. A shop, a career, friends—'

'No, don't count them,' she implored, interrupting me. 'My blessings. I know what I've got, and believe me, it doesn't add up to a great deal. I've got no husband, no children, and at forty-four, never will have now. I'm scared, Hattie. I look into the future and see a great big void.'

'Well, no children maybe, but the husband – a man … For heaven's sake, Maggie, there'll be others!'

'But I had a man,' she said sadly. 'One I loved. I had Henry. I don't want others.'

'He wasn't yours. You never had him, Maggie. He didn't belong to you.'

'I know.' She sighed. 'And I always felt bad about that, Hattie, you know? Knew I was deceiving and robbing Davina.' I'd never heard her say her name before: only 'the neurotic' or 'the stick insect'. 'But I've been robbed too.'

I swallowed. I'd always felt that. That Henry had taken her best years. No – not her best years, but her last chance to have a family, at any rate. She'd met him when she was thirty-five: still gorgeous, not beautiful but very foxy and sexy – endless legs – and he was undoubtedly a terribly attractive older man. Handsome, wealthy, well connected, he was known to his set as Golden Balls on account of everything he touched: but not Maggie, it seemed. Because although she'd played the part of the glamorous girlfriend perfectly, she secretly wanted to be a wife. She would have married Étienne and had his children, and she would have married Henry and had his too, if he'd let her. But she'd been coerced into a different role: bundled from pillar to post, so that the girl who looked like she was in complete control really wasn't.

'Anyway,' she went on in something more like her normal tone, 'I'll be fine. Life goes on, and any other cliché you care to mention. And your sister's been sweet. I'm embarrassed to say I had a sob on her shoulder yesterday.'

'Oh – is that where you are?'

'Yes, I came down yesterday to see how Rod and Kenny were getting on, and she made me stay the night.'

'Oh, good!' Yes she would. Laura was kind like that. 'You told her?'

'I had a breakdown in the downstairs loo, which she overheard. She battered on the door until I came out. Forced me to spill the beans. I think she was a bit shocked.'

Not about Henry – she knew all about that – but that someone she regarded as a real toughie and was secretly scared of – just as Maggie was rather scared of Laura with her perfect life – should dissolve and open up to her. 'I always think she looks down on me,' Laura would hiss nervously whenever she came to the shop, as Maggie slipped haughtily away. I believe they envied and feared one another in equal measure.

'In fact your whole family have been wonderful,' Maggie remarked. 'Your mother has obviously already married me off to the local squire down here, who's about sixty, according to Laura, shaking her head across the table at me and mouthing "No".'

'Mum's there!'

'Oh, the entire clan. And under the circumstances, we had a very jolly dinner last night. Your father tells me, eyeing me firmly, that there's a lot to be said for the single life.'

I laughed.

'As does Kit, who's divine, incidentally. I can't think why you've kept him tucked away.'

'He tucks himself away,' I said quickly.

A lot of women – and men – had fallen for Kit over the years and been disappointed, for Kit didn't really bat for either side. Mum insisted he was just waiting for the right girl, but Laura and I weren't so sure. He was very much a spectator. Kit had more friends and more god-children than anyone I knew, and was happy for it to remain so.

'He's taking me out for a curry in Thame tonight, although your mother thinks we should go to the pub where the squire props up the bar. Hugh, on the other hand, thinks we should go behind the bar, because he says the landlord makes so much money swindling pissed locals I could marry him, divorce him in a year, and move to Acapulco on the proceeds.'

I smiled. She was raising her game, as she always put it, and I blessed my family for helping her.

'Maggie, stay there. Don't rush out here for Fréjus, I can cope. Stay and recuperate a bit.'

'I might, if you don't mind. That's what I was ringing to say. I don't fancy crossing the Channel on my own right now, might throw myself overboard. The magic pills I got from Dr Owen have surely got their work cut out.'

'You got them!'

'Oh, yes. I thundered into his surgery on Friday night with no appointment and thumped his desk so hard his paperweight had an involuntary snowfall. He leaped up and wrote me a prescription in the manner of a man with an AK45 at his head – surely preferable to a mad, menopausal woman with rotating eyes. I left with a year's supply. Popped at least six on the way out to make up for all the ones I've missed.'

I giggled. 'And?'

'Oh, according to the packet, the worry lines will disappear in a matter of days, the complexion become dewy, the thinning hair achieve bounce and my equilibrium and memory will all be miraculously restored. The theory is, that in a matter of days, shiny-eyed and with the body of a twenty-six-year-old, I shall sprint past Henry in Lillie Road and have him swivelling in disbelief as he rues the day.'

'And the reality?'

'The reality is I still feel like shit. The jury's out, Hatts. I'll let you know.'

I smiled and bid her goodbye: wishing her luck and loads of love.

I sat there in bed, hugging my knees. Maggie, as ever, five years my senior, was the trailblazer. The one having an affair with the married man, 'because,' as she'd airily put it, 'that's all there is left in the man-pool.' The one now popping the radiance pills. But it seemed to me, suddenly, I wasn't far behind. Wasn't aeons away, as I'd always nonchalantly told myself. Maggie was now in a place I would be too some day. Of course I had Seffy, but Seffy was a teenager, would soon be on a gap year, at university. Blink and he'd be gone. Back for weekends, obviously, and Christmas and Easter … but gone, effectively. And I'd be … well. I'd be building my business, with Maggie, in my house, which I adored, in a city I loved … I bit my lip. Blessings.

I sat, pensive, on the bed. My hand still hurt, but a plaster had replaced yesterday's bandage. I picked at it. After a bit, my reverie was broken. Footsteps came running up the stairs: then voices on the landing, arguing. I froze, arms locked around my knees. I recognized that voice. It sent a bucketful of adrenalin shooting through me, but it also had me leaping into action. I dived for the baggy T-shirt I slept in, pulling it over my head – just as the door flew open.

There, framed in the doorway, beaming broadly, blond, tanned and quite delicious, stood Ivan. Behind him, a breathless Monique was remonstrating with him angrily in quick-fire French, wagging her finger. She broke into English.

'I tell him no! I tell him you no down yet, you sleep and I no know him, but still he persist!'

Ah, yes, Ivan did that. Persist. I felt the blood pumping through me.

'It's OK, Monique, I'm awake. And actually, I was expecting him.'

Throwing up her hands with a '*Zut!*' she went away, grumbling.

Ivan shut the door behind him with a wicked grin. And a decisive click.

'Stay right where you are,' he commanded, eyes feasting about my crumpled person and the crumpled bed. 'I'm coming in with you.'

He put the flowers and the bottle he was holding on a table by the door, then, with a practised eye, crouched to a diving position and launched himself headlong. As I rolled to the left, he measured his length into an empty bed.

'Oi!' He demanded into the pillow as I got to my feet. 'What's going on?'

'Lovely to see you, Ivan, but I'm getting up and having a shower.'

'Then I'll have one with you!' he roared, as in one fluid movement he was up and after me, following me to the bathroom.

'You will not.' I turned at the door, kissed him firmly on the lips, then shut and bolted it behind me.

'What kind of a welcome is that?' he bellowed through it in mock indignation. 'I've just driven eighty miles!'

'I kissed you!' I yelled back as I reached in to turn on the shower and let it warm up. 'What more d'you want?'

There was a pause, then: 'Where would you like me to start?' In gleeful anticipation. 'Shall I run you through my entire, hectic schedule, or just point out the highlights?'

'No,' I laughed. 'You will not. And when I come out, Ivan, it's breakfast I'll be wanting, not sex.'

'Who said anything about sex? Just a little cuddle!'

'Not even that.'

'I brought you flowers!' he wailed. 'Champagne!'

'I saw,' I said, as I got under the hot stream of water and turned my face up to it.

Just as Henry had.

A few minutes later I got out and towelled myself dry, rubbing my short hair, which could dry in the sun in the square, I decided, where I fancied a coffee and a croissant. My T-shirt and jeans were already in the bathroom so I quickly pulled them on and reached for my make-up bag. I was about to apply my usual faceful, when I regarded my reflection soberly. A few laughter lines around the eyes and mouth, the skin not quite as taut and peachy as it once had been, but hey. I heard the door go next door; rested the heel of my hand on the side of the basin. Had he disappeared in high dudgeon? Unlikely. After a moment, I replaced the eye shadow in the bag, applied a touch of mascara instead. Then I slicked on some clear lip loss and came out.

Ivan was lying on the bed, hands clasped behind his head, long legs stretched before him, looking over-innocent. Beside him on a tray, was the champagne and a jug of orange juice. A single sweet pea lay alongside. He patted the bed gently.

'Sure you won't change your mind?'

'Quite sure, thank you.'

'I've got you your breakfast.'

'Don't fib.'

He reached down beside the bed and produced a baguette, complete with a saucer of butter and jam, all clearly nicked from Monique's basket downstairs. He patted the bed again; eyebrows waggling. 'Tempted?'

'Not in the least, thank you. I want breakfast in the square.'

He sat up, blinked. 'I want, I want … You're a very demanding woman.'

'That's me all over. Sorry.'

He watched me cross the room to collect my handbag. Then he flopped back on the bed, clamped the French stick bolt upright between his legs, and stared at it in mock horror. 'But what will I do with this!' he wailed.

'We might have it at lunchtime,' I promised, managing to suppress a smile as I made for the door.

'Really?' He brightened.

'Possibly.' I reached for my door key.

'It's only fair to warn you, it'll be very hard by then.'

'That's a risk I'm prepared to take.'

He sighed; hauled himself off the bed, tossing the bread stick behind him.

'Heartless wench. All right, lead on Macduff. Where are we going, anyway? I mean out, obviously, which I consider an entirely retrograde step when I could be cuddling up to your delectable self in here, but which of the teeming, heaving eateries out there do you favour?' We clattered downstairs as he grumbled on. 'As opposed to a morning of splendid isolation, spent in that dear little lit bateau, with yours truly?'

I linked his arm as we emerged in the sunshine. 'We'll play it by ear.'

In the event we plumped for the smallest, quietest café in the corner by the church, where we sat in the dappled shade of a plane tree. Ivan chatted about his acquisitions in Montpellier – pretty good, considering there were still so many tourists about paying ridiculous prices for things one would normally get for a song, and also he'd done particularly well in the flea markets of Nice.

'Exhausting, though.' He slumped back in his chair and ruffled the back of his blond head, looking tired. 'Too many people, too many rip-off hotels, and a great deal of tat. But happily, one or two finds.'

'Such as?'

'An Aubusson rug in St-Paul-de-Vence?'

'Sounds good. Needs work?'

'A bit, but I know a man who can. Oh, and a secretaire from St-Maximin, which I'll French-polish and restore myself when I get home.'

Ivan was a bit of a craftsman on the sly. He secretly dreamed of a workshop: a sawdusty, sunbeam-lit environment with a bench full of lathes and tools, restoration projects always on the go. I'd never seen anyone drool quite so lasciviously when he came upon an exquisitely tooled drawer, or a piece of inlaid marquetry, and although he trawled the French markets for fashionable, shabby-chic treasures like the rest of us, England was where his heart really lay: in the solid cabinetmaking of his homeland, where his hero, Chesterfield, had planed and lathed. In a bygone era Ivan would have been a cabinetmaker himself; in this era, where no one had the time or the patience to wait a year for a piece of work, he flogged them. I always thought it was a shame he hadn't gone to college and learned the trade properly, and for his birthday – no, I don't know which one – I'd bought him an antique plane. He'd been speechless.

Baubles, however, as he disparagingly called them, were what sold on his particular stand just off Camden Passage – he only had space for one piece of furniture on which he spread the jewels – and in St-Maximin, he'd had a lucky find. A fabulous old garnet ring, which he was convinced was Louis Quinze.

'What d'you think?' He drew it out of his pocket and we peered at it in the dappled sunshine.

'Could be,' I agreed, holding it out to catch the light. 'The gold certainly looks old enough, and it's got some sort of mark inside too.'

'Ees come out of a cracker!' wheezed a fellow trader, Ricard, who'd come to join us. He pulled out a chair and sat down heavily. 'Twenty euros from Monsieur Devreaux in Rue de la Concorde. Am I right?'

'You're wrong, actually, Ricard,' said Ivan, pocketing it. 'But how lovely to have the pleasure of your unsolicited company. Will you be sharing our repast as usual?' He offered him the croissant basket. 'But not the bill?'

Ricard roared with laughter, skin like that of an old rhino, and, stretching across, helped himself to a cup of coffee. One of Ivan's Camden Passage cronies, Ricard was a character to be tolerated: he was also a competitive little Frenchman, and ignoring Ivan, whom he regarded as small fry, leaned in to quiz me mercilessly on what I'd found so far, pooh-poohing everything as junk, but his beady eyes giving him away. Particularly when I mentioned the mirrors.

'A pair, eh? I saw a pair of Napoleonic ones sell in Christie's for £60,000 last year. Not in that league, I suppose?'

I took a sip of coffee. 'Not far off.'

Sylvie, an Irish girl, also from Camden passage, pulled out a chair to join us. I'd only met her once, but Ivan and Ricard knew her well, and as she sat down, crossing the slimmest, brownest legs I'd ever seen, flicking back her long blonde hair, talking to Ivan since Ricard was ensconced with me, I felt that familiar pang I always experienced when a young girl cosied up to Ivan. Just chatting, he'd say casually later, with perhaps some reference to her vapidity. Not that Ivan was unkind, but he knew I was insecure. I knew they had adjoining stalls, though, and couldn't help wondering how he could resist her endless legs and sunny smile. Perhaps he didn't? Don't be silly, Hattie. Nevertheless I found myself reaching in my bag for my sunglasses. Those un-made-up eyes, which had seemed so frank and interesting in the gloom of the hotel bathroom, doubtless now looked tired and old under the glare of this Provençal sun, and beside the gleam and sparkle of Sylvie's laughing hazel ones.

'All *merde* and rubbish in Nice – and St-Paul-de-Vence, as usual,' Ricard was saying. I pretended to listen, but wondered, with a horrid lurch, if this was the girl I'd seen him with outside the Slug and Lettuce? Long blonde hair … I'd only seen the back of her then, their hands. But surely she'd been shorter? Less blonde?

Rattled, I dived into my bag again, this time for my lipstick, for a surreptitious slick. Sylvie turned to me with a smile.

'There's a plan to go down to St-Tropez for lunch. Dominique and Matt are going, and obviously Ricard too, if someone buys him lunch—' Ricard guffawed along with the rest of us. 'Are you and Ivan up for it?'

I liked the way she'd teamed us as a couple – not everyone did – and the way she'd asked me first. What I didn't like was the way she was getting up off her chair where she was obviously getting hot in the sun, pulling down her tiny denim skirt, which hardly covered her bottom, and reseating herself in the shade. It was the unconscious gesture of a beautiful young girl, irritated that her skirt was sticking to the backs of her legs, and rejigging it, unaware of the mesmerizing effect she was having on the men. Ricard watched, Gauloise stuck to lower lip with a lascivious, elderly eye: Ivan, it seemed to me, with untamed lust.

'Thanks, Sylvie, but actually, Ivan and I have already catered. We're having a French stick back at the ranch.'

Ivan's eyes, glazed in admiration at the endless legs, came round to meet mine in joy. I smiled into them, pleased I'd had that card in my hand. But as I pushed my sunglasses up my nose and crossed my legs, noticing my heels were cracked, I wondered, uneasily, just when my trumps would run out.

19

Early one morning, some days hence, Ivan and I were disporting ourselves in our habitually wanton fashion in a different location. Different town, different hotel room, this time in the Esterel hills, where we were poised to attend the final fair of the season. The final thrust, as it were. We were deeper south, so it was hotter, but luckily, our room had a roof terrace, which appealed to Ivan's al fresco nature, and which was hosting the morning's action. From this vantage point we had a glorious view of the rolling Massifs one way and, on a clear day, the twinkling Mediterranean the other, although not half as twinkling as the merry blue eyes that gazed down at me in my prone position. My own eyes, despite my increasingly déshabillée state, were firmly covered by the ubiquitous sunglasses. In these glaring conditions, they stayed resolutely in place, in true Jackie O/Posh Spice style, depending on your era – the former for me, definitely – and despite Ivan's entreaties for me to remove them. Recently I'd been known to run naked to the loo in them.

'But I can't see you!' he wailed, pausing a moment to try to whip them off.

'So much the better,' I muttered, reaching up and pulling his lips down to meet mine by the scruff of his neck.

One foot in a pot of bougainvillaea, another over a forty-foot precipice and hopefully not in the grave, I'd been in more comfortable positions. Despite the contortions, though, with lightning reflexes, I still managed to reach out and grab my mobile when it rang, in the pocket of my jeans beside me.

I stared at the number aghast.

'Oh God. Oh God, quick – geddof, Ivan,' I hissed. 'It's Mr Marshcroft!'

'Who's Mr Marshcroft?' he murmured, nibbling my earlobe. 'Can you shift that pot of mint, Hattie? It's going right up my nose.'

'Seffy's housemaster – quick!'

Being over eighteen – please God – and not the recipient of a private education, his formative years having been spent in a comprehensive in Soho, where his parents ran a patisserie, this didn't engender much fear in Ivan's breast. With a superhuman effort I kicked out wildly, so that with a grunt, he did at least shift sideways, enabling me to roll out commando style – in all senses of the word – and stagger to my feet. Grabbing a few shreds of clothing and pushing my specs up my nose, I fled to the bedroom.

'Mr Marshcroft!' I gasped. I dived under the duvet, thanking God telephonic technology hadn't quite got to the visual stage. 'What can I do for you?'

Through the French windows, Ivan was getting languidly to his feet like a tall, blond lion. He stretched his arms high above his head in a salute to the sun, then reached for his jeans. *Tot*ally gorgeous.

'Mrs Carrington, sorry to disturb,' Mr Marshcroft was saying. Never having had a Miss on his parent register, he was incapable of uttering it.

'Hattie,' I muttered as usual.

'Hattie,' he went on uncertainly, 'and nothing to be alarmed at, either.' This always rang huge great clanging bells in my head and I sat up straight. Oh God, what? How much alcohol, how peroxide was his hair, how sick, and more to the point, where? On one horrendous occasion at his last school, it had been on his housemaster's head.

'But Seffen spent the night away from school last night, which I'm afraid we have to take very seriously.'

I frowned. 'Away? What d'you mean? Where was he?'

'At St Hilda's.'

'St Hilda's!' The girls' school in the next town. Oh dear God.

'There was a social there last night, which we took a load of boys to, and Seffen managed to miss the coach back, yet, at the same time, got another boy already on the coach to cover for him. Both boys are being suspended for a week.'

I shut my eyes. Oh, Seffy. Oh, for God's sake. After all that's happened. All my entreaties. How could you?

'Well, of course,' I said, dry-mouthed, 'that's … extremely reprehensible. Although I'm sure – I'm sure there's a rational explanation …?'

'According to Seffen, he genuinely lost track of time. And somehow found himself miles away, which of course he shouldn't have been, in the grounds of the school.'

'With a girl?'

'Yes, with a girl. Who didn't make it back to her dorm until two in the morning. Seffen finally arrived here at three, having walked.'

'Oh – so he did make it back?'

'Eventually, but three in the morning does not, in my book, constitute the same night.'

'No. No, of course not.' My heart was pounding. I licked my lips. 'He was doing so well.' I said, in a small voice.

'He was, and will continue to do so, I'm sure.'

Mr Marshcroft was a decent sort: he knew Seffy's history, and was very much onside. I thanked him for that remark from the bottom of my heart.

'I've talked to Seffy, Hattie, and I do genuinely believe he missed the bus, and then panicked. Obviously he should have rung a member of staff instead of getting one of the boys to cover, but you do see, we do have to suspend him. To set an example.'

'Yes. Yes, of course.' I swallowed. 'Um, I'm in France, Mr Marshcroft, at the moment. But my sister, or my parents, will I'm sure collect him.'

'If you could make the necessary arrangements ...'

'Yes. Yes I will.'

I clicked the phone shut. Sat very still on the bed. All the fun and frivolity of the last few days turned to dust and ashes in my stomach. Suddenly the unexpectedly late September heatwave was too hot. The view, too shimmering and headache-inducing. The room, once a chaotic love nest, was now just a seedy jumble of clothes and bedding. Likewise the antics, the frolicking, the laughs with Ivan, running into the sea like children, having long lunches, too much to drink, watching the stars from the terrace wrapped in a blanket, all now seemed totally irresponsible. My son, aged fifteen, had spent the night walking eight miles in the dark, having been in the woods with a girl, whilst I'd been rolling around in bed, eating chocolate ice cream with my toy boy.

I punched out a number.

'Seffy.'

'Oh, hi, Mum.'

For some reason this nonchalant response completely threw me.

'Seffy, how could you?' I burst out. 'After all we've said, after all your promises, all we'd discussed – how could you jeopardize your position like this?'

'Oh, great. Nice of you to listen to my version first.'

'Your version! You were snogging in the woods with some girl – or worse – and missed the bus back! What else is there to listen to?'

'Well, thanks for your support, Mum. For that supreme vote of confidence. Nice to know you're there in a crisis.'

I swallowed; gulping down some air. Then I threw my head back and gazed at the ceiling, blinking as my eyes filled. 'I'm sorry. Sorry, my darling. I just ... What happened?'

'Like the man said, I missed the bus.'

'That's it?'

'Yes, that's it.' He was punishing me now.

'Right. Well, that's – that's understandable. You lost track of time.' Silence. Which Seffy was so good at.

'And – and we'll talk about it when I get back. I'll ring Laura, or—'

'I've already done it. Grandpa's coming.'

'Oh, you've—'

'Well, I knew you were in France getting all loved up. Didn't want to disturb.'

'Seffy, I am here on business!'

'Whatever. Anyway, Grandpa's coming. Gotta go, Mum. I need to see the head man.'

'Do you? Oh, Seffy, please please be contrite, apologetic. Not lippy. Not clever, please—'

'Crawl?'

'Yes! Seffy, we cannot afford for you not to. You've been suspended, for heaven's sake! That's incredibly serious.'

'Could be worse, as we both know. But, yeah, don't worry. I'll go in on my belly. Relax.'

Relax. Relax, he said. I clicked the phone shut. Then opened it again. I immediately rang Dad, thanking him profusely, assuring him I'd be back soon. I felt slightly calmed at hearing his steady, gentle tones.

'Don't worry, Hattie, all's well. I'll talk to the lad.'

And actually, he was the best man for the job, I thought. Better than me, who'd be shrill, hysterical.

Ivan appeared in the doorway, naked from the waist up. It didn't transport me.

'Problem?' He cocked his head, thumbs linked in the belt hoops of his jeans; leaned against the doorframe.

I nodded. 'Seffy's been suspended.'

He frowned. 'Oh. Drink?'

'No, thank the Lord. Not this time. No, he missed the bus back from a social at a girls' school. Walked back at three in the morning.'

Ivan threw back his head and laughed. 'Atta-boy! Nice one.'

'No it is not a Nice One, as it happens,' I seethed. 'The school takes a very dim view, and quite right too. He's fifteen, Ivan! Too young to be caught doing God knows what with a girl!' I was on my feet now, flying round the room; snatching up articles of clothing, throwing them on, struggling into linen trousers. 'And Seffy's on very thin ice as it is. This is all we need.'

'Yes, I agree, but it could have been an awful lot worse. Drugs, bullying … Getting caught with a girl isn't so bad. Could have been a boy.'

I swung round. 'Ivan, this is not funny, and until you have a child of your own, you'll never understand,' I spat. 'But then, you're far too much of a child yourself, aren't you?'

He blanched. 'Well, thanks for that.'

'My pleasure.'

I threw my passport in my bag.

'You're going?'

'Of course I'm going. Ivan, my son has been sent home! Suspended!'

'But the last fair's today, in a couple of hours. You could get what you want and then go back. Surely Laura or your parents could collect him. What difference does a few hours make?'

'The world of difference to me,' I snarled through gritted teeth, zipping up my bag with a flourish. 'If you think I can concentrate on Provençal china and bits of Luberon glass whilst Seffy—' I broke off: covered my mouth and swallowed a sob.

'What?' Ivan peeled himself off the doorframe. Came languidly in and sat down on the bed. 'Watches telly in Laura's playroom? With a bacon sandwich? Waits a few hours for his mother to finish her business trip and get back tomorrow as planned? Doesn't actually curtail her plans because he's been out of order? You've at least got a booking on tomorrow's crossing, unlike today, when you've got a sweltering ten-hour drive from here to Calais, and then how d'you know you'll get on the ferry? And what are you going to do when you arrive back in the middle of the night anyway – wake him up? Remonstrate with him? For heaven's sake stick to plan A and stop panicking.'

'Ivan, I am not panicking.' I swung around, fists clenched. 'All I know is Seffy needs me, right now. I feel it here,' I thumped my heart, 'OK?' I glared at him. 'And don't worry, I'll pay our way out of here.'

His face tautened with anger at this. That was uncalled for, unnecessary, and I knew I was lashing out, losing it, that I'd hurt him. But I'd snapped my moorings. I spotted a few bits of underwear under the bed, but my case was already zipped and overstuffed so I threw them in my handbag. I dragged my luggage to the door. Ivan watched in silence. Not, I noticed, offering to carry my bag out and downstairs to the lorry – no, he let me struggle on down on my own.

I arrived in reception in a heap and rang the little bell on the counter violently, meanwhile rooting in my bag for my credit card.

A beautifully coiffed madame appeared. She regarded me with interest, and I had the impression she'd been listening to the fracas on the first floor via her open reception window all along. Enviably chic, eyebrows raised, she attended to this stressed-out Englishwoman – crazy hair, crazy eyes, crazy clothes thrown on in a hurry, black pants showing through white linen trousers – who'd no doubt been jilted by her handsome young gigolo upstairs and was hurrying out to her lorry even now. Lorry! *Alors*, these English women, no style. She seemed to be trailing items of a personal nature too, as the zip on her overstuffed bag burst.

'*Madame, madame* ...' She tripped elegantly after me in pencil skirt and kitten heels, offering dirty underwear, a man's deodorant because these days I needed the extra protection it afforded. Taking them from her I glanced up and saw Ivan, leaning over the balcony, smoking a cigarette, calmly witnessing the scene.

Muttering my thanks to madame, who, I felt, was off to wash her hands pronto, I climbed into the cab. Thank God the lorry started – it didn't always – and thank God it was pointing in the right direction too, because a three-point turn in this vehicle was not easy. At least I could perform one, though, unlike Maggie, who, on one memorable occasion when I hadn't been with her, had got lost in the Dordogne, and simply carried on until she found a roundabout – sixty miles – which unfortunately was a mini one on a council estate, so she'd ended up in someone's sitting room.

I pulled out into a stream of traffic amidst blaring horns, and drove off down the dusty road. There. Thank God. At least I was on my way. At least I was doing something.

Five miles out of Valensole, though, I metaphorically hit my forehead with the heel of my hand. Madness. Complete and utter madness. Ivan had been right, of course he had. I shouldn't panic. I should go later, on the crossing I'd prebooked, not turn up and hope for the best. And of course there was nothing I'd be able to do when I arrived at four in the morning and Seffy was fast asleep. I should conclude my business here, and go tomorrow. Damn. What had I been thinking of? Well, half of me, I knew, had been acting on impulse: on knee-jerk, maternal reaction. The other half … what? Had been waiting for Ivan to take the lorry keys from me? Confiscate my passport? Some masterful gesture to force me into the Little Woman position? Was that what I wanted? I took a deep breath. Yes, sometimes, actually. Quite a lot, in fact.

On I drove. I tried to calm down. But it seemed to me all the scents of a Provençal autumn were sweeping through the open window like a cosh. An over-heady, over-evocative mixture of orchards, rosemary and thyme assailed my senses, swelled my head. Had I really been testing Ivan back there? And why was I angry with him, as well as Seffy? Because, like Seffy, he was still in short trousers, and what I really wanted was a man? Why? Why was I so incapable of making my own, rational decisions these days, as I always had done?

Suddenly I lunged impulsively – and dangerously – for my phone. Clicked it on. Battery low. In fact, battery non-existent. I glanced feverishly left and right for a handy turning place, getting hotter by the moment, hands damp on the wheel. But the road was long and narrow, and anyway, I couldn't go back now, could I? What would I say? I glanced at my watch. Apart from anything else, he'd be on his way to the fair. With Ricard ... Sylvie ... My tummy flipped. Was that why I was so furious? Because yesterday ... OK, yesterday his wallet had fallen out of his jeans, and when I'd picked it up and handed it back to him, a photo had slipped out. Just the corner, and all I saw was a girl's arm, that's all, but he'd stuffed it back in so quickly. He so obviously didn't want me to see ...

I put the mobile slowly back on the dashboard. Replaced my hand on the wheel. Suddenly it buzzed as a text came through. I grabbed it. It was from Ivan. Some of it was missing, but it was the usual sexual innuendo. Something about it being 'nice in back of lorry, kiss kiss.' I tossed it aside in disgust. Did he really think I needed that right now?

No, I did not. I set my jaw and drove on. What I needed was to pay attention to the road, which might be deserted, but was winding and bumpy, as French roads can be. And as so many other roads had been for me too. Suddenly I was back at the wheel of another lorry, my Bedford, in Croatia, rushing to the hospital, having heard that Ibby's family were dead. I caught my breath, wondering why that had sprung to mind. I never went there. Never. I gave my head an impatient little shake, and headed north.

Naturally the lorry had a puncture in a village just outside Normandy, and naturally it took hours at a local garage to get it fixed. Three men in overalls stood around shaking their heads, sucking their teeth, and muttering, '*Catastrophe…*'

By now it was evening and I was practically crying with exhaustion. I'd been driving for nine solid hours, and it was almost with a sense of relief that I was told I'd have to stay overnight and get the lorry fixed in the morning. The tyre was kaput: needed to be replaced. I left the lorry with the posturing mechanics, who were enjoying themselves now, grumbling about having to jack it up with all the furniture within, and actually discussing the possibility that I might have to unload it. I did what I always do *in extremis*, and threw money at it. Bade them take whatever steps were necessary, and repaired to a hostelry just off the square. Miserable with exhaustion, I trudged upstairs with yet another hotel key in my hand, to yet another empty room, and thence, to a hot bath.

Afterwards, wrapped in a towel, I rang Dad to tell him what had happened. That I'd be back tomorrow.

'That's fine, sweetheart, there's no rush. Seffy's here – we're at Laura's – he's just had some supper. There's nothing you can do, anyway. He needs to figure this out for himself.'

'And he's doing that?'

'Who knows? I haven't quizzed him. Just picked him up and brought him back here.'

Whereas I, of course, would have bombarded him with questions. Shrieked reproaches. I nodded; a lump in my throat.

'He used to be such a good boy,' I whispered.

I thought of all the prizes he'd won at prep school, all the glowing reports: 'Seffy is a credit to the school, both in the classroom and in his general conduct.' Up until a year ago or so, when it all seemed to go wrong.

'He's still a good boy,' said Dad firmly. 'He's just doing some growing up, that's all. It's a phase.' I nodded; couldn't speak.

'Oh, and Hugh's postponed his shoot till next weekend, by the way, so you won't be launched straight into that tomorrow.'

'Well, that's a relief. If I found a gun lying around I might be tempted to turn it on myself.'

He chuckled. 'Now that would be inordinately foolish. Relax, Hattie. All will be well.'

I nodded and put the phone down. Encouraged, actually. For when my Dad said all would be well, I really and truly believed it. Believed he would make it so. As he always had done, ever since I was a little girl. But Dad wouldn't be around for ever, I thought with a lurch. His steady hand on the tiller wouldn't always be there. And neither, at my stage in life, should it be the one I looked for. As I stood at the window in my dressing gown, looking out at the cobbled square from the semi-darkness of the room, I felt a cold hand reach in and squeeze my heart. Loneliness. Oh, I recognized it all right. It was a feeling I'd had increasingly recently, and one I dismissed, always. With a shake of the head, or a quick call to Maggie or Laura, for a laugh. But as I got into bed, it seemed to me my legs looked heavier. A bit more like Mum's. And as I pulled the covers over my shoulder and flicked back my hair, I knew one or two in the centre were grey now. Hardly any, the hairdresser assured me, you've got fantastic hair, but maybe a few highlights?

I found myself considering Hal's hair: quite grey at the temples, and he'd been so dark. But of course, it suited men. Made them distinguished. Added *gravitas*. And Hal had been quite gawky, as a youth. Well, he wasn't gawky now. And then I found myself wondering what my life would have been like if I'd gone out with him, as he'd badly wanted: taken that path in life, the sensible one, the one I knew deep down I should have taken. What if I'd married him?

Hal, with his half-amused, half-ironic smile. His watchful, clever eyes. I was amazed to find his younger self still precisely preserved in my mind, as if he'd been waiting there patiently all those years, for me to turn back the pages, and for him to step out. Yes, there he was at his desk in his room in hall, writing an essay. He had his back to me as I lay on his bed, chatting away to him, tossing a tennis ball up high, seeing if I could throw it so it didn't quite hit the ceiling. On he wrote. I complained about his music: Albinoni, always classical, couldn't we put something else on? The Jam? He'd say he couldn't work to that and I'd say – well, why was he working anyway? Because, he told me, if he didn't, he'd be up all night, as I would – why not do it now? Irritated, I'd throw the tennis ball at him, and with lightning reflexes he'd reach out and catch it, carry on writing, and oh my God, my God, it was so clear. Like a reel of film. And I'd felt so happy in those days, so carefree. I watched myself get languidly to my feet, saunter across to look at his books, wonder aloud how anyone could decipher those dry legal tomes: tease him. He'd grunted, failed to answer me, and then I'd been annoyed, I remembered: stomped out.

But now, years later, I liked the memory. Liked his single-mindedness, his drive, his ambition, which at times, I'd felt, had been too directly focused on me. I hadn't wanted to be under the same scrutiny he afforded his law books. Hadn't wanted those steady dark eyes to pick me out quite so precisely as he walked into the union bar. I wanted to be with my mates, having a laugh, not just alone with him. I wanted to tell him a girl couldn't withstand being made so significant, that it was suffocating. So when he came in, I'd get up and drag him across to join us at our jolly, beery table, even though I knew he wanted to sit alone with me, at a different table. Now, I realized, I'd like to be so significant. So cherished. And I'd like the classical music too. We could go to concerts, his arm gently guiding my back as we found our seats at the Wigmore Hall. Supper afterwards. I caught my breath in the dark, imagining this much, much safer place than the one I was in now. This dreary hotel room in northern France, waiting for my lorry to be fixed.

And then I slipped right down the precipice and imagined a lovely home, a family, a big country house. Children, ponies in the paddock, dogs in the boot room, like Laura and all her friends. My husband, like their husbands, a successful lawyer. Dinner parties, a little job – yes, still a job, still the interior designer, but with backing from my husband. No pressure. Not a big disaster if it doesn't work out, darling. No panic. That was it. That would be nice. Oh, and I'd shut for a month at Christmas while we went skiing, and in the summer too, while we were at our house in France. No, wouldn't shut, because my partner, Maggie, would take over. Maggie, who had to work all year round, who didn't have the option, the luxury, the cushion to break her fall. Wouldn't that have been nice, I thought as I shut my eyes, which I realized were wide open and staring, even though I was exhausted. Would still be nice.

Still my mind wouldn't rest, and I was *so* tired. Because now I was wondering, feverishly, whether Céline would carry on working. After children. Would she go back to the office in Paris in her Armani suit, having efficiently popped a baby off the breast, or would she, in a few years' time, be wandering around that glorious Seillans garden? Down there on those terraced lawns, beyond the olive grove, by the river, one hand holding a golden-haired toddler's, the other, on her slightly swollen tummy, barefoot and pregnant? Tears of self-pity gathered in my throat, as I realized it was all I'd ever wanted to be. Barefoot and pregnant. I wanted someone to take my shoes away.

20

The following morning, however, sunglasses firmly in place, sharp little white shirt over three-quarter jeans, I was Hattie Carrington, chic West London antiques dealer again, not the snivelling, self-pitying wretch of that hotel bedroom. Bangles jangling up tanned arms, Chanel No. 19 wafting out through the window, I was at the wheel of my lorry, getting the usual admiring glances from the other truckers as I rumbled up the ramp aboard the ferry. Never mind that there's more to life than getting admiring glances from six-bellied tattooed truckers. Never mind that I'd had to almost bribe the ferry port officials to let me on this boat, and not the one I was actually booked on, which sailed a mere two hours later. Oh, no, I couldn't get that. Out of the question. Not with the rest of the antiques gang, the likes of Ivan, Ricard and Sylvie, who'd no doubt worked the Fréjus fair brilliantly, got heaps of bargains under their belts, enjoyed a jolly lunch in town before packing up and driving *en masse* to Reims for supper and a stop-over, before a sensible three-hour drive this morning. I had to save *some* face. Had to pretend my desperate, pitiful flee from the hotel bedroom had been in some way worth it.

I sighed as I slammed the cab door and headed for the ship's stairs and upper decks. Thank God I'd forgotten my phone charger: thank God, for once, Ivan couldn't get in touch with me. For a woman who compulsively checked her inbox for text messages, rang 1471 to check her answer machine was working, and had been known to yell, 'Ring, damn you!' at her mobile, I was, for once, relieved to be incommunicado. Not to be answering awkward questions. Why, I wondered as I sat alone at the bar on the lurching ferry, watching my *café au lait* slop into its saucer. Why was my life like this?

I finally achieved Laura's house some hours later, via a circuitous route, that involved a stop at my house in London. There I'd had a quick wash and brush-up, and deposited the lorry, swapping my mode of transport for something more feminine. By the time, then, I eventually crunched up my sister's drive, with its splendid pleached limes and its sylvan views, I'd driven eight hundred miles in two days and was, frankly, shattered. Cranky, too. The calm, the quiet, the other-worldliness, the wood pigeon cooing tastefully from the treetops didn't soothe me as it usually would: in fact it's fair to say that for once I found the whole deeply privileged way of life downright irritating.

I parked at the front in the gravel sweep, got out and stretched my weary limbs, arms high over my head. Just then, I heard voices. I dropped my arms. Around the corner, I caught a glimpse of the tennis court, through the rhododendron bushes. Two boys in jeans, one of them Seffy, were knocking up. Oh, marvellous, I thought irritably as I shut my car door. Talk about the prodigal son. Bring him home to Auntie Laura's plush pad, and then arrange for a local lad to pop over and play ball. No doubt they'd be taking a dip in the pool later.

Maggie's car was in the drive too, which for some reason, annoyed me further. Still here. When what I really wanted was to conduct a family row in private. A row? No, I wasn't going to do that. Had vowed not to, remember? Something was undoubtedly bubbling up within me, though, and without troubling the house, I walked across the manicured lawn to the court to greet my son. Be nice, I told myself. Be calm. Smile. As I approached, the boys were picking up balls, their game clearly over, chatting amicably.

'Seffy.' My voice had unaccountably taken on a harsh, unattractive edge. Seffy glanced round, wary.

'Oh, hi, Mum.'

See? Again. That nonchalant: 'Hi, Mum.'

I opened the gate and walked in. 'Seffy, can you leave your friend to finish up here, please. We need to have a word.'

No, I would not be introduced, be made by Seffy to be polite and smiley: I would not be manipulated by the situation.

'Sure. Luca, can you manage? The balls and rackets go in that hut over there.' He pointed.

Luca. I was taken aback. Right back. I hadn't seen him for years. Had deliberately missed his last visit a couple of years back, finding him a sulky, shifty boy on my previous encounter. Yet here he was, this towering great lad, all tawny tousled hair and testosterone: a man almost.

'Oh – Luca.' I was covered in confusion as Seffy knew I would be. I felt his amused eyes on me. Fifteen love to my son. I reached for my manners. 'How marvellous to see you again. Gosh, it's been ages.' I advanced, hand outstretched. 'I'm Hattie, Seffy's mum. Laura's sister. You probably don't remember.'

'I remember,' he said, in his heavily accented English. We shook hands, and I glanced at the other one, the withered one – thank the Lord the left one, as Laura always said, so he could at least shake hands, so important for a man. It was still shrunken, but perhaps not quite so obviously as when he was a child. Had he seen me glance? I wasn't sure: but then I'd been wrong-footed. Forewarned, of *course* I wouldn't have.

The eyes, I noticed, still didn't meet mine. They slid away, dark and narrow, in a thin oval face, as Seffy's never did, even when he was caught with his trousers down.

'How lovely to see you,' I gabbled as it became transparent I couldn't just sweep Seffy away and leave Luca to clear up like the village boy I'd thought he was. And how ghastly was that? 'Are you here for long?' That sounded dreadful too, the implication being I hoped he wouldn't be, but then, as I said, I was thrown. Nervously, I began picking up the balls, stooping round the court like a baboon, or a cotton picker, whilst the boys leaned on their rackets and watched

'Yes, I stay about a month,' Luca said. 'My university course has an exchange year, so I am travelling the while, and staying a bit with my father.'

'Oh how marvellous!' I breezed as I scooped some more, thinking Seffy could at least *help*, and not stand arrogantly by. I staggered to the wire basket, up to my chin in balls, and dropped them in. Not one went in the basket. We watched as they bounced cheerfully around the court.

'Seffy, for God's sake – pick them up!'

He rolled his eyes. 'So-rry. You told me not to.'

'Well, I've changed my mind!'

I plastered on a smile. Then, embarrassingly, adopted Luca's own pigeon English, as sometimes happens when I address foreigners. 'And what is it that you are studying?' I asked slowly. 'At the university?'

He gave me a withering look. 'English.'

Of course. What else? Because in another few years he'd be here, installed in the house, lord of all he surveyed. And to run the estate properly, he surely needed the lingo. My heart lurched for Laura, with this ticking time bomb in her midst.

We were leaving the court now, heading across the lawns towards the house, and I felt my conversation dry up, because a natural question would be, what d'you want to do when you leave university? – and I couldn't think of anything else to say. Perhaps he sensed it.

'See you, Seffy.' He raised his racket, and giving me a sly, knowing smile, peeled off languidly in the other direction, past the rose garden, towards the stable yard. A bright red, low-slung slick of a car was parked there on the cobbles. I had an idea Ferrari was the word I was groping for.

'Yeah,' Seffy, raised his own in response. 'See you.'

I watched as, a sweatshirt over his arm, Luca sauntered off, plucking car keys from his pocket. Quite the dude. Not at all what I'd expected the awkward boy to grow into.

'What's he like?' I asked, curiosity getting the better of my own troubles.

Seffy shrugged. 'He's OK. He comes across as a bit pleased with himself, but when you get chatting he's all right.'

'Well, you're obviously chummy enough to have a game of tennis together?'

'Laura asked me to. I think she likes to get him out of the house. I could hardly say no, could I? Anyway, it was something to do.'

He bashed the ground with the head of his racket, and it occurred to me it wasn't as much fun as it sounded, being sent home from school. Which of course was why they did it. To concentrate the mind.

'I'm really sorry, Mum,' he said in a much smaller voice. 'It was such a stupid thing to do. I'm sorry I'm such a loser.'

Relief, love, joy, flooded my heart. That was all it needed. All it took, to stop me in my tracks, melt me, open my arms and hold him tight. We hugged, Seffy already towering above me, dark head bent. I could hear his heart hammering.

'You're not a loser,' I said fiercely. 'You just lost track of time, that's all.' I was instantly on his side. 'And I'm horrified they didn't do a proper head count, send someone to look for you. It is totally irresponsible of the teacher in charge to leave without you. Indefensible – and I shall tell them so.'

He shrugged and we walked on. 'Yeah, well, he's in the shit too, obviously, the beak. But we all make mistakes. I'd rather you didn't make a fuss, Mum.'

'No. No, well, all right.' I agreed. 'I won't, I suppose, if you don't want me to. After all, this isn't hugely serious, is it?' I glanced at him anxiously. 'You've only been sent home for a few days?'

'Till the end of the week, but then it's an exeat, so ten days in all.'

Of course, next weekend was an exeat, which helped. Everyone would be going back to school together: it was much more easily forgotten about. Seffy wouldn't be arriving back in a classroom suddenly. Ivan had been right, it could have been a lot worse. I breathed; started to relax.

'And the girl? Was she in big trouble?'

'A bit, but of course she wasn't miles from home like me. She was only about an hour late getting back to her dorm, and she slipped in without being seen.'

'Right. Do I know her?'

'You've met her, I think. Cassie Forbes?'

I stopped. 'Cassie Forbes? Cassie *Forbes*?' My head whipped back. I stared at him. His eyes were opaque. Impenetrable. But then, something sharp, something knowing was there as well. I felt fury mounting.

'Oh you stupid, *stupid* boy! What are you doing messing around with her?' The ghastly, hateful words were out before I could check them. Instantly, Seffy's shutters came down.

'We weren't messing around, we were talking. And anyway, why should you take against her so much? She's a nice girl, you said so yourself.'

'Yes, yes,' I breathed, raking my fingers quickly through my hair, 'she is a nice girl. I don't know why ...' But I did. Did know why. Dominic and Letty's child. I didn't want him to go there. 'Sorry. Forget it, Seffy,' I said shortly. But my son wasn't finished.

'What's the problem, Mum? Why the violent reaction?'

'No reason, no reason, you're quite right. I'm being ridiculous. And you're just friends, so that's lovely. Anyway, let's go in. Look, there's Laura.' I spotted her through the kitchen window.

'Well, we are just friends at the moment, but I really like her. She's really nice. Fit, too.'

Don't rise, don't rise. Somehow I knew he was lowering the worm, dangling it in front of my nose to reel me in, but I wouldn't take it.

'It's just, I worry, Seffy,' I said, keeping my voice level with a struggle. 'You know, we left the last school because it wasn't right, and now you're starting with a clean sheet. It would be a shame to—'

'We did not *leave* the last school,' he roared, making Laura turn, even through the glass. 'I was expelled, as you well know, for drinking a bottle of wine and inadvertently setting fire to the common room as I fell into a drunken stupor with a lit cigarette. We did not decide it wasn't right for me, for pastoral and academic reasons, as you're so fond of telling people, as if I could pick and choose. *I was fucking well kicked out!*' His face was white with anger; eyes ablaze. He never swore at me. I felt myself shrivel inside, as if a hand had reached in and scrunched me up, like a desiccated old leaf.

'No. No, you're quite right. We do both know that. But I like to protect you, to—'

'Lie,' he said fiercely. 'You like to lie. You call it glossing over the truth, but the fact is, Mum, you can't face reality.'

I felt myself rock back in my shoes at this: with the force of his venom.

'I tell anyone that asks that I was sent down, but you, you have to big it up, don't you? You have to blag and lie your way out of everything, and d'you know what? Sometimes it's downright evil.'

We were by the kitchen now and I reached out to hold the wall with the flat of my hand. To steady myself. I could feel my eyelids flickering under the force of his invective, his onslaught; could already hear Laura's footsteps running down the passage from the kitchen towards us. Through half-shut eyes I looked into my son's furious, glittering ones. It seemed to me I looked down the passage of time, right back to the beginning of everything; right to the core of my soul.

Laura's hand was on my arm. 'Hattie!' She gave me a little shake. 'Seffy – what's wrong?'

Seffy's face in that instant crumpled. Collapsed like a puffball that's been pricked, and even though he turned and ran, I saw his eyes fill as they had when he was a little boy. For some reason, a moment when we were on holiday, years ago in Croatia, on the Dalmatian coast, sprang to mind. He must have been about ten. He'd built a fort on the beach. Not a castle you understand – he was too old for those – no, this was an intricate Camelot affair, complete with arrow slits and roads and a drawbridge. A child, running backwards, pulling a kite, had accidentally trampled through it, wiped it out in moments. It was that same, aghast look he had on his face, as if his world had caved in.

Laura took me inside and I managed to babble something innocuous. About how shocked I was at Seffy being sent home, and how, stupidly, I'd balled him out. How cross I was, especially after all that had happened. But then I stopped. Because you see, I couldn't remember if Laura had been told the lie: about Seffy choosing to leave the last school, and move elsewhere. Luckily she was prompting me, sitting us both down, her hand still on my arm.

'I know, because he was sent down before, of course you're worried.'

Yes, yes, I had told her, that's right. It was Mum who didn't know. Dad did. Seffy had told him. My mouth was very dry, though, and I was glad of the glass of water she put in front of me. I drained it in rapid gulps. It seemed to clear my head, as if I'd rinsed my brain under a cold tap.

283

'Stupid of me. I yelled at him, you see,' I repeated, dimly aware I was fabricating again. 'Got cross, and he exploded.'

'But at least you've cleared the air,' she was saying, 'which is no bad thing. Let him cool down now, and then talk to him later. Much better. Honestly, sometimes I think if Luca and I had a stand-up-knock-down like you and Seffy just have, it would be so much healthier.'

'I saw him,' I managed to mutter, managing to move on, to progress the conversation as one normally would. 'He was playing tennis with Seffy. He's changed, for the better, I thought. Slightly less shifty? More charm?'

I reached for the Evian bottle to replenish my glass. I needed to rehydrate, to be calm: to breathe.

'Well, he's *grown up*. And he *is* much improved, but we're still so polite with each other, Hatts. However much I try, he still won't meet me halfway. Still keeps me at a distance. And of course, that puts me on the back foot and I get all brittle and insecure. And yesterday – oh God, yesterday I behaved *so* badly, after what was, after all, only an accident. But still. You know what Daisy's like about those wretched bantams.'

She was at the sink now, drying up glasses in that automatic, feverish way women do when they're trying to calm themselves: clinging to a simple domestic task.

'What happened yesterday?' My mind was still buzzing, and I could feel my heart pumping.

She turned. 'Oh, of course you don't know. Hugh took Luca for a wander with the air rifle, down by the lake. He's shooting here next weekend and he doesn't exactly get his eye in much in Florence. He shot one of Daisy's bantams by mistake.'

'Oh Lord. She'll be devastated.'

'She is. I rang her at school yesterday. I mean, they *do* drop off their perches now and then, and the fox got one last winter, but this was the mother of all the chicks. And the fact that it was Luca seemed so heinous to Daisy. "He murdered her!" she kept saying. "Mum, he murdered her!" And of course her being so upset made me upset, so when I came off the phone and he sauntered up and asked – rather nonchalantly, I thought, but perhaps he was nervous and it came out wrong, you know how he never looks at you – asked how she was, I said, "Well how d'you think? You've shot her pet!" And ran upstairs. Not very clever. A bantam isn't a pet, and he didn't do it on purpose. It didn't make for a very pleasant evening, though. I realized I'd overreacted and came back down and fell over myself trying to apologize and Hugh tried to smooth things over, but it didn't help that I heard Luca mutter to Seffy, who'd just arrived back with Dad, 'It's only a fucking chicken.' Dad had to take me in the kitchen and talk to me, tell me to breathe, to count to ten. Where would we be without Dad?'

'I don't know,' I said, knowing I'd thought that exact same thing very recently.

'Anyway, he stayed for supper which helped – Dad, I mean – and was brilliant with both boys. He doesn't get the cold glittery eyes like I do. Luca's OK with him, and – oh, I don't know.'

I thought of Seffy's glittering stare just now. And in that moment it occurred to me that these boys had a lot in common. Both somewhat displaced, not actually part of a family. Away from their home countries, cuckoos in other people's nests. Or at least, that may be how they felt.

How they'd been made to feel. A nauseous feeling rose in my throat. I thought of Seffy, in the woods behind St Hilda's, kissing Cassie Forbes: two young people finding each other, very sweet, very special. Experiencing perhaps, those first glorious shafts of love. I shut my eyes tight, teeth clenched. My head was spinning furiously, and when the door slammed violently above us, it gave me such a start, my hand shot out, and sent my water glass flying, smashing to the floor. Granted the subsequent commotion and sound of running footsteps were urgent and unsettling too, but then I managed to knock the water bottle over. It spun around the table hideously, spilling everywhere.

'What now?' said Laura as she lunged to set the bottle upright. We scrambled around picking up pieces of glass, waiting for the footsteps to come inevitably closer. They did, and as the door flew open, Maggie and Ralph de Granville burst into the room.

'I cannot work with this man!' Maggie was bright red in the face, fists clenched. She glared at Ralph, who looked similarly ruffled.

'And I cannot work with this woman!' he growled furiously. He threw his shoulders back and strutted across the room to take up a position by the sink. Spinning on a sixpence to face us, he folded his arms and tossed his head back. 'She's ignorant.'

'Ignorant!' Maggie roared.

This was possibly the worst insult you could hurl at my highly intelligent, supremely cultured friend. 'I'll tell you who's ignorant. Anyone who hangs a streak of unframed dirt on the wall and calls it art, or – or puts a ridiculous lump of rock in the middle of the floor and calls it a table. Anyone who hoodwinks people, basically. Deceives them into pouring good money into pretentious crap. Who proselytizes phoney rubbish and gets their clients to adopt it like the emperor's new clothes – *that's* ignorant. It's despicable too!'

'Oohh …' Ralph seemed to shudder from the top of his beautifully coiffed hair, right down his skinny spine to his toes. 'As opposed to borrowing some tired, whimsical ideas from a clichéd, hackneyed parody of a bygone, pastoral era, perhaps? Ooh, let's have another set piece, with a pair of Louis Quinze chairs, and yet another bit of artfully draped antique velvet over a rickety iron table. No innovation, no flair, and, most importantly – no ideas!'

Maggie's face was suffused with rage. 'I'll have you know it is entirely the innovative twist I put on my classics that *re*invents them, that brings them right up to date. That bergère with the scorched wood frame, for example, or … or the chaise with arms painted matt black in the study – all the things you *don't* see because you're blind to anything that wasn't made five minutes ago. Just because it's contemporary, doesn't mean it's good, you know.'

'And just because it's old, doesn't mean it's attractive,' he spat back. He sucked in his cheeks and looked her up and down. 'You're an excellent case in point, if I may say so.'

Maggie's breath was rarely taken from her, but it seemed to have been sucked right down to her elegant black patent boots. Not for long, though.

'How dare you? You're about as antique as they come, pulling in your middle-aged stomach and posturing away with your tired old luvvy manner. Dyeing your hair and—'

'I do *not* dye my hair. This is entirely natural!'

'You've got roots!'

'Which is more than I can say for you,' he snarled. 'My family, I'll have you know, are descended from the very French salons you crave to imitate: from the de Granvilles of Allègre with a beautiful château in the Loire that you will never in your wildest dreams re-create!'

'My wildest dreams would certainly never include anything of yours.'

'Except my Peruvian Rouge, of course. You couldn't help yourself, could you? Little tea-leaf.'

Maggie gave a howl of rage. Hands raised like claws, she launched herself, harridan style, across the room. Luckily Laura and I, who'd been watching this exchange like a Wimbledon final, heads swivelling this way and that, were alive to it and instantly between them, backing them away, calming and cajoling whoever we felt we had the most influence over, making soothing noises the while.

'Come on, Maggie, this is no way to behave,' I implored her.

'I'm sure we can resolve this and all play – work – together,' my sister soothed Ralph.

'She stole my paint! My rouge!' Ralph pointed furiously over Laura's shoulder. 'I have twenty-two essential colours in my range, mixed exclusively to my own palette and specifications, and what do I find as I stroll through one of her bourgeois little room sets, tripping over yet another hideous chaise longue? *My Peruvian Rouge on its arms and legs!*'

Maggie turned her head away, arms folded defiantly, and in that gesture, I knew: knew she was guilty. 'Did you, Maggie? Did you take his paint?' I found myself asking, as one would a child.

'As if,' she spat disingenuously.

'Why can't you share?' my sister enquired of Ralph in a motherly fashion. 'Let her look at your colours, and maybe she'll show you hers?'

Ralph's lip curled. 'There is nothing of that woman's I would ever wish to view,' he said disdainfully.

'And nothing I should ever wish to show him.'

'Thief.'

'Poseur.'

'*Voleuse.*'

'*Bâtard!*'

The two of them glared at one other. Then they tossed their heads and flounced from the room: unfortunately – for no doubt a grand, sweeping exit was what both were after – simultaneously, so that the desired effect was rather marred. They collided in the doorway, jostling furiously to get through, to be first out.

Laura and I listened to the sound of their ever-decreasing stomping footsteps, which eventually died away as they marched off in opposite directions through the corridors of this great house. Then we sat down heavily together at the kitchen table.

Laura blinked at the Evian bottle. 'Sod that for a game of soldiers.' She threw it in the recycling bin, opened a cupboard, and seized a bottle of gin. I, meanwhile, busied myself getting the glasses, the tonic, the ice and lemon.

21

Supper that evening threatened to be a petulant affair. Two taciturn boys whose habitual mode of communication was monosyllabic at the best of times, a brace of warring interior decorators – both of whom, I'm sure, Laura was regretting having asked to stay as long as they liked – Laura and I, both shattered by the upsets of our respective children, and Hugh, blinking a bit as he tried to referee. Sensibly, Laura had plumped for a quick sausage and mash in the kitchen. As she fried the sausages, Ralph cleverly sidled in and installed himself on a stool by the Aga, arming himself with a drink and a clutch of amusing decorating anecdotes. By the time Maggie arrived slightly later, he was making his hostess laugh uproariously, and generally stealing a march on his rival. Maggie, witnessing the hilarity, turned on her heel and stalked into the scullery to sulk.

'Conscious card,' she muttered as, grasping the situation, I went to find her. She was sitting on the draining board, smoking furiously. I steered her out, in the opposite direction to the kitchen, handing her a glass of wine.

'He's just trying to be amenable,' I soothed.

'He's just trying.'

'Yes, but you know what it's like when you're doing up someone's house. If you're staying, you have to sing for your supper rather. We know that.'

'He doesn't sing, he brays.'

'OK, he brays,' I said wearily. 'Come on, Maggie, forget about Ralph for the moment. Show me the house. Show me what you've done while I've been away. I deliberately haven't looked, because I wanted you to show me.'

'Really?' She brightened. 'I thought you'd looked and didn't like it, because you hadn't said anything.'

'Don't be ridiculous, I've been walking round with my hands over my eyes. Come on, I want the grand tour.'

We started upstairs and worked our way down to the front hall, taking in all the rooms she'd had a hand in, and all those that were Ralph's too. In actual fact, I decided, what Mr de Granville had achieved in the more formal areas of the house – the drawing room, hall, master bedroom, et cetera – was really rather good. Just as what Maggie had achieved in the informal rooms – the playroom, the sitting room, the children's bedrooms – was excellent too. Maggie, of course, would beg to differ.

'Look at this!' she spat as we went into the drawing room. She waved an incredulous hand at the vast lump of rock she objected to by the fire. 'Hideous! Just downright despicably hideous.'

I rather liked it. Long and elegant, it was a huge piece of granite, to be sure, but a welcome change from the ubiquitous stool or coffee table, and contrasted well with the marble mantle. He'd set it on a simple cream rug between creamy sofas, punctuated by the odd enormous granite-coloured cushion. I marvelled at its smoothness. Reached out to—

'Don't touch it!' she snapped. I snatched back my hand as if I'd burned it. 'It's what he wants!' she hissed. 'He wants everyone to fondle it, to coo and use words like "tactile". Useless lump of old rock.'

Except not useless, because smooth enough to set a tray on, with coffee, as Laura liked to do after supper; to sit around; perch on, even. And OK, perhaps it was a talking piece, which Maggie despised, claiming good pieces should blend in and not be discussed, but the rest of the room blended in rather beautifully around it. He'd hung simple linen drapes at the windows, but unexpectedly, the drapes were heavy with tassels at the top for a traditional, luxurious twist. There was, admittedly, an imposing modern sculpture in the corner by the window, but on closer inspection I realized it was of a philosopher, Descartes. So in fact, Ralph's style was contemporary but with a twist of the ancient: a nod to the past. Whereas ours, I thought, going slowly back to revisit the sitting room, which Maggie had done with lovely old French chairs but upholstered in red leather – practical with children – was old, but with a nod to the future: a contemporary twist. So two not so very different styles met in the middle.

'Look at this!' she squealed as she marched me on to the dining room, throwing wide the door.

I gaped. Almost didn't recognize Hugh's heavy old ancestral furniture. The sideboard, cleared of dusty old crystal and silver, had a vast modern canvas hung above it – presumably the 'streak of dirt'. But it was a red and vibrant streak, and it worked brilliantly, bringing out the russet in the piece of mahogany below, bringing it alive. The dining table was set with enormous pewter plates, going way back before this oak table was made, and wrong-footing one. Ralph hadn't tried to update it, but taken it back further in time, to when hairy men threw bones over their shoulders to the dogs. The panelling he'd dared to paint a lovely soft grey, just the sort of grey Maggie and I might have used, and the chairs he'd recovered in rough hessian and scattered around the sides of the room. Benches instead, for everyday use, heavy oak ones, ran either side of the table.

'Ooh …' I said, sitting down. 'I like it!'

'You don't!' she snorted.

'I do,' I said disloyally, and rather bravely. 'I think he's done a great job. And I love these huge plates. Yum.' I picked one up.

'Platters,' she told me. 'We're not allowed to call them plates. Have to use a stupid bloody pretentious word.'

I put it down.

'Yes, but you get cross, Maggie, when customers talk about our "sofas and settees", muttering under your breath, "Bergère".'

'Only because it grates,' she said, throwing her head back and scratching it energetically. 'And it's incorrect.'

'Well, that's how he feels,' I said, getting up. I peered at the painting. 'Is this the streak of dirt?'

'Streak of piss, more like.'

'Who's it by? It looks like a Kandinsky.'

'It's a copy. But not. If you know what I mean. In the style of.'

'Clever!' I marvelled, swinging round to her, knowing she knew it too. Could tell by her short answers and the way she was chewing her thumbnail. 'Come on, Maggie, you've got to admit, the guy's got style. And he hasn't got where he is on reputation alone. We know that's not possible. He's earned it. You're only as good as your last commission.'

She sighed. 'Yes all right, he's got something, I admit. But why does he have to be such an arrogant ponce?'

I shrugged. 'Who knows? Insecure? Or maybe he was born like that. Have you bothered to find out?'

'Why would I?' she retorted. 'And anyway, I've been far too busy with my own rooms, actually, to really bother looking at his.'

'Which are fab,' I assured her. 'Laura's thrilled.'

'Is she?' She looked anxious.

'Absolutely. She told me.' She had. Had said the two designers had worked brilliantly, better than she'd ever hoped for. And that Hugh was thrilled too. But she'd said it in a quiet, Laura-ish way I didn't like, which told me she had a lot more on her mind. Luca, probably. I didn't dwell on that now.

'And it's taken your mind off Henry?' I asked tentatively.

'Yes, it has,' she said in some surprise. 'I mean, obviously I've had my moments. Had to run to the bog occasionally, rent my hair, beat my breast. But coming down here, being out of London, away from his patch ... well, it's helped. And a damn good row with another decorator always takes your mind off things, doesn't it?' She grinned. 'How about you? How's your love life?'

For some reason I thought of Hal.

'Oh. Ivan's ... good.' I walked over to the tall French windows. Gazed out. 'Lovely.' For a reason I couldn't quite fathom, I didn't want to talk about it. 'And France was good too. I got some terrific things in Montauroux for the shop, and for here too, come to that. I'll bring them down next weekend.'

'Good. I tried to ring you but your mobile's always off. Too busy with Ivan, I expect.'

'Yeah, Ivan and I had a great time.'

'Bonking for Britain.' She grinned. But as ever with Maggie, I felt some disapproval behind the smile. Just as I had always cautioned her about Henry, so she would put the brakes on me too. We knew where our duty lay. We wanted one another to be happy, but we would never entirely encourage each other's hopeless relationships. I had other girlfriends who'd say, 'How exciting, a younger man! Lucky you!' But I knew that behind the apparent envy lurked a deeper knowledge: that the relationship was doomed and they were all set to view the car-crash with their popcorn. Only Maggie voiced caution, and I considered it the true hand of friendship. But now Henry was gone, would she disapprove even more, I wondered nervously. Now she was in the clear, as it were?

'You didn't get a peek at his passport, I suppose? Discover just how young our Romeo is?' Ah yes, she would.

'No.' I cranked up a smile. 'And as usual I kept mine firmly in my underpants.'

'Which I suspect is the first place he'd look.'

I laughed. Then my smile faded. I narrowed my eyes to the view, to the fields beyond: suddenly I wanted her caution. Her hand on the brake.

'It's all bollocks, though, isn't it, Maggie?' I said softly. 'Me and Ivan? It's going nowhere.'

I felt my heart leap with fear. Waited for her to rush in. Agree. Held my breath. She didn't answer. I looked at her anxiously. As usual she disarmed me.

'Oh God, who knows,' she sighed eventually. 'Who's to say what's a right or a wrong relationship? What, at the end of the day, can we do, but follow our hearts?'

She fingered the silk curtains thoughtfully. Dropped them and smiled ruefully. 'I can't make your decisions for you, Hatts. They have to be your own. From here.' She made a fist and thumped her chest.

I nodded. And then I wondered why I wasn't telling her about Hal. Under normal circumstances this would be the moment for some You'll-never-guess-who-I-met chat, but something made me open my mouth, then close it again.

'Is he back?' She eyed me knowingly.

'Who?' My heart pumped.

'Ivan.' She frowned. 'Who did you think I meant?'

'Oh. Um, I don't know. Yes, Ivan probably is back by now.' I could feel myself blushing. 'But I came home before him, because of all this wretched business with Seffy.'

'I heard. But don't be too hard on him, Hattie.' She put a hand on my shoulder.

I said it before she could, not wanting to hear it. 'I know, it could be worse.'

I moved away quickly, crossing to the door.

By the time we all sat down for sausage and mash, we were pretty well oiled. Laura and I had obviously had a head start with the gin, but Maggie and Ralph had evidently shifted a fair amount too. Seffy and Luca were both on beer, and only Hugh, it seemed, was sober. Ralph, it became increasingly clear, had cast himself as the life and soul of the party, which, because she wasn't speaking to him, forced Maggie into an unattractive corner, rendering her snappy and brittle. His tales of warring clients, a husband who wanted every room a different shade of yellow and ran from room to room shouting, 'More sunshine! More sunshine!' whilst his wife plopped a speck of blue in each to turn them closer to urine, got more outrageous and no doubt more apocryphal. But we all laughed anyway, apart from Maggie, whose mouth tightened disdainfully. He'd obviously got his feet firmly under this particular table, I thought as I toyed with my mash. I wondered how long he'd been here? It wasn't unusual for a decorator to stay a while in big houses. In fact, with a complete revamp, it often happened. One became part of the family, a retainer, rather like a nanny, both parties finding it hard to let go, and that was obviously what was happening here. The wall-to-wall commissions Ralph had referred to were clearly not as seamless as he'd made out: either that, or the charms of staying in a stately home, complete with full board and lodging, were irresistible.

Maggie and I had occasionally found ourselves on the receiving end of similar hospitality, together with other country house artisans: picture experts, furniture restorers, who'd been called in to treat woodworm, moth, general decay. We'd all sit around a sea of mahogany of an evening, eyeing each other suspiciously. On one occasion, in a mausoleum in Cheshire, I'd asked the girl beside me, who was painstakingly cataloguing the library, how long she'd been here. 'Oh, about nine months,' she'd replied vaguely. So there was nothing unusual in Mr de Granville's continued presence at my sister's table. And Hugh and Laura were clearly being treated to a practised charm offensive, but at least he was trying, which I always felt one should, and I was rather annoyed with Maggie for not. I was the sister. The one allowed to Be Myself. She didn't come into that category. I found myself wondering, rather uncharitably, whether she'd go back to London tomorrow like me and Seffy, or stay on.

'Oh, no, I thought I'd stay a few more days,' she said airily when we took the plates through to the dishwasher in the scullery next door. 'Laura said to stay as long as I liked, and Christian's very happy holding the fort. And, of course, you'll be there tomorrow, won't you? Shall I get the salad, Laura?' she called over her shoulder as she rooted around in my sister's fridge. *Quite* familiar. 'Or shall we go without tonight?'

'Go without, Maggs, I think,' came back the cry. 'But there's some cheese, if you wouldn't mind bringing it.'

'Sure,' sang back Maggs.

'I'll get it,' I muttered.

'No, no, it's in the kitchen, I got it out earlier.' And Maggs trotted off to retrieve it from the side, beaming at Laura as she took it to the table, turning her back on Ralph as he got up and tried to help, both falling over themselves to be of service. Which of course was delightful. My best friend and my sister, who historically had regarded each other warily and with some antipathy, getting on like a house on fire. I scraped the plates in the scullery. Splendid.

But … why was I the one leaving? The one going home? Because stupidly I'd already made it plain I didn't want Seffy having a lovely time here: playing tennis, helping himself to beers in the fridge, having a holiday, when he should be having a punishment. I wanted him to kick his heels in London, with no friends around to meet on the King's Road, just his mother for company, or even an empty house when I went to work. Yes, Maggie already knew that. I'd told her as we'd toured the house together: said that a bit of contemplative time was what I felt he needed, and not, I thought, glancing through the open door at him joking with Hugh, who was showing the boys how to decant port through muslin, not to be quite so relaxed.

As I gazed at my son a myriad of emotions seemed to surge and well up inside me, until I thought I'd explode. I stood very still as the full force of it hit me, then exhaled a shaky sigh to relieve the pressure. Just then, Seffy's eyes came round and rested on mine. I held them for a moment: gave a little smile. He didn't return it.

I found myself the first to look away.

The days passed quietly and slowly in London; indeed, they seemed to shuffle past in slippers for, of course, not only was Seffy away from the charms of the Abbey in a poky little town house, I was too. And I'd never thought about my house like that before, never. It was my home, my sanctuary, my refuge, and yet somehow, with Seffy in situ at a time when he shouldn't be, when it wasn't the holidays, when his friends weren't horizontal on the floor with him, or playing loud music upstairs so I'd thump the ceiling with a broom roaring, 'Turn it down!' it seemed strange. Muted. Especially since, this time, he didn't seem to listen to music at all, or even watch much television. In fact, he barely troubled technology. He read quite a bit, I noticed, and when I came in from work, I'd find him on the sofa in the bay window, somewhere I often sat because it was light, but not Seffy: a grown-up position, with a view of the street, not the scruffy television and computer end, with a bag of crisps. It was a contemplative place to sigh and reflect. And when I picked up the book he'd been reading from the floor when he went to the loo, I dropped it as if it were hot. Poetry. Poetry! And not only that, but Marvell, and even I knew what he wrote about.

'What are you doing with this?' I'd said in a brisk, accusatorial tone as he came back, as if I'd discovered him with *Tits 'n' Bums*, or *Asian Babes Do It Sideways*.

He shrugged, 'Found it in the bookcase.'

'Oh. Right.'

Yes, and one glance at the inside cover confirmed that it was indeed mine: my name in a flamboyant hand in violet ink, when I was going through an exotic phase: 'Harriet Carrington, 1989.'

I'd bought it because Hal had recommended it to me. Me, the English student, him being Law, had introduced me to Marvell's 'Coy Mistress', as he had to Bach, and cooking with herbs and garlic, and would have done to so much more. So much more I hadn't accepted: had shut the door on. I shut the book now, deliberately losing Seffy's place.

'That Ali G film's on later. Shall I order us in a takeaway and we can watch it together?'

'*Borat*. No, it's OK, I've seen it. And I'm not that hungry. I'm going upstairs.'

And up he went, trailing long ripped jeans, showing plenty of boxer shorts and *taking the love poems with him*.

'He's fifteen!' I hissed down the phone to Maggie later.

'Well, gosh, how lovely, that's great, isn't it? Not only does my godson have a great brain, but a wonderful sensitive side too.'

'You don't think it means he's at it?' I chewed the inside of my lip. Shut my eyes tight.

There was a censorious pause. 'No, I don't think it means he's At It,' she said drily. 'And don't you bloody well read his diary, either.'

'No, no, I won't,' I breathed, ashamed.

And then did the equivalent. Maggie, childless, wasn't to know this meant Facebook, which, I discovered, I could make neither head nor tail of: lots of teenagers waving their arms and sticking their tongues out. After a sweaty twenty minutes or so, glancing constantly over my shoulder in case he came down, I gave up. But then – oh, Hattie, how low can you go? – his phone. Which he'd left on the sofa as he'd dripped upstairs with his book. I pounced on it. Glanced furtively upstairs. Then tapped into his messages.

A couple from his friend Will at school: 'Bad luck, mate, could happen to anyone.' Another: 'Yeah, Davis is stressed, but then Davis is a dick.' This, a reference to the master in charge of the fated trip.

Then one from my father detailing pick-up arrangements – the wonderful texting grandpa – ending with, 'All love, my boy, and chin up' which made my eyes fill. Then nothing more.

I lowered the phone. Breathed again. Dropped it quickly back on the sofa, feeling like a heel. I walked smartly to the kitchen, hands tucked under my armpits as if to balm where I'd touched the phone – burned them.

Of course, he could have deleted any messages from her, I thought feverishly later, as I washed up a solitary bacon and egg pan. Seffy hadn't emerged, even though I'd deliberately billowed doors to waft the bacon smell upstairs. He could have erased her from the memory bank, but he'd be more likely to erase Will and Dad, surely, and keep a sweet missive from a girl? A girl, who, I told myself as I dried my hands, was firmly locked up in her all-girls' boarding school. Just as Seffy, after this coming weekend, was once again locked in his. Quite.

I glanced at the clock, ticking too audibly in this empty kitchen, which suddenly had a stagnant, old-lady feel to it. The dishcloth neatly folded over the taps: the single plate and knife and fork drying on the draining board, not enough to trouble the dishwasher. And I never minded that usually, because I knew Seffy was always coming back. That soon we'd be two, or many more, with his friends. But tonight I glanced up towards his unusually silent bedroom; tonight something cold crept over my soul and I had that horrid feeling again, the one I'd had in the French hotel bedroom. The one about being alone.

It was only ten o'clock and normally I'd watch the news and then go to bed, but it was one thing to watch it alone because your boy is at school, and another to watch it alone because he's in, but doesn't want to be with you. Which I suddenly knew, with a sharp intake of breath, was the reality. Feeling something like physical pain, I sat down and bent double. My head was low and my hands clenched as if in prayer, but my eyes wide and staring.

After a bit, I sat up straight. Breathed deeply to compose myself. Then I flicked off the lights, and went to bed.

Friday night, for both of us, I felt, couldn't come quickly enough. We were bidden to Laura's for the shooting weekend, and yet again the shop was to be left in Christian's capable hands. Yet again I wondered what on earth Maggie and I would do when his arthritis really did incapacitate him and we had to find someone else to hold the fort. Who? Who could we call upon at a moment's notice and say – could you do this weekend and then nothing for a month, but maybe three days in November? Oh, and then a couple of weekends? And who else would be so pleased and proud about it, as Christian was when Seffy and I popped in to drop off the keys at his home in Munster Road, *en route* to Laura's?

'And don't feel you have to open dead on nine thirty, Christian. We all know no one buys antiques in London till midday.'

'We all know *malheureusement*, no one buys antiques at all any more in London. Too busy going to crappy Ikea. But I open *normalement*. On the dot as usual. *Ça va*, my boy?' This, together with a beaming smile and embrace for Seffy, who'd got out of the car to join me on the doorstep.

'*Ça va*, Christian,' grinned Seffy, instantly enveloped in a breath-squeezing, rib-crushing bear hug, which normally we'd exchange an amused grin about, but not today, I noticed.

'You come and see me soon and we get that GLC French around your belt, hm? I, Christian Dupont, will teach you more than any fool *inexpérimenté* teacher, yes?'

'I will,' promised Seffy. 'I'd like that,' he added truthfully.

Seffy spent a lot of time with his godfather, often choosing to help him in the shop if I wasn't about. I'd arrive back from a commission in the holidays and find them in the back room together, putting the world to rights, smoking furiously – Christian, I hope.

'And you notice I not ask you why you at home in term time?' he asked with a twinkle in his eye as we kissed him goodbye and turned to go.

Seffy turned back, grinned. 'Yeah, I did notice that. Thanks.'

'Is because I know it's a long story. And maybe not one for your mother.' He winked as we got in the car.

'Oh, don't worry, Christian. I know all there is to know,' I assured him breezily from the window as I started the engine.

'So you think,' he nodded thoughtfully, keeping his eye on Seffy. 'But I not so sure.'

We waved goodbye, but this last remark had the effect of making me breathe more shallowly. My lips tightened as we addressed the predictably heavy Friday afternoon traffic and headed for Hammersmith roundabout.

'Christian's very French, isn't he?' I said airily to my son as we finally achieved it. 'He thinks any red-blooded fifteen-year-old boy has only one thing on his mind!'

Seffy shrugged. Looked out of his window at the passing shops.

'Thinks, just because he was chasing girls down boulevards on his Vespa at your age, so are you!'

He turned back to me slowly: cold eyes letting me dig my hole.

'Thinks everyone is – you know – at it.' Those ghastly words again. The eyes stayed on me. Watchful. Hateful, almost. I felt prickly with fear. Reacted violently.

'Seffy, it is both rude and intimidating to employ the Death Stare that you young people are so fond of, so kindly cut it out!'

From friendly banter to vituperation in seconds flat. He turned away. But I wasn't finished. I would draw him out.

'Seffy – would you please answer me!'

He came back to me. Under hooded eyes sent me a long flat stare. Then he shrugged. 'What? I have no idea what you want me to say. You think Christian has a dirty mind. I disagree. I think he has a fine, astute mind.' It was said lightly, evenly, but it had the effect of rendering my breath even shorter. My tongue flicked out to moisten my lips.

'Right. Well. How marvellous. Christian's a smart man. Bully for him. Let's leave it at that then, shall we? Unless you've got anything else to add?' Silence. 'Right, well, then I suggest we do.'

Rattled, I swung into the empty bus lane, ignoring dire warnings of cameras recording my every move, and with the eye of London Transport and God's too, no doubt, upon me, lurched off into the traffic.

Laura was clearly in a Friday night flap when we arrived. She had a shoot dinner for twenty-six that evening, which she loathed. Hugh had gone to collect the girls, but Charlie's school didn't have an exeat so he wasn't allowed out, which she also loathed. Particularly when Charlie knew his sisters were home.

'Why do we send them away at eight?' she wailed when she'd greeted us in the hall. Seffy trooped off to the playroom to watch the television. 'What is the point? To make little men of them? To meet the right people, or something equally crapulous?'

I hadn't, with Seffy, but knew Hugh had quietly insisted with Charlie. And since he rarely insisted on anything, Laura had given in. But as she wiped her eyes and blew her nose, I knew it was the greatest and hardest expression of her love for Hugh. I suspect he knew it too.

'Charlie's fine, you said so yourself,' I soothed, giving her a hug. 'Having a ball. Rioting in the dorms, in all the teams – loving every minute of it.'

'Boarding school mothers always say that,' she said miserably. 'So no one can accuse them of being a heartless witch. If I said my baby loathes being away from home and cries down the phone to me you'd say, well, what the bloody hell are you up to, wouldn't you?'

'I suppose.'

'And if I said every male in Hugh's family since the Domesday Book has gone away to school at eight and I didn't have any choice, I'd go from witch to doormat in moments.'

I sighed.

'Anyway,' she sniffed, 'I might drive across on Sunday, and just spring him. Tell them I need my boy for the day and that's that.' She stuffed her hanky up her sleeve. Gave another almighty sniff. 'You didn't bring yours then? Speaking of boys.'

'Who?'

'Ivan. I sent you an email since you never answer your phone. I thought you might like to ask him down this weekend.'

'Oh!'

A few weeks ago I'd have been thrilled. Touched she'd taken him seriously, delighted to be in a position to ask. But … would he have come? To meet the family? In my heart I knew the answer. Could see the amused gleam in his smokey grey eyes. 'What – meet the parents? I thought we said we wouldn't do that?'

'Um, no,' I mumbled to her now, turning to mount the stairs with my luggage. 'But, thanks. He's busy this weekend.'

We had said that, months ago when Ivan and I had first met. On that first, sexy, steamy night, after a dinner party at my friend Eliza's house where I'd sat next to him, then dragged him, literally, back to my place. Over breakfast in bed, we'd established some ground rules. I didn't want to meet his pretty young mum in the patisserie in Soho, whom I imagined was probably about my age, and he didn't want to meet my ageing Ps in their smart house in Primrose Hill. This was to be a fun, frivolous relationship with no strings attached, and we'd cemented the deal with another bout of frenzied lovemaking.

We'd also decided no texting during the working day. I didn't want that silly schoolgirl heart thump when the phone vibrated in my pocket, and he was delighted not to go through the motions he felt obliged to do with younger women. That's not to say my heart didn't still leap when he rang in the evenings or at weekends, so with that in mind, these last few days, I'd gone one step further. I'd turned the whole blinking lot off. The answer machine was on permanently at home, the mobile was off, and I only answered my work phone when I could see who was calling. One or two clients had commented in surprise, 'I did try your mobile' but no business was lost, and on the whole, life went on. The world, I discovered, continued to rotate on its axis. No one died. But I hoped, as a consequence, that whatever Ivan felt for me, which I knew to be largely sexual, would dwindle. I hoped he'd take the hint. So that when I eventually told him – as of course I would; I knew the rules – the deed, effectively, would already have been done.

He'd rung my landline once – left a breezy message. Rung the shop too, left a similar one there. I hadn't exactly been inundated, though. And I must admit, I'd expected a bit more. But as I sat on the edge of Laura's spare room bed and finally allowed myself to turn on my mobile, as I'd promised myself I would when I was away from Lonely Old Home and could trust myself, a few hours before a smart dinner party, not to ring him back, my hands, I noticed, trembled slightly.

I knew my inbox would overfloweth. It did indeed. With all manner of people – work, friends, Laura, as she'd said – but only one from Ivan.

'Ring me when you're about.'

I stared. Looked at the date. Four days ago. Well, that said it all, didn't it? I raised my eyes slowly to the pale green silk, stretched across the walls on batons, which I dimly recognized as being a nice touch by Mr de Granville. Casual, nonchalant, offhand. Hardly renting his hair. I realized I was severely taken aback. Downright shocked. I absolutely knew we hadn't been a serious item, nothing special, with no longevity inherent; knew, when I took up with Ivan, I was dipping my toe in the peripatetic London singles scene, but I hadn't realized quite how disposable I'd be. But then again, that was what I'd wanted, wasn't it? It made the split so much easier for me. Which was marvellous.

I got up off the bed, quelling the lump in my throat. I put my things mechanically in drawers: hung up my dress for tonight. Then I went quickly downstairs, in search of company.

I found Laura running through the front hall to the dining room. She was bent double clutching a huge pile of plates, looking harassed.

'Bastards,' she muttered. as she went.

'Who?' My voice was tinny.

She stopped, turned, wild-eyed. 'Oh. The bloody bin men. They come on a Friday, but if I forget to take the rubbish to the bottom of the drive, they won't come up. Now I've got a fortnight of stinking ordure waiting to greet my guests in all their finery tonight.'

'But surely it's round the back?'

'Trust me, the slightest breeze and it's round the front. They'll be asphyxiated on the spot. I'll be scraping them off the doorstep. I'll have to take it all down to the tip.' She hurried on to the dining room.

'I'll go, if you like.'

She stopped. Turned back. 'Oh, Hattie, would you?' Relief cleared her face. 'But you've just driven all the way from London.'

'It's fine, I'd like something to do.' True. 'Just tell me where to go.'

'Maybe Seffy could go with you?'

'No, no, don't worry,' I said quickly, 'I'll go on my own.' I strode off towards the back door. Really on my own. No Ivan now, no Seffy ... no. That way madness lay. Breathe. Just breathe. 'Where do I go, Laura?'

'I'd ask Maggie,' she was saying, following me to the back door, 'but she's gone to collect Kit. His car's broken down again.'

'She's *still* here?' I was feeling raw, and couldn't keep the incredulity from my voice. Disingenuous too, for I knew. Had spoken to Maggie – had obviously spoken to my business partner. But I realized I'd wanted to say it. Say something harsh.

'Oh. Yes.' Laura looked flustered. 'Just finishing off, and she's been invaluable. Such a help with this party, doing the flowers and everything, and I asked her because I felt it was a way of thanking her – and you, of course – for a job well done.' She regarded me anxiously.

I was such a cow. Trying to make my sister feel guilty for still housing my friend, when for years it was what I'd wanted? What was wrong with me?

I gladly buried my face in my handbag, delving for my car keys.

Outside, I helped her heave the shiny black bags into the boot of my car, thinking I might just drive it into a handy ditch, or a wall. Have done with everything. Go to the devil, as well as the tip. Instead, minutes later, I was bouncing down the back drive with five huge sacks of rubbish as baggage, which, I felt, was entirely appropriate.

As I drove I narrowed my eyes to the sunset. I remembered him watching me over the balcony: Ivan, I mean. Bare-chested, cigarette dripping from his hand as I scurried off to the ferry. Amused, chilled. An expression that reminded me … yes, of Seffy's, in the car. And something else too … pity. I froze. Clenched the wheel. That I didn't need. From anyone. I was the one who needed to grow up. I was the fool. A thumping great one. A meal ticket too. I swallowed: put my foot on the accelerator and roared down the lane. And as the saying went, there was no fool like an old fool.

The tip, when I reached it, was empty. It also threatened to be on the point of closure, according to an angry notice in red capitals warning six o'clock sharp and no later. There was no one about to enforce this, though, so I drove on through the menacing spiked gates and parked. Then I set about the glamorous task of heaving the heavy bags of rubbish out of the boot, across the yard, up the flight of steps, and throwing them over into the vast skip. Yuk, yuk and yuk. Face screwed, I tossed the last one in. Laura was right. Two weeks in the sun had rendered the contents ripe, rank, and threatening to spew. Even though nothing had actually split, I couldn't wait to get back and wash my hands. But as I got back in my car, I witnessed one of those moments that, in retrospect, you really wish you hadn't. Wished that you'd arrived ten minutes earlier, or later, so the quandary wasn't yours.

A frail, white-haired couple, beige clothes flapping around thin limbs, were struggling up the steps, fresh from their Nissan Cherry, a huge bag of rubbish between them. They'd managed to get it to the top of the steps, but couldn't raise the muscle, or the energy, to throw it over into the skip. They tried again, failed. Discussed. The old lady stood back to let him try alone, as instructed. Still no good. I could bear it no longer. Taking the keys from the ignition, I got out, nipped up the steps in my stripy Converse shoes, and aware of a vicarious thrill of now being comparatively young, as opposed to comparatively old, muscled in with a breezy, 'Here, let me.' In a trice I'd taken the sack from their bony hands, and like a chieftain in some Highland Games display, swung it, and hurled it, so it sailed right out to the middle of the skip. Along with my car keys. Which had also been in my hand.

I stared aghast. The old couple, unaware, cooed their thank yous.

'Ooh, you are kind, dear, thank you so much.'

'My keys!' I spluttered as they pawed me gratefully. 'I've thrown my car keys in too!'

Immediately their wrinkled faces collapsed. Hands went to mouths. Rheumy eyes widened in horror. We all turned to gape, then back to each other, appalled. We cast about wildly, for some handy man to assist – but no. No tattooed, gum-chewing hero was going to emerge in wife-beating vest and filthy trousers from the empty hut that cringed below in the yard; no greasy Alsatian would strain on a chain beside him. No Stig of the Dump.

I gulped. Swung back. I could see the keys, glinting with a smart red leather tag, atop a bag. There was nothing for it, I'd have to go in.

The elderly couple twittered in consternation as I gingerly lowered myself into the vast skip, an eight-foot drop at least.

'Oh, my dear, is that wise?'

'Probably not,' I agreed, and as soon as my feet touched plastic, and one disappeared, I realized wherein lay the real problem. These shiny, slippery, disgusting bags full of rotting food were like veritable quicksand, and if I wasn't careful I'd disappear down the side of one, and thence another, never to be seen again. This fluttery old couple were unlikely to whip out a mobile and call for help, and I imagined the headlines: 'Woman Dies in Dump'. Or even, when some *Daily Mail* journo had spotted the Ivan angle: 'Spurned Older Woman Commits Suicide in Dump'.

Quick as a flash I lay flat on my stomach. I'd watched enough 007 films to know instinctively that prone was the way forward. If I was to achieve my keys, glinting ten bags away in the evening sunlight, I had to spread the weight. Had to crawl, commando-style, towards them. Nose and mouth clenched, I inched my way across bags of a heave-making revolting nature, some of which had split, spewing forth their disgusting contents. Finally I was within snatching distance. I lunged, grasped – and slipped sideways down a crevice. Hugging a bag in a full-on embrace to stop myself falling, the red leather tag in my fist, I whimpered with panic, eyes bulging in terror. I could hear the elderly couple at the side, twittering in consternation. I clung on. Then, slowly, slowly, eased myself out of the crack, out of the … kipper bones … the ancient yoghurts, the mayonnaise, the coleslaw, the – oh, dear God – *nappies* … and crawled back, slowly, hyperventilating gently, towards the side. Towards freedom.

Getting out, however, was not so straightforward. Whilst I'd lowered myself impulsively and easily down an eight-foot skip wall, without bionic springs, I couldn't just as easily leap out. Whimpering now, I piled bag upon bag of rancid rubbish into a rotting, tottering pagoda up which to climb. I placed my foot just so – and the bag split under the pressure. Chicken vindaloo squelched over my witty little shoes and right up my legs. I told myself it would all end soon. Soon be over. I clamoured aboard the top one, declined the delicate arms that flailed over to help lest I snap them, and heaved myself over the side.

Much consternation and agitation then ensued, but even my new friends backed off sharpish at the pong that was emanating from me; at the sight of me, slathered from head to toe in household waste. They thought twice about laying their papery hands on my ketchup-smeared arms. Off they scampered to their car, croaking their thanks, whilst I, walking – appropriately enough – like The Thing From the Swamp, arms and legs away from my body, dripping with – oh, let's just call it goo – went to mine.

Not wanting to brush myself down for fear of what I might brush, longing to strip, to shower, to scrub, to flay even, longing for an out-of-clothes-and-body experience, I found an old newspaper to sit on. Then I opened all the windows – hands trembling, I noticed – and sped back down the lanes to Laura's. Chin raised, lips clenched, I could almost hear the shower running. Could almost sniff the Lifebuoy. No: don't sniff.

I crunched up the gravel drive and parked in a creative fashion at the front, making a mental note to hose the car out later. Eschewing the grand portal and steps, I ran, arms still hanging like a baboon's, around the side of the house to the back door, but as I beetled past the herb garden, past the scullery window and turned the corner, Laura appeared, already dressed in a beautiful navy silk dress. Already coiffed and fragrant.

'Oh!' She halted in her tracks. 'Hattie. Good God, whatever's happened? You're *covered* in muck! You've got spaghetti and – oh yuk, teabags, and something gross in your hair! Is that a condom?'

She stared at me in horror and since I hadn't dared glance in the rear-view mirror, could only imagine the gory scene I presented.

'Long story,' I gasped, as she backed away, hand to nose. 'Been in the tip.' I could hardly speak.

'Hattie, you don't have to get in.' Her blue eyes widened in dismay. 'You just drop the *bags* in. You don't actually have to— Oh.' Suddenly her face changed. Was covered in confusion as she glanced over my shoulder. I too swung round at the footsteps.

'Oh! Hi, there, how lovely,' flustered my sister, putting on her most social smile. I gaped in horror. 'Um, Hattie, I don't know if you remember – well, of course you do, how silly of me. And of course, you saw each other the other day. Um, it's Letty's brother-in-law, Hal Forbes.'

23

Obviously I wanted to die on the spot. And, horror of horrors, he was advancing steadily, in a crisp checked shirt and jeans. Smiling, moving in for a kiss. A polite social one, of course, two perhaps, one on each cheek. Not to be borne.

'No! No, I stink!' I warned. 'Unclean!' I took a hasty step away, stumbled, and reared back into a rose bush. My feet went out from under me as I landed, tits up in the thorns.

Hal blinked down, astonished.

'Hattie's been in the tip,' Laura purred, hastening to help. 'She's from London,' she explained, as if I were cerebrally challenged. 'Didn't realize you don't actually have to get in, just pop the bags over the edge. She thought we—'

'No, no, I knew that,' I gasped, struggling to get up. 'But there were some other people there, and I threw my car keys in the middle and— Ow!' My ankle had gone. I sank back, wincing.

'What, like after a dinner party?' Laura's eyes popped above me.

'What?' I squinted up at my sister.

'Car keys in the middle? Well, not us, obviously,' she flustered nervously. 'Hugh and I never do. But ... isn't that what swingers do?'

'But at a tip?' Hal frowned, mind clearly boggling at visions of unsavoury characters – unshaven tattoo artists, rancid bag ladies – gaily tossing keys to souped-up Escorts, untaxed Mondeos ...

'No – *no*,' I breathed, struggling to my feet and wishing Laura would just *shut up*. She had offered to help me, but thought better of it on seeing my outstretched hand. 'I *threw* my car keys *accidentally* in the middle, as I endeavoured to help a sweet old couple throw *their* rubbish away.' I was vertical, finally. 'And now, if you'll excuse me …' I glared at my sister as if she, personally, had pushed me in, and turned, mustering what shreds of dignity I could, on my heel.

Feet swimming in my shoes – to say they squelched barely hints at their condition – I limped away in a haze of eau de dump, trailing alphabet spaghetti in my wake.

Some time later, having nearly taken my skin off in the shower, I threw my clothes in a plastic bag, and hastened them to Laura's laundry where I set the dial to boil. Clad only in a towel, I hurried back to my room to get dressed for dinner.

Hal again. On my patch, again. But then … it was his patch too, wasn't it? As he'd neatly pointed out in France. His family had grown up at The Pink House; indeed, I'd first met my brother-in-law there. It was only natural Hal might be here, having dinner, perhaps even shooting tomorrow, but still … Laura might have warned me. But then again, I'd been pretty much incommunicado all week, hadn't I? Perhaps she'd emailed me that too? I miserably cast off my towel. And I couldn't have looked more terrible. Couldn't have *smelled* more terrible. I shuddered as I recalled. Well, if that doesn't put him off, nothing will, I thought as I shimmied into an evening dress. I stopped. Stared at my reflection in the cheval mirror. Put him off? He's engaged, Hattie. And why on earth would he be On in the first place?

Nevertheless I found myself taking an inordinately long time over my make-up. I removed my mascara when it clogged and reapplied it. Told myself I always wore scent behind my knees at a dinner party. But I eyed myself carefully as I removed some pearls from my ears and switched them for something more glitzy. More shimmering. I've always had to be on the lookout for subversive behaviour. Skulduggery. But it wasn't just me, I decided defiantly, as I slicked on some lipstick and pressed my lips together to seal it. Something in his eyes, Hal's eyes, had arrested me. I'd spotted it in France and, despite my disgusting state, I'd spotted it again today, from the depths of the rose bush. Something lit from within. He'd disguised it quickly enough, but not before I'd seen. He was pleased to see me.

Minutes later, heart fluttering, I went along the galleried landing, one hand brushing the banister rail, the other smoothing down my dress. I realized I was spectacularly nervous. It had occurred to me, in my bedroom, that she would be down there too – Céline. Undoubtedly. And I had to meet her, make polite conversation. Plaster on a smile. And all the while, might I be thinking... it could have been me? It should have been me, even? I stopped, my breath taken momentarily. That I could *think* such a thing.

On I went. Already I could hear the muffled chatter and clinking of glasses, sounds of pre-dinner drinks in full swing. But as I got to the top of the stairs, I was halted again, by voices much closer. They were coming from the room my brother always stayed in when he was here. His voice, together with another very familiar voice, was raised; laughing. The door was ajar. I pushed it incredulously.

Maggie was sitting on the bed, hands clasped under her chin, as Kit paraded in a full-length cassock.

'Ooh, yes, I love it!' she cooed as he gave a twirl. 'Definitely the blue. It matches your eyes. Oh – hi, Hatts.'

She got up from the bed, looking a little sheepish, I thought. She kissed me, covering any confusion.

'The blue? As opposed to?' I enquired coolly, kissing my brother. 'Hi, Kit.'

'The grey,' he said serenely. 'For Sunday's service. Maggie thinks the blue is more suitable for Harvest Festival.'

'Does she now,' I said drily, knowing Maggie very well. Recognizing the shine to her eyes, the flushed cheeks. 'But surely not for dinner, Kit?' I enquired lightly.

'Oh, no, I'm just about to change. Now off you trot,' he shooed us both out. 'Just showing Maggie because she was interested.'

I bet she was, I thought, as she scuttled out ahead of me, all ready to party on down. She was wearing elegant black silk trousers and an ivory top, prattling some spurious nonsense about what a lark my brother was. But she didn't get very far as, at that moment, Mr de Granville appeared from another bedroom. They stopped, glared at one another and then, just like a French farce, Maggie disappeared firmly into her own room, muttering something about forgetting her evening bag.

'So *exhausting*,' Ralph murmured, shaking his head as he fell in beside me. I took it to be a rather friendly tone and glanced up, surprised. He was looking particularly dashing in his black tie, floppy hair curling on his collar.

'To be so despised,' he explained, with a wry smile.

'Oh, she's all right really,' I assured him. 'I think the two of you just got off on the wrong foot. She can be a bit insecure.'

'Well, if she's insecure she should be tethered,' he snapped in more like his usual voice. 'Put on a lead and not allowed to snap at one's ankles like a yappy little terrier.'

'Oh God,' I grinned. 'She'd hate to be thought of like that.'

'Would she?' His face cleared. 'Excellent. I shall make it my analogy for the evening. Might even refer to her as Nipper.' He bared his teeth.

I giggled.

Ralph swept back his hair. 'Sweet of your sister to ask me to stay on this weekend,' he observed lightly.

'She wanted to thank you. She's thrilled with what you've done here and I'm not surprised, it's fab.'

'Why, thank you, flower,' he drawled, but looked genuinely pleased.

'And of course she's not averse to having a trophy designer at her dining table,' I reminded him.

'Just as I'm not averse to being one,' he shot back.

As we descended the huge sweeping staircase – and privately I was glad not to be doing it alone – we encountered two portly, middle-aged men at the foot of it. They were removing coats and straightening cummerbunds, brushing dandruff from shoulders. One, with bristling eyebrows, was addressing the other, very florid one.

'I say, awfully sorry to hear about your wife,' he remarked as we followed them to the drawing room.

'What about my wife?'

'Well, I gather you've split up.'

The florid one turned even pinker. 'Do you fancy my wife?' he demanded.

'Er, no. Of course not.'

'Well, neither do I,' he barked, stalking off to find a drink.

Ralph snorted with delight. Whispered in my ear: 'Rather sets the tone for the evening, doesn't it? They're far friskier than us Londoners, you know. He'll be shacked up with someone else's wife before the night is through. Oh, hello, what did I tell you?'

Following the florid one in, we watched as indeed he lost no time in accosting a tall, buxom lady in a low-cut turquoise dress by the door. As he slipped an arm around her waist he growled, 'Evening, Fiona. What fucks like a tiger and winks?'

'Gerald!' she brayed. 'I've no idea!'

He gave her an extravagant wink, then swaggered off to the drinks tray. She broke into peals of delighted laughter.

Ralph rolled his eyes at me. 'See? I rest my case.'

I grinned and glanced around the room. It was heaving already, noisy too. Despite the throng, the first person I saw, looking gorgeous in his dinner jacket, on the other side of the room talking to an elderly gent, was Hal. He must have changed here, I thought. He'd been in jeans in the garden. Was he staying, then? Which bedroom, I wondered. Which *bed*room, Hattie? And which one of these lovelies was his intended? His affianced. For lovely they all were, the women, and I don't know why that surprised me. The hair was much longer than in London, clothes different too – more glamour, less restraint. Fashion rules seemed to have been thrown away. If it was sexy – wear it, seemed to be the code. There was more velvet, more jewellery, higher complexions from hunting, firmer thighed too, I suspected under those silky evening dresses. I felt slightly pale and underdressed in my simple Armani shift and kitten-heel shoes. These women were high of heel and low of cleavage, tanked up, and as Ralph had rightly observed, raring to go.

'Some people have come a long way,' Laura had remarked to me earlier, 'so we party hard.' I could believe it.

Across the noisy, braying heads I spotted Letty, in a low-cut, fuchsia-pink number. Her cheeks were flushed, eyes overbright. She gave me an extravagant wave.

'Oo-oh!' she shrieked, muscling through. 'How lovely! You look terrific!'

Her cheeks were boiling as she kissed me. I had a feeling she was well oiled already.

'Have you seen Hal?' she yelled. 'I gather you two met in France – had dinner even!'

'Um, yes.' I flushed, glancing round warily and hoping Céline wasn't in earshot. 'Well, supper, really. Just to – you know – catch up.'

'Oh, I do know,' she roared, with massive innuendo and a sharp dig in the ribs. She was clearly disastrously pissed. I began to feel a bit panicky. So loud.

'Um, lovely to see you, Letty, but I'm just going to catch Seffy. Won't be a mo.'

'Oh, Yes, I saw Seffy earlier, helping the girls. Someone pointed him out. Isn't he divine? No wonder Cassie can't stop talking about him! She's *so* annoyed she can't get out this weekend – bloody schools.'

I gazed at her as Seffy came up with a bottle of champagne, butler for the evening.

'Top up, Mum?'

'Thanks, darling.' I said, distractedly, still looking askance at Letty.

'Where's your glass then?'

I turned. Came to. 'Oh. I haven't got one yet.'

He rolled his eyes. 'Does help. Oi, Biba!' He beckoned to his cousin, who was bobbing about with a tray of full glasses. She pushed across as Letty moved on.

'Hi, Hattie,' she grinned, offering me a drink. 'Don't you love the outfit?' She and Daisy had dressed as French maids for the evening, in killingly funny little skirts, bibs and mop caps. She dropped a curtsy, eyes lowered. 'Ma'am.'

'Love it,' I assured her, rallying.

'We tried to get Seffy to put Dad's tail coat on, but he wouldn't.'

'I don't want to look like a bloody Etonian.' Seffy moved off with the bottle.

'And, by the way, I think your ex is gorgeous,' Biba hissed in my ear. 'Mummy told me you went out with him at university.' Her eyes roved across the room as I coloured.

'Well, no. Not strictly true.'

'But fancied his brother more, who was married to Letty!' She pulled a face. 'I think this one's way better looking. I've seen pictures of the famous one. He was Foreign Secretary, wasn't he? Dad said he was really well known at the time, all sort of Kennedy-ish and young statesman-like, and then those famous diaries came out when he died. So sad he was killed, but honestly, Hattie, this one's really fit. *And* unmarried!'

Was it my imagination or was Seffy, who'd turned ostensibly to pour more drinks, listening intently?

'Well, engaged, Biba,' I mumbled. 'Getting married next month.'

'No, apparently not. He's called it off – *again*.'

I stared at her. 'What?'

Her blue eyes were very bright and I had an idea she'd sampled a few glasses from her tray herself.

'Yes, apparently for good this time. I was just talking to Letty. She said his heart's simply not in it and he can't go through with it. The fiancée's devastated, apparently.' She pulled a mock-sorrowful face. Then shrugged and grinned broadly. 'Oh, well.' She nudged me.

'Is she here?' I managed.

'Who, the ex?' She looked at me incredulously. 'Rather doubt it, don't you? You're hardly going to pitch up for a dinner party if you've just been dumped. Second time apparently, after hundreds of years. Letty says she thinks he's in love with someone else, always has been. God, I love middle-aged gossip. You lot are way more interesting than we are. Oh, look out, Daddy's trying to get everyone in for supper. I said I'd help, he's so pathetic.'

She scooted off towards her father, who, in his amiable polite way, was tentatively suggesting to the roaring, pissed throng, that perhaps they wouldn't mind awfully going through to the dining room … food hot and all that …

Biba beetled to his side and cupped her hands round her mouth.

'Supper time!' she yelled.

Everyone swung around, laughing. She earned a sheepish grin from her father.

I joined the flow back across the hall, and through the double doors to the dining room. The grey hessian-covered chairs, all twenty-six of them, were now around the long table, and everyone was cooing and admiring Ralph's décor, the painted panelling, the modern art. Ralph looked pleased, but actually, nicely pink too, I thought. Not totally immune to these admiring comments. He pushed his hair back somewhat shyly, smiling delightedly when he was pointed out. And the effect he'd created was truly beautiful: bathed in candlelight, the gleaming mahogany was covered in bowls of white roses and sparkling silver, the flickering light softening sharp noses, ruddy jowls, non-existent chins. Jewels sparkled and skirts rustled as everyone found their place, and as I moved to mine, I just knew – of course I knew – that he'd be there, beside me, holding out my chair for me. I advanced with a thumping heart.

'Hal, how lovely.' And this time we exchanged the peck we should have traded in the rose garden. 'I'm approachable now.'

'You've scrubbed up.'

'I have, but it was nip and tuck. I considered coming as I was, then thought, nah, make an effort.'

'Shame. I rather liked the in-the-bush-backwards look. It had a certain dishevelled charm, although you smell a bit better now.'

'I should jolly well hope so. Chanel have got problems if I don't.'

He laughed, and after that, it was easy. We talked about the house and my work here with Maggie, and then we discussed country life. After a bit we got on to old friends: ones I hadn't seen for years, but he had.

'Remember Kirsten?'

'God, yes, the pious swot. She hated me.'

'High-class tart in Park Lane now.'

I put down my fork. 'I don't believe you.'

'No, OK, she runs an escort agency. But still, much the same thing.'

'Good *heavens*! She was so Miss Jean Brodie! So disapproving. They're always the worst, of course.'

'Or the best,' he remarked, eyebrows raised.

I laughed, and it occurred to me he was flirting. Which years ago would have been anathema. This was a more relaxed Hal: less serious, less intense.

We turned, briefly and politely through the main course, in Hal's case to a tall blonde woman with hooded eyes, and in mine to a sweet old chap who couldn't hear a thing and bellowed 'What?' a lot, bending his head, practically in my Bourguignon. By the time the pudding arrived Hal and I had found each other again. And it was so like old times. So much easier than in France, with this cushion of twenty-odd others around us. Plenty of noise to fill any awkward silences – not that there were any. It was like slipping into an old coat, I thought.

He smiled up at Biba as she refilled his glass. Together with Daisy and Seffy she was circling with the wine, although Daisy, I noticed, had ignored Luca, who'd held out his glass as she approached. He blushed as she passed him by, her head high. Biba spotted and quickly dashed to fill it. Luca was deemed too old to serve and old enough to eat with us, at the head, I noticed, opposite Hugh, albeit fifteen feet away.

'I won't, thanks, Seffy, Biba's already been round.' This, from Hal, over his shoulder to my son, with a smile. Then they shared a bit of banter about Seffy knowing how old soaks like us knocked it back, and maybe he should hover with the bottle?

'You've met Seffy?' I said, surprised, as my son moved on.

'Oh. Yes.' Hal looked momentarily flustered. Caught out, even. 'We ... met when I popped up here once, to see Hugh. Had a chat.'

'With Seffy?'

'Yes.'

'Oh, right. What about?'

He paused. It was our first awkward moment.

'Oh, you know ... life's rich pageant, that sort of thing.' He cleared his throat and made a pretence of asking his neighbour for the cream. I wondered if he was embarrassed about having sought Seffy out. About wanting to meet him because he was mine. Perhaps. I was flattered.

'He's a lovely boy. A credit to you.'

I met his eyes. Smiled. 'Thank you.'

'You've done very well, Hattie.'

My heart kicked in at this. What did he mean?

'Thank you,' I said mechanically again, but his eyes were still on me, and suddenly I didn't want to talk about me and Seffy any more, or how well I'd done.

'You haven't mentioned Céline,' I blurted, and he instantly glanced away. A cheap trick, but it worked.

'Céline and I ...' He swallowed. Gazed at his plate.

I put a hand on his arm. 'I'm sorry. That was unfair of me. I already know. You've split up.'

'You know?' He looked back quickly.

'Biba said Letty told her.'

327

We glanced down the table. Letty was hunched forward, trying to spear a profiterole: frowning with the rapt squinty-eyed concentration of an inebriate.

'News travels fast,' he remarked. 'It was only a few days ago.'

'But it's over?'

'Oh, yes. For good, this time. I can't go on kidding myself, Hattie. I should marry her, of course: she ticks all the boxes. Always has done. She's beautiful, smart, clever, kind … but there's a problem.'

'Oh?' I knew what it was.

He looked at me. 'I don't love her.'

Nevertheless I caught my breath. His eyes were unashamedly soft; vulnerable even. Yet despite their transparency, despite the fact he was the one showing his hand, it seemed to me I was also revealed.

'Right,' I managed. 'Tricky then.' I played with the stem of my glass.

'Not really. Only fair to do the right thing. I couldn't subject her to a married life of being enormously liked, could I?'

'I … suppose not.'

For some reason a snapshot of the life I'd envisaged for Céline sprang to mind. The one where she was strolling down by the river, in that idyllic garden in France, a toddler on one hand, another on her swollen tummy. Except it wasn't Céline in the Cath Kidston frock. It was me. Hadn't Biba said he'd always been in love with someone else? And how many serious girlfriends had he had time for when he'd been with Céline for so many years?

'Hattie, look …' he said quietly. 'I know this isn't the time or the place, and there are millions of people around

328

us, but there's something you need to know…' He paused, glanced about to make sure we weren't being overheard.

I lunged for my wine. Yes? What did I need to know? Although I already knew what it was, but would love to hear it. Would love to hear those words. Which no one, not counting immediate family, had actually ever said to me. How sad was that? His eyes came back to mine and I felt every sinew tighten, every pulse quicken. I was poised to catch every nuance.

'I know,' he said in a low voice, 'about Dominic.'

I felt my eyes widen in astonishment. Not what I had expected. Not at all. About Dominic? Yes, of course he knew about Dominic. What did that have to do with anything? With the here and now? With Hal and me? Years ago it had been pertinent, sure, but not now, years later, when we were both mature adults, when so much water had flowed…

'But, Hal, that was aeons ago.' I frowned, annoyed. I felt cheated of my words. I'd *wanted* my words. 'I was young, immature. We've been through that, and anyway—'

Whatever else I was going to say in my defence, however, was lost, in the sudden smashing of china and glass. Followed by a thump on the table. It was a perfectly awful clatter. The entire dinner party swung round as one, to see Letty, having nose-dived into her profiteroles, sprawled on the table. Her head lolled, her eyes were shut, her mouth open: red wine spilled into her hair. She was out cold.

24

Hal scraped back his chair and leaped to his feet, moving quickly round the table to his sister-in-law. The men on either side of her were also up, but dithering, with that embarrassed look of not wanting to get involved, or touch. Funny how men really want to touch, or really don't. Under Hal's instruction, though, one of them hoisted Letty's arm around his neck, and as Hal took the other, they got her to her feet. Her face was smeared with chocolate and cream where she'd fallen in her plate; her dress too. Eyes flickering slightly, head lolling, feet dragging in her pink high heels, she was half carried, half dragged, ignominiously from the room. Laura and Biba scuttled after.

A silence fell as we absorbed the shock. Poor, poor Letty. In front of all her friends, her neighbours. My cheeks burned for her. Most eyes were lowered to the table; then darted around surreptitiously to gauge reactions. Following Hugh's anxious lead, conversation was resumed in muted tones. As I mechanically picked up my spoon to address my profiteroles, I realized I felt utterly deflated. Like a pricked puffball. Fearful too. What did Hal know about Dominic? What did he mean?

The chatter in the room had gained momentum now, and the woman to my left leaned across Hal's empty chair, resting the heel of her hand on it, to enquire after my children: 'Oh, just the one? At which school?'

Keep going, her eyes seemed to say. We keep going, you see? For form's sake. For Laura and Hugh. D'you see?

Yes, I did see, actually. They were my family, and I felt a flash of anger at what I perceived to be her impertinence. But on the other hand, what nice friends to have. And this one was gorgeous. And she'd been next to Hal. Divorced, it transpired. Perhaps he was in love with her, I thought wildly, irrationally. Perhaps Laura had deliberately put him next to her, not me?

'Oh, yes, I hear Lightbrook's awfully good. GCSEs?'

Soon, I agreed. Next year. And then endured a long ramble about her own brood, and their numerous achievements. But I wasn't really listening. Could only nod and smile at what seemed appropriate moments, longing, as I was, to run out and join Hal and his drunken sister-in-law and say – what? What are you talking about, Hal? But not wanting to either. Fear making me sit tight, like a child gripping a musical chair. Hugh's eyes flickered round the table, imploring everyone to please, just carry on. Assuring us his wife would sort it out, Biba too, who was frightfully cool under fire. It would be her telling her mother to go back in as Laura flapped: telling her she'd put Letty to bed, deal with her – 'Just go, Mum.'

And sure enough Laura did return, resuming her place with a nervous smile. Eyes lowered, she assured the murmured enquiries to either side that all was well, and answered her husband's gently raised eyebrows with a smile and a nod. But I knew Hugh's eyes were for Laura, who was so easily upset: for her welfare. He cared more about his wife's equilibrium than any drunken guest's, he was making sure she was all right, and my heart ached suddenly. For what I didn't have. For the years of concern and protection I'd missed, as I'd forged on alone, chin up.

After a bit Laura caught my eye, and those of a few close girlfriends, eloquently suggesting we might go through to the drawing room for coffee, which we did, along with a few men too: those who liked to get home and always joined the women, bullying their wives into downing a quick cup and then getting their coats. As we made polite conversation by the fire – no sign of a prostrate Letty in here, she must be upstairs – people began to drift hallwards, thanking Laura, Hugh, who'd emerged from the dining room now with the other men. A gathering collected in the hall, bursts of hearty laughter and cigar smoke filtering through, as the party began to break up. Daisy was helping to find coats and wraps, the other children clearly still ensconced in the drama offstage, except, here was Biba, stealing into the room, flushed, to whisper in her mother's ear.

'All well?' I moved across to listen.

'She's asleep in the Green Room,' Laura reported, as Biba, with a ravishing smile, slipped away to find an elderly lady her stick. 'Hal was going to take her home, but she's so comatose she may as well stay. And it would be too embarrassing to drag her through the hall in front of all these people. Some are going but the hard core – the Tapners, the Rankins – stay all night, I'm afraid.' She jerked her head towards a bright-eyed group clustered round the fire, still roaring heartily and sinking brandy now. 'But you go up,' she, said quickly. 'I'll have to stay for form's sake, but even Hugh eventually goes to bed and leaves them to it. Honestly, Hattie, it's half-past one.'

'Well, I might,' I said gratefully, noticing Maggie was of the hard core element by the fire, colour high in her cheeks, smoking and flirting furiously, looking like she was powering on through till dawn.

'Oh – and if you see Hal up there, would you tell him he can have the bed in Charlie's room? If he's staying, that is. Tell him it's the one he got changed in, he came straight from London.'

'Right.' I brightened. A cup of strong coffee had steadied my nerves. I was looking for an excuse to talk to him.

I slipped away and beetled down the passage to the back stairs, eschewing the front hall where everyone was gathered, taking them two at a time. I found him softly shutting the Green Room door across the landing.

'Is she ...?'

'Sleeping.' He smiled. 'Rather soundly, obviously. But she's been sick, so I think she'll be all right. Nurse Biba forced her to put her fingers down her throat. Teenage rules, apparently. One wouldn't want to drown in one's own vomit, would one?'

'Oh Lord. Yes, Biba's frightfully efficient like that.'

'And Letty complied beautifully. I'd take her home, but I'm not sure she'd want to be carted out in front of the neighbours. I'll stay and take her tomorrow.'

It occurred to me there wasn't much that would surprise her neighbours now, but I let it go. And I liked the fact that he was staying with her. That was so like Hal. Not to bolt and leave her. There was a silence. This end of the house, the nursery end, away from the front hall, was quiet. Dark too.

'Laura says you can sleep in Charlie's room. It's where you got changed, apparently.' My voice sounded odd. Unnatural.

'Thanks.' He didn't move an inch. Certainly not in the direction I'd vaguely indicated. Stood before me in the gloom, his eyes watchful, steady.

'Um, Hal. What you said earlier, about Dominic.'

'Is none of my business,' he said quickly.

'Yes, but can I just ask, did you just mean—'

'Shh, Hattie.' He put a finger on my lips. We gazed at one another. And whatever else I was going to say, or ask, or struggle to explain, was lost, because he leaned forward and kissed my mouth.

Then he kissed me again, lightly, then again. Instinctively we moved away from the top of the stairs, down the dark corridor, where he pulled me against him. This was not the hesitant, student Hal of years ago: this was not the boy I remembered. This was terrific.

Along with my thumping heart, footsteps were audible suddenly, coming lightly up the stairs. We sprang apart. Hal pushed his hair back.

'Is she all right?' Laura whispered urgently, crossing the landing and coming towards us down the corridor.

'Fine,' said Hal, as I straightened a picture behind me where my head had leaned. 'She's sleeping soundly,' he said, as Laura quietly opened the Green Room door a fraction and put her head round. 'Nothing eight hours' kip won't cure, I'm sure.' I think we all knew this wasn't true.

'Poor thing, what a nightmare.' She shut the door softly. Sighed. 'Well, there's nothing else we can do for her tonight. She'll just have to sleep it off. You're down that way, Hal.' She indicated further on down the corridor. Ran a hand through her hair. 'Hugh sweetly told me to go to bed too. I'm shattered. He says he'll deal with the Rankins. Hang them out to dry when they've drained the cellar. Come on, Hattie. Night, Hal.'

'Night.'

There seemed nothing else for it, but to allow my arm to be linked by my sister's as she moved off towards the main part of the house and our bedrooms. But as I raised my eyes to Hal's to say good night, I was aware of such a light, such a force, indisputably matching the intensity of that kiss, it fairly took my breath away. There was no doubt who he'd thrown his beautiful French girlfriend of six years over for: no doubt where his heart lay – had lain, slumbering, all these years. I felt myself on the receiving end of such passion, I felt humbled. I flashed him an inadequate look in return, then fell into step beside Laura, amazed she couldn't feel the heat on the back of her legs.

Once in my room I instantly went to the mirror, wanting to see what he'd seen. Pink cheeks, shining eyes: so we'd both lit up. I smiled. And what now? Might he – and this was truly thrilling – corridor creep?

I brushed my teeth thoroughly, took my make-up off, but not my mascara. Chose, not an old T-shirt, but a rather lovely white cotton nightshirt I'd bought in France. I got into bed and lay there, heart pounding. Hang on. Might just have a quick wash. Pits and parts, as Mum would say. I hopped back into bed, still a bit damp. Would he think it odd? That I'd washed? Was damp? I nipped out and dried very thoroughly.

The minutes passed. Ticked on. Don't be silly, Hattie, he's not that sort of man. He's mature, sensible. He's everything your life lacks, everything it should have: everything you need. I gave a great sigh of relief in the dark. After all those years of being Out There. Come in, Hattie Carrington, your time is up. I felt so warm, so cosseted, it wouldn't surprise me if I finally fell asleep with a beatific smile on my face, like a lost soul who's been anointed. Either that or the cat who's got the cream.

I was woken, an hour or so later, by a certain amount of giggling and whispering outside. Was it him? Instantly awake, I slipped in one fluid movement to the door: opened it in time to see the shadowy figure of an indeterminate male disappear around the gallery, and then Maggie's door shut softly. Right. Corridor creeping wasn't off *her* agenda then. I fell back into bed and, instantly, into a deep sleep.

The following morning dawned bright and chilly. A faint mist was already lifting from the hills, the sun breaking through and peeping in at the windows. It was Saturday, the day of the shoot. Breakfast was laid in the dining room – the kitchen deemed too small when a house party gathered – and as I came downstairs and went into the great panelled room, Hal was striding around in Mr Darcy breeches. I nearly fainted with excitement. Biba and Daisy were serving breakfast to a clutch of quiet, hung-over guests at the table, faces hidden behind their newspapers, whilst Hal helped himself to bacon from the sideboard, closing a silver domed lid.

'Morning.' The smile he gave me as he returned to the table with his kidneys flipped my heart right over.

'Morning,' I breathed.

What, all for me? my brain said. I took in his height and stature as he sat down. This handsome, well-put-together man, clad in expensive Harris tweed and moleskin; Church's brogues. But I wouldn't rush. Wouldn't hasten to bag a place beside him at the breakfast table, like something out of the lower fourth. Would linger to chat to the old codger who'd approached the sideboard with me, who was making noises about the fine weather as I collected my scrambled egg. Let Maggie, who burst in now and bustled to my side dressed in a Londoner's idea of country clothes – tight black cashmere jumper and skin-tight jeans tucked into Russell and Bromley riding boots – be the over-excited one.

'Isn't this killing?' she breathed. 'I keep thinking I'm in *Gosford Park*!'

'Was there much sex in that ?' I enquired mildly.

'What?' She frowned, confused. 'No, I don't think so. Or if there was it was all hushed up and repressed – why?'

'Just wondered.'

'I meant the tweed knickerbockers and the kidneys for breakfast bit.'

'Ah.' I nodded as if the dawn had come up. 'That bit.'

'Look at your brother!' She hissed, clutching my arm. 'Doesn't he look divine?'

Kit had materialized, clearly straight from the shower, looking a bit damp round the edges. He tucked his checked shirt in and yawned.

'Divine.' I agreed. 'What time did you go to bed, Maggie?'

She was still drooling and I saw Kit flash her a grin back.

'Hm? Oh,' she coloured as she came back to me, 'not long after you went up, I expect. Although I did sit and chew the fat for a bit.'

'Oh? Who with?'

'You know, those die-hard friends of theirs. The Harrisons, a few bankers. Some barrister chappie.'

'Kit?'

'Um, yes, he was there.'

'Right.'

Why was I cross? Why? He wasn't off limits, was he? And wouldn't we, as a family, all very much like him to be on limits? And Maggie was my best friend.

'Morning, darlings. I say, isn't it a perfect day? And what a feast!' My mother, resplendent in a lovat-green deerstalker and a matching, swirling cape swept through the double doors making quite an entrance, as my mother can. Even heads buried deep in *Telegraph*s glanced up.

'Hi, Mum, you look lovely.' I kissed her and she gave us a twirl. 'Thank you, my love, and so do you. And Maggie – look at you! Dressed to kill?' She popped an imaginary gun.

'Hope so,' grinned Maggie, giving her a hug. I'd forgotten she was firm friends with my mother now.

'Anyone I know?' Mum breathed in her ear.

'Er, well. A bit.' Maggie had the grace to blush.

'Ooh, how thrilling! Well, I won't pry, but I'm delighted for you. You show that dreadful Hugo chappie what he's missing.'

'Henry,' corrected Maggie, but I noticed her face didn't tauten at his name: no look of pain haunted her eyes.

Dad approached, in tweeds, which surprised me.

'I thought your shooting days were over?' I said as he kissed me. 'Thought you saw it as more of a spectator sport these days?'

My father, who'd shot a lot in his youth, and was indeed a very good shot, had quietly hung up his gun a few years back. He'd been invited to a very smart shoot in Norfolk, which he'd later described as mass slaughter, not unlike the Somme. The sky had been black with birds, he'd said, in fact you couldn't see the sky: and it was big, in Norfolk. Hundreds were killed, and then buried in pits. Hugh didn't run anything like that sort of shoot: the numbers here were low, the birds generally high, so sporting, and it was the day out that mattered. The walking in the great outdoors, lunch with friends, the conviviality, not who'd shot what and how many. And everything was either eaten – most people went home with a couple of brace – or given to the local butcher to sell. But Dad had lost the stomach for it, none the less.

'I'm going to stand with Seffy,' he said, nodding at my son across the table, already devouring a pagoda of bacon, eggs, beans and sausage, beside Luca, doing the same.

'Oh, Dad, how kind. I hadn't thought ... '

Hadn't given a thought to the safety of my son. Seffy usually shot under Hugh's auspices, but of course Hugh would be busy. My father, naturally, had been alive to this.

'Well, in point of fact he doesn't need anyone – he's perfectly capable on his own – but it makes me feel better.'

'Me too,' I said with feeling. I wasn't wild about fifteen-year-olds with guns. 'Thanks, Dad.'

My parents moved away to greet their granddaughters. Daisy was bustling around clearing plates, and Mum was exclaiming at Biba, who was still running in with trays of bacon.

'But, darling, Mummy tells me you were on duty last night till two. You are marvellous.'

'I think you'll find Biba's got it all worked out,' observed Dad, giving his granddaughter a huge wink. 'No flies on her.'

'Six pounds an hour, Grandpa,' she grinned. 'And double money after midnight. And let me tell you, I notched up a few of those last night. I was still running around at three a.m., and being backstairs girl gives you a totally different perspective!' She rolled her eyes at Maggie, who looked flustered.

As Biba hurried on, Dad raised his eyebrows.

'Whatever did she mean by that, d'you suppose?'

'Nothing for you to bother about,' soothed Mum, leading him off to meet and greet. 'Oh, look, there's Luca.'

She skirted the table to bestow a ravishing smile. Luca got awkwardly to his feet, his sallow, sulky face flushing slightly as Mum engaged him in animated conversation, as she did so well, I realized. Dad approached too, to shake hands heartily. They were so good at this, I thought, watching. At making him feel welcome, included. Drawing him out. It occurred to me that if I could turn out just a fraction like my parents, if I could put half the effort and kindness into life that they did, I couldn't go far wrong. So accepting. So much grace. Turn out? If I was a blancmange I'd have been on the plate long ago.

'A terribly attractive man has just asked me if I want to beat,' Maggie breathed tremulously in my ear. 'I might have to go and lie down. What does he mean exactly? And where does this flagellation take place? Are we completely naked? Will there be an audience? So many questions. He has got the most heavenly regional accent, though. Shall I say yes?'

'Do, but I hope you're not disappointed. You'll be fully clothed and it takes place in dense, prickly undergrowth as you flush the pheasants out with a stick. It's exhausting. I'd go with the guns, if I were you.'

'Go … with the guns.' She savoured this, rolling it around in her mouth. 'Another very sexy option. Is that go, as in All The Way?'

'No, it's go as in perch behind on a shooting stick, freezing your butt off', remarked Dad, overhearing. 'Oh, and murmuring admiringly when he hits something. Try to keep quiet when he misses everything – whatever you say will be wrong – and on no account wrestle the gun from his hands and offer to have a go yourself. I'd ignore my daughter and beat. It's much warmer, more exhilarating, and the company is often a deal more entertaining.'

'Right,' she agreed uncertainly. I could tell she rather fancied herself on a shooting stick behind a man with a gun, but out of politeness to Dad she turned to the tall, ruddy-faced chap standing with his group of beaters drinking coffee behind her. I recognized him as Hugh's gamekeeper. Maggie laid a jewelled hand on his arm.

'I'll beat,' she purred, fluttering wanton lashes.

Oh *Lord*. I'd have to take her home soon.

'I think,' she dithered, vacillating. 'Hang on.' She'd spotted Biba across the room: hastened away to canvass her opinion.

Meanwhile Ralph de Granville was making a late entrance, looking dashing and debonair in a subtle Harris tweed flecked with pink, which surprised me. Not the pink – I just wouldn't have had him down as a sportsman. Yet here he was, picking his bit of card from Hugh, which told him which peg he was on, and downing a quick cup of coffee. Hugh lightly clapped his hands and cleared his throat, mildly pointing out, whilst glancing at his watch, that if we were to start at ten, which was kind of the plan, we needed to shake leg, a bit. If no one minded. The rest of the men duly collected their bits of card, and then Hal, Seffy, Luca, the Harrisons, the Rankins, Hobson-Burnetts, Tapners, my parents et al., plus the seven or eight beaters, all drained coffee cups and filed out across the hall and down the back corridor.

The wives, I noticed, looked glamorous in clever feminine variations of tweed or anything else sludge green or brown: moleskin trousers, skirts, leather boots. It was jeans and Barbours for the teenagers, but with a twist: a beaded scarf, perhaps, over an old jumper. Before I joined everyone in the yard where I knew they'd gather for a few last-minute instructions, I peeled off to the loo. I gazed at my reflection in the mirror. Smiled. It occurred to me that for once in my life, I was in the right place at the right time. Here I was at a country house party, with a handsome, charming, successful, single man, who adored me. Even as I'd sipped my coffee back there in the dining room, even as I'd talked to my parents, I'd felt his eyes on me; devouring me. Savouring me, even, as he ostensibly mantalked to Mr Harrison, discussing drives, the merits of a twelve bore or a twenty: even then I'd known where his mind really was.

The loo door handle rattled behind me. I exited, and I cannoned straight into Maggie, who was furtively plastering on her Pearl & Shine in the unsatisfactory reflection of a hunting print in the gloomy corridor.

'Oh, it was you in there. I might have known. You could have let me in.'

'Too late – they're off. Come on.'

I took her arm and steered her out. Through the back door we saw Hugh, helping people into the back of open Land Rovers, lorries. Some were setting off on foot, some on quad bikes, but there was a general revving up for imminent exodus.

'Ooh, what fun, which one?' Maggie's eyes shone as she took in the various modes of transport.

'Whichever you like.'

She dithered.

'Come with us, luv.' From the back of a truck, a huge, burly man extended an enormous outstretched hand. Maggie took it eagerly, clambering aboard to settle amongst an earthy assortment of red-cheeked farm workers, their sons, and other locals who'd fancied a day out. Most were in tatty jeans and wellies, some with overexcited terriers on bits of string.

As they made a space for her to sit down, she turned. 'Come on, Hattie!'

'Um, actually,' I shored up a ravishing smile for Hal as he leaned down from the back of an open-ended shooting brake to offer me his hand, 'I'm going with the guns.'

I flashed her a grin. Couldn't resist a giggle, even as I caught her astonished face. As she bounced off down a track, looking outraged, holding on tight with her new friends the beaters, I settled myself down amongst the men of my choice. The ones in the Savile Row suits.

25

Two benches facing each other ran either side of the shooting brake, with six or seven guns and wives squeezed on apiece: like a tube train, I thought as we rumbled along. There the similarity ended, though. We were much closer, elbows and knees touching, and I doubt these people troubled public transport much. It was all very jolly and convivial, and on the floor between us, four or five black Labradors trembled and steamed with excitement. One rested its huge head on my knee. On we rattled, chatting companionably, this truck full of canine and human lasagne, down a bumpy track to the first drive, the one over the hill in the bottom meadow. As we bumped along, I realized it wasn't just knees, but bottoms and thighs which, by necessity, had to touch. Press, even. I tried not to think about my left buttock against Hal's. Panting with excitement – the dogs, not me – the Labradors were soothed by the jewelled hands of the wives, who were all terribly good-looking; friendly and inclusive too.

Imogen Harrison opposite, with honey-coloured hair, a wide smile and a hundred-acre voice, was telling me of a shoot she'd been to years ago, where Lester Piggott had been a guest, new to the game. As he aimed his shotgun at a pheasant running along the ground, his host had enquired mildly, 'You'll wait till it takes off, won't you, Lester?' to which the jockey had replied, 'No, I'm waiting for it to stop.' How everyone roared in our rickety-rackety lorry and 'haw haw haw!' how I roared along with them. Yes, terribly funny.

'Was that the Witherston-Parkers' shoot?' asked a distinguished, silver-haired man beside her.

'Yes, Piggy and Fluff. And of course Piggy didn't bat an eyelid!'

We all roared again, and this time I was right on cue, didn't miss a beat.

That'll be me soon, I thought, eyeing Imogen avidly: pearls in my ears, cashmere round my neck, beautifully coiffed hair under a charming tweed hat with velvet rim, and those smart leather welly boots with ties round the top. I must ask Laura where to get them. Although Laura tended to wear jeans and some hastily borrowed garish plastic boots of her daughter's. Yes, me and Hal: laughing with our friends as we weekended up in Scotland, fishing perhaps, or deerstalking. Bambi's mother sprang to mind. No, just fishing. And maybe even with Imogen and her husband? She looked nice, I thought. She smiled as my eyes devoured her.

'You're Laura's sister, aren't you? We didn't meet properly last night.'

'Yes, Hattie.'

'Well, if you're staying, do come to supper tomorrow night. We're having a few people over. Hal's coming, aren't you, Hal?'

But Hal was engrossed with the chap beside him, laughing heartily at another shooting anecdote.

'I'd love to,' I smiled back, happily. Had she already clocked us as a couple? How thrilling. 'Are you local, then?'

'Yes, only a mile or so that way.' She pointed.

'Oh right. In the village?'

'Well, the castle.'

'Ah, yes, of course.'

345

Fuck me. I knew Laura and Hugh's friends lived in stonking great piles, but I hadn't really paid much attention. I would now, though. I'd be mugging up on all the grand estates. I should clearly know who lived in which. Could I Google them? I wondered. Or was there a book I could buy? Yes, of course, there was Debrett's. Golly. Never thought I'd be popping that in my Amazon basket. Needs must, though, and I was pretty sure I'd have this aristocracy lark under my belt in no time. Just so long as the accent didn't get on my wick, I thought nervously as a thoroughly inbred woman on my left whinnied spectacularly in my ear.

Imogen was stroking a Labrador's head as she chatted away to me, sweetly actually, asking about London, what I did, genuinely interested, and as I chatted back, I chummily stroked the head of the Lab beside me. But when it moved, I realized I'd been stroking Hal's knee, clad in soft moleskin. He crossed his leg away and I burned with shame. Should have made a joke of it there and then. Imogen would: 'Thought you were the bleedin' dorg!' but Hal was still engrossed with his neighbour and the moment had passed.

We rumbled down a snaking track into the valley bottom and shuddered to a halt. Someone came running round to let us out and as I jumped down into the crisp, frosty grass, I cast Hal a glance. He grinned back, eyes shining. Well, of course they were shining: I'd fondled him in public, already. And I was going to be so restrained, so poised. Exercise some caution, for a change. I sighed. Oh, well.

Maggie came marching up.

'Cow,' she hissed in my ear. 'What's that?' She jerked her head at my shooting stick. 'A seat.' I opened it. 'You perch your backside on it as you drool behind your man at his peg.'

'Right, I'll have that,' she grabbed it. 'If I'm going to be forced into the role of subservient peg totty I'll bloody well do it in comfort.' I grabbed it back and we giggled as an unseemly tussle ensued.

'Maggie, behave.'

'Don't you tell me to behave. You're the one fluttering your eyelids at that sexy Hal Forbes. Why he hasn't been snapped up yet I simply can't imagine.'

'Actually, Maggie …' I lowered my voice to confide, to divulge, for until we share our secrets with our friends they lack a certain dimension, when suddenly, she clutched my arm.

'Look – isn't that the girl we met in the village? With Seffy?'

My laughter dissipated, my excited gossip with it, as I turned. A few yards away, Cassie and Seffy were standing together, heads bowed, talking softly. They'd clearly just clambered off the back of a throbbing quad bike.

'It is, isn't it?' repeated Maggie. 'She's gorgeous. Oh, don't look like that, Hattie. You're far too possessive. Let go, for heaven's sake. Cut those apron strings. What's her name again?'

'Cassie. Cassie Forbes.'

She looked across at her name. Smiled shyly at me.

'Cassie.' I executed a tight smile. 'I thought you couldn't get out this weekend.' It sounded awful. Accusing. I felt Seffy's eyes on me.

'Oh, well, sometimes we're allowed out for the day if we're not in a team, and I wasn't so …' She trailed off, a bit pink.

I rallied. 'Oh – well, how lovely! Yes, how nice that you could join us. Is Mummy here?'

Mummy. So cheesy-sounding, in my effort to be chummy. And no, of course she wasn't, she was sleeping off the mother of all hangovers, as I well knew. So Cassie blushed some more.

'Um, no. She's – a bit busy today.'

Seffy's eyes were cold now, at what he perceived to be my cruelty to his friend. Friend, or girlfriend, I wondered, heart thumping.

'Are you going to watch me, Hattie?' called Biba, looking gorgeous in jeans and an old hacking jacket rolled up to the elbows. 'Daddy's let me loose with the twenty-bore.'

'Under my strict supervision,' warned Hugh, hustling her away. 'Come on then, Biba, find your place and stop posing.'

People drifted away down the wide, sunlit valley to take up positions facing the sloping beech woods. My new friend Imogen materialized beside me.

'Shall we stand with Hal? He's an awfully good shot.'

She had a well-behaved black Labrador on a lead on either hand, and I wondered vaguely if it was the law. No, look, there was a yellow one over there.

'Um, yes, why not?' I mumbled distractedly.

Maggie had already beetled off up the hill with my stick. I couldn't quite make out which tweedy back she was accompanying, but I didn't really care. I was thinking about Seffy and Cassie. As we crunched through the frosty autumn leaves, Imogen prattled away beside me in a lovely familiar fashion, about her children, as women do: finding common ground. Hal took his place and we stood back a bit to watch. One was on her gap year, she told me, another at university; the eldest son in the City. It occurred to me she didn't look old enough for such grown-up children but perhaps she'd married young. How young? As young as Seffy and Cassie? Don't be silly, Hattie. But I could feel myself becoming a bit precarious. A bit unsteady. Perhaps Imogen was older than she looked? Early fifties, even? And perhaps a life of luxury was the answer; the way to keep one's bloom. Is that how you got through the menopause?

'Sorry?' She looked startled, and it occurred to me I'd voiced the question out loud: 'Is that how you got through the menopause?' She flushed, staring at me.

I cleared my throat. 'Through ... the maze of paws. In the morning, when you come down. Two dogs is a lot.' I faltered, endeavouring to look a bit unhinged, which wasn't hard.

'Oh. Yes,' she agreed uncertainly. 'But actually one belongs to our housekeeper,' she added shortly.

'Ah!' I greeted this piece of information as if it were the key to life itself. The veritable Holy Grail. Nodded hard. 'I see.'

After a bit, unsurprisingly, she moved away. Muttering something about a friend on the next stand, taking her dogs with her. Still feeling raw and unconnected, I sat numbly on a log. Watched as Hal, a few feet in front of me, scanned the sky keenly, gun poised. A pheasant flew over, low and slow, an easy target: he raised his barrel, and left it: it flew on. Then another, higher, faster this time – he fired and it spiralled down. The sound of gunfire rang out down the line, filling the air, and dogs scampered excitedly about, retrieving. It was a beautiful day, clear and bright: a bit tricky for the guns, I was told – too much glare – but lovely for us, the spectators. Enjoy, enjoy, I told myself furiously. Don't think so much. Don't spoil it.

The guns were spaced about thirty yards apart, so I could see Angus Harrison to my left, and then further up the valley Kit, and, surprisingly, no Maggie perched behind. That would disappoint her. She must have hustled off prematurely with my stick in the wrong direction. I felt a pang of relief, then checked myself. I mustn't mind so much: must be more charitable. It was just … Laura and I had never been quite sure about Kit's sexuality. We were pretty sure he wasn't gay, but we weren't entirely sure he embraced heterosexuality either. So what was the one in between … asexual, was it? The occasional girlfriend had been produced but we're talking light years ago, and they'd been mousy, shy: nothing like Maggie. And I didn't want him to get hurt, I decided, pursuing my feelings to their source. Maggie was so much more worldly. Sharp elbows, too. I wasn't sure Kit stood a chance.

Beyond Kit stood Luca, looking tall and handsome in his well-cut Italian shooting gear: a softer, lighter tweed, in a different league to the English cloth. I marvelled at how well he handled a gun, his bad arm not at all evident, aiming now at a high bird, dispatching it economically. Another swirl of feathers came crashing to the ground nearby with a thump. All eaten, I told myself firmly as it twitched convulsively before lying motionless. All eaten, and what a fantastic life they'd had, out here in the wild.

Think of battery hens, cooped up in ghastly conditions, dark and overcrowded, pecking at each other, and which we bought without blinking in the supermarket. These birds enjoyed a far superior existence, and apart from anything else, stood a chance of getting away, I thought, as Luca missed a high one. It soared away into the stratosphere.

Daisy was behind Luca, instructed by Hugh to pick up for him. Not a particularly apposite choice, but her father had been busy at the time, distracted by organizing his day. I'd witnessed Daisy open her mouth to protest, and Hugh say, 'Just go, Daisy,' annoyed that she wasn't delighted to accompany her stepbrother: forgetting, perhaps.

I watched Daisy trudge off sullenly now, hands in pockets, to retrieve a woodcock he'd brought down. It had been an excellent shot – woodcock are tiny – and it had been flying high. He turned to Daisy with an involuntary grin of boyish pleasure. She scowled back, and instantly his face reverted to a mask. He swung back again to take aim at the sky.

Beyond Luca, right on the brow of the hill, I could just make out Ralph de Granville, looking dark and dashing. Quite a few admirers were clustered behind him, perched on shooting sticks. I couldn't make out who, exactly, but he always attracted a crowd. Seffy, I knew, at number seven gun, would be just over the brow of the hill, out of sight, with Dad. Dear, dependable – trusting – Dad. Tears, ridiculously, pricked my eyelids. Why so emotional, Hattie? I blinked them back. Made myself concentrate on Ralph, silhouetted against the hazy golden light, like an old shooting print that had been retouched.

The barrel swung round as he took aim, and a cock pheasant dropped, in a flurry of red and brown, to the ground. He seemed to be shooting well. Hugh would be pleased. He wanted his guests to have a good day, and I tried to take pleasure in that, in everyone else's enjoyment. Why, then, were there nail marks in the palm of my hand? Quite deep? I unclenched my fists. Breathed slowly, in and out; the scent of autumn sharp in my nostrils.

'D'you want me to pick up?' I called with forced jollity to Hal.

He knew me well. Turned. Raised quizzical eyebrows.

'Do you want to pick up?'

'Not really,' I muttered gratefully.

He laughed. Then turned back to execute an impressive right and left, before and behind, bagging a hen, then a cock, over the bare treetops, which formed a bristling line, their dark branches standing to attention like witches' broomsticks. I had picked up once, years ago, on my first shoot here: running eagerly to help Laura, who was standing with Hugh. I'd seen her scoop a brace expertly from the ground, two fingers crooking round their colorful necks, and had hastened to follow suit. But then shrieked and promptly dropped mine. Laura had turned.

'It's still warm!' I gasped in horror.

'Of course it's still warm. It was alive two seconds ago.'

'And – oh, yuk – I think it *moved*. I can't, Laura.' I felt sick.

'Then don't,' she said calmly, coming across to pick it up herself. I'd gazed in awe at my supermodel sister, striding off in her tight jeans, hands full of dead animals.

'Practice,' she'd grinned back at me. Adding, 'Like so many difficult things in life.'

I knew at the time she'd meant Luca: practising liking him. Carla too, who, in those days, made her life a misery. I knew she meant you could get used to anything if you jolly well put your mind to it. Bucked up. Behaved. Persuaded yourself otherwise. I gazed at the bristling tree-tops knowing this was true. That you could persuade yourself to believe something you wanted, until it became the truth. That a tiny spot of self-deluding dissonance could spread like an ink stain to colour your entire life. And sometimes it was a good stain. But sometimes it was ugly.

I clenched my jaw, trying to lift myself out of my mood, which wasn't good, I knew. I concentrated on Hal's back, on the controlled swing of his body following his gun, whilst his feet remained constant. I wanted to chat, to raise my spirits, but that wasn't done. The odd remark, yes, but not a constant stream of chatter whilst your man performed. Your man. My man. I felt better. Mum would be so pleased, I thought, hearing her chortle at the peg to my left. She was behind the rather good-looking, silver-haired Angus Harrison. I smiled, despite myself, as she clapped her suede-gloved hands prettily in appreciation. Mum was a terrific flirt, but that was all. She should have been French, really. She took that great Gallic delight in entrancing men, but only adored my father, who never turned a hair – indeed, rather enjoyed the attention his still very attractive wife engendered. Trust. Yes, that was it. Mutual trust, and love. And, most importantly, kindness. They had all that, my parents. I watched as Mr Harrison popped another. Mum cooed.

He turned to smile, delighted, flicking back his silver hair. He could flick all he liked: in a few hours' time Mum would be sailing away with Dad in their ropey old Datsun back to their house in London, without ever giving Mr Harrison another thought. She was like Laura, a one-man woman, but although Laura had got Mum's looks in spades, she hadn't the confidence to flirt. Was always right by Hugh's side at a party. Not that she was shy, she just hadn't mastered the art of harmlessly enjoying other men's company – which was an art, I decided, watching Mum throw back her head and laugh at something Angus said. She saw me and waved.

'All right, darling?'

I smiled. 'Yes, thanks.'

A one-man woman. That's what I'd be, I thought, staring at Hal's broad shoulders. Had always wanted to be. Those wretched tears were stinging my eyes again. I'd just fallen in love with the wrong man. Fallen in love with his brother, the married one, and hadn't stopped loving him, even when he'd died. Not for years. Years and years. I thought about my box, under my bed, full of cuttings: how I'd get them all out, on every anniversary of his death, pore over them, and on his birthday too, and any other spurious excuse you cared to mention. Had done so right up until quite recently. Up until … well, yes, I suppose it did coincide with me feeling much better about myself, meeting new people. I formed this thought carefully, voicing it carefully, even to myself: protecting myself. Self-preservation: that's what it was all about, and if I was to protect myself now, to stop myself getting hurt, then I needed Hal beside me. I exhaled very slowly, with relief. Oh, how achingly happy I'd be, and how safe. In fact, so safe, and so secure, I wondered if I'd ever, ever talk to Seffy, properly. The thought rocked me: the possibility that I'd ever be brave enough. But with Hal beside me, with his quiet wisdom, maybe, just maybe, I'd find it within myself. Whatever else I'd thought, on that bright, sunny day, as I'd sat on my log behind Hal, hands clenched tightly in my lap, whatever else I'd pondered, or determined to do, was lost to posterity, as a shriek rang out in the valley. A man's shriek. Ghastly, primeval, penetrating. The shriek of a man in pain.

Everything stopped. The shots, the flurry of dropping birds, the dull thudding, the beaters tapping tree trunks and thrashing through the undergrowth towards us. Hal and I swung round. Beside us, Mr Harrison was already running towards his next peg, towards his neighbour, Luca, who I could see was on the ground. He was on his back, covered in blood. Blood was pouring from his face, his neck, red and fresh, and he was lying motionless. Daisy stood over him, hands over her face, screaming. She screamed one, long, continuous shriek after another, a girl's scream, different in tone and pitch to the one we'd just heard, but equally terrifying. Between them, the shotgun lay on the ground, still smoking.

26

I leaped to my feet and raced after Hal. Ahead of us, Angus Harrison was already falling to his knees beside Luca.

'Is he dead? *Is he dead?*' Daisy was backing away now, her face contorted with horror. Luca's arms were flung out crucifix-style, his legs splayed. Angus's head was sideways on Luca's chest, listening for a heartbeat.

'No,' he said finally. 'He's not dead. Someone call an ambulance – quick!'

I whipped out my phone and punched out numbers with trembling fingers. Hal, on his knees now at Luca's head, had a handkerchief balled to stanch the flow of blood. A red stain instantly spread though the white cloth like blotting paper. The rest of the shooting party were running through the valley from all directions, converging on us now.

'What happened?' Hugh barked, flinging down his gun, white-faced, as I waited for an operator to answer.

'It exploded!' Daisy wailed, shaking her hands in the air as if they were wet. 'The gun just exploded in his face!'

'Ambulance,' I breathed as a calm, female voice asked which service I required.

'Both barrels have blown,' said Hal, glancing at the gun, which was twisted and peeled back like a banana skin, a horrific sight.

'There's been an accident,' I managed into my mobile, as more people clustered, gaped in horror, then backed away, hands to mouths. As I was asked for further details I tried to keep my voice steady. 'A shooting accident. We're on the Saxby Abbey estate, Little Crandon.'

'Oh my God!' Laura was on the scene now, falling breathless to her knees beside her stepson. I saw Maggie gasp; back away, like others who'd clustered, but hung back: looking, but not looking. One, a doctor he said quietly, authoritatively, elbowed his way through, an elderly man with snowy hair and a paunch, like a monk. He crouched down, issuing instructions, whipping his necktie off and using it to help Hal.

Laura was beside me now, seizing my arm, shaking it. 'Have you got an ambulance?'

'No, the village is Little Crandon,' I said, trying not to panic, shutting my eyes and holding my hand up to her, trying to concentrate, 'but we're on the Abbey estate, out in the countryside. I don't know where exactly, and I don't see how you can—'

'Here.' Hugh took the phone from me. I listened as he explained precisely how the ambulance could get to us, down a lane, then a track. 'But it won't get any further down the valley – hurry.' He handed me back the phone. 'We'll have to get him to the top of the hill.'

'Can we move him?'

We turned to the doctor.

'We'll have to,' he replied, looking up at us soberly. 'He's losing too much blood to wait for paramedics to stretcher him out. Get a four-by-four down here – now.'

Someone fled away for an off-road vehicle. We were in a deep valley with steep sides, like a cutting; a beautiful sun-dappled valley, miles from the road.

Daisy was sobbing now, in her mother's arms, as Seffy and Biba arrived breathless, their young faces pale and horrified. Biba screamed, clutching her mouth, her eyes huge with horror. As I moved quickly to comfort her, I saw Seffy hold Cassie, who turned her face away; buried it in his neck.

'Come on, come away.' Someone, a familiar voice, had the sense to urge them – Dad, of course. 'Nothing we can do here.'

He was assisted by Maggie who, catching my eye, eloquently let me know she'd usher them off too, look after them, also good in a crisis. I gave Biba to Mum, who wrapped her in her arms, and then the grandparents led the teenagers away, in a huddle up the hill. But not Daisy: she wouldn't be parted from Laura when Mum tried to take her.

Hugh was crouched down by his son's head, talking to him, saying his name over and over, trying to reach him. Angus Harrison, on his feet now, looked gravely at the gun on the ground; didn't touch it.

'Why did it explode?' someone asked quietly.

'Must have got blocked,' he muttered. 'Mud, usually, is the classic.'

'Mud where?'

'In the end of the barrel. But he'd have had to have stuck it in the dirt – like this.' He demonstrated with a jabbing motion downwards. 'Madness.'

'I did!' sobbed Daisy suddenly, jerking her head up from Laura's breast. 'He handed it to me while he unwrapped some new cartridges. Didn't even look at me, didn't ask, just handed the gun back, arrogantly, and I was cross and jabbed the barrel in the ground. I didn't know!' She wailed in horror as it dawned.

Hugh looked like he'd been shot himself.

'Oh, Daisy,' breathed Laura, before she could stop herself.

'Oh, Daisy!' Her daughter screamed, wrenching herself away. 'You see? Oh, Daisy – you've killed him!' She turned and ran, arms and legs windmilling in all directions, out of the valley, away up the hill. Laura moved like I've never seen her move, like a missile, after her.

And then, bouncing over the horizon, tumbling down the hill, a green Land Rover careered towards us, stopping in a spray of mud. The back door flew open and finally, finally we could all cling to activity, as four or five men, under the monk-like GP's instruction, carefully lifted the bleeding boy, only a boy, I thought with a lurch as his thin, frail arm, the withered one, dangled – someone held it up quickly – into the back of the Land Rover, to lay him on the bench along one side. And then they all got in, the men, to cushion Luca, support him from the bumps, one holding his head, all on their knees, all blood-splattered, the driver slammed the back door and ran round to leap in the front and take the wheel.

We watched as slowly, carefully, the Land Rover crawled up the hill, out of the valley, all of us holding our breath collectively, willing it not to jerk. But the driver, the game-keeper, Dan, whom Maggie had taken a shine to earlier, knew the ground like his own body. He coaxed that vehicle around ruts and over the brow of the hill, to softer ground, a meadow, to a track where he could crawl along and meet the ambulance, which even now could be heard wailing towards us out of the distance. A wave of relief rippled palpably amongst us and I felt my shoulders relax slightly. I exhaled slowly.

I was aware of Hal beside me, which surprised me. Hugh, of course, had gone, Angus Harrison too, and some other men. I thought Hal had been amongst them. He'd been at Luca's shoulder, lifting him.

'Oh, I thought you'd gone.'

He looked at me. 'I wanted to make sure you were all right.'

Don't ask me why, but in that moment, as we made our way up the steep hill, I was transported back to the days when Hal waited for me outside lecture theatres, with cups of coffee: that same penetrating look on his face. Once, when I'd been to see a musical with some girlfriends – a silly show, it may even have been The Chippendales in the King's Theatre – and we'd come out giggling, recounting bits, there he'd been, in his greatcoat, waiting, and my laugher had died as my friends had caught his expression and knowingly peeled off. My heart had sunk. Why, of all things, should that spring to mind, I thought angrily, guiltily even, as we, the straggling remains of the shooting party, made our way up the steep hill, out of the sunlit valley.

The children were in the kitchen with my parents when we got back. Mum had made them sweet tea and they were sitting in a shocked huddle around the table, cradling their mugs, white-faced.

'Is he going to be all right?' Biba said immediately, as I came in.

'I'm sure,' I soothed automatically.

'We don't know,' said Hal quietly. More honestly. We didn't know.

'It wasn't Daisy's fault,' blurted Biba, eyes glittering. 'How was she to know you shouldn't get mud in the end. She doesn't shoot. It wasn't her fault!'

'Of course it wasn't,' Mum murmured, swooping to put an arm round her as Biba burst into tears again.

'Where is Daisy?'

'Upstairs with Laura,' said Seffy.

'Best left, love,' said Dad, putting a hand on my arm as I made to go. Yes. Of course.

Outside, the sound of people packing shooting paraphernalia into cars, drifted through. Guns were being zipped into slips, gumboots coming off, shoes on, cartridge bags thrown in. But there was no cheery banter to accompany the activity. No end-of-day laughter or chat, as there had been when we'd all set off. It was eerily quiet. Through the window I saw the Preston-Coopers, who were supposed to be staying, loading smart overnight bags into their car; the Palmers, too. Time to go. No one wanted weekend visitors hanging around at a family crisis; they'd make themselves scarce. Even Maggie was nowhere to be seen. Angus Harrison put his head round the kitchen door.

'You'll give them our love?'

'Of course.'

He nodded gravely. Departed. Nothing more to be said. It shocked me, though, that he thought the worst. These men shot regularly, most Saturdays in the season: a barrel exploding in someone's face was clearly a rare accident.

'I'd better go,' Cassie said uncertainly, sensitively.

'There's no need,' Seffy told her, quickly.

'No, but my mum ...'

'I'll walk you back.'

They got up from the table. I watched them move to the back door together.

'Hal could run you back,' I said quickly, and when I turned, enquiringly, Hal's eyes were already on me.

'Sure,' he agreed, grabbing his keys. He strode out ahead of them, before the youngsters had a chance to demur. I watched them go. Thanked him silently for that.

'Now then, young lady.' Dad turned to Biba. 'You and I are going to hose down those dogs. Daisy won't thank you for leaving them in that state.'

The two Labradors, who'd been in the river, were always under Daisy's self-imposed wing. Ordinarily she'd be cleaning them in the kennels.

'No – no, you're right.' Biba still very distressed, but knowing this was something she could do for her sister, followed my father out. They took the dogs with them.

The large house, so recently full of noise and laughter and the expectation of a glorious day ahead, was suddenly ghostly, denuded. I looked at Mum opposite me, gazing wearily into her tea. Her ash-blonde hair was a little awry; her shoulders sagged in her Italian cape. I leaned across; held her hand.

'Why don't you go and have a lie-down?'

She looked up at me gratefully. 'Oh, darling, would you mind? I feel all in.'

'Of course not.'

'I won't sleep, of course. So you'll let me know the minute ...?'

'Of course I will, the moment they phone,' I assured her.

As she went, gathering her handbag, it occurred to me she looked older: in stocking feet now, shoes in her hand, her bunions from years of high heels hurting, no doubt, face lined and tired. And it struck me they wouldn't be around for ever, these parents of mine. And they'd most likely die unaware; uninformed … No, Hattie, don't go there.

I got up from the table shakily. Went to the sink, clutching the tops of my arms, gazing out of the window. The thing that I loathed and feared most in myself, which on good days was a small seed in the corner of my mind, always there but small, but on bad days was a huge swollen growth, the size of a watermelon, filled my head like an abscess. Veined and thin-skinned, it seemed ready to pop. I held on tight to the edge of the sink; shut my eyes. Breathed deeply. No. I wouldn't let it pop. Couldn't let it pop. And, if I willed it enough, it would deflate. Crumple back like an airbag, or a child's balloon, days after the party. I waited for that to happen. The kitchen clock ticked on in the empty house. Minutes passed. I stayed there, at the window, holding on, in so many ways.

A car came up the drive. Hal's car. I exhaled slowly. That was quick. Good. The car forked before it got to the house, went slowly down the back drive, probably to the kennels, I realized, where Seffy had no doubt spotted Biba and Dad. Gone to see if there was any news. No, no news. A bad sign, I thought. Surely if it was good, Hugh would ring? I looked at the phone on the dresser. I can't, its shape seemed to say. And I thought how often I'd stared at phones over the years, willing them to ring. Ring. Ring! I'd breathed at one, my face close. It had been a different shape from this neat, compact little handset on the dresser: bulkier, squarer, the receiver attached with a coiled cord.

I opened the window for some air. Could hear the others with the dogs, Hal and Dad raising Biba and Seffy's spirits: giving them a job to cling to. They'd probably be hosing down the kennels too, now. And I remembered how good Hal was at that, at taking one's mind off things: remembered coming out of my finals, my face white with shock.

'Not one question. Not one bloody question! I was promised *King Lear*. It was all *Macbeth* and *Hamlet*!'

'So what?' he'd shrugged. 'It's only a fraction of the marks.'

I'd extracted a Number Six from a crushed packet with trembling fingers, leaned against the wall and sucked hard as hordes of students flowed past discussing the paper.

'It's a quarter. The tragedies are a quarter!'

'A fraction, like I say. Not a complete tragedy.'

'Not funny, Hal. I was so bloody stumped I ushered in Goneril and Reagan anyway, said Shakespeare had had enough of neurotic females after Ophelia, wanted a bit of bite.'

'Which will impress the examiners no end. Shame you didn't usher in the Brides of Dracula too: they had bite. Come on, I thought we'd go to the zoo.'

'The zoo?' I'd blown out a line of smoke in astonishment. 'No, no I need a hostelry, Hal, need to do some sorrow-drowning. It'll take at least a bottle.'

He'd insisted, though, and we'd spent a very crazy day at Edinburgh Zoo, making the animals feel at home, which Hal said was important. Said it was rude to stare, as everyone else did – how would we like people to walk past our houses staring in? Said we had to be supportive, inclusive. So we'd lumbered past the elephants swinging our arms from our noses, chattered and screeched at the monkeys, waddled like penguins past their pool. I smiled, in spite of myself now, remembering the aquarium. Hal in his huge coat, being a swooping sea turtle, the odd looks: giggling like children, which we weren't much more than, of course, *King Lear* forgotten. And how Hal had laughed when I'd been the koala bear, opening my eyes wide, crouched up on a bench, clutching my hand-bag to my tummy as my baby. A wonderful laugh, his head thrown back to the heavens, brown eyes glittering: lovely. My heart gave an exultant little kick, a little – see? kick, and I could feel the thing in my head, my abscess, shrink down, back to the little pea-sized lump. Better: much better.

My hands had already unclenched from the rim of the sink when he came in through the back door, glancing quickly at me to check I was OK.

I smiled. Gave a little nod. And we knew each other so well, we didn't really have to speak.

'But no news from the hospital?' Hal asked.

'No, no news.'

He came across. Held me close. And it felt so right. So safe. I stayed in his arms, my head on his chest, in the quiet, ticking house. I felt every muscle relax: felt my bones liquefy. At length, I raised my head.

'Where's Seffy?'

'I left him down there.'

'At the kennels?'

'No, at Cassie's.'

I stared. 'What?'

'Well, Letty wasn't there. She'd left a note saying she'd gone to London. Quite normal, according to Cassie.

Apparently she just disappears on a whim, leaving Cassie alone, which is rather worrying.'

'So they're on their own? Seffy and Cassie?'

'Yes. Seffy said he'd walk back later, but he didn't want to leave her just yet.'

'Of course he doesn't!' I stormed, breaking out of his embrace roughly. I stepped back. My breathing was laboured.

'What d'you mean?' He looked startled.

'Well, for God's sake, Hal, use your head! Two teenagers alone in an empty house – of course he doesn't want to leave her! What would you do? What *are* you doing, even, right now? Getting cosy, that's what!'

'Oh, I don't think—'

'You don't think? You don't think? Well, you're not a parent, Hal. You don't think they'll be snogging away down there? Getting to first base? I can't *believe* you've been so stupid!' I was out of control. Unsafe in every way. Didn't recognize my horrible, rasping voice.

'They'll be getting down to it, Hal, you mark my words. Oh, you stupid, *stupid* man!'

I swung about wildly, casting around for my car keys – my bag, where was my bag? On the chair – no. Oh, on the dresser.

'Unlikely, don't you think?'

'*Unlikely?* Oh, no, most, *most* likely, you have no idea.' I was rummaging for my keys, frantic fingers fumbling. Not in my bag. Where then – in my coat? I was in a race against time, and I couldn't find the wherewithal to get there, to stop him. Where were my *sodding keys*?

Hal cleared his throat. 'No, I meant, unlikely, seeing as she's his sister.'

My hands froze on the pile of papers I'd been upending in my search: a pile of Laura's bills — milk, newspapers. Odd, how, in that moment, I remembered she owed the milkman £40. The whole world seemed to stop on its axis, like a Ferris wheel. And I was at the top, left hanging: swinging in my cart.

27

I stayed staring at the pile of papers. Felt the blood drain from my face. Slowly, I turned. 'What did you say?'

'You heard.' Hal's eyes were steady. Not aggressive, but focused.

I found a stool; reached out and dragged it to me. The earth had tipped beneath me and my legs wouldn't carry me. I was aware of his gaze, but felt oddly detached from it. No, Hal couldn't have said that. Couldn't know that. This couldn't be happening. If it were happening, if my world were unravelling like this, full tilt, at breakneck speed, life wouldn't be going on like this. The gardener, for instance, outside the window, wouldn't be raking the gravel in those slow, languid strokes. The sun wouldn't be dancing and dappling those yellow and green leaves in such a frivolous fashion. If Hal knew Cassie was Seffy's sister, the radio, on low in the corner, certainly wouldn't be reminding me to get down to DFS now, for yet more slashed prices, more sensational bargains.

'And that's not all!' went on the excitable voice. 'Any three-piece suite you buy before the end of the month comes with a free, Scotch Guarded cover, and a five-year guarantee!'

I turned my head to face my informer, feeling robotic in my movements. My mouth was sticky, but my voice seemed about to engage, to make a break for it.

'You know?' I heard it say.

'Yes, I know.'

I stared at Hal. Almost challenged him. Very nearly didn't believe him. But his eyes told me it was true. That he could see right through me, right around me, right inside me: knew everything about me. Could see my heart, soul, mind and spirit. It was as if, with all the thoroughness of the drugs squad, I'd been strip-searched, and all my dirty little secrets were now on display, spread about for all to see.

My voice became the only animate thing in the room.

'How did you know?' It came out in a whisper.

'Seffy told me. Or at least, told me he suspected.'

I clutched my mouth. 'Seffy!'

Hal gave me a moment. But a million moments would never have been enough. Eventually he went on, slowly, methodically; as one would to a patient coming round from an anaesthetic.

'Said he suspected Dominic might be his father and you his real mother.'

'But – but no. I mean how …? That simply isn't possible. How can he have?' I was frozen with terror.

'He came to see me. Tracked me down. Rang first, of course, leaving a polite message at my law firm, informing me that he was Hattie Carrington's son, asking if we could possibly meet. He left his email address. I answered, and the following day he was downstairs in reception. We went for a drink. He asked me if you and my brother had ever had a relationship. I had to say quite possibly, you'd been caught in his office. OK, he said, when? When would it have been? He wanted dates. Precise timings. He wrote it all down in a notebook. Very calmly, methodically. He told me he'd found some stuff at the back of your wardrobe in a box. Had forced the lock while you were away. Wanted to know why it was so secret, so permanently barred. Then he had the box mended. He'd found all the clippings about

Dominic that you'd kept, all through his glittering career: articles, profiles. The obituaries and retrospectives after he'd died. Reams of it. Years and years in a small box. A first edition of his diaries too, published posthumously, of course.'

I tried to make sense of what he was saying. My head was still shrieking – what? *What?* This couldn't be happening. Seffy *knew*?

He asked if I'd take a DNA test to see if it matched his, or was close. As his uncle and nearest relative on that side of the family. Not strictly true: Cassie is, of course. But he didn't want to alarm her until he knew for sure.'

'When?' I managed at length, mouth very dry now. 'When was this?'

'About a year ago.'

A year ago. I couldn't speak. Stared at him.

His eyes held me. I was having difficulty breathing. Shock had sucked the air from my lungs. What I could muster was coming in shallow bursts. A year ago.

'Why didn't he say anything?' My mouth formed the words but my mind was racing frantically ahead. My son knew. Knew he was mine. I was struggling to catch up. Having to stumble to my feet with each well-aimed kick to the head.

'He figured if you didn't want him to know, he wasn't going to rush to tell you. Initially, of course, he didn't think that. Initially, when we first found out, he was very angry. And extremely distressed.'

Suddenly I dropped my head into my hands. Of course he was. Because what I'd done was the most wicked thing a mother could ever do. Disown her child. But I'd had to do it. Couldn't tell the world he was Dominic's: had had to protect Dom, his career, his reputation. Back then, years ago, he was constantly in the papers. Constantly jetting off, Kissinger-style to the Middle East, Sierra Leone Kosovo, even ... There he'd be on the six o'clock news, our man in some war-torn territory. My man. Young, clever, handsome. A man to be trusted. Trusted with our country's safety. And there I'd sit watching him, with Seffy in my arms, or later, toddling about the tiny sitting room. Dom would sweep back his mane of blond hair and talk to camera, troops in battledress ranged behind him, talk to me, look me in the eyes, his voice deep and sincere, telling me a peace treaty was imminent. 'We're working hard: trust me.' How could I wreck all that? Throw in a grenade, a lovechild, watch his life implode? Tarnish his name? Oh, no, I'd had to protect him. I'd loved him so much I would do that, at all costs. But what a cost.

And then later, when I thought I could tell Seffy, when Dom died, thought I could tell the world, it was almost worse. He became a martyr, a hero. Our own Foreign Secretary, victim of a heinous terrorist attack. The funeral all over the papers. His memorial service televized, dignitaries, heads of state attending, the Duke of Edinburgh on behalf of the Queen. All that sorrow and reverence. How could I? I just couldn't. But ... maybe a couple of years down the line? When it had all blown over? But then his diaries had come out, posthumously, to great acclaim. A huge publishing phenomenon, a forward by Letty, his widow; a picture of her and Cassie. So I couldn't. And then ... well, then it had been too late.

'I must go to him,' I whispered, stumbling to my feet, but my knees were like a rag-doll's. Hal came across and pulled up a stool beside me.

'Wait. Wait a bit, until you're composed. He's known for over a year. A bit longer won't make any difference.'

Over a year my son had been living with the knowledge. Why hadn't he said? Railed at me, accused me of treachery, yelled in my face about betrayal – left me, even? Suddenly I went cold. A year ago he'd been expelled from his London day school for smoking and drinking, and eventually, albeit unintentionally, setting fire to his common room. A very unsettled mind in this profound and intense boy, the child psychologist's report had read. A troubled child, his headmaster had said, of this model pupil: this previously straight-A student. Is everything all right at home, Mrs Carrington? And I'd thought it was. Hadn't known. Why hadn't he said?

'Why didn't he say?' My voice, from somewhere small and remote.

Hal shrugged. 'You'd kept it a secret from him for fourteen years. Why shouldn't he keep it secret from you? Actually, I think he was so angry he thought he'd exact some revenge. But then, more recently, as we talked – at length – I hope he understood a bit more. I think he was just very sad, Hattie.'

Many things struck me about this: Hal and Seffy knew each other well. Had investigated DNA together, had talked at length. Jesus. All this had existed, perhaps been staring at me, whilst I'd been carrying on with my world. The whole of last year was not the way I'd perceived it at all. But 'very sad' pierced me most. My boy. The person I loved most in the world. I thought of all the times I'd almost told him, but had lost my nerve: times when I'd sat on the side of my bed, screwing up my courage, hands tightly clasped, knees together, while he was downstairs watching Sky. How I'd reached for my box, in the cupboard, to take it down and show him: talk to him. But had always bottled it. Thought – tomorrow, I'll do it tomorrow. Or next holidays, when he's home. And then, the moment had passed. And the box had gone back in the wardrobe. But ridiculously, because I'd almost done it, I felt that was better than not having tried. Told myself I'd passed some sort of honesty test.

Always, always, you see, I'd shrunk from his reaction. Knew his shock and horror at my not telling him earlier, when he was young, would be too much for me to bear. That I'd shrivel in his eyes. Yet I'd already shrivelled. Had been quite desiccated for over a year now. I remembered questioning his appalling behaviour last summer. Remembered his rudeness, coldness: 'How *could* you behave like that, Seffy?' I'd put it all down to teenage hormones. That day he'd thrown the vase across the kitchen, smashed the window. I'd put that down to stress from having been expelled. But he'd known.

'I think a bit of him was still hoping you'd tell him. That you were maybe waiting until he was sixteen.'

I seized this like a lifebelt. Sixteen. Would I? No. No, the unattractive truth was – I thought I'd got away with it. To my shame, I knew I wouldn't have told him. Was too cowardly. Loved him too much: no, correction, loved his *love* too much, which, I now realized, I had been without for some time. He'd withheld it. How hurt he must have been to do that. I doubled up on my stool and pressed the heels of my hands to my eyes. It seemed to me some old wound in my chest had started bleeding.

'Once I'd started down that road of deception,' I whispered into my fists, 'I couldn't stop. Everyone thought he was adopted. Everyone had believed my story. It was like a rolling stone, gathering more and more moss and becoming enormous. And at the point when I really thought I might tell him, could tell him, a couple of years after Dom died, Letty published the diaries.'

'And you didn't want to tarnish Dominic's memory.'

I jerked upright. 'How could I suddenly appear with Dominic Forbes's lovechild? Have the nation turn its eyes on us? At a time when everyone was remembering him again, going all misty-eyed. And how much worse would that have been for Seffy, too? Dominic was a *huge* political figure – huger still for being blown up by terrorists – a national hero. I couldn't let the tabloids loose on us, on my son. They'd have had a field day.'

'Yes, I did tell Seffy that. Said you were protecting him. I've explained that.'

'Oh – have you, Hal?' I reached out – seized his arm. 'You've explained why I did it?'

'As much as I could, yes. I've always batted for you, Hattie. Always will.'

It hung there in the air: his love for me. A constant reminder. Reproach, even. My hand came back to my lap.

'But Seffy didn't see it like that. He only saw you protecting Dominic. And yourself.'

'No, never myself,' I said fiercely, fists clenched. 'I couldn't have cared less what they said about me, wrote about me. But Dom—'

'You loved very much. And his memory. Seffy would say more than him. A greater love.'

I hung my head. 'Not true,' I whispered. 'No one ever more than Seffy. But with each passing day it became so much harder. So impossible to do a U-turn once I'd told him he was adopted.'

'So why did you do that?' I swung round at the voice. Seffy was standing in the doorway behind us, white-faced.

'Oh, Seffy.' I got up and stumbled towards him. He backed away, hands up, stopping the traffic. His eyes were hard and narrow. Impenetrable.

'No, Mum, I want to know. Why did you?'

'Darling, look—'

'*Just tell me.*'

My breathing was very erratic now and I wondered if I'd faint. I groped for my stool behind me. Sat down. I knew this was very important. The truth. I gave myself a moment.

'Because that was the lie I'd told since you were born. That I'd adopted you in Croatia. That was what everyone thought – Granny, Grandpa, Laura, all my friends. And I knew, when you were about six, that should have been the moment to tell everyone. Let them know I was about to tell you the truth, that there was something they should know. But I lost my nerve. Found myself telling you what they all thought, instead.'

'That you'd adopted me. You denied you'd even given birth to me. Thanks, Hattie.'

I gazed at him in horror.

'Well, I've called you Mum for fifteen years. Maybe now I'll call you Hattie, when in fact you're my mother.'

There was a warped logic to this, I couldn't deny.

'Every day I thought I'd tell you,' I whispered. 'I swear to God, Seffy, not a day went by when I didn't consider it. I thought I'd tell you when you were ten, then eleven. Thought you'd be old enough to understand why I'd done it. But as time went by, I knew you'd understand less. I'd done such a terrible thing, and it was getting bigger with every passing moment.'

'It defines me, Mum.' Seffy's voice trembled. His face was ashen. 'Knowing who my parents are. It defines everyone. It's so basic, so fundamental. You denied me that.'

'I'll go,' Hal said quietly. I'd forgotten he was there.

'No, stay, please,' said Seffy. 'I don't want to be alone with her.'

The wound in my chest erupted and gushed through my insides, flooding me. I felt my frame crumple as I hid my face in my hands.

'Seffy,' began Hal, 'you have no idea how much interest you would have attracted. Will still attract, if you—'

'Come out of the closet?' Seffy turned on him. 'Why shouldn't I – of course I will! Today's papers are tomorrow's fish-and-chip wrappings; why should prurient press interest be more important than me knowing who I am?' His eyes were blazing. 'Knowing I have a real mother, a dead father, a sister in Cassie – who was horrified, incidentally—'

'You told her.' My hands fell from my face.

'Of course I told her. I got to know her, gradually, then we talked for hours in the woods at the dance.'

Which was why he hadn't made it back to the coach on time. They weren't snogging at all. Were talking about being brother and sister. About sharing the same father.

'Seffy, I'm so sorry.' My voice came from somewhere very distant. Very dark. 'And I'm sorry that that is so inadequate.' My stomach had turned to ashes long ago. The silence ached between us.

'It's a start,' said my son, at length. 'Any sort of apology is a start.'

Oh, thank God. A tiny shard of light. He turned away, though, seeing the hope in my eyes.

'And talking has helped. To Hal. To Cassie. I hated you, Mum, more than you can ever imagine, a year ago. But listening to Hal, and more recently Cassie, who could see ...' He hesitated. 'Well, she could sort of see, although she didn't condone it, how it had happened.'

I exhaled through barely parted lips. Oh, bless you, Cassie. Sweet, sensitive Cassie. I dug my nails into the palms of my hands. Don't speak. Don't hope.

'Or at least, she could see how hard it was, once you'd started down a path, to turn back. To say – hang on, everyone, actually, he's mine.' I couldn't look up. Meet his eye. His voice continued in my ears. 'And the odd thing was ... I always felt you were my mother. Never felt adopted. But maybe all adopted children feel like that, is how I explained it to myself.'

'I love you so much, Seffy,' I said in a low, quavering voice, raising my head. Daring to look. 'So much.'

'I know.'

This much he did know, whatever I'd done.

'But that whole Bosnia bollocks ...' he said savagely.

I bowed my head. 'I know.'

'That whole elaborate lie.'

'It had to be elaborate.'

377

'Putting maps on my bedroom wall, taking me there when I was little. Swimming out into the sea and showing me the mountains where my supposed father fought for his country.' His eyes were like ice now, or fire. Both.

'You were so fascinated,' I whispered in shame. 'So consumed by it all, at nine, or ten—'

'Ten,' he corrected viciously.

'Begged me to take you there to see. What could I do? Deny you that? And it wasn't a complete lie. Don't forget I was pregnant there with you, had you there. To some extent your roots were there. You were born there.'

'But my father wasn't a fucking guerrilla, was he?'

'No. No, but … the awful thing was, Seffy, I came to believe the lie myself, almost. Because I wished your conception had been otherwise, I found myself going along with it.'

'Taking me to the village, trying to find the house—'

'With my heart in my throat. Hating myself. Wondering how I could be doing it. But knowing, in some odd, mis-shapen way, it was out of love for you. Protecting you. So who's child am I? you'd have asked. Oh, a married man's, a politician I once worked for, who had a wife and child already. Your trusting little ten-year-old face.'

'No, you were ashamed of me knowing that about *you*. Ashamed of yourself.'

'That's true,' I gulped.

'And Dominic was dead by then, anyway,' he said obstinately.

'Yes, he was.' I dug deep. Shut my eyes for courage. Spoke slowly. Carefully. 'But what I feared most of all, Seffy, was your censure. Your face. Your eyes. The shock. Then the recoil. That is what I have cowered from all these years. That's why I couldn't do it.'

The air felt charged between us. I think because it was the truth, and Seffy recognized it. At length he spoke. Unsteadily, though.

'And did you think you'd ever tell me?'

I dug deep again. 'I know you'd like me to say yes,' my voice wavered, 'and that it would help both of us if I could. But I have to tell you, Seffy, your mother is a coward through and through. I was ashamed of myself, and I knew you'd be ashamed of me.'

'Plenty of people have affairs.'

'I didn't have a love affair with your father. It didn't last months, weeks, even.'

'How long?'

'Just once.'

'Only once?'

'Yes, one day. One day in May.'

They waited for me. Seffy and Hal. I shut my eyes. That one day could change so many people's lives.

'I wasn't even a mistress. Didn't have that distinction.'

'So how …?'

I took a huge intake of breath to steady myself. 'It was the day of the reshuffle. Dominic, your father—'

'Dominic will do,' Seffy said harshly.

'He'd gone to see the Prime Minister. To find out which job he'd secured – if anything – in the cabinet. It was a very big deal. I waited, I remember, at the window across from Parliament Square. I remember tension gripping my body, remember the huge love I had for him, the hope, his anxious face as he'd gone. He came back elated. He'd done it. Got it. Got Foreign Secretary. He embraced me, swung me round. Kissed me. We were so happy and that felt so good.' I bent my head.

'So – what, you went in his office?' Seffy's voice. 'In broad daylight?'

I swallowed. 'We locked the door. Pulled the blinds.'

The shock, in Laura's kitchen, was palpable.

'D' you see now?' I said, looking up. 'You want the truth, Seffy, but what if it's not palatable? What if your mother's a – a—' I broke off again, gulped air.

'But you loved him?' he said abruptly.

'Oh, yes.' I blinked, astonished. 'With all my heart.' Hal turned away at this, but Seffy didn't.

'So, no,' I said sadly. 'In answer to your question, I don't know if I ever would have told you.'

'Not even if I'd gone out with Cassie?' His eyes challenged mine.

I nodded. 'Yes. Yes, that … would have driven me.'

'Which was why Seffy was not so very displeased with creating that illusion,' Hal observed quietly.

'Forcing my hand,' I said numbly.

'Yes.'

No one spoke. Silence flooded the room. It roared in our ears as we all digested the past: how it had caught up with the future. How the past always catches up, eventually.

'Tell us about Bosnia,' said Hal, eventually, and that 'us' caught me. Yes, we were us, now. The three of us. Why should that disconcert me? I wanted to ask how often Seffy had seen him. Just that once in London? Or more regularly? Time would tell. Right now, it was my turn.

'I went out there, to Split, not knowing I was pregnant. It didn't occur to me, so much else had happened. But I knew I had to get away. Letty had come up to London to congratulate Dom, had come into the office and no, she hadn't found us. An hour or so earlier she would have done, but she walked in just as I'd leaned over his desk to kiss him goodbye.' I remembered her face as she'd stood there in her black and white dress, eight months pregnant.

'So I went away. And because Kit was there, Bosnia seemed like a very good idea. I wanted ... a difficult place. Not an easy, sunny beach. I wanted to prove to myself that I wasn't a thoroughly unpleasant person.' I remembered Hal's note on my bed. I swallowed. Went on: 'So I went to join Kit. And it was grim, of course it was grim. It was a war zone, and people were in far direr straits than me. That, at least, helped. I felt I was doing some good, even if it was minuscule. And then after a few months, I realized I was pregnant.' I breathed out shakily. 'And I was horrified. And if you want the whole truth, Seffy, if you want it warts and all, full disclosure, I thought – well, if I work my cotton socks off, heave heavy boxes into lorries, drive across mountains until I'm too tired to see, negotiate rocky paths in trucks with no suspension and bounce about savagely enough, well, then maybe I'll lose it.' I looked up. 'I was very young. Pregnant with a married man's baby.'

Seffy acknowledged this, I could see. He nodded.

'But you clung on in there. You were persistent. You weren't going anywhere.'

'But didn't it show? People must have known. What about Kit?'

'I hid it for as long as I could – baggy tops, that sort of thing – and of course people didn't know me, didn't really know my size. But yes, it did eventually. But by then Kit had gone away. He left almost as soon as I arrived. I was in Croatia, on the coast, and he was right in the middle of the country, in Sarajevo, incarcerated in the siege. We had no contact with each other for five months. By the time we saw one another again, you'd been born.'

'Where?'

'In Dubrovnik.'

He waited. The big empty house waited too. Ticked on. I licked my lips. 'The place ... I went to find with you, the little house in the village, in the foothills, that was where I'd lived when I'd worked at the depot. With a family called the Mastlovas. Refugees themselves. The daughter, Ibby, and I were pregnant together.'

'They knew you were?'

'Oh, yes. In time. And that was our bond, mine and Ibby's. We talked about it a lot, with our limited language. She was due just a few weeks before me. And very happy about it.' A sudden, vivid picture of the pair of us sitting together in the dusty front yard, stomachs swollen, children playing, chickens pecking in the dirt, Ibby knitting a tiny shawl. She'd tried to make me as happy as she was about my unborn child. I remembered her passing me the needles with a laugh, telling me to knit on, then getting up to go back into the house to start supper: but my eyes had filled; one hand on my huge bump, tears spilling, a ball of creamy wool tumbling off my lap, unravelling on the ground.

I cleared my throat. 'When Ibby went into labour they all went to the hospital – the whole family – and the car was blown up by a shell. By the time I got there, she'd delivered her baby, but died from her wounds. Perhaps it was the shock, but I went into premature labour. Her baby only survived a few hours, but mine was born – you were born – soon after.'

I saw the harassed young doctor, who'd delivered Seffy, leaning over me. Then I saw something my mind had blocked for years. Heard it too. Voices shouting, screaming in the corridor about a kindergarten being bombed: the ward door flying open. A man, his face racked with anguish, his little girl in his arms: one leg just a bloody stump, half her head blown off. The man shrieking, forcing the limp, mutilated body into the obstetrician's arms, there in the maternity ward: a desperate man, desperate for help. They say the mind blocks these sorts of memories to protect us. Does it also protect us from the consequences resultant of such appalling chance and timing? In which a terrible wrong can seem like the only course of action? Or do we have to work out the whys and wherefores for ourselves, years later. I took a breath to steady myself.

'I fled. I left you, Seffy, on that hospital bed.' Seffy's eyes widened in shock. 'I fled in terror and disbelief at all that had happened.'

There was a silence as my words were absorbed.

'Didn't anyone try to stop you? Find you?'

'No one had time. Dubrovnik was a city in chaos, remember. Injured were arriving constantly. Bloody children in despairing arms. And no one knew who I was. I got a lift on a lorry and went back to the village, to the empty little house. Very empty. All dead. The whole family. And taciturn as they were, they'd been my family, all those months. And there I was, without my baby. I was … well, I wasn't well. In my head. Traumatized. All sorts of labels would be stuck on me now, I recognize that.' I took another deep breath. Let it out slowly. 'People do extraordinary things in war, Seffy. Not always good, brave ones. Although those are the ones you hear about.' My shoulders sagged, then I composed myself. 'I don't remember much about those few days, except I know I sat in the dark, by an unlit fire, the dogs on my feet. I was in shock, I think.' I raised my head. 'Two days later, I took one of the Bedford lorries, and went back to the hospital. I was told the baby had been taken to an orphanage.' I looked at my son, very calm now. 'You need to know, Seffy, that I didn't go to that orphanage to reclaim you. I went to see that you were really there. Safe and well. To place you, in my head. Some kind people might say I was not in my right mind at the time, but I think it's important you know that.' I was aware of Seffy watching me intently but I couldn't read him.

'I went to the orphanage with a friend I drove convoys with. It was run by nuns, in a disused castle in a bombed corner on the outskirts of Dubrovnik. Kindly, gentle nuns. Not an altogether terrible place. They did the best they could. But still ... dismal lines of cots. No place for a baby to grow up. The moment I saw you, something kicked in. My heart, I suppose. It started beating again. I told them immediately you were mine, that you'd been born to me in Dubrovnik hospital, that I wanted you back. No one believed me. I told them there were records, birth certificates. Of course there weren't, there was a bloody civil war on; no one had taken the time to write anything down. I told them to examine me, then they'd know. They wouldn't. They said a lot of mothers had lost their babies in the war, came in claiming orphans.' I gave a wry smile. 'The final irony was, I couldn't have you. I told them I'd be back. I was. With the help of the UN, friends in the right places, and my humanitarian connections behind me, I adopted you. We came home two weeks later. Me and my Bosnian child. Ibby's child. That was my story, my *raison d'être*. I told everyone it was her baby who'd been taken to the orphanage, and that I'd gone and claimed him. And I had papers to prove it, signed by the mother superior. Papers to show to my parents, the world. Which was why, in my head, I was able to believe I'd adopted you.'

It seemed to me the breath that came out of me as I exhaled went on for ever; had been waiting to come out for so long. It seemed to wrap around us, this air, this silence, enveloping the three of us, suspending us in time. A numb calmness took hold of me and the wound in my chest no longer wept, no longer seeped. It was done. The thing was done.

28

It seemed to me we held those positions for a long time. Hal leaning on the dresser, arms folded, Seffy with his back to the sink, looking down at his shoes, me on my stool, gazing at my hands, like three characters in a play oblivious to the curtain coming down at the end of an act, still there when it's raised for the next.

Running footsteps in the room above vaguely stirred me. Down the backstairs they came, along the passage, until the door flew open. Laura stood there: face pale, but alight.

'He's going to be all right. He was knocked unconscious by the blast but he's come round and he hasn't got any serious head injuries. Hugh just rang, he's going to be OK.' She covered her face and burst into tears.

It took me a moment. Then, feeling numb and displaced, I got up and crossed the room to hug her. 'Thank the Lord. Oh, thank God, Laura,' I managed to whisper.

Seffy hugged her too and she fought for composure. She gave a mighty sniff, threw her head up to the ceiling and blinked hard. 'He's on a drip, and very groggy, obviously, but he's conscious. Admittedly he's got this almighty gash across his forehead and his face is completely peppered by the shot, but heads do bleed – ferociously, apparently. Apart from the gash, though, it's mostly superficial.' She blew her nose vigorously. 'Hugh says it looks much, much worse than it is.' She nodded emphatically; tucked her hanky back up her sleeve.

'I'm so glad, Laura.' Hal crossed the room to join us and squeezed her shoulder.

'He says obviously he'll have to stay in for a bit, for observation, but there's every chance he'll be out in a few days. He's not even in intensive care any more. I'm going to the hospital now. Daisy wants to come too. Where are the others? I must tell them.'

'They're down at the kennels with the dogs. Mum's gone up for a lie-down.' My voice, from somewhere.

'I'll go down and tell them. Will you tell Mum when she wakes up?'

'Of course.'

And off she flew, down the passage and outside towards the kennels. Luca. I'd quite forgotten. I heard Daisy thunder downstairs and then run down the back passage and on out to the cars.

'Mum!' she cried as she ran across the gravel. 'Come on!'

A door slammed as she leaped in her mother's four-by-four, glancing about impatiently.

Well, thank the Lord. One young girl who wouldn't have to wrestle with her conscience for the rest of her days: one young girl whose life hadn't been brought to a standstill as she tortured herself with what she may, or may not have unconsciously inflicted on her half-brother. That sort of mental anguish was not something one wanted to lug around for ever, and despite being completely shattered, I felt the gentle easing of my own lead weight, hitherto dragging behind me. Seffy knowing was frightening, but not as frightening as it might have been had he been ten or eleven, surely? All his young trust destroyed? At fifteen he understood a bit, I felt. I straightened up a little. And I like to think I'd have told him at some stage, anyway. Nonsense. I caught my breath, aware that even in the privacy of my own head I couldn't be completely truthful.

I heaved up a sigh and let it out shakily. From a selfish point of view, though, at least he'd had a year to grapple with this. At least it wasn't fresh. Pumping. But a year without me to help him, I thought with a lurch. On his own, except … no, he'd had Hal. As we heard Laura's car take off at speed, I thanked Hal silently, fervently. Once he'd got over his own shock, that Seffy was his brother's child, I know he'd have spoken well of me. Wouldn't have painted me as too black a figure, would have urged Seffy to look at it from my point of view, even if he didn't entirely understand himself. Because he loved me. I knew that viscerally, and was comforted by it. He would have said: Seffy, she was young, she was frightened. She came home from Dubrovnik with her lie all packed up – at what point could she have unwrapped it, said, stop, this is Dominic's child, I want to get off the roundabout? Surely once we take that first fatal step into fiction, into that world of imagining, we're sucked down until we almost start to believe it ourselves?

Another lie. I never for one moment felt Seffy was anything other than mine. My own boy. And it had been torture to deny him publicly, too. When, at the age of eight, I'd gone to collect him from school and he'd said excitedly: 'Miss Taylor did her assembly on adoption today, because of me, because I'm special, because I was chosen,' I'd almost fainted. The lie had rippled out of my control, beyond my immediate family and friends. It was in Seffy's hands, not mine. I'd rendered him culpable, and he was spreading the word. That should have been my moment. To grip it. Tell him the truth. Talk to the teacher, squash it dead. But I'd ducked it. His trusting hand in mine as we'd walked home, clutching a wet painting, Seffy chattering away, about how all his friends wanted to know where Croatia was. The lump in my throat had been an immovable blockage.

His friends. Different ones now, of course, at a different school: Will, Tom, Ben – whom Seffy would have to tell. Would he? How? Put an advert in the school magazine? Seffy Carrington, not adopted after all. I imagined his, friends' astonished faces. The questions: 'So why did your mother …?' 'Because my father was famous. Married too.' 'Oh, I see.' But not seeing. Thinking: God, you poor bastard. Pity. Which any fifteen-year-old boy wants about as much as a pair of frilly pants. Easier now he was an adolescent, Hattie? Easier than being nine or ten? I don't think so.

I thought of Hal trying to placate Seffy, rationally, sensibly. It occurred to me he knew so much about me. Had known, when we'd had dinner in Seillans, at his house in France. He'd been seeing Seffy for a year. If, for a moment I felt that I was the one deceived, manipulated, it passed quickly. Not only did I deserve to be in the dark, but if Seffy's love was to be delivered back to me, it would be mostly due to Hal. And I mustn't assume anything. Mustn't assume deliverance. My son's face right now was an inscrutable teenage mask, but as Biba burst in through the back door, he rearranged it accordingly.

'Have you heard? He's going to be all right! There was masses of blood, apparently, but he's going to be OK!'

I hugged her as she flew to embrace me. Dad followed her in, beaming and rubbing his hands.

'Thank God,' he said warmly. 'What a relief.'

'I'm so glad for Daisy,' whispered Biba in my ear. 'I mean – obviously I'm so glad for Luca, that he's not badly hurt, but, Hattie, can you imagine if …?'

'I know,' I said quickly as she welled up. 'I know, Biba, but he's not.'

'No,' she said quickly. And then she turned and held her arms out to Seffy. So big-hearted, always the demonstrative one.

I saw Seffy smile into her hair as he held her. I didn't presume to catch his eye and smile, although I wanted to, but it occurred to me she'd have to be told. Biba. And Daisy, and Laura and Hugh, and Mum and Dad. For a moment the enormity of what I'd done, the scale of my deceit, threatened to overwhelm me. Made me feel faint. Made me think I may not be physically capable of seeing everyone reel in astonishment, these lovely nieces of mine, these elderly kindly parents: my father, coming to hug me now. Felt I'd sink in shame. Disappear into the stinking, bubbling mire that was the real me, as these good people stood about gaping in horror, absorbing the shock.

'Oh, Dad!' I gasped into his shoulder.

'I know, love, huge relief. Huge. The lad's going to be fine.' He patted my shoulder and moved on to clap Seffy on the back, but Hal must have seen my face, my distress. He was meeting my eye, sending me a clear message of support: Don't panic.

And now Dad was rounding up the troops, saying he was starving, absolutely ravenous, and was taking everyone out to eat.

'Biba, wash your hands and face. You've got mud all over you from the dogs. Seffy, wake your grandmother. Tell her all's well and that we're going to the pub.'

Lunch was originally to have been in the little lodge in the woods where two ladies from the village would have been ready and waiting with shepherd's pies, a trestle table laid for the jolly shooting party, carafes of wine. But Hugh would have rung ahead and cancelled, so now, here was Dad making alternative arrangements: buoying everyone up, restoring equilibrium.

'What about Maggie, is she still here? Go tell her to come.'

'No, I saw her go,' Biba was saying, washing her hands at the sink. 'She asked me to thank Mummy. Said she didn't want to be in the way. I think she's gone back to London with Kit.'

'Kit! Our man of God. The one we might have needed in a crisis. Jumping ship.'

'I'm sure he just didn't want to be in the way, Grandpa.'

'I'm joking, my sweet. Kit would be here if we'd needed him, but he doesn't like to lurk portentously in his cassock at such moments. And I don't blame him. Oh, look – here's your grandmother.'

More hugging and exclaiming as Mum appeared, looking slightly creased and dishevelled, but the light had returned to her eyes.

'So relieved,' she kept saying quietly as she was embraced. 'So relieved.'

Biba found her handbag for her, and someone else – Seffy – popped back upstairs for her shoes, which she'd left in the bedroom: 'By the bedside table, I think, darling.'

I watched him go, marvelling at how normal he looked. But then, he hadn't just had his life turned upside down. That was my province.

Mum sat at the table and got her compact out, powdered her nose. Then she popped some lipstick on, listening as everyone chattered around her, as Laura and

Dad told her how Luca had said a few words, was conscious, had squeezed Hugh's hand, was really quite *compos mentis*. At length she smiled; stood up.

'Right!' She snapped her handbag decisively and hung it over her arm. 'Well, I for one need a very large gin and tonic. Are we off?'

They were. Trooping out to the car, talking excitedly. Dad was saying that Laura had texted him, that she and Daisy were going to come on from the hospital, meet them at the pub. Hugh would stay with Luca, and Laura go back after lunch to relieve him. It was all arranged. All organized through the miracles of modern science, he said waving his mobile incredulously, the technological powers of which never ceased to astound him.

'Coming, Hattie?' he turned.

I unstuck my tongue from the roof of my mouth. 'Um would you mind if I didn't, Dad?'

'Not at all,' he said, quick as a flash, catching something in my voice.

'I think I'd just like to be on my own for a bit. Might go for a walk.'

'A splendid idea, very restorative. But we need you, Hal. You're our driver. I can't work that damn Land Rover of Hugh's and my little Datsun hasn't got belts for all these good people. Would you oblige?'

Hal hesitated, then: 'Of course,' he said politely, for what could he do but agree to transport everyone in his much larger estate car? Only the set of his shoulders betrayed the fact that this hadn't been in the script.

Out they went. I watched them go from the window, wondering how it was that my father could do that: know instantly that, for some reason, I needed some space – from

392

Hal too, I realized guiltily – and then achieve it for me, with no questions asked, no enquiring looks, even. And none later either. He'd wait. Bide his time. And then be silent as I told him, as he always was. Never butted in with questions, knew how to listen. But what a story. I'd be changed for ever in his eyes. I shrank from that. Knew I'd be changed in everyone's eyes, but my dad's, after Seffy's, I feared the most. Would it be too much for him, I wondered. Would it – not kill him – but age him, considerably, to know what I'd done?

The demons were huge again now, that growth bulging to life in my head, popping up with its leaping veins, skin straining. My breathing became shallow, and it occurred to me I shouldn't be on my own. What might I do? Nothing. Don't be stupid, Hattie, you're not that brave. I held on to the sink, temples throbbing. Listened to the quiet of the huge house, which was never really quiet: the distant rumble of the washing machine in the laundry, the peacock, shrieking on the lawn outside like a distressed child, the ticking of the long-case clocks in the hall, the endless creaking – there must be thousands of old floorboards and panels, all of which realigned occasionally, so that at any one time the house seemed to groan, as if it constantly sighed, folded its arms, rearranged itself. I heaved one up myself. Of self-pity? I hoped not. I deserved none. It occurred to me I should have gone to the pub, was once again ducking the moment, not facing Seffy, but I knew I wouldn't be capable of polite conversation. Knew we both needed some distance. Another floorboard creaked, but this time it couldn't just be an ancient floorboard, it had to be perpetrated by a footstep. I turned.

The door opened and Kit wandered in. Barefoot in jeans and a T-shirt.

I stared. 'Oh. We thought you'd gone.'

'Gone where?' He yawned sleepily, ruffling the hair on the back of his head. He crossed the room.

'With Maggie. Biba said you'd gone to London with her.'

He frowned, padded to the sink and ran the tap, reaching for a glass. 'No, I just helped her take her bags to the car. She's been here for ages, had loads. Anyway, I hate London.'

'Yes, I know. But I thought you two ...' I trailed off.

He turned, rolled his eyes. 'Give over. You're as bad as Mum, and I thought I could at least count on you and Laura. Have they all gone?'

'Yes, two minutes ago, to the pub. Luca's going to be all right.'

'I know. I heard Biba telling Mum. I was in the room next door.'

Right. But didn't burst in and say, 'Wow – great news! What a relief!' Didn't get involved. Just listened; digested, and was quietly pleased. My little brother, who never invested. Never emoted. I don't know how I could ever have imagined him with Maggie.

'Great, isn't it?' he mused, reading me. 'A priest who can't get involved. Father, I have sinned, and let me tell you how – no, no, my son, I'm afraid I don't do feelings. Can't advise you.' He smiled ruefully. 'At least I'm not Catholic. Don't actually have to preside over confession. Saint Augustine would not be impressed.'

He knocked back the glass of water. Then set the empty glass on the draining board; gazed bleakly at it.

'You do listen to your parishioners,' I said quietly. 'I know you do. Give great comfort.'

'Do I?' He shrugged. 'Not sure. I mean, yes, I listen, but most of me shrinks from it, deep down. Always has done.'

'I know.' In self-defence. 'I'm the same, Kit.'

'No you're not,' he said softly. He turned his back on me and looked out of the window. 'You feel everything very keenly. You just can't express it to others. Can't tell them how you feel. I don't even feel it.'

'Feel what?' This was surely the deepest my brother and I had ever got.

He shrugged. 'Love? You know. Stuff everyone else feels. I'm deficient in the Emotive department.' He made ironic quotation marks in the air; gave a wry smile. 'But, hey, why be gloomy? Not everyone's got all their faculties, have they? Look at Luca, poor guy, without a proper arm. Or Sheba.' He nodded at the cat dozing on the window sill. 'Stone deaf. It's only a minor disability, the one I have.'

'What about God?'

He frowned. 'You mean, do I love him?'

'Yes.'

He pursed his lips thoughtfully. 'Yes.'

'Well, there you are then. Eminently capable.'

He smiled. 'Yes, here I am, then. Although, he might quite like me to love others, don't you think?'

'Not if you have to force it. Dissemble. You're true to yourself.'

He looked at me properly. 'You make it sound very noble, Hatts, but actually, it's more to do with fear. I can protect myself this way. I know what it will cost me in equilibrium, you see, and I'm aware I'm not robust enough. Know there's not much to spare. So I'm economical with myself.'

There was a silence.

'Kit, can I ask … well, what d'you think made you like that?'

He raised his eyebrows, and implicit in that look was – you have to ask? In that moment I knew. Sarajevo. Which we'd never talked about. But where I knew, in that incarcerated city, at that time, in those few months, he'd witnessed terrible atrocities. Like speeded-up film, snippets of things I'd heard about rushed through my head: the massacre at Markale marketplace, where I knew Kit had been, with friends, some of whom were killed as they lined up for water; the old man he lived with, Lyjodo, a Muslim, beaten to death in front of him; the rape camps no one talked about; the ten thousand killed in one city, most of them civilians. *Ten thousand* seemed to shriek at me as the last few frames snapped by: then silence. Darkness. In the quiet, a pilot light was lit within me. I waited for the flame to steady, then took a breath. Dug deep.

'Kit, I know you don't do feelings, emotions, have shut yourself off from all that, but I just have a hunch you're the one person who can help me right now. The one person I should tell – must tell – before I talk to anyone else. And I want you to be totally honest with me. Tell me what you – or God, if you like – would think. Whether I'm damned to hell and damnation for ever.' I swallowed. 'It's about Seffy.'

He met my eye. 'I know about Seffy.'

I stared. 'You know about Seffy?'

'Yes.'

'That he's mine?'

'Yes.'

I felt the breath being sucked out of me. Kit's eyes were steady.

'You mean … you've always known?'

'No, only recently. You did a very good job, Hattie. No one knew. But Seffy told me.'

I felt the kitchen move slightly; the walls shift.

'He came to see me last summer, at Blenheim. Came from school, on a Sunday. Slipped into the back of a service I was taking. Gave me quite a shock.'

I collected my jaw, licked my lips. 'And … and what did he … what did you …?'

'Oh, we walked back to the vicarage together and he explained it all very matter-of-factly. He'd known by then for a few months. Had grown accustomed enough to the idea to explain without too much emotion.'

'But why didn't you tell me?'

'He asked me not to. But he did ask me to tell Mum and Dad.'

I shaded my eyes with both hands as if the light coming through the window was too bright for them.

'We've known for some time, Hattie.'

I moved from my stool, groped for a chair. 'Why not, me?' I didn't recognize my voice. Also, I knew: Hal had already told me. 'Because I hadn't told him for fifteen years?'

Kit hesitated. 'A bit. Perhaps. But no, mostly … I think he still sort of hoped you might …'

'Tell him,' I finished in a whisper.

Kit was silent.

'Thought that his mother might, if he was very lucky, claim her son, in time. Given time. But I never did.'

Why, then, should I be the first to know? Why should I presume that privileged position, when I hadn't afforded it to him? How very presumptuous of me.

'And Mum and Dad …' The walls of the kitchen were closing in now, like my humiliation.

'Were joyful, to use a biblical word.'

'Joyful?'

'Of course. Why not? He's ours. Seffy's ours. Oh, stunned and shocked to begin with, naturally. But then, given time … yes, really joyful.'

I nodded. Understanding. Slowly.

'As you must be,' he said gently.

'Have always been,' I said brokenly. 'Have always known he's mine, you see. Always been quietly joyful.' My mind was racing in circles, like a dog after its tail. I tried to imagine the scene, Kit, sitting my parents down – what, here?

'I had a chat with Dad first, in London,' Kit said, reading me, 'who told Mum. Not Laura, because Seffy knew she'd have to tell you. But he did tell Christian. He was the only one who already knew, incidentally. Said he'd suspected from the very beginning.'

'*Christian?*'

Kit frowned. 'Who you worked with?'

'Yes, I know who Christian is!'

My mouth wouldn't close. I dropped my head in shame. What must they think? Me again. See?

'That you've had a tough time, Hattie.' I'd said it out loud. 'A sad, lonely old time of it.'

Suddenly I was in Dubrovnik hospital, giving birth, in terrible pain. All around was noise, confusion, mayhem; shelling in the street, the school opposite hit: people running for cover, windows shattering. I remember thinking as I pushed, as I gripped some strange hand, I can take the pain, but I can't take the confusion; can't take the terrible chaos. Please, please, make it go away. I just want some shush. And then Seffy was out in moments, and in my arms, and the ward I was taken to was full of people, sitting on the floor, on my bed, wrapped in soggy, bloodstained bandages, eyes blank. I remember the man bursting in with the child; I remember getting off the bed where Seffy was wrapped in a blanket, backing away in horror. Remember stumbling to the door, and once outside, vomiting in a sink. Then being physically incapable of going back in. Just groping blindly down the crowded corridor, down the stairs, out into the dusty street, and away. Still bleeding heavily. Getting a lift on a lorry, part of a convoy, just having to get away. How odd. I'd never gone there before, in my head. Never remembered actually abandoning him.

Kit seemed to be sitting beside me now at the kitchen table. His hand closed over mine, and I realized, in that gesture I had more than I could ever have hoped for. Shocked and horrified, initially, this family of mine, but they wouldn't totally condemn me. There had been moments along the way when I'd had to wrestle with the feeling that life hadn't been altogether kind to me. Could it be my family felt that way too? Felt I'd been dealt a rotten hand? If they did, I knew it was down to Kit, who, like Hal, would have smoothed the way. Shed a little light on what had happened to us out there.

'If you're such an emotional cripple, Kit, how is it everyone turns to you in a crisis, hm?' My voice was unsteady. 'How is it that Seffy sought you out first, as I did? Riddle me that one, Batman.'

He gave a small smile. 'Perhaps it's because I'm always hanging around like a bad smell. Perhaps it's the dog collar. Perhaps they think I've got a hot line to God. Or maybe it's because I don't have the usual appendages – a wife, children – so they see themselves filling some shoes. It could also be,' he said lightly, 'that they know I'm careful with myself, *ipso facto* I'll be careful with them.' He got to his feet and walked to the window. 'It could be any number of reasons, Hattie, but one thing I can tell you with absolute certainty. It's got nothing to do with me being some kind of life authority. Some kind of Solomon. I haven't got anything figured out. I'm no wise man.'

He ran the tap, filled his glass again, and drank it down quickly. Perhaps, I thought watching him. But perhaps not.

29

Luca came out of hospital a few days later and there was something parabolic about his return. This prodigal young man with his Ferrari, his Armani clothes, his Rolex watch, his savvy, cunning ways, the biting tongue, the caustic remarks that could cause Laura and the girls to dissolve and Hugh to rush around performing damage limitation; this sharp young blade, when he walked into the kitchen with Daisy that day, just looked different. Granted he was heavily bandaged, his arm in a sling and his head in a white turban like a First World War hero, but it wasn't just that. It was his eyes. Where previously they had been wont to flash at one before slithering away, now they were steady and ... what was the word, I wondered, as we all got up from the lunch table to exclaim, embrace him – but not too hard, Daisy warned ... yes, humble. The eyes were humble. And vulnerable. His guard seemed to have slipped, and when he sat down to join us, Mum, Dad, Seffy, Hugh, Laura, Biba, Hal and Cassie – oh, yes, Hal and Cassie – and when we made polite, gentle enquiries, that guard didn't go up again either. He didn't shy away as he usually did, or give evasive answers. In fact, when he'd assured us he was feeling much better, he cleared his throat and said the whole episode had been entirely his fault. That he'd been a fool to hand Daisy his gun in the first place, that it had been an arrogant gesture, and he'd compounded the insult by telling her, 'In Italy I have a loader.' In other words, he was unused to such parochial shoots. In short, he'd provoked her, and was entirely to blame. This, in his heavily accented English, to his entire stepfamily, when historically two words were an achievement. Our mouths were open, but Daisy wasn't having it.

'Bollocks, it was entirely my fault, as I've told him a million times. I've been brought up in the country, I know about guns. And I certainly know it's a heinous crime to mess around with one, to dig it in the ground and—'

'You didn't know it was dangerous,' he interrupted.

'OK, I might not have known that, but Daddy's always said, you never ever treat them with anything other than total respect.'

'But you don't shoot, like Biba.'

'That's got nothing to do with it. If I'd got just a fraction more mud in it I'd have killed you.'

'And if your aunt had balls she'd be your uncle,' remarked Dad.

'What?' Daisy was flummoxed, but Luca grinned, understanding.

'If if if – the fact is, I'm still here, eh?' He widened his eyes at her and prodded his chest. 'So shudda your face, as they say in Firenze.'

'Yeah, shut it, Daisy,' agreed Seffy, as Biba laughed.

Lunch continued then in a relaxed fashion, and as coffee appeared, the younger element drifted off into the playroom to play Ping-Pong or watch television, taking Luca and Cassie with them.

'How extraordinary,' Mum was the first to exclaim quietly once they'd departed. 'He seems to have completely mellowed. It's almost as if the blow to the head has done him some good.'

'It's Daisy,' Hugh said simply. 'She's reached something inside him, I'm convinced. She hasn't left his bedside these past few days, and even when he drifted off to sleep she kept talking to him, weeping a bit, too. It's almost as if something's thawed.'

It was true. Even when Hugh and Laura had come home at night, Daisy had insisted on staying at the hospital, talking a nurse into letting her sleep in two chairs pushed together, claiming she could sleep anywhere. But not sleeping; holding his hand, waiting for him to wake up, getting him water if he needed it. And boy, had they talked, according to Hugh.

'I'd slip away,' he admitted to us now, 'or hide, embarrassed behind my newspaper. It all got far too heavy for me.'

'What kind of things?' Mum urged.

'Oh, you know. Daisy asking him all about how he felt growing up. Being part of this family, but not, if you see what I mean.'

'And what did he say?'

'That he'd felt hugely jealous. Had done all his life. This big, happy scene that he wasn't really part of, but would have been, if his parents had stayed together, had more children. Said he resented Laura for being so maternal when Carla wasn't, that he took it out on her by being surly and difficult. Oh God, you've no idea what Daisy got out of him.'

I could imagine, though. An open, warm-hearted girl, one of a pair, whom, as Luca had so rightly observed, Laura had done a brilliant job with. Charlie too. Children didn't grow up on their own, they were brought up. And

Luca had never had the benefit of that with Carla and a string of nannies. Resented his half-siblings who had.

'When she said she wanted him to be a proper brother, and not just some random guy who appeared from Italy now and then, I got stuck firmly into the crossword, I can tell you.'

It didn't escape any of us, though, that, despite Hugh's protests, he'd misted up somewhat.

'Good for her,' said Dad, gruffly.

'I'm amazed you stayed so long, Hugh,' observed my mother, gently. 'And you mustn't blame yourself, you know. You and Laura have always bent over backwards to make him feel one of the family.'

They had, but there was no disputing how the young Luca must have felt: damaged, both physically and mentally, with the rest of the Pelham clan always before him, as a shining, undiminished foil.

'And then they talked about the house,' prompted Laura, who clearly already knew this story. I realized Hal was being included as family around this table, and if part of me found that faintly unnerving, as if events were running away with me, I dismissed it instantly.

'Oh, the house,' groaned Hugh, sinking his head in his hands. 'At that point I very nearly legged it to the fire escape. But Daisy made me stay. "No, Dad,"' he straightened up, aping his daughter, eyes wide, '"We need to do this." And Luca, with practically no prompting, sat up in bed, and looking heart-rendingly vulnerable in his pyjamas and his bandaged head, his poor arm lying on the blanket, explained falteringly that he'd always felt it was his trump card. His only card. These Pelhams, these half-siblings of his, they had everything – looks, good humour, loving parents, a beautiful home – but oh boy, not for long. He, Luca, the cuckoo in the nest, but the oldest cuckoo, could turf them out in a few years' time, and would too. Would inherit and become Lord Many Acres, marry a beautiful English girl, re-create the Pelham dynasty. Only this time, on his terms.'

Dad inclined his head thoughtfully. 'And why not? It's his birthright.'

'Except his heart wasn't in it, he said. He didn't want to live in a freezing, rattling Victorian abbey, be squire of all the dank misty landscape he surveyed. It wasn't in his genes. His heart was in Italy, which he loved. Florence in particular, the Tuscan hills, which, let's face it, are hard to beat. But as you know, the Abbey can't be sold. That's the deal from the trustees. It has to be passed on. So he's passing it on to Biba.'

'Me?' Biba appeared in the doorway, Ping-Pong bat in hand. She looked astonished. 'I wasn't listening, I just came to get some balls from the drawer.' She went pink.

Hugh held out his hand to her. 'Come in, darling.'

'Why me?' She stayed stock-still where she was.

'Because you're the eldest.' Hugh let his hand fall.

'Yes, but Charlie—'

'It doesn't have to go down the male line, that's not in the brief. This is 2009, my darling. It's to be yours.'

'I shall give it to Charlie,' she said fiercely, colouring up. 'Honestly, Dad, it's lovely, but there's no way.'

'We'll see. We'll think on it,' her father said gently. 'It may be that Charlie doesn't want it either. The important thing is, the here and now. No one's to be turfed out. It's to stay as our family home for the duration. Thanks to Luca.'

'And I shall make it up to him,' said Laura suddenly, after a brief silence. She looked fiery. Determined.

'There's nothing to make up,' Dad assured her. 'You've always done your best by him.'

'Yes, but if I'm honest, Dad, I always felt he had his finger on the trigger. Was always a bit scared. But now, oh, now it'll be so much better. He'll never feel insecure again.' Her eyes shone.

'Oh Lord. She's on a mission,' groaned Hugh, shaking his head.

'Let the poor lad up for air occasionally, eh, love?' remarked my father, reaching for *The Times* and shaking it out to read over his coffee. He rattled it noisily and disappeared behind. 'Let him take a breather from the bosom of the family now and again, hm?'

Hal and I smiled about it later as we strolled in the garden by the river, hand in hand.

'Funny, isn't it?' I said, shading my eyes over the stream at the mallards splashing and flapping off into the hazy autumn sunshine. 'To the casual observer, this family has got everything. But for a long time, it hadn't. Everyone's been frightened of Luca, tiptoeing around him. But if everyone had just been a bit more honest with each other, it might have saved a lot of heartache over the years.'

Hal raised his eyebrows. I coloured. 'Which is rich coming from me, I know,' I tumbled on quickly. 'But being honest renders one so vulnerable, Hal, that's the trouble. And I had so much to lose.'

'You've gained a lot,' he observed, narrowing his eyes into the distance to where Seffy and Cassie were playing doubles against Biba and Daisy: we listened to the thwack of balls. The shouts of laughter.

'Seffy's gained her. I can't lay claim to Cassie in any way – it would be disingenuous. I feel I've knowingly disowned her all these years. I can't suddenly turn round and say – hey, great, you're my son's sister, welcome!'

'No, but you'd be amazed how flexible and forgiving young people can be.'

This I knew to be true, my own family being the most recent, potent example, and they weren't all young. One by one they'd sought me out over the last few days, to say how pleased they were about Seffy, how happy. Not how duped or misled they felt they'd been all these years. Laura and I had talked for hours in her room, thrashing it out moment by moment, going back years, to when we'd shared the flat in Pimlico. To Dom. The girls, who'd been told, tiptoed in towards the end, sitting on the bed hugging their knees, wanting the whole story again, from the beginning, *please*, Hattie, their mother protesting, saying it was not for their ears. But I felt it most definitely was: that I owed them all, and I'd begin again, telling my sorry tale from the beginning. And to my surprise, it became a little easier each time. Marginally less shameful. Mum and I walked to the village one sunny afternoon on some spurious errand to buy cheese, sat on a bench by the pond, and found we weren't back until dark, minus the cheese. My family's acceptance and understanding was a huge comfort to me. And, I'm ashamed to say, a huge surprise. Dad, though, aside from a squeeze of my shoulders when I went to bed one night, and a gruff assurance that he was beyond thrilled, didn't say much. It worried me initially, even though I knew it wasn't his way to roar in and ask questions. When he casually mentioned, though, that he might take me on a jaunt to Venice next month, for a long weekend, as he'd taken Hugh and Laura the previous year, I knew that would be our moment.

With Cassie, however, I'd felt indescribably awkward. Had almost avoided her. But she'd tracked me down, and to my shame had told me how pleased she was, this bright-eyed, eager girl with flushed cheeks, to find Seffy, and to find me, she'd added generously. I'd caught my breath, mortified. After all, I'd slept with her father. Why should she be generous?

'Oh, Cassie, I'm totally undeserving of that.' I'd been peeling potatoes at the time, and the sink had been a good place to hide my face: I hadn't broken off, so in effect had my back to her as I peeled faster. But she'd leaned on the draining board beside me, picked up a knife to help, and said she didn't altogether blame her father. Yes, it was terrible to cheat on Mummy, but her mother was … fragile. Could be tricky. Volatile. Everyone thought her parents had the perfect marriage – all the obituaries said what a loving, close couple they were – and that, understandably, Letty had been driven to drink through her grief. But … was that entirely true? Perhaps she'd drunk before? Cassie looked at me closely. I put my knife down; wiped my hands carefully. 'Perhaps Daddy had been unhappy, or they'd been unhappy together?' she asked.

I remembered him gently remonstrating with Letty when she was pregnant: knocking back the Chablis in the garden, eyes over-bright.

'I think if Hal wasn't so loyal he might confirm my suspicions,' she told me now, eyeing me closely.

'But he never has?'

'No. I did once ask if Mum drank before I was born, but he just said something noncommittal, like – everyone likes a drink occasionally.'

Yes, he would be loyal to Letty. Of course. His sister-in-law, the widow, the wronged wife. And maybe that was all it had been back then. Liking the occasional drink. I'd only met her once – who was I to judge? I asked Cassie where she was now.

'In the Priory. Oh, she's there a lot,' she said, seeing my shocked face. 'Books herself in. Or Hal and I do it for her.'

I realized then what Cassie had had to deal with. On her own. All this time. Why she could badly do with Seffy and me. Hal, of course had always been there for her, but now … well, now there would definitely be something more supportive and homogenous about the grouping. Seffy and Cassie, and me and Hal. Lovely for her, I hoped. Lovely for Seffy, too.

As Hal and I walked on in the autumn sunshine that afternoon, it struck me we were strolling by a river much as we would in France one day. Maybe next summer, in his garden, with Seffy and Cassie perhaps playing backgammon up on the terrace under that pagoda dripping with bougainvillaea, their laughter filtering down to us. Later we'd all have supper outside, candles flickering in the dusk, cicadas chattering in the long grass, a huge bowl of pasta, or perhaps a fragrant bouillabaisse. The four of us talking and laughing into the night, and if my fantasies seemed to encompass the bigger picture, rather than the minutiae of a heartbeat, well, look where heartbeats had got me before: entangled with men who were careless of my emotions, who made free with my spirit. No, an equable life with Hal, free from the vagaries of passion and despair was my focus, and for once I wasn't getting ahead of myself. I knew, you see, Hal's plans for me were long term. Knew there was nothing flighty or ephemeral about this man, knew his love was constant, and I felt so safe. So comforted and wrapped, as if I'd finally landed somewhere soft, after all those years of being Out There.

As we strolled and chatted now by this very English river, the water rushing clear and bright over the pebbles, shivering around the tall bulrushes at the edge, as we strolled on in the fading light, we came to the little stone bridge. That's where we paused, and where I turned to face him: and that's where he took me in his arms, and a million miles from that snatched kiss on the landing, kissed me properly, for the first time.

30

The house I was looking at was capacious by most people's standards, but by mine, it was downright huge. It was in Notting Hill, an area I wasn't overly familiar with, but could quickly get used to, I decided, as I leaned over the black wrought-iron first-floor balcony, peering down to the garden square below. A cool enclosure full of gently yellowing plane trees and rich autumnal vegetation winked back at me: a tasteful oasis from the buzzing bars and shops I knew lay only a convenient stroll away. I inhaled the air, savouring its gentrification, narrowing my eyes at the terrace of identical creamy stucco houses opposite. Four storeys, with a flight of steps up to a pillared front door, complete with shiny brass knocker: three tall windows on the first floor giving onto a filigreed balcony like the one I was leaning on now. Similar, but look closer, and they were all different, in terribly refined and subtle ways, to do with the planting of the box hedge in the front garden, the window boxes full of expensive tumbling plants, the colour of the front door. Different room configurations within, no doubt too. Behind me, Torquil the estate agent was eulogizing about this particular one's hidden depths.

'Working fireplaces in the dining room and also in here, in the drawing room, of course, and French windows in all south-facing rooms. This room is 480 square foot, if you're interested. And upstairs, five bedrooms, which, with the kitchen and breakfast room below, totals 3,400 square feet. A staggering footprint, I'm sure you'll agree.'

Indeed it was. Staggering. Certainly compared to my own humble little footprint in Fulham. And so much square air space too, I thought, coming back inside and craning my neck up at the ornate plaster rose in the centre of the ceiling, miles away in the stratosphere. I considered my own cringing little eaves. But then, Hal had said look for something with generous proportions. So I had.

Hal was in Zurich, or – no, Geneva, I think. On the last leg of a legal tour, finalizing a deal worth zillions, whilst I, the expensively dressed girlfriend, was putting a toe in the property market. Seeing what was out there, as they say. All of which was really quite precipitous considering he'd only kissed me properly – what, ten days ago? Obviously there'd been a great deal more than just kissing since then, but still: to be standing here in the new Marc Jacobs coat he'd bought me and my spiky black patent boots, viewing sod-off London houses was undoubtedly fast work. Not mine, I hasten to add. It was all down to Hal, who didn't hang about. Had bags of get up and go, as opposed to my own habitual sit down and stop.

Still, I felt a bit of a fraud dressed up like a trophy wife, viewing houses my wildest dreams wouldn't stretch to: there was something not quite real about it, as if I were looking through a wall of glass.

Personally I would have thought his Holland Park house, which I was now very familiar with, having spent quite a few nights there, would have fitted the bill. These past few mornings I'd woken up flushed and incredulous in his sexy wooden sleigh bed, marvelled at the huge modern canvas on the opposite wall and thought it entirely sumptuous and spacious. But as Hal said, it had history. I must admit, I did feel faintly guilty as I padded around the interior-designed drawing room – the work of one Helmut Bing, a towering German decorator – in Hal's white towelling robe, wondering what on earth Céline would think as I tried to get to grips with the terrifying gadgets in her double-O-seven kitchen. Cappuccino makers that took off like rockets, toasters that took your eye out, but could I locate a humble kettle? Then there was the shower, so forceful I buckled at the knees and was nearly beaten to the granite floor, accustomed as I was to squeezing a few parched drops from my own eccentric plumbing. So yes, Hal was right. History dictated we move on. But also, he'd pointed out, it was a question of layout. We were looking for a family house now, not only for Hal, me and Seffy, but for Cassie and Letty too.

'And of course you've got the separate basement flat, which Mr Forbes stipulated,' Torquil was saying. 'Another eight hundred square feet.'

'Yes. Yes, that's perfect.'

Or would be if Letty agreed, which Hal sincerely hoped she would, so that Cassie could spend more time with us, absorb family life. Letty too, if she wanted. All of which would be lovely for the children.

Was I nervous about that? About Letty being amongst us? I crossed to the marble fireplace. Ran a finger over its smooth creamy surround. No, not now, strangely enough. I had been, hugely. But now I knew Cassie had been to see her mother at the Priory, had told her about Seffy's parentage. To which the response had been weary indifference.

'Oh yes, I always suspected he was Dom's.'

'You did?' Cassie had said, astonished.

'Yes. I saw them kissing in your father's office, darling. Seffy would be exactly the right age to be conceived around then. She said she'd adopted him in Croatia and that was very good of her. I've always liked her for that. She could have blown my world apart, but she didn't. I thought she might later, when Dom died, but she kept her counsel. It's right that Seffy knows now. A few years too late, if you ask me, but she probably lost her nerve. We all do that. God knows, I've lost more than nerve. And she's had a tough time, Hattie. Give her my love.'

I'd listened to this with eyes and mouth open as Cassie repeated it verbatim. She knew? Or – at least had always suspected? I remembered how sweet and eager she'd been when Maggie and I had first encountered her in the village. Appreciative, perhaps? One person – the only person – who understood what I'd done? I felt relief. And something unclench and lay down within me. One by one the scrunched-up bits of history were unfurling and smoothing out: there … and there …

It occurred to me Hal had never suspected, and he too knew about the kiss. But men were less imaginative in so many ways. No doubt he couldn't believe I'd be so devious. But Letty could. Only she wouldn't call it devious. She'd call it resourceful. No, I had no qualms about Letty living below us. But she, apparently, did.

'I like my house,' she'd said stubbornly to Cassie.

'I know, Mum, and this way we wouldn't have to sell it. Hal's offering us the flat in London rent free. We could still keep The Pink House and go there at weekends.'

'We'll see.' Letty had waved a weary hand. 'We'll see. I have to go to my therapy class soon, darling, spill my tortured beans. No doubt make some hideous raffia mats, too. And I'm awfully tired. Might need forty winks first.'

Cassie had crept out.

'And then through here,' Torquil was saying, 'we have double doors into the study, as Mr Forbes requested …'

He led me through into a wood-panelled room, one wall entirely lined with books, overlooking the back garden. I gazed out. Another refined, walled enclosure, old-fashioned white roses still flowering against ivy and a gnarled miniature apple tree.

'Yes, he'll love this,' I agreed.

Perfect for Hal to hole up in, I thought, working late into the night, as I knew he did, being brilliant and scholarly, and making his company, probably the biggest and most highly regarded commercial set of solicitors in the City, a great deal of money. Earning every penny of his seven-figure, equity partner salary. Which was a long way from human rights, I'd teased him the other night, reminding him how he'd once wanted to save the world.

He'd laughed. 'Full of high ideals and principles back then. But you've got to live in the real world, Hattie. And anyway, I still do *pro bono* work.' He'd tossed me a brief tied up in pink ribbon: an immigrant family, over here from Zimbabwe, minus the mother of the three small children. He was trying to get asylum for her, remove her from the hostile regime. I closed it quietly, retied the ribbon and shut up. Right. No flies on him. Got every angle covered, hadn't he?

I'd placed it humbly on the floor beside me. I was lying on the sofa in his house at the time, behind him as he worked at his desk, just as, it struck me, I used to lie on his bed in halls of residence, throwing a tennis ball at the ceiling. I smiled. Glanced at the sofa table beside me. A huge bowl of smooth sandstone balls – *objets d'art* no doubt, Helmut's style but not mine – presided. I picked one up consideringly. Hal got up from the desk, came round and kneeled beside me.

'Not thinking of tossing it at the ceiling, are you?'

I stared. 'How did you know?'

'There's nothing I don't know about you, Hattie Carrington.' He stopped my protesting mouth with a kiss and removed the ball from my hand. 'Absolutely nothing.'

The kiss developed, and the sofa was abandoned in favour of the bed. I'd suggested we stay put, or utilize the rather enticing Aubusson rug in front of the fire, but Hal wasn't having any of it. He was very much a bedroom man. Didn't linger there much, either. Liked to get up and go. Back to work, mostly. I was pretty sure I could lead him astray later, though, when his case had finished. Instigate a few entire days horizontal. I smiled, then realized I was smiling rather wantonly at Torquil.

'Oh, I'm sorry?' I came to.

'I said would you like to see the bedroom?'

'Oh – yes, I would! Very much.' And I trooped out after him, only slightly pink.

Walking back through Portobello Market half an hour later, which I found in full swing, I thought how extraordinary it was that not so long ago, and for many years, my life had had more than a hint of make-do-and-mend about it. I did what I could. Now, strolling down this bustling street, fresh from viewing 26 Maidwell Avenue, I had to quell the idea that I'd somehow got too lucky. Up until now I'd never quite got the man, never quite got the family life that, say, Laura had – never quite got the breaks. Life had been, not a disappointment, but a compromise. I was used to working my socks off on a date, battling with the bank manager, with Seffy's schools, or at auctions when I knew I'd be outbid on a piece I badly wanted – never quite making it in so many ways. Now, it seemed, I'd simply been plucked and carefully placed on the other side of the winning post without even breaking sweat: I'd arrived. So this was what it felt like: odd that the euphoria wasn't more overwhelming, but then one could hardly go about with a permanent rictus grin on one's face; that wouldn't be realistic.

I smiled down at my patent boots as I threaded through the crowds. The cries of the traders echoed around me, and my practised eye caught the stalls of bric-a-brac I'd once sold: pseudo antiques. We'd talked, Hal and I, about me going it alone in a bigger shop, with his backing – really making a name for myself – but I hadn't wanted to. The fun, I'd told him, the whole *raison d'être*, was working with Maggie. The shop was our baby, our thing, and all right, we weren't up there with the Helmut Bings of this world, but we did OK, and I didn't want to change that. He'd smiled, and I think been pleased. (In fact I had to dispel the feeling I'd somehow ticked a box, shown myself to be a Good Person.) However, it has to be said, a fleeting glimpse of myself in swanky Holland Park premises – or Chelsea Green perhaps – tucked snugly between other expensive dealers, 'Harriet Carrington' in swirly gold lettering on the shop front, *had* flitted briefly to mind. But it was gone in a moment. What, no Maggie? No cradling coffee cups behind the counter on Munster Road, flicking through *Heat* and gossiping for hours?

'No reason why you can't still do it with Maggie? Still be partners?' Hal had said later, and this *had* bought my eye. Maggie and I together, in tasteful grey cashmere, as opposed to our high-street takes, in terribly chic premises betwixt Theo Fennel and David Linley: nipping to Bibendum for lunch, instead of to the sandwich bar. Now you're talking. I'd said I'd think about it. See what Maggie thought about Hal injecting shedloads of cash into our business, see if she'd mind. I could already hear her, though. 'Mind?' she'd squawk. '*Mind?* Of course I don't bloody mind! How flipping marvellous, all our dreams come true! Don't be a fool, Hattie, say yes instantly. Now. Chelsea Green or Pimlico?'

I smiled. No, Maggie was very tired of The Struggle. She wouldn't say no to a leg-up. Something made me hesitate, though. We'll see, I thought, walking on. I did need to contact her, though. I was feeling faintly guilty that recently, she was doing more than her fair share at the shop. I'd worked three days this week, but she'd done five the previous one, and the weekend. As I headed towards the tube I texted her: 'Let's work together tomorrow.' Two minutes later she texted back: 'Good idea, been missing your ugly mug.'

I smiled. Pocketed my phone. I'd missed hers. And her wit. I put my collar up against the stiff breeze that was whisking tissue paper from oranges around my feet and thrust my hands in my pockets.

As I walked, my mind turned to Seffy and I wondered what lines his thoughts were running on now he was back at school. We'd talked long and hard about how to handle our new – to the rest of the world – mother-and-son relationship, but of course, he'd already had months to consider it. Was way ahead of me.

'No announcements, no big deal, no chats with housemasters, OK, Mum?'

'OK,' I'd said uncertainly 'So ... still a secret?'

'No, not a secret. But I'd just like it to gradually seep out, on a need-to-know basis.'

I was frantically wondering how this would work when he gave me an example.

'I mean, say, for instance, I meet a girl at a party, and she comes to lunch or something, you're my mum. Not my adoptive mum.'

'OK,' I said slowly. 'And then she hears from a friend you're adopted?'

'And I say – oh yeah, Mum was protecting another family. Letty and Cassie. And I tell her the whole story. I just want to play it straight, OK? Tell it how it is. No more lies.'

'Right.' I instantly felt tiny.

'No, I don't mean lies,' he'd said quickly, seeing my face, 'that's harsh. It's just, the truth is so simple. I tell her I found out recently and I'm thrilled, which I am. End of story.'

My face was obviously one of worry and guilt.

'Don't forget, Mum, what seems huge to us, will only be huge for them for five minutes. People only really invest in themselves, they don't spend too much time dissecting others. It'll be fine.'

I nodded uncertainly again.

'And how much better that it's this way round? Rather than the kid who thinks he's biological, then discovers he's adopted? There's got to be an element of celebration in our story, surely? And that's how I'm going to play it. Low key, but pleased, OK?'

'OK,' I said, knowing better than to choke out how I'd always wanted to claim him, always wanted the world to know he was mine. Had always inwardly celebrated. He knew. Knew all that. So a gradual seep into the consciousness it was. And I did quietly thank the Lord he hadn't got to the girlfriend stage without knowing. I had at least spared him explaining to a girlfriend of three years, say, when he was twenty, that his mother had disowned him. I shuddered. That word. Which I made myself say in my head occasionally, but which shrivelled me. I bowed my head to the pavement and walked on.

And Hal would help us through all this, through the inevitable fall-out, I thought with a rush of relief as I raised my eyes, simultaneously shaking my head at a lad trying to sell me two bags of satsumas for a pound. The voice of reason would echo in those tall Notting Hill rooms without doubt.

Seffy was pleased and amused by our relationship, Hal and mine, which I'd shyly and tentatively intimated at. Well, no, completely broached actually, in an email to him at school, desperately wanting, in the spirit of full disclosure, for him to know everything, almost before it happened. After some initial enquiries about rugby trials, etc., I'd written: 'Hal and I are becoming close after all that's happened, which is lovely. I hope you're pleased too?'

He'd rung me that evening, amused.

'Are you asking for my blessing, Mum?'

'No! I mean, well, I don't know.' I'd coloured. 'I just …
well, I didn't want you to hear second-hand, that's all.
From Cassie, or someone. And of course it affects you
too, so …'

'I like the guy, Mum, you know I do. He's been very
good to me. I approve. Go to it, my child.'

I'd laughed, but actually, there was more truth in this
than was comfortable. I had behaved like a child in many
respects and Seffy had been so grown up, so mature.
I straightened my shoulders. Not any more. I'd slip right
back into the mothering role and Seffy could be a child
again. And Hal … oh, what a father figure he'd be. My
heart thumped and I felt my pulse quicken. He was so
well read, so intelligent, so focused. Seffy's real father's
brother: it was as close, I realized, as I could ever get to
providing Seffy with a father, and he'd been staring me in
the face all this time, all these years. The family unit I
craved and knew Seffy did: knew, when he returned from
friends' houses, having sat around tables with parents and
siblings, all noisy and convivial, and had come back
thoughtful to just Mum. Well, now he had Hal and Cassie
too. We could do all that, the four of us. We could be that
family. Something resembling the Bisto advert in the fifties sprang to mind and I believe I even had a pinny on. It
was never too late.

Unable to keep the smile from my face I narrowed my
eyes to the sun, saluting it almost, feeling it on my cheeks
as I rounded the corner, past a stall full of ancient clocks
and watches. One, a long-case, or grandfather clock, with
a glorious sunburst face caught my eye, but it was a face
beyond that stopped me in my tracks. Behind an adjacent

stall full of church candles and ecclesiastical memorabilia, statues of Madonna and child, old incense burners and antique altar cloths, leaning languidly on a trestle table as he chatted to another trader, throwing back his leonine head and laughing, was Ivan.

31

He was wearing a soft checked shirt I didn't recognize, rolled up to the elbows over a white T-shirt and jeans, and had an enquiring light in his eyes as he listened intently to his friend. As the punch line was delivered he threw back his head again and hooted with laughter, right up to the heavens: that familiar, joyous, uninhibited bark of delight, booming out through the noise of the traders, the bustle. As his eyes came back, full of mirth, they caught mine, just before I'd managed hurriedly to put my sunglasses on. He stared, astonished.

'Hattie.'

I hadn't seen Ivan since I left him in that rumpled hotel bedroom in Fréjus. Hadn't spoken to him, even though he'd left a message on my answer phone, and on my mobile. Hadn't returned his text. I knew he wasn't good for me, you see. Knew he was too fast, too loose, too transitory, too young and just *far too much*. Knew I was aiming not just too high, but off centre. That it would be my undoing. I had therefore ruthlessly and effectively blanked him from my mind, which I am eminently capable of doing: see blanking my biological son for fifteen years. I can, with a supreme effort of will, successfully perform miracles. I can close my mind to something unpalatable or upsetting in the name of self-preservation. Been at it for years. And I'd done it with Ivan. This, surely, was a test then. I met his smoky-grey eyes, albeit through my Ray-Bans. Had I been successful? Of course.

'Ivan.'

I smiled, kept my voice steady.

His guard went up. The initial surprise and openness disappeared from his face at my cool rendition of his name. He matched my glacial demeanour ice-block for ice-block.

'How have you been?' I enquired.

'Fine, thanks. And you?'

'Good, thanks. Yes, really well.'

A silence.

'I like the new shirt.' I didn't, actually. Well, I did, but it had thrown me, this indication of the speed at which he'd transformed himself into a separate being, with a separate life. I knew all his clothes, you see.

'And I like your coat.'

'Thank you.'

Another silence.

'This isn't your patch?'

'Hm?' He was staring at me.

'Portobello,' I said. Work with me, Ivan, keep this conversation going. We need only do it for two minutes, for form's sake, then I can walk on by.

'Oh, no. But there was a fire at Camden. Some idiot left a fag burning.'

'Oh, how awful.'

'So, Ned,' he nodded at his friend who'd turned away to serve a customer, 'said I could share his stall here for a few weeks while they get their act together at Camden. Not much to share really: I lost most of my stock.' He shrugged ruefully.

'Oh Lord. Did you?'

'Yeah, but hey.' He ruffled the hair on the back of his head. 'Sometimes it's good to start from scratch again. Get rid of all the dead wood. Makes you evaluate what you really want in life, don't you think?'

He was eyeing me carefully now. Did he mean me? Was I dead wood? Was he deliberately being hurtful? I swallowed. Didn't hurt at all.

'Yes. I suppose so.'

'You get used to something, start acting through force of habit, mechanically. And not all habits are good. I can see that now. I've rather gone off the jewellery. I like the religious artefacts now, and clocks. Clocks are my thing.'

'They're lovely,' I said, reaching out to stroke a mahogany long-case, tenderly. I snatched my hand back. They were. But I was a bad habit. Move away, Hattie. Nod, smile, say, 'Lovely to see you,' then walk on. That'll be it for ever. His eyes were much too smoky, his throaty voice dug up too many memories. Too many laughs. Shaking with laughter, in fact, in bed, beside each other, facing the ceiling, or on a mattress on the floor.

'And you?' A quizzical gleam in his eye.

'Me?'

'You got to Seffy on time?'

'Oh – yes, I did.'

Of course. He'd gone missing from school. And I'd run all the way back from Provence.

'And?'

'And yes, he's back. Back at school. All's well. It's … a long story, but all's well.'

'Good. Give him my love.'

How funny. That was what did it: the damage. Him giving Seffy love. I felt a bit faint.

'I will.'

It occurred to me I'd behaved very badly. He was fond of Seffy and of course I should at least have let him know he was all right. But the thing is, when one is trying so hard to stay afloat, bailing out like fury, one does rather jettison anything that might threaten sinkage. I'd tossed Ivan overboard, knowing he could have me plummeting in moments. Did I, for instance, want to be forever wondering where those steady grey eyes were resting in Camden Passage? Where that laugh was barking out, head thrown back, throat exposed? Wonder what fun he was having, and with whom? No I did not.

I took a tissue from my coat pocket, went to dab my nose, but actually, surreptitiously wiped my lipstick off. Then I removed my sunglasses. I'd put a spot of mascara on for the estate agent this morning, but other than that, I was bare-faced. There. That's me, Ivan. In the bright sunshine. Thirty-nine.

'Lovely to see you, Ivan. I must be off.'

I smiled and turned to head off down the street. My heart was pounding. Steady, Hattie, steady. A nice sedate walk, no scurrying. Glance down at those Calvin Klein boots. Lovely, aren't they? You see? You're almost there. Couldn't be easier. Now. Around this corner, and you're home and dry. No pounding footsteps behind you – good. No 'Hattie – wait!' ringing out. Excellent. I hovered, just on the corner of Pembridge Road, fingering some Brussels lace on a stall. Put my glasses back on, and carefully snuck a look back up the street. Portobello was teeming, but I could see him, turned away now, only a speck in the distance, though my razor-sharp eyes picked him out. He was talking to Ned again. Back to three minutes ago, where he'd left off his conversation. Whilst I, I realized to my absolute horror, was back to square one.

I felt the last few weeks unravel as if a thread had been pulled on the neck of a jumper. My mouth dried and I turned and walked quickly on, listening to the sound of my heels clip-clopping down the steps to the tube, clinging to movement.

At Sloane Square I got a taxi, a luxury I could afford now. I sank back in the black upholstery and fished the particulars for 26 Maidwell Avenue from my bag. I read them as if I were studying for finals, letting the glossy photographs seep in. That glorious first-floor drawing room, and all that fabulous space upstairs: that long attic room on the top floor that stretched the length of the house, and which I'd already earmarked for Seffy to have a pool table in, a wraparound sound system, big screen across one wall. All the cool toys his friends had and we didn't. He'd be up there with Hal, in the evenings. Did Hal play pool? I wasn't sure, but the next clip of film in my head featured a broad back in a checked shirt leaning over a pool table in a pub in Fulham, where I'd seen someone else play, a brown forearm stretching down a cue, a throaty laugh ringing out as, with freakish good luck, he pocketed the black.

Breathe, Hattie, breathe. I did, with studied concentration; my hands gripping the particulars as if my life depended on them. The taxi rumbled on. Past the fire station, past World's End, not home, but to Maggie's. To discuss the new shop with her. To hear her squeal, jump up in the air and declare, 'Oh, yes, *yes*! God, what a star that man is, Hattie, and definitely Chelsea Green, not Pimlico. So nineties, don't you think? Too many ageing poofters. Or even Chelsea Harbour, what d'you think?'

And I'd get caught up in her glee, make plans, ring estate agents, discuss putting Munster Road on the market. No more stepping over sacks of rubbish, no more down-and-outs sleeping in our doorway – or, perhaps, a better class of down-and-out. And then my phone rang in my bag as I received a text. Never have my hands scrambled so feverishly, never have my fingers so eagerly shot back the screen to receive the message. My eyes scanned it quickly.

The message read: 'How No. 26? Did you like it? Hx'

I stared. Crushing disappointment had swept through me.

'Loved it,' I punched back.

I replaced the phone carefully in my bag and folded my hands on top. After a moment, I fished it out again and added, 'And I love you too.'

Then I turned my head away to gaze out of the window. The taxi rumbled on.

The shop was shut as we crawled past over the speed bumps on Munster Road, as I knew it would be. It was gone five and we closed on the dot mid-week, particularly at this time of year when business was slow. The paint was peeling a bit, I noticed, on the door, and around the front. Needing doing. But there was no point doing it if we sold; someone else would only want it a different colour. A single Louis Quinze chaise longue resided in the window on a Persian rug, testimony to our 'less is more' style: a pendulous Parisian chandelier hung above, and that was it. Tasteful, expensive, minimalist, although it looked a bit forlorn, I thought, that empty sofa, in a shabby shop front, unlit and after hours. A bit tired. But then the run-down newsagent's next door didn't help, plus the endless billowing litter. I had a sudden glimpse of Maggie and I, arriving at the shop together one morning, dressed slightly too young, as London women often are, and too thin: still in tight jeans and little jackets and shiny boots, but before we put the key in the door, as we turned to camera, our faces were lined and faded, stark against our dyed hair. Our liver-spotted hands clutched skinny lattes from Starbucks. I shuddered. No. Thank goodness we were moving on, I told myself.

Maggie's house was also in darkness, which made my heart sink as I got out of the taxi. I'd already paid the driver, and he was trundling away even now. Still, I could easily walk to my house, I reasoned; it was only a few blocks away. I pushed open her gate and walked up the brick path. She grew the same plants as I did, which always made me smile: a tangle of unpruned honeysuckle and roses prevailed. Except … I didn't really want to go home, I realized, hadn't been there for days, was afraid to be alone there with my thoughts. What might I think, walking around my empty little house? No, I'd find Maggie wherever she was. Ring her. She'd be in a bar somewhere, with a girlfriend or two, maybe Sally and Alex. I'd join them.

I rang the bell, knowing she wasn't in, but pressing it long and hard anyway, my eyes shut, almost leaning on it, taking out some of my pent-up emotion. No answer. And the curtains were drawn upstairs as well as down, as if she was away, even. Damn. I turned to go, wondering what plan B was. Obviously to ring her, but if she was out of London … maybe I'd ring Sally. I fished my phone from my bag, just as a voice, in a low undertone, filtered through the bay window.

I frowned. Turned back. Hastened to the window and pressed my face to the glass. I couldn't see anything through the chink of curtain. But I could definitely hear movement.

'Maggie!' I banged on the glass, as it simultaneously occurred to me that she might be being burgled. Would I frighten thieves away? Might the door burst open any minute, and down the path hurtle a pair of six-foot youths with knives, ready to thrust at anyone in their way? Indeed, the door did fly open: I shrank back instinctively. There stood Maggie, in her white towelling bathrobe, looking flushed.

'Oh.' I gaped. 'Sorry – were you in the bath?'

'Yes, I bloody was! But I'm out now. Couldn't get away from the interminable doorbell ringing. Thought the street was on fire. Are you all right?'

'Yes, why?'

'You look terribly pale.' She peered at me.

'Do I?' I felt my cheek. 'Bit tired, probably. Maggs, can I come in?'

She hadn't exactly held the door wide and swept me through.

'Um ...' She bit her lip, looked up and down the street. Her voice dropped. 'Bit awkward at the moment.'

'Oh?'

I suddenly realized she didn't look particularly damp around the edges. Perhaps she hadn't been in the bath at all. 'Oh!' It dawned. 'You're entertaining,' I hissed.

'Might be.' She scratched her neck; looked sheepish.

'Ooh, Maggie, you old dog. That was quick. Wait till Henry gets to hear, eh?' I peered around her.

'Well, quite.'

I was craning my neck right round the door now. 'Any-one I know?'

'Noo, noo,' she lied, because you see, I know my best friend well. Can spot a whopper at three paces. I snapped my head back and stared at her in astonishment.

She looked sheepish. Shrugged. 'Needs must,' she muttered.

Needs must. My brain whirred furiously. 'Not Carlos?' I hissed eventually. Carlos owned the sandwich bar on Munster Road and had been flirting furiously with Maggie for five years. He was easily fifty, small, round, hirsute, swarthy, but very, very determined. He'd recently promised Maggie, *sotto voce* as he handed over her egg mayonnaise on brown, that, 'one day, 'ee would 'ave her little tooshy.' Maggie confessed she found this both terrifying and faintly thrilling, and over lunch we'd speculated exactly how hirsute he'd be, where it began – neck and wrists – where it all ended …

'He hasn't 'ad your little tooshy, has he?' I gasped.

'Certainly not!' She pulled her dressing gown tightly around her. I stood there, racking my brains.

'Norman! Ooh, Maggie, is it Norm?'

Norman, from the pub opposite, was a strange young man with hooded eyes and a brooding, psychopathic expression but who, when Maggie shamelessly batted her eyelashes at him, occasionally shifted heavy furniture for us. Gormless Norm, who sent Maggie hot stares from behind the bar when we popped across for a lager, and who, I'd tell her, looked exactly like Anthony Perkins in *Psycho*, then I'd rock crazily in my chair like the mother. Once, when he'd collected our glasses – I swear this is true – he carefully licked the rim of Maggie's half-pint glass on the way back to the bar.

'Norman!' She was incandescent with rage. 'How dare you! Now bugger off, Hattie. You've got your own blissful little love nest smouldering away on the other side of town, how about leaving me to mine?'

'Blissful little love nest?' I snapped to attention. 'I thought you said it was needs must?'

'What are you, the FBI? This isn't *Channel 4 News*, you know.'

'So who's the lucky—'

'*What the bloody hell is going on?*' a familiar voice boomed out, but one I couldn't instantly place. It drifted from within, certainly, but not from upstairs. From down.

I peered around Maggie's shoulder in its general direction, then back at her. She was going very pink. In fact, she avoided my eye completely and regarded her bare feet instead. From out of the sitting room, clad only in a length of burgundy chenille curtain fabric worn around his waist toga-style, revealing a bronzed and perfectly toned torso, came Ralph de Granville.

'Good God.' It was out of my mouth before I could stop it. 'I thought you were—'

'In Italy?' Maggie cut in quickly.

'Or gay?' enquired Ralph, not in the least abashed.

I flushed. 'Oh, no.'

'Lots of people do,' he conceded. 'And I don't always disillusion them. They like the idea of a gay decorator, feel far more comfortable with it. Can't quite grasp the idea that a red-blooded heterosexual would want to finger their drapes.'

'Oh, no, I've *never* thought that,' I said, the colour of the red chenille swathed around his middle.

'Yes she did,' Maggie admitted as he put his arm around her. 'We both did, didn't we, Hatts? But happily,' she giggled as he nibbled her ear, 'he's all man.'

The breath had all but left my body. I was bereft of speech. I gazed, stupefied. All man.

'Can I offer you a cuppa? I was just going to put the kettle on.' He turned to me cheerfully. 'Meanwhile, I'll leave you girls to discuss my finer points.' He flashed me a wink. 'Builder's, if it's all the same to you. Can't be doing with the flowery Lapsang muck. I drink enough of it in my line of work.'

'Oh, um …' I faltered.

'Come in, deary, you'll catch your death.'

This last was delivered in his habitual camp manner, and I realized he was demonstrating how he could turn it on. Up until then his voice had been quite normal. Bloke-ish South London, in fact.

'No, no, I won't stay,' I said hurriedly as he strode off to the kitchen, no hint of a wiggle now.

When he was out of earshot I turned to Maggie.

'I can't believe it!'

'I know.'

'I am completely floored!'

'Not as floored as I am,' she purred, still with what I realized was a post-coital glow.

'But … half of London thinks he is!'

'More fool them. Their loss is my gain,' she grinned, wrapping her dressing gown around her.

I gaped at her, again bereft of any meaningful dialogue. She looked like the cat who'd gulped the cream.

'You might have told me,' was all I managed, eventually.

'I was going to, but I knew you didn't like him.'

'Didn't like him! *Didn't like him!* Bloody hell, that's rich, coming from you. Only because *you* didn't. You hated him. Couldn't be in the same room with him!'

'Because I was afraid of him. Funny, isn't it?' she mused. 'Can't get enough of him now.' She went a bit misty-eyed.

I stepped inside out of the cold, shutting the door a bit behind us, keen to get to the bottom of this.

'But how the hell did it happen?' I hissed, glancing down the hall. 'I mean, how on earth did you two ever get it together?'

'We had a fight one day – one of many, I might add – at Laura's. It was when you'd gone back to London. We were arguing about that vase of his in the hall, with the cherubs on, remember? He kept putting it there, on a table, and I kept taking it away because I felt it interfered with the karma of the kitchen?'

I did. Some silly squabble about how three paces from the kitchen was still *her* territory, and when she flung open the door, all she could see was *his* hideous vase, intruding.

'So I picked it up and marched off with it, planning to plonk it in the dining room, his space. He blocked my way down the corridor, telling me to put it back, *now*. I refused. Told him to bugger off. We stood there facing each other, hissing and spitting like two cats, getting closer and closer until we were nose to nose. There we were, eyeball to eyeball, still trading insults, when suddenly, he put his arms around me and kissed me really hard on the mouth, like something out of a Cary Grant film. No – *Gone with the Wind*, at the end. Clark Gable.'

'Good God.'

'I nearly dropped the bloody vase, which, as you know, is worth a fortune, and of course I couldn't hit him or anything, didn't have a free hand. I couldn't even wriggle, he's so strong. And then, after a moment, I realized I was enjoying it. Really enjoying it. So I sort of ... succumbed.'

'Like Scarlett!'

'I suppose.' She looked abashed. 'And of course I was paralysed with shock too, because I'd always *always* thought he was gay.'

'Well, *quite*!' I agreed.

'But he's not. He's just really artistic and creative. But people don't understand a man who rearranges bedcovers for a living, so he affects this dandy camp bit, which becomes something of a habit when he's working. Look at that chap on the telly—'

'Laurence Llewelyn …?'

'Thingy, exactly, and he's as straight as they come. And, of course, it goes down brilliantly with all his female customers, who love the idea of a gay best friend. Goes down well with their husbands too, incidentally, who don't necessarily want some gorgeous hunk in the master bedroom discussing king size or super king. I mean, it's the tennis coach with knobs on, isn't it, if you'll excuse the expression. And imagine how many frustrated housewives would be wrestling Ralph into their boudoirs if they knew he was up for it?'

'There is that,' I said with feeling. Ralph was distinctly gorgeous, and some of the women of Kensington and Chelsea were panting as they opened the door to the milkman. He'd be dragged in by his velvet lapels. She'd quite stolen a march.

'Good for you, Maggs,' I said admiringly.

'Isn't it?' she agreed coquettishly, rearranging her dressing gown again. She blinked in astonishment. 'And I thought I'd got to the age when getting lucky meant finding your car keys.'

I giggled.

'And it's not just that,' she went on with a little frown. 'He really wants to be with me, you know? I mean, not just in bed.' She peered at me. 'Is that normal?'

'Well, if someone likes you, of course it is.'

'See? I forget. It's been so long. Can't think what I've been doing all these years.' She looked dazed. 'I tell him I'm going out to get some milk, and he jumps up and says I'll come with you. Or I potter to the shop for an hour, and he comes too. He really likes the shop, incidentally. But with Henry, all I could think about was how long he'd stay at the flat afterwards, which wasn't long.'

'But that's so lovely, Maggs,' I said, delighted.

'Isn't it?' she blushed. 'He's practically moved in.'

'Has he?' I gaped. 'Already?'

'Yes!' She glanced round in case he overheard. Lowered her voice. 'He's got this incredibly cool pad in Docklands, but seems to want to spend all his time in *my* poky little house.'

'Tea's ready!' A voice boomed – yes, boomed – from the kitchen.

'And he's got so many brilliant ideas for our business,' she confided breathlessly. 'In fact, he thinks we ought to go into business together, just him and me. Not that I ever would,' she added hastily. 'And I'm sure it's just – you know – pillow talk. But he seems to really like what I do. He admires me, and I was never sure Henry ever did. Just thought I had a sweet little job, something I did during the day, to keep me out of mischief. But Ralph really gets me, you know?' Her eyes searched mine.

'Yes. I think I do.'

'Says I'm a strong woman, and doesn't make that sound like a bad thing.' She paused, reflective a moment. 'And oh, Hattie, we have such a laugh!' Her eyes widened in sudden delight. 'Really hold-your-stomach laughing. About all our funny customers, all those X-ray women. You should hear him take off Mrs Barty-Clifford – "Aim orf to Glorstishire for the weekend" – should hear him take them all off, actually. Honestly, it's like talking to you. Like joking around with a good mate, and I could never be like that with Henry. So – well, uninhibited. D'you know what I mean? Always felt I was being someone else to

437

please him, to fit in with his idea of me. Does that make any sense?'

'Yes. Yes, it does.' I gazed at her. Didn't want her to say any more. Didn't want her to stir anything else up. I almost didn't recognize her, either. The light in her eyes. Her happiness. There was a lump in my throat.

'How long has this been going on?'

'Well, a bit,' she admitted.

A bit. Suddenly a light went on in my head. I blinked. 'Oh my God. Was that Ralph I saw leaving your bedroom that night at Laura's? After the dinner party? Corridor creeping?'

'Might have been.'

'Might have been – it was! *And* you were with him at the shoot the next day!' Perched behind him on the brow of the hill on a shooting stick. I thought back feverishly. Remembered how surprised I'd been to see him walk into the breakfast room in macho tweeds, quite late, but oddly, how it had suited him. How lit up Maggie had been that day. And I'd thought she was lighting up for the beaters. She'd had a night of passion.

'Tea's up, ladies.' Ralph came back down the hallway with a tray. He took it in the sitting room. 'One lump or two?' This, over his shoulder to me, in his old camp voice.

'You old fraud,' I grinned.

He shrugged cheerfully. Then came back rearranging the chenille around his waist. 'Yeah, well, sorry about that. Sorry to hoodwink you, but there's not much call for muscular decorating in SW3, I'm afraid. Everyone wants you to be in touch with your feminine side. And of course,

I'm much keener on being in touch with Maggie's.' He put his arm round her shoulders and pulled her in towards him. Two pairs of eyes shone rather magically at each other. I stared, transfixed. Ralph remembered me. Turned.

'You coming in or what? The neighbours are having a field day. Afternoon, Mrs Watson!' he called over my shoulder through the open door with a wave. 'Yes, that's right, she's got a new lover.'

Maggie giggled.

'Um, no. I'm going. You two … carry on.' I turned and stepped back outside. They were fairly oblivious to me, anyway.

'Oh, did you want me?' Maggie remembered suddenly; poked her head around the door as she went to shut it. She narrowed her eyes thoughtfully at me. 'You all right?'

'Yes, I'm fine, honestly. Really fine.'

I walked off down the path, giving a cheery backward wave over my shoulder, shutting the little gate behind me.

Right, I thought as I headed off back down the street. Well, that was that. No danger of a chin-wag with *her*. No chance of skirting round the subject until her eagle eyes steadied and she thrust in with a rapier like, 'What's up, Hatts? What's the problem?' She was far too distracted for that. And I was pleased, actually. Pleased I hadn't voiced any doubts about the way my life was going. Because once they're out, those doubts, there's no retracting them. They're there for good. Remembered for ever. Yes, thank goodness. A reprieve. And I was thrilled for Maggie, really thrilled. A man who was looking for a strong woman for a change. Well, Maggie was certainly that. And I'd always felt she'd needed a he-man like Henry to match her blow for blow, not a sensitive, creative type. How wrong we both had been. I could suddenly see them together, Ralph and Maggie, not just now, but in years to come: Maggie, obviously bossing him by then; Ralph making wide eyes and creeping around theatrically – 'Yes, my love, anything you say, my love.' Making her laugh. Which was what it was all about, wasn't it? That wretched lump in my throat again. Good luck to them, I thought as I walked on in the twilight.

'Good luck, Maggie.' I said it softly, into the dusk.

I realized I was walking home, heading down some very familiar streets, which I hadn't intended to do, and not pausing to ring Sally or Alex. But I didn't feel like Sally now. Didn't feel like sitting in a bar with single women, having just a little too much to drink, going home poorer and slightly worse for wear. I didn't know what I wanted, or if I did, I certainly wasn't disclosing it to myself. Home it was, then.

As I turned the corner and started down my road, trying to keep my thoughts at bay, I saw a figure emerging from the passageway that ran alongside the house, where Seffy kept his bike. I stopped in shock. Then walked on. Oh, of course, it was Christian. He'd been watering my plants whilst I'd been living in sin on the other side of town. He smiled: raised his hand when he saw me.

'You no supposed to be here!' he called.

'I know,' I said when I'd reached him, kissing his papery cheeks. 'But I popped in on Maggie for a chat.

Haven't seen her for a while. This is a treat, Christian.' I raised my game for him: it was a relief to do so. 'You are such a star to do my plants, particularly when they're so pathetic. How are you?'

'Ah, you know, I survive. One day they find a cure for arthritis, no doubt, but until then,' he shrugged, 'like your plants, pathetic. And you with your shiny new lover? You flourish?'

'Oh, yes, I flourish.' I walked smartly up the path. 'Are you coming in?'

Christian and I had talked long and hard when I'd popped in to see him last week: about Seffy, about what I'd done, and about how he, Christian, had always suspected, so it was odd that I couldn't quite look him in the eye, I thought as I fumbled now for my keys. I'd laid myself bare to pretty much everyone: everyone had had a jolly good peer into my soul, but Christian had almost been the hardest. Perhaps because he'd helped me so much back then, when Seffy was a baby. I felt I'd betrayed his trust.

'Well, for a moment maybe, but only to show you the terrible state your roses in.'

'Roses?' I flashed him a grin. 'Didn't know I had any.'

Christian despaired at my garden, pointing out that although he watered it, it was no earthly good if I didn't dead-head, prune or weed. We walked through the musty, closed-up house, with its stifling smell, and out the other side via the French windows to the sorry patch of lawn and straggly flowerbeds at the back.

'Dismal!' He groaned, shoulders sagging dramatically, hands raised to the heavens. 'Neglected! No form!'

'I know,' I laughed. 'But actually, Christian,' I hesitated, 'it'll be someone else's problem soon. Hal and I are moving to Notting Hill.'

'Ah?' He turned. 'He propose?'

I smiled. Christian, sweetly old-fashioned, wasn't at all sure about cohabiting.

'Not exactly. He asked if I'd spend the rest of my days with him.'

'Same thing. And you say?'

'I say ... said, that I was honoured. And very flattered. But I asked ... if I could have a bit more time.' I thought back to us standing there on the stone bridge, the river rushing beneath us, both Hal's hands holding mine. 'I said I thought I needed some space, after all the Seffy business.'

'And he say?'

'He was very understanding. Said he completely understood, wouldn't rush things. Was happy for us just to be together. Which we are.'

'And when he ask you again?'

'He may not.'

'He will.'

I licked my lips. 'I'll say yes.'

I was surprised to hear myself say it. But I knew Christian was right, knew a life-time contract was what Hal wanted.

'You accept because you feel you owe it to him? To everyone? To Seffy, your family? To yourself even? To not be problem any more? To make up for everything you've done?'

I stared, astonished. 'No, Christian. Of course not.'

He shrugged. His mouth sagged theatrically at the corners.

'And of course this man Hal, you owe him even more, hm? Owe him huge amounts. He look after Seffy this whole year, guide him through traumatic time. Be there for him. And Seffy, he like him very much, yes?'

'Yes,' I whispered.

'He be good father figure, too. Good influence, good role model. Successful lawyer, yes?'

'Yes.' I was answering as if in a trance, his watery old eyes holding mine.

'And this sister, Cassie, maybe you owe her, eh? And the mother you wronged – Letty. Give them back a family. So whole sorry mess come good, come full circle if you marry Hal. Whole thing make sense of the past, *n'est-ce pas*? All boxes ticked, with this Hal.'

I looked down at the ground.

'Except one,' he added softly.

I held my breath.

'Do you love him?'

I felt the ground crumble a little beneath me. Couldn't answer.

'Do you, Hattie?'

I glanced up quickly. 'Love. *Love*.' I spat it. 'I'm thirty-nine years old, Christian. I've made a pig's ear of everything so far—'

'You don't deserve love? Is that what you say?'

I stared. 'Yes. Yes, OK, that's what I say. Sometimes other things take precedence. Like – like duty, honour—'

'Capitulation, compromise. You don't love this man, but you settle for him. But he a good man, Hattie. You do him a great disservice to marry him, hm? You remember that.'

He fixed me with his eyes for a moment. Then turned and went back through the French windows into the house.

'You're wrong, actually, Christian,' I shouted after him, when I'd found my voice. 'He's spent most of his adult life waiting for me, putting his life on hold. He's been engaged for years, but didn't marry because of me. I do him a great service!'

He turned. Came back. His eyes no longer watery: they were like flints. 'And how long it last, hm? This charity marriage? How long till you no bear the sight of him?'

I was having difficulty breathing. I blinked rapidly. We stood there in the dusk.

'I can't, Christian,' I whispered at length. 'I'm in too far. Too deep.'

'You can,' he said, more gently. 'You can, or you never get out.'

I took a breath. Let it out shakily.

'But then it's just me again.' I gulped. I thought of Maggie and Ralph. My sister, all my friends. 'Me, on my own again. Seffy will be going off to university, and I'll be—' I stopped. My breathing was shallow. 'I'm frightened, Christian.' The first honest thing I'd said. And the truth does surely ring. 'I'm scared. Of this house, of the shop, of being alone. Spinster of this parish. I'm so afraid.'

His face softened. He held out his arms. I walked into them.

'He is my friend, Christian,' I pleaded into the tweedy lapel of his jacket. 'My very good friend. Has been for years. He's not just anyone.' Tears were welling now.

'It's not enough,' he said firmly. 'Not enough. Courage, *mon amie*. You will be all right.' He gave me a squeeze. 'Quite all right.'

Hal listened in silence when he got back from Geneva. It was late, and he was tired, and I hadn't wanted to tell him then: had wanted to wait until morning, but he'd seen my face. He sat by the window in a tubular steel-framed chair, still in his suit, slumped forward with his elbows on his knees, staring at the space between his feet as the light faded in the tall windows behind him. I hadn't faltered. I hadn't even cried. I'd got through it quite eloquently for me, albeit quietly. And it had sounded surprising rational. Maybe because, as Christian had said, it was the truth, finally echoing in this huge room, ringing around the chandeliers, the modern art on the walls.

'You don't love me,' he said finally, flatly. It was the one thing I'd left out.

'No. At least … not in that way.'

'There is only one way, Hattie.' He looked up at me, and not in his habitual way that made me feel small, guilty, as if I didn't quite match up: that reproachful way that made me feel as if I was still in a gymslip. Just sadly. 'Only one way, and that's the way I love you. With all my heart. You're right. We can't go on.' He got heavily to his feet. 'I won't try to persuade you otherwise. Won't tell you we could manage with just my love. Christian's right, it's not enough.' He turned to look out of the window, his back to me. He put his hands in his trouser pockets. 'And the awful thing is,' he went on softly, 'I knew. Knew your heart wasn't in it. But I was banking on you feeling a little bit indebted. And rather exhausted with life. Banking on you not being honest with yourself, because I knew you were capable of doing that. You mustn't be too hard on yourself, Hattie. I've been manipulative. Only because I love you, but still, it's not nice. I'm culpable, you see, not you. I knew you too well, and I used that knowledge to my advantage. I'll sleep in the spare room tonight.'

He turned and crossed the room past me. I watched him go, sitting on the sofa, tears stinging my eyes now. He picked up his jacket from the table on the way, slung it over his shoulder and disappeared down the hall. Vulnerable. And therefore, lovable. I heard the bedroom door close behind him and felt very sad. I swallowed, taking huge gulps of air. But ... oh, I was so relieved. I exhaled shakily. I had no idea I'd feel so relieved. As if a whole heap of coal had slowly rolled, gathered momentum and tumbled from my back. I sat a little straighter in the gathering gloom: listened as he brushed his teeth, pulled the chain. The mechanical sounds of a husband, I realized, getting ready for bed. Something I'd always wanted, very badly. The lovely, cosy familiar sound of routine, one that I probably wouldn't ever have now.

And maybe his love would have been enough for a while. Maybe too, if we'd married, his ardour would have dampened a bit, which would have helped, I realized. Hal had campaigned for me all these years, but I wonder if he knew what it felt like to be championed: to be rendered so endlessly significant, the focus of such intensity. It made me want to wriggle out from under his microscope and roll off the slide. I truly believed he'd conjured up an idea of me that didn't exist. I could never live up to his expectations. He'd become possessed by a fixed idea of me that had only grown in my absence over the years. I could only be a disappointment.

I took another deep breath and let it out slowly. And I fervently hoped he'd be happy. Meet someone. Céline hadn't been right. I wasn't right. But someone would be. Someone would make him very happy, and he deserved it. But I had a feeling it would be a while.

Sometime later I dimmed the lights and left a note, saying how much easier it would be if we didn't wake up here together in the morning. I hadn't cleared out entirely, but would be back another time for my things. I thanked him for everything he'd ever done for me, which was immeasurable, I knew. I wanted to say how I hoped we'd be friends for ever, but didn't. I knew he wouldn't take it as a compliment. Then I packed a few things in a small bag, left my key on the table in the hall, looked around one last time at the beautiful, spacious flat, but in a new, semi-detached way. Then I slipped out into the night.

Days passed. At home, on the other side of town, I pulled up my drawbridge and felt somewhat removed from the world for a while. I didn't want to share my new single state with anyone quite yet. Not Maggie, who was seamlessly entangled with Ralph. Not Seffy, who'd be surprised and disappointed. Not Christian, who'd pro-voked it – a bit of me didn't want him to know he'd been spot-on quite so quickly – and certainly not Laura and the rest of my family, who were still breathing a sigh of relief and thanking the Lord that finally, *finally*, the tricky sister, the difficult daughter, the one they worried about, had landed on her feet. Was going to marry sensible Hal. No, I kept my counsel. Which wasn't hard, because no one asked. As Seffy had so astutely remarked, we consider our own lives to be endlessly significant, but others take only a passing interest. They have their own to be getting on with.

There was also a quiet satisfaction in being the only one who knew. Aside from Hal, of course. But I was pretty sure, being a man, and a very particular type of proud, guarded man, he wouldn't be sharing quickly. Wouldn't be running any touchy-feely colours up a flagpole – hey, it's me, top lawyer Hal Forbes, I've been dumped. Would lick his wounds quietly for a while, as I would mine. But I was quite lonely. And once or twice – and I cringe to admit this – I had to resist the temptation to send him a text: 'Are you OK?' Happily I recognized the dishonesty inherent in that and tossed the phone back in my bag. After all, hadn't I promised myself I'd be scrupulously honest from now on?

After a while, though, I did email Seffy at school. Explained about Hal and me, and how sorry I was. I'd debated long and hard about ringing him, but I wanted him to have the luxury of thinking about it before he was bounced into a response. Or was that my luxury, at hearing his considered response, as opposed to his instinctive one? The thorny old truth again. Anyway, he must have been at his computer, because two seconds later, he rang.

'If that's what you've decided then fine, it's not a problem, Mum.'

I felt relief wash over me. 'But you're so fond of him, so close to him now.'

'Still can be, can't I? He's still my uncle. I'm not the one marrying him, though, am I? Relax. We were OK as we were, we'll still be OK.'

I shut my eyes. Thanked him silently. Blessed him inwardly. Muttered something about seeing him on Sunday. But when I replaced the receiver, I stood a little straighter. And as I went about my supper, my solitary boiled egg and soldiers, there was less tottering. Fewer hair-line cracks.

But I did feel my life shrinking again: a shrunken life. I was necessarily drawing back from people who would ask about Hal, and therefore isolating myself. It seemed to me, though, as I put one foot in front of the other and went about my business, that at least my soul was intact. No compromises. I didn't have that terrible feeling that, any minute, I was about to be found out. By Seffy. By Hal. There was great comfort in that. I felt I was getting to know myself again.

I found myself cleaning my little house from top to bottom, wanting to thin out all the rubbish, pare it down. De-clutter. I mended the curtain rail, painted the kitchen – even weeded the garden. And I got a plumber in for the downstairs loo – a nice chap, who found a rather chatty housewife who didn't draw breath. He couldn't get out of the door quick enough. I also worked long hours in the shop, sorting out the accounts, a job long overdue, whilst Maggie went to Italy with Ralph to fondle marble, amongst other things. I busied myself, as they say in women's magazines.

Weekdays were fine, Saturdays OK, Sundays downright dangerous. I felt unsafe on Sundays, especially in the evenings. Something lurked ominously within me, waiting to break out. Luckily the museums and art galleries were open and I got to know the V&A pretty well. They don't turf you out until quarter to six, if you're interested. And when they do, if you're still feeling precarious, there's always the Brompton Oratory round the corner. I'm not Catholic but wished, as I joined the queue for evensong, I could kneel and genuflect like the mysterious-looking foreign women: draw comfort from it. I did once. Then felt a fraud.

One weekday evening, when I was coming home from work past the Slug and Lettuce on the Fulham Road, I saw, amongst the café tables on the pavement outside, a sheet of blonde hair. Its shiny perfection and brightness amid the bustle seemed almost allegorical, and just as I was wondering where I'd seen it before, Ivan stepped out of the pub and made for that very table, a pint in one hand, a spritzer in the other.

He saw me and stopped. 'Hattie.'

'Ivan.'

Damn. *Again*. Gorgeous. *Again*. Tanned, pink shirt and jeans. Damn.

He recovered first. Spoke first, albeit flustered. 'Good to see you. D'you want a drink?'

Two young people outside a pub, whilst an older woman shuffled by, back from a solitary day's work, dressed, appropriately enough, in navy blue. A mistake. I'd thought it very Jean Muir at the time but actually, it was more Anita Brookner. Oh, and my heels were in a Tesco bag so I was practically in carpet slippers.

'Oh, no thanks. I've got to get on.'

He put the glasses down. 'Hattie, this is my sister, Ingrid,' he said carefully. A woman with a vacant expression turned her head. Smiled, but looked far away. She was middle-aged.

'Hi!' In my surprise I stuck out my hand. He didn't have a sister. I knew that. And there was something not quite right about this girl. I was aware of my features not knowing what to do with themselves. My hand was still unshaken: she stared blankly at it, her face flat. Eventually, I pocketed it. At that moment she proffered hers, hesitantly. I quickly took it.

'Here, sit a moment.' Ivan held out a chair. His eyes were asking me to sit.

'Oh. Well, yes, OK. Just for a moment.' I sat. How could I not?

'What will you have?' he asked quickly.

I looked at Ingrid's glass.

'A spritzer, thank you.'

He went back in. I chatted to Ingrid. Well, I chatted, she listened. Ivan returned with a glass, and the three of us exchanged pleasantries in the electric glow of outdoor heaters, about how the street had changed, new shops springing up: helping Ingrid along a bit occasionally. Mostly she sat open-mouthed, listening, but at one point she laughed until I thought she'd never stop. Ivan smiled and waited for her. At another moment, she reached out and took his hand. He held on tight. I drank my wine quite fast, but not overly so. Then I thanked him, said goodbye to Ingrid and went home.

I paced around my sitting room for a bit, arms tightly folded across my chest. Then I got my mobile out. To remind myself of my new life, my new, much healthier, slim-line protected self, I scrolled back through my texts. Way back, to the one Ivan had sent me when I was beetling frantically home to Seffy from the hotel in France, when he'd suggested something in the back of the lorry would be nice. Leaning laconically over the balcony rail with a towel around his waist. Some of it was missing I knew, but I'd get the gist. It would help.

In the way texts have of sometimes recovering themselves, none of it was missing now, and it was there in its entirety. I went hot. On an impulse I punched out his number. He answered, but simultaneously, my doorbell rang.

'Hello?'

'Oh.' I was flustered. Too many bells in my head. 'Hang on, Ivan, there's someone at the door.'

I flung it open, annoyed, to behold him on the doorstep. We gazed at one another, phones clamped to respective ears. Then we laughed foolishly and put them away. I stood back to let him in. He looked awkward, but I was hardly at ease either.

'Where's Ingrid?' I asked: casual but curious.

'She's gone home.'

'Oh.'

'She lives with her family in Dawes Road.'

'Her family?'

'She was adopted before I was born.'

'Right.' I was astonished.

He looked defensive. 'You're not the only one with secrets, Hattie.'

'No. No, quite right.' Once again I had a sense of my own importance. Small. Quite small in the scheme of things.

His face softened. 'She's ten years older than me and things were very different then. Mum was very young. She couldn't cope. They both worked long hours in the café. It was a different world. I don't blame my parents.'

'No.'

'But I'm not terribly proud of it.'

'But … you see her?'

'Just once a month. Probably not enough.'

'It's something, though.'

There was a silence.

'Do your parents know?'

'That I see her? Dad does. Mum doesn't. He says she'd be too hurt. Too ashamed.'

I nodded. How extraordinary. She'd disowned a daughter. Ivan didn't know about Seffy. But the parallels didn't escape me. I stared at him. Then turned away quickly and went to the window, fingers twisting about together.

'Ivan, at the risk of sounding like a private detective, those pictures in your wallet, the blonde girl. Are they Ingrid?'

'No, they're Claudia.'

'Claudia?' I turned back.

'Yes.' He pulled the wallet out of his jeans pocket and opened it. 'She works in Camden Passage. She held some of the pieces for me.'

He crouched and spread the photos on the coffee table. I approached cautiously. All were of pale, new pieces of furniture – lime, perhaps: chairs, small tables, lamp bases, bowls, all in the same style, all with very clean lines. One or two of the smaller pieces were held by a girl.

'You made these?' I picked one up.

'Yes, I told you in France,' he said impatiently. 'Also tried to interest you in a terrible old garnet ring, but, hey . . .' he muttered in an undertone.

'What?' I frowned.

'Nothing.'

I shook my head, confused.

'I know you told me you were making things, but why didn't you show me the pictures?' I hadn't really been listening, though. Had been thinking I looked so old compared to the girl. Me, me, me.

He shrugged. Shuffled them back together and stuffed them in his wallet. 'Because they're not as good as I'd like them to be. Yet.'

'I think they're very good.'

'One or two are all right, but your standards are high, Hattie.'

I glanced up, surprised. There was an edge to his voice. It sounded like an accusation. Was he suggesting I'd be critical?

'You've got years of experience in the trade. I'm just a new boy.'

'Hey – not so many years!' I joked, or tried to.

'No, not so many. You're thirty-nine.'

'Yes.' I said, taken aback. Thrown even.

'And I'm thirty-two.'

I boggled. 'Thirty-two? Are you? I thought you were much younger!'

'I know.' He gazed at me unblinking. Then he threw his head back and laughed: that glorious, abandoned throaty laugh. His eyes, when they came back to me were still amused. Quizzical. 'How much younger?'

'Well, twenties ... late twenties at the most!' I blustered, genuinely astonished. Seven years. Only seven years. Not so much, surely?

He leaned forward and parted his hair at the temples. 'Grey – see?'

I peered. 'A bit. But you're blond; hardly shows. Not like me.' I almost bent my head to part and display my own roots: thought better of it.

'But … why didn't you say?'

'Why didn't you?'

'Well …' I was flummoxed. 'For obvious reasons! Women don't – you know – advertise it.'

'You didn't want me to think I'd landed an old maid. And I didn't want you to think I'd done nothing with my life.'

'What d'you mean?'

'I'm thirty-two years old. I've got a stall off Camden Passage. What d'you think I mean?'

'Oh, but …'

'You're only a few years older, but you've got a ritzy shop in Fulham, have had for ages. A proper business, written up in *Interiors*. You own your own house, I rent a room in Crouch End. We come from different backgrounds and mine has nothing to offer but a disabled sister.'

My mouth dropped in astonishment. 'But you're you!' I wanted to add: all sort of blond and gorgeous and funny. Instead I spluttered stupidly 'You're Ivan!'

'And you're you. Smart and sophisticated and savvy and beautiful – you're Hattie. With landed gentry at the Abbey. My mum runs a café.'

I felt overwhelmed. Here we were, the pair of us, with what felt like cupboards full of skeletons, rows of hang-ups, yet on opening the cupboard door, others might give it a once-over, a cursory nod and say, looks OK to me. I'll take it.

Would he? Is that what he was saying? Would I do? And was he asking?

I felt my heart beat very fast, as if it were making a run for it. But I was afraid. I loved everything about this man. I loved the way he moved so effortlessly through life, striding on cheerfully in an uncomplicated manner. This little room seemed brighter already. When he'd gone, I knew I'd be back to carefully threading my way around it, avoiding invisible land mines, everything becoming much harder. I leaned back on the windowsill. He was perched on the arm of a chair. We regarded one another in silence.

At length I reached into my pocket.

'I've just reread your text to me in France.'

'The one you didn't answer.'

'Because I misread it. Some of it was missing. I didn't know what it said. I glanced at it: 'Got you a flight from Nice in hour. I'll take back lorry. xx' I raised my eyes slowly. 'You'd do that for me? Drive back while I flew?'

'I'd do anything for you, Hattie.'

The words hung in the air between us. Suspended. His eyes were steady: didn't waver.

And that should have been my moment. To cross the room, walk into his arms, as he surely would have opened them. My moment to let someone in again. And not just anyone. Instead, I got to my feet and moved carefully towards the front door.

'Have you eaten?' I plucked my coat from a hook, not looking at him. Put it on and opened the door.

'No.'

'Then let's eat. And talk. I have a lot to tell you. There's a great deal you don't know about me, Ivan. You may not feel you'd do anything for me, once you know.'

He stood up: tall, blond and it seemed to me, dazzling. Filling the room. He attempted to look grave but his mouth twitched. 'My, that sounds serious. Ominous, even. Yes, by all means let's eat, and you can tell me all about yourself. I'd be surprised if it influences me, though. I think you'll find you're stuck with me whether you're a closet vampire or not.'

I glanced up at him as we went out into the night. It occurred to me I would be very surprised if it influenced him too. As I straightened up on the doorstep from locking the Chubb, he smiled at me.

'Spill your beans, Hattie Carrington,' he said softly. 'But it had better be good. I could have knocked us up an omelette apiece in the time it takes to order a couple of steaks — one rare and sophisticated for you, one common and burned to a frazzle for me, in Le Bistingo. But sure, you go à la carte, sniff that wine and toy with your artichoke hearts. After all,' he jerked his head back to the bedroom window, 'it might be a while before you eat again.'

Ditching my prissy demeanour, I threw back my head and laughed into the night. It struck me, as the sound combusted like a lightning bolt, that I hadn't heard that sound from my own lips for quite some time. Joyous. Uninhibited. And it also struck me, as we set off down the road together for the future, matching each other stride for stride that although it wasn't the meaning of life, it was surely the whole point?

A house in the south of France.
A holiday of a lifetime.
What could be nicer?
What could possibly go wrong?

Chapter One

Somewhere over the English Channel travelling north, closer to the white cliffs than to Cherbourg and whilst cruising at an altitude of thirty thousand feet, a voice came over the tannoy. I'd heard this chap before, when he'd filled us in on our flying speed and the appalling weather in London, and he'd struck me then as being a cut above the usual easyJet Laconic. His clipped, slightly pre-war tones and well-modulated vowels had a reassuring ring to them. A good man to have in a crisis.

'Ladies and gentlemen, I wonder if I could have your attention for a moment, please. Is there by any chance a doctor on board? If so, would they be kind enough to make themselves known to a member of the cabin crew. Many thanks.'

I glanced up from *Country Living*, dragging myself away from the scatter cushions in faded Cabbages and Roses linen I fully intended to make but probably never would, to toss attractively around the Lloyd Loom chairs in the long grass of the orchard I would one day possess, complete with old-fashioned beehive and donkey. I turned to my husband. Raised enquiring eyebrows.

He pretended he'd neither heard the announcement nor sensed my eloquent brows: he certainly didn't look at them. He remained stolidly immobile, staring resolutely down at the Dan Brown he'd bought at Heathrow and had taken back and forth to Paris, but had yet to get beyond page twenty-seven. I pursed my lips, exhaled loudly and meaningfully through my nostrils and returned to my orchard.

Two minutes later, the clipped tones were back. Still calm, still measured, but just a little more insistent.

'Ladies and gentlemen, I'm sorry, but if there is a doctor or a nurse on board, we would be most grateful if they would come forward. We really do need some assistance.'

I nudged my husband. 'James.'

'Hm?'

His shoulders hunched in a telltale manner, chin disappearing right into his neck and his blue-and-white checked shirt.

'You heard.'

'They mean a *doctor* doctor,' he murmured uncomfortably. 'A GP, not a chiropodist.'

'Oh, don't be ridiculous, you're a foot surgeon! Go on.'

'There'll be someone else,' he muttered, pale-grey eyes glancing around nervously above his glasses, a trifle rattled I could tell.

'Well, obviously, there isn't, because they've asked twice. There could be someone dying. Just go.'

'You know I hate this sort of thing, Flora. There's bound to be someone with more general expertise, more –'

'I really think, young man,' said the elderly woman in the window seat beside him, a well-upholstered, imperious-looking matron who'd removed her spectacles to regard him pointedly and reprovingly over her tapestry, 'that if you do have medical experience, you should go.'

She made him sound like a conscientious objector.

'Right. Yes. Yes, of course. *All right*, Flora, you don't need to advertise me, thank you.'

But I was already on my feet in the aisle to let him out, gesticulating wildly to a stewardess. 'Here – over here. Make way, please.' This to the queue of people waiting patiently beside us for the loo. We were quite close to the front as it was. 'He's a doctor.'

'Make way?' James repeated incredulously under his breath, shooting me an appalled look as the entire front section of the plane turned to look at the tall, lean, sandy-haired, middle-aged man who'd unfolded himself with effort from his seat and was now shuffling forwards, past the queue to the bog, mumbling apologies and looking, in his creased chinos and rumpled holiday shirt, more like a harassed librarian than a paramedic in a hurry.

I sat back down again, feeling rather important, though I didn't really sit: instead I perched on the arm of my aisle seat to get a better view. Luckily, a steward had redirected the queue to the loo at the back and I could now see that a little crowd of uniformed cabin crew had gathered around a young girl of about nine who was sitting on the floor, clearly in distress. In even more distress was the very beautiful woman in tight white jeans and a floral shirt standing over her, her hands over her mouth. She was pencil thin with a luxuriant mane of blonde hair, and her heavily accented voice rose in anguish.

'Oh, *mon dieu*, I can't do it again – I can't!'

I saw James approach and address her and she gabbled back gratefully in French, clutching his arm. I'm reasonably fluent, but at that range I couldn't make it out, but

3

then she switched back to English, saying, 'And I have only one left – please – help!'

She thrust something into my husband's hand, at which point I was tapped on the shoulder from behind.

'Excuse me, madam, would you mind taking your seat? We're experiencing a spot of turbulence.'

The glossy, lipsticked smile on the expertly made-up face of the stewardess meant business. The plane was indeed bumping around a bit. Reluctantly, I lowered my bottom, which obviously meant I missed the crucial moment, because when I craned my neck around the stewardess's ample behind as she passed, the crowd at the front were on the floor and James was crouching with his back to me, clearly administering something. They'd tried to move the girl to a more secluded position and shield her with bodies, but a plane doesn't yield much privacy. The blonde, clearly the mother, was the only one standing now, pushing frantic hands through her hair, clutching her mouth, unable to watch, but unable to turn away. My heart lurched for her. I remembered the time when Amelia shut her finger in the door and almost sliced the top off and I'd run away as James held it in place with a pack of frozen peas, and also when Tara coughed up blood in the sitting room and I'd raced upstairs, screaming for her father. You knew you had to help, but you loved them so much you couldn't bear to watch. There was a muffled collective murmuring from the crew and then, without looking indecently ghoulish, I really couldn't see any more, as the mother had dared to crouch down, obscuring James as well.

I went back to my magazine. An interview with a woman

4

from Colefax and Fowler informed me that, on the paint-effects front, Elephant's Breath was all over. Everyone was coming into her Brooke Street showroom asking for chintzes and borders now. Borders. Blimey. I had rolls of the stuff in the attic. Did Laura Ashley circa 1980 count? Probably not. My mind wasn't really on it, though, and I narrowed my eyes over my reading glasses. James had straightened up and was answering a series of quick-fire questions from the mother, whose relief was palpable, even though strain still showed in her eyes. My husband, typically, made light of it, brushing away what were clearly effusive thanks, and came back down the aisle, perhaps less hunched and beleaguered than when he'd gone up it, as quite a few passengers now regarded him with interest. I got up quickly to let him slide in and sit down. The ordeal was over and relief was on his face.

'Well?' I asked. The matron beside him was also agog, needlework abandoned in her lap.

'Nut allergy,' he reported. 'She'd taken a crisp from the girl beside her and it must have been cooked in peanut oil. The mother realized what had happened but had never had to administer the EpiPen before, and she cocked it up the first time. She had a spare one but was too scared to do it in case she got it wrong again. The stewardess was about to have a stab.'

'So you did it?'

He nodded. Picked up Dan Brown.

'Did it go all right?'

'Seemed to. She's not dead.'

'Oh, James, well done you!'

'Flora, I have given the odd injection.'

'Yes, but still.'

'I say, well done, young man,' purred his beady-eyed neighbour approvingly. 'I couldn't help overhearing. I gather you're a surgeon?'

'Consultant surgeon,' I told her proudly.

'Ingrowing toenails, mostly,' said James, shifting uncomfortably in his seat. 'The odd stubborn verruca.'

'Nonsense, he trained as an orthopaedic. He's done hips, knees, everything, but he gets a lot of referrals from chiropodists these days, when it's out of their sphere of expertise.' I turned to James. 'Will she be all right? The little girl?'

'She'll be fine. It just takes a few moments to kick in.'

'Anaphylactic shock,' I explained to my new friend across his lap. Like most doctors' wives I considered myself to be highly qualified, a little knowledge often being a dangerous thing.

'Ah,' she agreed sagely, regarding James with enormous respect now, her pale, rheumy eyes wide. 'Well, that's extremely serious, isn't it? I say, you saved her life.'

James grunted modestly but didn't raise his head from his book. His cheeks were slightly flushed, though, and I was pleased. Morale could not be said to be stratospheric in the Murray-Brown household at the moment, what with NHS cuts and his private practice dwindling. When he'd first decided to specialize, years ago, he'd chosen sports injuries, having been an avid cricketer in his youth, but that had become a very crowded field. He'd seen younger, more ambitious men overtake him, so he'd concentrated on cosmetic foot surgery instead. A mistake in retrospect, for whilst in a recession people would still pay to have a crucial knee operation, they might decide to live with their unsightly bunions and just buy wider shoes. He'd even joked with the children about getting a van, like Amelia's boyfriend, who was a DJ, adding wheels to his trade, morphing into a mobile chiropodist, perhaps with a little butterfly logo on the side. 'A website, too!' Amelia had laughed, 'I'll design it for you.' But I'd sensed a ghastly seriousness beneath his banter. He spent too much time in what we loosely called 'the office' at the top of our house in Clapham, aka the spare room, pretending to write articles for the *Lancet* but in fact doing the *Telegraph* crossword in record time, then rolling up the paper and waging war on the wasp nest outside the window. Not really what he'd spent seven years training at St Thomas's for. This then, whilst not the Nobel Prize for Medicine, was a morale boost.

I peered down the aisle. I could see the young mother standing at the front of the plane now, facing the passengers, her face a picture of relief, casting about, searching for him. I gave her a broad smile and pointed over my head extravagantly.

'He's here!' I mouthed.

She'd swept down the aisle in moments. Leaned right over me into James's lap, blonde hair flowing. 'Oh, I want to thank you so very much,' she breathed gustily in broken English. 'You saved my daughter's life.'

'No no,' muttered James uncomfortably, but going quite pink nevertheless. He tried to get to his feet, his manners, even on an aircraft, impeccable.

'No, don't get up,' she insisted, fluttering her pretty, bejewelled hands. 'I will see you later. I just wanted to say how grateful I am, how grateful we all are. My Agathe – you saved her!'

'Well, I administered an EpiPen, but not at all, not at all,' James murmured, gazing and blinking a bit. She really was astonishingly beautiful. I marvelled at the yards of silky hair which hung over me, the tiny frame, the vast bust, the enormous blue eyes. Was she a film star, I wondered? She looked vaguely familiar. A French one, perhaps – well, obviously a French one – in one of those civilizing arty movies I went to with Lizzie occasionally at the Curzon when James was watching *The Bourne Identity* for the umpteenth time. I didn't think this was the moment to ask and watched as her tiny, white-denimed bottom undulated back to its seat.

Once off the plane at Stanstead, on the way to Baggage Reclaim, I saw a father point James out to his son, perhaps as someone to emulate in later life: where all his GCSE biology studies could lead, and the reason he, the father, enforced the homework. The boy stared openly as he passed, as did his younger sister, and I surreptitiously got my lippy out of my handbag and gave a quick slick in case anyone should want his autograph. By the time we got to the carousel, however, most people seemed intent on getting out of the place and had forgotten the heroics. Including the mother and child, who hadn't yet materialized, I realized, glancing around. Perhaps they were hand luggage only? Had swept on through already? Hard to imagine what they were doing on easyJet at all. But then, just as James returned from the fray with our battered old suitcase, I saw them enter the baggage hall. The little girl seemed fine now and was skipping along in front, holding a man's hand. He couldn't be the father, I thought; too thuggish and thickset. Indeed, there seemed to be a couple of similar heavies in tow, whilst the mother strode along in their midst, in sunglasses. Were they staff? Certainly the small, dumpy woman carrying all the Louis Vuitton hand luggage must surely be an employee, and the swarthy man with the cap couldn't be the husband either.

The blonde seemed about to sweep on through, but then, just as she neared the exit she spotted us. She whipped off her sunglasses and came striding across, beaming.

'*Alors*, there you are! *Regard* – look at my *petite* Agathe. As right as what you English bizarrely call rain, and all thanks to you, *monsieur*. My name is Camille de Bouvoir and I am eternally grateful.'

James took her tanned, extended hand. 'James Murray-Brown.'

'Orthopaedic surgeon,' I purred. 'And I'm his wife, Flora.'

She briefly touched the fingers of the hand I'd enthusiastically offered but turned straight back to James.

'I knew you were a surgeon. I could tell by those hands. So sensitive, yet so capable.'

'Aren't they just?' I agreed, although no one seemed to be listening to me.

'And I would like to repay your skill and kindness.'

'Oh, there's really no need,' demurred James, embarrassed.

'May I take your email address? I somehow imagine you would be too modest to get in touch if I gave you mine.'

'He would,' I confirmed, scrabbling around in my bag for a pen and withdrawing a distressed tampon instead, but Madame de Bouvoir had already produced her iPhone. She handed it to me wordlessly and I tapped away dutifully, very much the secretary to the great man. Very much peripheral to proceedings.

9

'I will be contacting you,' she promised, pocketing it as I handed it back to her. 'And now, Agathe wants to say something.' She gently shepherded her daughter forward. '*Cherie?*' The child was as slim as a reed, with widely spaced almond eyes in a heart-shaped face. Although not yet on the cusp of puberty she was very much in the Lolita mould: destined for great beauty.

She took a deep breath. 'Thank you so very much, *monsieur*, for saving my life. I will be for ever grateful to you and thank you from the bottom of my 'eart.'

She'd clearly practised this small, foreign speech on the plane with a little help from her mother, and it was delivered charmingly. An elderly couple beside us turned to smile. James took the hand she offered, bowing his head slightly and smiling, for who could not be enchanted?

'*Mon plaisir,*' he told her.

Courtesies having been observed, Mme de Bouvoir then kissed James lightly on both cheeks three times. She briefly air-kissed me – only once, I noticed, as I lunged for the second – and then, as a socking great pile of Louis Vuitton suitcases were wheeled towards her by one of her chunky attendants, she sashayed out of the concourse ahead of the trolley, bestowing one last lovely smile and a flutter of her sparkling hand.

James and I gave her a moment to get through customs, where no doubt she'd be met by a man in a uniform, before we waddled out with our bags.

'Great. You know exactly what that will be, don't you?' muttered James.

'What?' I said, knowing already: even now regretting it.

'Some poncy restaurant we've been to a million times

already. We'll have to sit there pretending we never go any-where smart and endure a lengthy, excruciating meal, which we're force fed anyway on a regular basis.'

'Not necessarily,' I said, with a sinking feeling. I grabbed my old blue bag as it threatened to slide off the trolley.

'We're probably going there tonight!' he yelped.

I avoided looking at him, stopping instead to look in my handbag for my passport. James froze beside me.

'Dear God, I was joking. Please tell me we're not out tonight, Flora. I'm knackered.'

'We have to, James. I've got to get the review in by tomorrow.'

'You're not serious.'

'I am.'

'Jesus.'

'How else d'you think we're going to pay for that bloody holiday? Shit. Where's my passport?' I delved in my bag.

'I've got it.' He produced it from his breast pocket. 'Where are we going?'

'Somewhere in Soho, I think. Oh yes, Fellino's. I have a feeling Gordon Ramsay's trying to take it over and he's resisting.'

'Hasn't he got enough bloody restaurants? Have you texted Amelia?'

'Yes, and she's outside whingeing about us being late. Apparently, we should have let her know the plane was ten minutes delayed. As if I haven't sat for enough hours in that wretched car park waiting for her.'

'Can't you ask Maria to put it in next week's edition? Say you'll go tomorrow?'

'I've tried, but apparently Colin's already let her down.

He was supposed to do the new Marco Pierre but he's got a sore throat, so someone's got to do one.'

'Oh great, so Colin's got his excuse in first, as usual.'

I ignored him. We were both very tired.

'You could google the menu on the web? Write the review from that? Say how delicious the tiddled-up turbot was?'

'Oh, good idea. Like I did at Le Caprice, only, unfortunately, the turbot was off that night, and the scallops, both of which I'd waxed lyrical about. I'd rather keep what remains of my job, if it's all the same to you.'

'But you know Fellino. Can't you ring him and ask what the special is? See what he recommends for tonight?'

'It's fine, I'll go on my own.'

'No, no, I'll come,' he grumbled. 'Blinking heck. Who goes out for dinner the night they get back from holiday?'

'We do, if we're going to go on holiday at all,' I said with a flash of venom. There was the briefest of pauses. James's voice, when it came, was light, but it had the timbre of metal.

'Ah yes, forgive me. For a moment there I thought I was the successful alpha male in this partnership. The high-earning surgeon with a career on a meteoric rise to the stars, providing for his family.'

Heroically, I held my tongue as, tight-lipped, we followed the other weary travellers down the corridor to the escalator. We climbed aboard wordlessly, passed through Passport Control, then trundled out through Nothing to Declare.